Estelle Ryan

The

Flinck Connection

The Flinck Connection
A Genevieve Lenard Novel
By Estelle Ryan

First published 2014

Acknowledgements

With every book it becomes harder for me to write the acknowledgements. These people are my pillars and words fail to impart the depth of my appreciation for each one. I am honoured to be surrounded by such incredible individuals who support, love and understand me.

As always, Charlene, for your interest, love and support. Linette, for continuing to be the best sister. Anna, for your interest and support. R.J. Locksley for your astute editing. Julie, Wilhelm and Kasia, Kamila, Paula, Jola, Ania S, Alta, Krystina and Maggie for your continued interest and support. Piotrek for allowing me to use your surname, and for being a good friend during your short time on this mortal plane. Ania B for being such an amazing woman and friend. Jane, for your love and support.

And to every single reader who has contacted me and who keeps in touch through Facebook – thank you. Every email, every comment carries great weight and is more appreciated that I can ever express.

Dedication

To Moeks.

Chapter ONE

"And I will always love you." The melodramatic, yet oddly memorable song jerked me out of a restful sleep. It took me a mere second to go from a state of relaxation to utter annoyance. I grabbed my smartphone from the bedside table where it had been perfectly aligned to the corners. As I sat up, a few things registered in my mind, the face flashing on my smartphone's screen being the most vexing. I swiped the screen.

"You changed my ringtone. Again." I hated when Colin did that. He had started this unacceptable behaviour the first time I'd met him eighteen months ago.

"Jenny, you need—"

"—to have my old ringtone back. You know how much I hate it when you do this. Why do you continue doing this? Will you ever stop being a thief and stealing into my smartphone?"

"Jenny!" The urgency in his tone not only stopped my annoyance, but also triggered a shot of adrenaline to enter my bloodstream. "You need to phone Millard."

"Why? What's wrong?" It wasn't just his tone that alerted me to a problem. For the last seven weeks, Colin and Colonel Manny Millard had been at odds.

Colin Frey was a thief, reappropriating art that had been taken during conflicts or illegally obtained. He did this to return these artworks to their rightful owners.

Even after knowing him for eighteen months and being

romantically involved with him for eleven months, I still felt conflicted accepting his profession. The fact that he was secretly employed by Interpol did nothing to aid my discomfort. Before he had entered my life, everything had been much simpler. I had successfully divided everything in black and white categories. Things had been either right or wrong. Colin had taught me that life consisted of grey areas.

One of those areas was his cooperation with Manfred Millard. An Interpol agent and lifelong law enforcement officer, Manny headed our team of five as we investigated art crimes. Our team existed on the order of the president of France, and the probes into art illegalities were second priority to any case the president requested us to look into. This position was well suited for Manny, but it was a daily conflict for him working with the rest of the team, especially Colin.

They shared a turbulent past and it often seemed they took pleasure in antagonising each other. Something had happened seven weeks ago between Manny and Colin that had caused renewed hostility between them. Neither one was willing to talk about it. Colin had stubbornly refused to talk to Manny. The current state of their relationship would not allow Colin to ask for Manny's assistance. That was why Colin's request for me to contact Manny was a surprise.

"Jenny, are you listening?" He wasn't as patient as usual when I got lost in my thoughts. There was an unfamiliar sharpness to his tone.

"I'm listening. Why do you want me to phone Manny? Why don't you phone him?"

"I'm standing in Claude Savreux's home office, looking at his dead body."

"Oh my God, did you... No, of course you didn't kill him.

Why are you there? What are you stealing? Are you talking about Monsieur Claude Savreux, the Minister of Defence and Veteran Affairs? Why do you want to steal from him?"

"Jenny." His voice was low, the tone he took when he needed me to focus. "Phone Millard, tell him to get people he trusts and a warrant or something that will get him into this house."

I took a moment to think this over. "Are you sure he's dead?"

"Very."

"Then I'm not going to phone Manny until you tell me why you are there."

A few hard breaths sounded through the connection. "Wake Nikki up and ask her. I have to leave. I don't want to overstay my welcome here."

"Nikki?" My voice raised a pitch and a few decibels. "You're involving Nikki in your crimes?"

Nikki was an eighteen-year-old student who had come into our lives five months ago. She was the daughter of the late Hawk, a notorious arms trader. When he had died, Nikki had been seventeen, not yet an adult. She had refused to be placed in the government system and threatened to run away. We had become her foster parents until she came of age three months ago, yet she was still staying with us.

"Jenny." He sighed. "Just wake her up and let her tell you. I've got to go. I'll keep an eye on the house until Millard arrives, but I'm leaving now."

Before I could give more voice to my outrage, he gave me the address and promptly hung up on me.

I trusted Colin with my life. I even loved him, despite his life being shadowed by unclear moral and ethical lines. He was also the only person whose physical touch and closeness

I could bear. Time and again he had proven himself to be a man of integrity. That was the reason I swiped my smartphone's screen and tapped on Manny's number.

"What's wrong, Doctor Face-reader?" Manny's voice was gruff from being woken up.

"Colin is in Minister Claude Savreux's house and he's dead."

"What? Who's dead? The minister?" His voice was decidedly clearer and louder. "Did Frey kill him?"

"Colin didn't kill him. I don't know any details. Colin phoned me to tell you to get to Minister Savreux's house as soon as possible. With a search warrant."

"Bloody hell." A grunt came through the connection. "Do you know what the time is?"

"Of course I do." What an inane question. "It's fourteen minutes past two."

"Exactly."

"Oh, and Colin asked that you get people you trust for this. I don't know why he would say this, but his tone implied that this was particularly important." I didn't want to tell him about Nikki's involvement yet, particularly since I didn't know how she had become entangled in this. With her unfailingly cheerful disposition, she had won the hearts of everyone, including Manny's. He was overly protective of her, hence my reticence in telling him.

"Oh, for the love of Pete," Manny said after a few quiet seconds. "Give me the address and let me see what I can do, Doc. I'll phone you in a bit and you had better have more information for me by then."

"How long is a bit?"

"A bit?" He groaned. "I will phone you in twenty minutes, Doc."

I stared at my smartphone after Manny disconnected the call. Was the death of Minister Claude Savreux a murder? I hadn't even asked Colin about that. He wouldn't have asked for Manny's help if he hadn't considered it important. The strain I had heard in his voice caused me great concern. He had seen something that had worried him more than he had wanted to say. I put on my dressing gown and slippers to go wake Nikki.

After months of Colin's persistence, I had relented and we had combined our neighbouring apartments. It had been a particularly difficult three weeks for me when the builders had broken through the wall separating the two living areas. In my apartment, we now had a larger sitting area with my two sofas and one of Colin's. I had refused to allow his unsightly recliner chairs in my living space. We had combined our libraries into a very large reading area on Colin's side. I spent many a night in one of the reading chairs while Colin and Vinnie watched some television show. Colin had converted one of his bedrooms to a multimedia entertainment area—a room I seldom visited. With two bedrooms left on Colin's side, Vinnie stayed in one and Nikki in the other. Colin and I were the only ones living in my side of the large combined apartment.

Vinnie was Colin's best friend, a large man with a violent criminal history, but with fierce loyalty towards his friends. I counted him as a very close friend and caught myself more frequently disregarding his past. Two years ago, I would've held it against him and refused to have any connection with him. Like Colin, Vinnie had proven to me that a man could be more than his past. He was the protector of our team, making it logical for me to first go to his bedroom before waking Nikki.

I knocked on his door and waited. After knocking for a second time and not getting an answer, I opened the door and turned the light on. The room was empty, the bed made. Vinnie wasn't home. He often went out at night, staying in touch with his criminal contacts in case we might need information from them. I sighed, turned off the light, closed the door and went to Nikki's room. It was physically painful for me to enter her room. Typical of her personality type, she felt comfortable in cluttered chaos. Her room brought panic clamping down on my mind. On mutual agreement, I never entered her room and she always kept the door closed.

Unintelligible mumbling answered my knock. I took it as an invitation and went into her room. I turned on the light and shuddered. The floor was covered in boots, scarves, books and shoulder bags. Nikki's reaction to the sudden light in her room was to pull her duvet over her head with a groan. "Go away."

I stepped over three pairs of shoes and stopped next to her bed. "Nikki, wake up."

She lowered the duvet just enough to peek over it. "What's wrong, Doc G?"

"Why is Colin in Claude Savreux's house?"

"I don't know. I don't even know who this person is."

There was no deception in her tone or the visible parts of her face. "Lower the duvet, please."

"Oh, come on! Seriously? You want to read me? Why?" She rolled her eyes, but lowered the duvet to her chest and laid her hands on top of it. In the short time she'd been living with us, she had learned that I needed to see the body as a whole to accurately read nonverbal cues. I didn't have the natural ability neurotypical people had to read and interpret body language. Having doctorate degrees and being the top in my field in reading body language enabled me to understand what people were saying despite their words. Right now Nikki was telling the truth.

"Colin phoned me five minutes ago to tell me that he was in Minister Savreux's house and that the man is dead. When I asked him what he was doing there, he told me to ask you."

Her eyebrows lifted and her eyes flashed open. "Oh, shit. Someone's dead. That's not good. I swear I didn't know whose house it was and I know nothing about him being dead."

"Take a deep breath." I had learned through experience that lowering my tone and speaking slower calmed Nikki when she was working herself into a panic. "I believe you about not knowing whose house it was. Just tell me why Colin told me to ask you what he was doing there."

Her fingers curled around the duvet while she took a few calming breaths. Her shoulders lifted to her ears in the turtle effect, nonverbal behaviour seen when someone felt unsure. She sat up, inhaled to speak, but stopped when I lifted my hand.

"The truth, please."

She nodded. "Yeah, yeah. You'll see the truth in any case. You know, it's sometimes really hard speaking to you."

"Nikki." There was a warning in my tone.

"Someone DM'ed me on Twitter. I don't know how they got my handle, because I've made sure to not have my name attached to it."

She spoke English, but I didn't understand her. "What is a DM and what is a handle?"

Nikki pushed herself up and leaned against the headboard. "My handle is my profile name on Twitter. A DM is a direct message. It's like an email, but it's sent on Twitter. I received the first one a week ago. I ignored it, thinking it was a kind of spam that sometimes makes it through the filters. But then I got one yesterday afternoon and it was much more specific. It told me to tell you about the message."

"Me?" How did someone know to reach me through Nikki? "Yet you didn't tell me. You told Colin."

She didn't respond, but fleetingly touched the back of her neck, conveying her discomfort.

I took a calming breath. "Who sent it?"

"I don't know. This person's handle is just a bunch of numbers."

"What did the messages say?"

"Hold on, I'll show you." She pushed her hand under her pillow and moved it around until her eyes widened and she smiled.

My mouth opened slightly when she lifted her smartphone. "You sleep with your phone under your pillow?"

"Of course. Don't you?"

"No. Why do you?"

"I check my feeds when I wake up in the middle of the night." Her head tilted back and she squinted. "That sounds bad, doesn't it?"

"Just show me the message." I held out my hand for her phone. She swiped the screen a few times before handing it over. I frowned at the screen. "*Tell Lenard! IMPORTANT! Flinck @ 224 Rue de Marge. Pervasive reach. 1+1=2.*"

"At least he can do math." Nikki twisted to look at the phone.

I pulled it closer to my chest. "How do you know it is a he?"

"I don't know if it's a he or a she, but whoever this is is rude." The confidence in her tone caught my attention.

"Why do you say that?"

"If someone tweets in capital letters, they are shouting at you. That's rude."

"Why didn't you tell me about this message?"

She shifted and clutched the duvet on her lap. "I didn't want to worry you. It's bad enough with Dukwicz still being around. That is why I told Colin."

Clearly, I had not been successful at creating the peaceful environment I had wanted for Nikki. Five months ago Dukwicz, a mercenary of international repute, had killed Nikki's dad, taken part in my and Colin's kidnapping, and then managed to escape capture. The president had asked us to find him, but after five months of non-stop investigation, we still had not located him.

Nikki's criminal father had tried to keep her away from his illegal activities once she'd entered her adolescence. I had hoped to prevent any of my work touching her life.

"See," she said, pointing at my face. "I didn't want you to look like that."

"Like what?"

"Stressed."

I looked at her young, open face, weighing my words. "You shouldn't worry about me. Every day is stressful for many different reasons. I stress when Vinnie cooks dinner, hoping that he will remember to clean up after himself. I stress when it rains, knowing that I will have to polish the floors to remove muddy footprints. I stress when you put a cup on the coffee table, because you spilled a drop and it might stain the wood. But I've learned how to deal with my stress. The worst form of stress is when I have a lack of information. The more I know, the safer I feel. So please tell me everything you know about these messages."

"Wow. That's kinda screwed up." She winced at her

indelicacy. "Sorry. You are just sometimes really hard to understand."

"I know. We can discuss this issue at a later, more opportune time. Now, I need to know about the messages."

She took the phone, swiped the screen twice and handed it back. "That is the first DM. It only said, *'Vermeer @ 89 Rue de Jonette'*. Nothing more. There are so many freaks hanging out on Twitter and Facebook, I didn't pay attention to it when I received it a week ago."

"Six days ago." The date and time of the message was above the five words.

"Yeah. Well, I totally forgot about it until yesterday's message."

I looked up from the phone. "Next time I would like it if you told me."

"Oh, God. I didn't mean to hurt your feelings." Her brows pulled together and her lips thinned in distress. She leaned forward and put her hand on the duvet, reaching out to me. "I trust you, Doc G. With my life. You are the best thing that could have happened to me. I just didn't want to worry you."

"I understand, Nikki." I could see she wasn't convinced. Inwardly I sighed. "I'm not offended or hurt. You made the best choice you thought available, even though your reasoning was greatly flawed."

"Ouch, but you are right. Sorry, Doc G. Next time I'll come straight to you."

"Or Colin if I'm not here. Or Vinnie when Colin's not available." I thought about this. "I think it would be better to tell Manny before you tell Francine anything."

Nikki smiled. "Why? Because she'll immediately tell me it's aliens or a government conspiracy?"

"Yes. Manny will be much more reasonable in his conclusions. And he has a gun." My phone vibrated in my dressing gown pocket once before a loud song about not being able to read a poker face alerted me to a call. I took the phone out of my pocket and almost smiled despite my annoyance at the changed ringtone. "Hello, Manny."

"Doc, what have you got for me?"

I told him what Nikki had told me and what I had read on her phone. "The person sending these emails doesn't seem to be very intelligent."

"Why, Doc?"

"Well, his math was insulting in its simplicity."

"Do you think he meant that if we add up his clues we will come to the right conclusion?"

"That is conjecture, but tolerable. There is another reason I think he's not very smart. Using 'pervasive reach' is redundant. Pervasive means to have a far reach."

"Okay, now can you tell me what the bloody hell Frey is doing at Claude Savreux's house?"

"I don't know yet. Let me put you on speakerphone and you can ask Nikki." I tapped the screen and looked at Nikki. She exhibited contrition again.

"Hi, Manny," she said, looking at the phone.

"Hello, lass." His tone softened considerably. Manny's affection for Nikki was undisguised. "Now tell me why ~~that~~ you sent that thief to a politician's house."

"I didn't send him there. And I didn't know it was a politician's house." She took a deep breath and relaxed her shoulders. "When I told Colin about the two DM's, he said that I was not to worry about it anymore and that he would look into it. He told me that I did the right thing to tell him and not Doc G. He also didn't want to worry her."

"Do you know anything about this Flinck person?" Manny asked.

"Yes." There was no trace of uncertainty in her answer. Of all the options available to her, Nikki had chosen to study art. She was in her first year, and I had made sure she understood that she had complete freedom to choose any specialisation she preferred. Four months into her course, she loved every minute of it and studied harder than most students. "Three weeks ago we looked into Dutch artists. Govaert Flinck was part of the Dutch Golden Era. That was a time in Dutch history when some of the best Dutch artists, scientists and tradesmen lived. They were internationally known. Um, as well as anyone could be internationally known before the internet."

"Doc, do you know anything about this Flinck? Anything more than being famous before the internet?"

"No." I shook my head even though Manny couldn't see. "In this case, Nikki knows more than I do."

"Nikki, did Frey do anything specific when you told him about the message?"

"Um, yeah. His eyes widened in the way Doc G says shows surprise."

"Hmm."

There was a moment of silence and I wondered if Colin was safe. I leaned towards the phone. "Did you organise people you trusted to go to the house?"

"Yes, Doc. I'm on my way to the house now. Hopefully they will have the warrant by the time I get there. As soon as we've cleared it and I'm sure it's safe, I'll phone you to meet us there. Maybe you can be of some help."

"I'll meet you there." I tapped the screen of my phone to end the call before Manny's inevitable arguments. Almost immediately, the same poker face song filled Nikki's bedroom again. I turned off the sound and stared at Nikki.

"What?" She shrank back against the headboard.

"I want you to go into my bedroom and lock that door until we come back."

"You won't let me come with you?"

"I want you to be safe. My bedroom has an enforced door with extra locks." My fingers curled into fists. This was very difficult for me. I bit down hard and spoke through my teeth. "You can sleep in my bed until we come back. It's important for me to know that you are protected."

"Where's Vinnie?"

"Not here." I walked to her door, my phone vibrating in my hand. "Give me five minutes to get dressed."

It took me four minutes to get dressed and one minute to calm my breathing. Rationally I knew that I only had to change the bedding after Nikki slept in my bed to make it mine again, but still I found this most perturbing. Colin was the only one I had ever allowed to sleep in my bed. For some irrational reason it was not only acceptable, but enjoyable to have him sleep next to me. The thought of anyone else—even someone I cared for—sleeping in my bed caused me great anxiety.

I found it interesting that Nikki's safety and my concern about Colin took precedence over my usual obsessions. Two years ago, my focus had been purely on maintaining my equilibrium and my routines. Now I was impatiently waiting for Nikki so I could make sure she locked herself in my bedroom while I went to this mystery address.

Chapter TWO

"Are you ever going to listen to me, missy?" Manny whispered through tight lips as soon as I got out of my car. "I said I will phone you when it is safe to come."

"Why are you whispering?" I kept my tone down, but didn't see the need to whisper. There was more than enough noise on the tree-lined, suburban street to wake the neighbours at this early hour. The officers in black uniforms couldn't prevent their boots from crunching over the snow as they moved towards the house at the end of the street. I had parked next to Manny's car, three houses from the address Nikki had received.

"We're not hosting a bloody street party here. If Savreux is dead, the killer might still be in the house." He shook his head and scowled at me. "You shouldn't be here. And you should've answered your phone."

"You were going to argue with me and waste time." I shrugged. My phone had buzzed the whole way to this house. I had checked every time, and ignored it when I had seen it wasn't Colin. "I didn't see the point in an inane debate with you."

His nostrils flared and he threw his hands in the air as he turned away from me.

"Hi, Doctor Lenard."

I jumped at the deep voice speaking quietly behind me and spun around, my hand pressing hard against my sternum. A tall man stood next to my car, his posture typical of soldiers—on constant alert. He was in full uniform, which included a black facemask, but I recognised the friendly eyes. Daniel Cassel was a team leader for GIPN, a rapid response team similar to SWAT.

"Good evening, Daniel. I keep telling you to call me Genevieve."

"Genevieve." He smiled. "Manny said you were coming. Do you have any more intel?"

"I told Manny everything I…" My voice tapered down when Daniel's body suddenly went still. It was the kind of stillness observed in animals when they became aware of a threat and stopped to analyse the sound. I was about to ask him what he had heard when boots crunched on the snow to our left. Daniel pushed me behind him and had his gun aimed at the sound before I could protest him touching me. To my right, Manny also had his gun aimed at the sound coming closer.

Manny's eyes widened slightly in recognition, but he didn't lower his weapon. "Please give me a reason to shoot you."

I peeked around Daniel. Colin stood a few feet away from us, lifting his eyebrows at Manny's handgun. Daniel's posture relaxed and he holstered his weapon. "Monsieur Goddphin. Pleased to meet you again."

Colin had introduced himself to Daniel a year ago, wearing a disguise and going by the name Sydney Goddphin, a seventeenth-century poet.

"Daniel." Colin nodded, but didn't take his eyes off Manny's handgun. "You can holster that thing now, Millard."

"Give me a few moments more. I'm enjoying this."

Neither one of them wanted to talk about the reason for the recent hostility towards each other, but this was reaching ridiculous levels. I stepped out from behind Daniel to stand in Manny's line of sight. Colin smiled when Manny swore and holstered his weapon, but then frowned at me. "You shouldn't be here."

"One of the few things we agree on, Frey."

"I suppose you are the reason for this nightly excitement, Goddphin?" Daniel lifted his chin towards the house at the end of the street.

Colin's eyes narrowed for a second as he made a decision. He nodded as if to himself and held out his hand to Daniel. "Colin Frey. You might as well use my real name."

"Colin Frey, huh? Well, well." Daniel shook Colin's hand, one corner of his mouth lifting. He had recognised the name, most likely from a criminal context. "Things are making more sense now. I take it you were inside the house?"

"Yes." Colin looked at me. "Did Nikki tell you about the DM's?"

"She did and I told Manny everything."

"Which he told me," Daniel said. "My guys are in place to go into the house, but I need to know if you have anything else to add."

Colin and Daniel started talking about the layout of the house, the best places to enter, and exits to keep an eye on in case the killer was still in the house and was flushed out. Manny was listening with interest to the conversation. Despite the fluctuating levels of animosity between Manny and Colin, they reluctantly respected each other's expertise, even if they would never acknowledge it in public.

Once Daniel was satisfied that he had a better overview of the house, he left to coordinate with his team. He seemed even more vigilant than the last time I had seen him. It might be because five months ago he had declared a house cleared of people and explosives when it hadn't been. We had entered that house only to be held at gunpoint, an experience that still hovered in the back of my mind. It had taken months before I had stopped obsessing about what could have happened, and only recently had I been able to limit checking the locks to my apartment to only three times throughout the night.

"It's going to take them a while to clear the house." Manny turned away from the street where he had been following Daniel's progress to the house, his focus now entirely on Colin. "What do you know about Claude Savreux?"

"Not much." Colin's shoulders lifted. "He's been on the news lately talking about the decision to send even more troops to CAR. That was pretty much when I stopped paying attention. Other than that I don't even know what kind of politician he is."

"He's the Minister of Defence and Veteran Affairs," I said. "Lately, he's brought a lot of attention to PTSD and that not only soldiers who have been in combat suffer from it. He's been on quite a few political talk shows, saying that the government needs to do more to look after their soldiers as well as other people suffering from PTSD."

"What else do you know, Doc?"

"I don't know much about his professional and personal life. He appears to be a civic-minded politician. But these bits of information I've learned from the news, not that the news is ever a believable representation of the truth."

Manny's eyebrows lifted. "You sound like Francine."

"No, no. This is not a conspiracy theory. This is a truth that has been proven often enough. Francine believes that governments feed the media whatever fodder they consider appropriate in order to keep the masses ignorant and controlled." Our IT expert Francine was prone to fanciful hypotheses. She was also my only female friend. I frowned. "This is of absolutely no relevance to this conversation. What do you know about Savreux?"

"The same as you," Manny said. "I didn't even know he lived in Strasbourg. I thought all these bigwigs lived in Paris. Okay, so we don't know much about Savreux. Frey, what do you know about this Flinck?"

"He lived in the seventeenth century in Holland and was one of the artists in the Dutch Golden Era. He was reputed to be one of Rembrandt's best students. Surely you know who Rembrandt is."

Manny looked towards the end of the street, ignoring Colin's baiting. "So? Was there a Flinck Golden Era painting in the house?"

Colin shook his head. "I went through most of the rooms in the house and didn't see any of Flinck's work anywhere."

"What the hell does that message to Nikki mean?" Manny didn't look at us as he asked this and I wondered if he expected an answer.

Before I could voice my confusion, a soft whistle caught our attention. Daniel was standing outside the house on the corner, waving at us to come closer.

I turned to follow Manny, but Colin stopped me with his gloved hand on my arm. He stepped in front of me, waiting until he had my full attention. "There is a dead man inside that house, Jenny. He's lying on a carpet that is now stained with his blood. Are you sure you want to go in there?"

When I had accepted the job as an insurance investigator at Rousseau & Rousseau, I had never imagined that I would see so many dead bodies. At times it had been traumatic, but my ability to compartmentalise had stood me in good stead. Despite this skill, I still gave Colin's question considerable thought before I nodded. "I'm sure. As long as Daniel and his team are there to keep us safe, I'll go in."

"Okay." He held out his hand and I placed mine in his. I was still wearing my driving gloves and therefore didn't feel the contact at all, yet it gave me the level of comfort that I had come to expect whenever Colin touched me. As we walked the ninety metres to where Manny and Daniel were talking, I thought about how powerful the mind was at searching for and finding safety and comfort when it was the thing we needed most.

"You guys know the drill," Daniel said when we stopped next to them. "Don't touch anything, don't move anything and if you see something suspicious, call me or one of my team."

He waited until we all agreed, stepped away from the front door and gestured us in. Manny walked in first, his posture slightly changed. Most of the times he was hunched over, creating the image of someone not paying attention to anything around him. It was an illusion. He was one of the most astute observers I had come across.

Colin didn't let go of my hand as we entered behind Manny. I had learned to appreciate their concern for not only my physical safety, but also my mental well-being. Yet I simultaneously found it irritating. There were moments it felt as if they considered me incapable of looking after myself— something I had done since the age of seventeen. I dismissed these musings and paid attention to the house.

It was a home befitting a politician. It had clearly been decorated by a professional designer, the furniture and finishing touches of the highest quality. Persian carpets covered dark wooden floors and the walls hosted paintings of old masters and more modern works. Working daily with insuring high-end possessions, I knew that just the frame on the painting above the eighteenth-century table was worth five hundred euro. We slowly made our way through the entrance and past what appeared to be a formal reception area to our right. Manny looked into the room and immediately the tension in his body increased.

"This where it happened?" he asked over his shoulder.

"Yes." Daniel walked past me to stand next to Manny. "The crime scene unit is going to have our heads for walking in here without any protective gear, but I wanted you to see the scene as it is before they get here with all their equipment."

Manny nodded and looked at me. "You up for this, Doc?"

"If you are asking whether I am ready to see a dead body, my answer is no. But I will go in nonetheless."

"Well then, shall we?" He didn't wait for an answer, and walked through the doorway. Colin and I followed.

The room was a textbook example of understated elegance. It was clearly a man's home office. A large, dark wooden desk dominated the left side of the room. There were no ornaments on the desk itself, but the coffee tables and mantelpiece held a few noteworthy works of art. To the right, in front of the fireplace, two deep leather chairs faced a leather sofa, the arrangement separated by a low, solid wood coffee table. I took in all the details, trying to memorise as much as possible. Later we would have photos of the scene, but the first impression was the most important to me. This impression included the ambience, smells, sounds and anything that felt out of place.

A few things registered in my mind. The lack of a fire was the first. It was mid-winter, yet that fireplace had not been used today. It was pristine, as if thoroughly cleaned a few hours ago. The second thing I noticed was the smell. It was disconcerting that I was familiar with that coppery smell. I looked towards the heavy beige curtains across from the doorway. On the carpet close to the curtains only two legs were visible, the rest of the body hidden by the desk.

I took a fortifying breath and slowly walked deeper into the room.

Bit by bit the body of a middle-aged man was revealed. A few times I had seen him on television, which made it easier to recognise his face. There were a few theories about facial expressions upon death. Some said that your face would be frozen in that very last emotion that went through you as you breathed your last breath. I held no such beliefs, but if I did, the last emotion Savreux had felt had been outrage. There was not a single indicator of fear, regret, sadness or even resignation visible on his face. Interesting.

I realised that I was focussing on his face in order to avoid looking lower. I had noticed his presumed cause of death, but hadn't wanted to study it too closely. Knowing that I could miss some important clue, I lowered my eyes to his throat and the dark purple line around it, and the deep scratches where Minister Savreux had tried to get to the garrotte.

Strangling someone was a rather personal method of murder. It required being close to the victim. More importantly, it necessitated physical strength to hold the garrotte tight enough around the victim's neck until he or she expired. It was physically demanding but effective. That led me to question the presence of the blood on his shirt. I stepped even closer, staring at what had once been a white shirt.

Dark panic started to creep up on me, the periphery of my vision turning black. It was hard to stay unaffected when facing such brutality. I sucked in a deep breath, closed my eyes and imagined Mozart's Violin Concerto in E Flat Major playing in my mind. This piece I usually used when I wanted my mindset to be one of rational work.

A few minutes later, the panic receded. When I opened my eyes, everyone was in a different place in the room, except Colin. He was still next to me, holding my hand.

"Okay?"

"Yes." I pointed to Minister Savreux's bloody shirt. "Look at all the holes. I count at least fifteen."

"Overkill," Daniel said from next to the desk. He was opening and closing drawers. "That usually happens when it is a crime of passion, when the killer knows the victim well."

"And wants to take out all his anger on the person." Manny stood a few feet away from the body, studying it with one eyebrow raised. "Who did Savreux piss off? Did he have some dirty secret that his wife found out?"

"He doesn't have a wife," a new voice said from the door. The tall, muscular man was still wearing his ski mask and helmet, also part of their uniform, making him hard to identify, but his voice sounded familiar.

"What do you know about Savreux, Pink?" As soon as Daniel said the name, I remembered. A year ago, we had saved the president's son, and Pink had been the IT and electronics specialist on Daniel's team. I still didn't know his real name, just his silly moniker.

Pink slung his rifle over his shoulder and removed his helmet and mask. "Hi, everyone."

Manny grunted a greeting. "Is he divorced?"

"No, his wife died of cancer about sixteen years ago and he never remarried. There are rumours about him having lovers, more than one at a time. Sometimes even together."

"Anything factual?" I hated tabloid-level gossip.

"If you consider photos as factual, then yes." Pink nodded

towards Savreux. "Until his wife died, he'd been quite an upstanding guy. Speculation is that she kept him on the straight and narrow. Once she was out of the picture, he did what he wanted. But he was always discreet. He never flaunted anything, not the money he inherited from his wife's estate, not—"

"Wait." I lifted my index finger. "Tell me more about the inheritance."

"All straightforward. He earned well while they were married, so there was never any suggestion that he had married her for her money. They lived quite modestly for such super-rich people. And before you ask, she got her money from her father who owned a huge clothing chain. She never worked a day in her life, but was always very involved in charities." He stopped to think for a moment while looking at Savreux's body. "That was something he continued even after her death. At every charity event, he mentioned her name and how he was doing this in her honour."

"Is it just me, or does this guy sound too good to be true?" Colin asked. He had left my side and was walking around the room. He stopped at the mantelpiece, looking closely at every ornament.

"Being a politician, the chances are quite good that we will find skeletons in his closet," Pink said. "None of them get to where they are without making enemies or stepping over the line a time or five."

"Doc?" Manny didn't have to finish his question.

"I understand the sentiment." Since I was not naturally adept at catching nuances, figures of speech and hints at the truth, Manny and the rest of the team had respected that by saying exactly what they meant. In this case, the meanings were quite easy to construe.

"What do you think?"

"I think it is far too early to draw any conclusions. I would only dare having an opinion about this man once I have gathered sufficient information."

"Oh, my God!" Pink's smile was genuine. "Now I remember why I liked you so much."

I didn't know how to react to this and didn't even bother with a social smile. I turned back to the body and pointed at Savreux's forearms. He had rolled up his shirtsleeves to reveal tanned and muscular arms. "I can't see any defensive wounds. He must have been caught by surprise, or he was subdued in some other way."

"Or he could have been drugged." Colin pointed to a whiskey glass on the coffee table in front of the sofa. Both Colin and I were intimately acquainted with being drugged. The mention of it brought uncomfortable tension to my throat and chest. I ignored it and continued to survey the body and its immediate surroundings.

For more than a minute, the only sound in the room was the ticking of an antique clock on the bookshelf. When I felt that I had seen enough, I walked over to where Colin was studying a large painting to the left of the fireplace. He was biting his bottom lip, his forehead was furrowed and his head tilted. He'd been scrutinising every centimetre of that painting for the last five minutes. "What are you looking at?"

"This is an original Jackson Pollock." His tone lifted slightly as he stood back, his arms folded. "This is… this is unbelievable. There are few of his paintings ever on sale. How did this man get a Pollock?"

"But that's not this Flinck artist we are looking for." Manny's voice and expressions no longer held the earlier animosity against Colin. "If that painting is not here, Frey, why don't you go through the house to make sure that it isn't hidden somewhere?"

Colin gave a single nod and looked at me. "Coming?"

"Yes." I wanted to see the rest of the house to get a better impression of Claude Savreux, the man. Even if a person's house were decorated by a designer, there would be areas showing the influence of the inhabitant. Already his home office revealed a man for whom portraying the image of old money was important. The decor told me that he had wanted to impress with the wealth of his collections, but not to overwhelm.

The rest of the house was not much different. On the walls were paintings that caused Colin's eyes to widen and a few times his pupils dilated, informing me of how much Colin loved looking at that specific work. Our pupils dilated when we wanted to visually absorb as much as possible from whatever was giving us pleasure. Pink followed us from room to room, dividing his attention between monitoring the environment, inspecting the rooms and checking his tablet. That last habit reminded me of Francine.

In the master bedroom, he shook the tablet. "Aha! I've got some more info on Savreux."

Colin turned away from a landscape painting that could have been a Monet or a Renoir. He had been standing close, his nose millimetres away from the canvas. "Scandals or boring biographical info?"

"Mostly the boring stuff." Pink's nose wrinkled, expressing tedium.

"It is in details others dismiss as banal or boring that one can often find important clues," I said. "Tell me what you have."

"Well"—Pink looked at his tablet screen—"when Savreux wasn't busy with his charity work, he was arguing with the president."

"The president of France?" The person we were working for?

"The one and only. According to these articles, Savreux and a few others have opposed more than one legislation supported by President Godard."

"What legislations?"

"One of those... well, it looks like the president was pushing for privacy reform. This is most likely a backlash from all the spying scandals recently revealed. You know, with those leaked documents showing how the US government has been spying on everyone and his dog."

"Why would any government spy on someone's dog?" This was most peculiar.

"It's an expression, Jenny." Colin chuckled. "You really should read that book Vinnie gave you for Christmas."

A few months ago, I had experienced my first true Christmas courtesy of my friends. The decorations Francine had put up in my apartment had caused me numerous panic attacks. Vinnie had spent even more time than usual in the kitchen, involving Nikki in all his cooking. Christmas Eve dinner had been extravagant to a point that I had considered planning a journey for next Christmas. As much as I hated travelling and all the panic surrounding a trip, it was much preferred to another Christmas Eve dinner. The excessive food, bits of tinsel under my furniture, tinsel finding its way to my bedroom had pushed very hard at my obsessive-compulsive borders.

The gift-giving had been pleasant though. There had been a pile of colourfully wrapped gifts under the tree—a tree

Colin had thoughtfully insisted had to be artificial since the pine needles would've driven me into a daily cleaning frenzy. Of all the gifts, Vinnie's book with the top one thousand metaphors and expressions had given everyone the most pleasure. It was still unread on the coffee table.

"Jenny?" Colin touched my arm to bring me back to the present. "Are you listening?"

"I am now."

Pink smiled. "I was saying that Savreux provoked quite a public attack on President Godard for the new legislation he wants to pass. President Godard's No Secrets law."

"Oh yes, I know about that." It had been in the news for a long time. I remembered the president using transparency of officials across the board as his key election campaign issue more than two years ago. "He wants all elected officials to open their finances for the public to see, personal and official finances."

"He also wants to limit the immunity from prosecution members of parliament and the ministers enjoy." Pink's smile was light and genuine. "There are a few very vocal guys unhappy about that. Minister Savreux was one of them."

"I'll have to read about this." I couldn't wait to get to my computers. "It might give us more insight into this murder."

"Especially since it is so close to next week."

"What's happening next week?"

"That's when President Godard is speaking to Parliament. He has been building his case for a long time and has gained a surprising support in the Senate and National Assembly for this kind of transparency." Pink was swiping the screen of his tablet as he was talking. "Hmm, the president's wife is also involved in this. She was on a talk show this week sharing her personal financial situation. She even had her bank statements there. Brave woman."

Pink continued talking about the No Secrets law, but I had stopped listening. I didn't believe in coincidences. In the average citizen's life, there were incidences of happenstance that I was willing to concede to. However, in the lives of politicians, events seldom occurred without being connected to either their own strategy or that of somebody planning to use them. I worked daily with the data of clients for whom every meeting was calculated, every person they were introduced to a possible ally in achieving their goals. These people's lives were filled with events or people so carefully introduced as to appear coincidental.

With this in mind, I refused to believe that the direct messages Nikki had been receiving, the art implicated in both, Savreux's death, and his connection to the president and his wife were happenstance. This intrigued me and I shifted impatiently. I wanted to get to my computers.

Chapter THREE

The quiet whoosh of the door to my viewing room took my attention away from the ten monitors I was looking at. My viewing room was one of the few places in the world I felt completely safe. When Phillip Rousseau had hired me to work at Rousseau & Rousseau, he had converted a room to my exact needs. The room was spacious, completely soundproof and had ten computer monitors mounted in a curve to give me all the viewing space I needed. The desk in front of the monitors was long and clear of any clutter—the way I liked it.

Phillip walked into the room, looking fresh and as elegant as always. His dark grey bespoke suit was complemented by a deep red silk tie and shoes that I knew he had specially made in Italy. He had been the first person in my life to treat me with acceptance and respect. Over the last seven years, our relationship had evolved to become much more personal now viewed him as the wise and honourable father fi had longed for as a child.

"Good morning, Genevieve." He stopped chair, staring down at me. He knew I did in lying or pretending, and therefore s as he was currently doing. As if try of mind.

"Good morning, Phillip. Why a

"What time did you get in?" Answ question confirmed that he was concei.

"I was here at thirteen minutes past four."

He waited for more, but I didn't have anything to add. After a few seconds, he sighed. "And you don't think it strange to be at your desk at such an hour in the morning?"

"I had work to do." I shrugged. "Colin broke into Minister Claude Savreux's house last night and found him murdered in his home office. I found the lack of knowledge I had about this man most disconcerting and wanted to learn more about him."

Phillip looked away, took a deep breath and turned back to me. "If Manny had not briefed me on the situation, your careless announcement would've been very worrying."

"What careless announcement?" I quietened when I noticed Phillip's expression. He wore that expression when I was not paying attention to my words or the implications thereof. I took a moment to think and nodded. "I can see how that sentence could be a cause of concern. I apologise."

He pulled a chair closer and sat down. "Did you find what you were looking for?"

"I've been through most of his personal history that's available online. I was just about to start with his professional history."

"Why don't you take a small break and join us for breakfast?"

I leaned back. "You are not offering a suggestion. What is happening?"

His quick glance towards the glass doors connecting my living room to the team room had me turning around to into the next room. When the president had asked to head our team for special investigations, Phillip rously offered to convert another room to the exact the team. At first, I had resisted the idea of my room to the team room with the sliding glass doors, but logic had prevailed. It granted me and the others easier access. It also gave them ample opportunities to interrupt my work, insisting I take breaks and eat. Their intentions were appreciated. The interruptions not so much.

The team room had a complex computer station to Francine's specifications. She was after all considered to be one of the world's best hackers. Manny had a desk that was always overflowing with files and little scraps of paper. I had a clear view of most of the room, especially the round table in the far corner where we usually had meetings. At the moment, most of the team were assembled around the table, looking expectantly at me. Colin wasn't at the table and I didn't know where he was.

"Vinnie brought breakfast. It's only croissants, muffins and other pastries, but it is enough to feed us for three days." Phillip stood up. "Tim is making coffee and should bring it in any moment now."

He walked to the glass doors, entered the code into the keypad and waited at the open doors for me. I glanced longingly at my monitors and my shoulders dropped as I got up. "I'm not eating any of those jam doughnuts Vinnie likes so much."

"Aw, come on, Jen-girl. There is nothing like a doughnut to give you more energy." Vinnie's voice in the team room. At almost two meters tall, a body of a wrestler, Vinnie had the personalit match. "But if you really don't want this, I of those special pastries you like so mu

I sat down in my usual chair at th the three plates of baked goods a separate plate were three pastn everyone else preferred. I hated the lips and fingers, creating a mess around my plate. These little pastries were neat. Only a few crumbs ever landed on my plate.

"Thank you, Vinnie." I turned to Nikki, who was seated on my left. "I didn't know you would be here."

"Vinnie insisted." Nikki communicated so many different emotions through her tone that it had taken me a few weeks to decipher those. Her expressions were easier to understand. Her lips were in thin lines, the top lip slightly curled. "He thinks I'm in danger. Again."

"Rather safe than sorry, punk." Vinnie loaded his plate with three muffins and two croissants, and licked his fingers. I shuddered. "Until we figure out what is happening and who is sending you those tweety emails, you're stuck with me."

"No!" Nikki turned to me, her face pleading. "Please, Doc G. I don't want a bodyguard. Vinnie scares off anyone and everyone who wants to talk to me."

"It was only once, punk. That dude had more jewellery on his body than my auntie Helen at Christmas dinner."

"I think the criminal is right, Nikki." As usual, Manny's expression conveyed affection when he looked at Nikki. "We don't know what any of this means, so I would rather err on the side of caution."

"Seriously?" She threw her napkin on the table. "Can I still ◌ to my classes?"

"Can't you afford to take a week off?" Francine asked from ◌d her computer. She got up and brought her tablet to ◌le. "It's only a week, girl. Give us the chance to figure ◌ and keep you safe at the same time."

"◌o you even know that my life is in danger?" Nikki ◌rms, her eyebrows raised.

"These direct messages were sent to you, Nikki." I said. "To an account that doesn't have your name associated with it. Take a moment to think clearly about this. Don't let your underdeveloped cerebral cortex influence your logic."

I didn't understand why there were chuckles around the table. It was common knowledge that the thinking part of the human brain only developed fully by the age of twenty-six. Most decisions made before then were not carefully considered, and actions taken were most often impulsive and regretted later on.

"Yeah, yeah, I know. Observe, assess, analyse and act. You've told me that a million times."

"Impossible. I don't recall the exact number of times I have…" I sighed when the *zygomaticus* muscles around Nikki's mouth relaxed into a smile. "You were being hyperbolic. Again. Well then, if you do as I advise, you will see the wisdom in taking a few days off while we observe, assess, analyse and act."

She picked up her napkin and forcefully placed it on her lap. "Fine. But I'm doing this with great discontent, unhappiness and rebellion in my heart."

"So noted." I ignored her redundant use of language. Even though she was annoyed, her micro-expressions exhib none of the exaggerated emotions she had laid claim

Our discussion was interrupted when Tim c team room, carrying a tray with a large the mugs. Timothée Renaud had started assistant six weeks ago. It had taker recover when his previous assista giving away confidential client da investigating. Another month had b right person for the position. I had given my vote of confidence when the twenty-nine-year-old man had stood up to Manny during one of the many interviews.

His nonverbal cues had been consistent throughout all six interviews, conducted separately with Phillip, Manny, Colin and even Vinnie. It was the latter's size that had had the most intimidating effect on Tim. The others' verbal manipulations had not affected him as strongly. I had watched the footage of the interviews seven times each. None of us wanted to repeat the loathsome experience of a close associate's disloyalty. Thus far, Tim had lived up to the expectations placed on him.

"Well, aren't you just having the little party here?" Tim rolled his eyes at the plates on the table and shook his head at Vinnie. "You got these pastries at that other shop? I've told you before, just walk twenty metres on and you'll find better quality goodies. Mind you, they might have a dress code."

"And what? I have to wear those skinny pants, that girly tailored shirt, and those shiny shoes to buy doughnuts?" Vinnie pushed a whole doughnut in his mouth and talked around it. "No, thank you."

"At least I don't cause old ladies to scamper away from me." Tim's effeminate pronunciation and mannerisms had convinced the others he was homosexual, but I had my doubts. His sexual orientation was of no concern to me and rather pay attention to how he stood up to Vinnie.

That was only once." Vinnie slammed one hand on the "What is it with you guys piling on me? Is it an 'I hate day today?"

love you, big guy." Francine patted him on his cheek when he uttered a disgruntled noise.

"I'll leave you lovelies to it then." Tim turned to Phillip. "I'll be at my desk if you need anything, boss."

Phillip nodded. "Thank you, Tim."

Vinnie poured coffee for us, serving Manny last. Francine had grabbed the first mug of coffee, not even taking her eyes off her tablet. I held her skills in the highest regard. Before I had met Francine, I had considered myself quite adept at finding information on the internet. She superseded my skills to such an extent that the only research I now did was superficial. There was no sense in wasting time when Francine could uncover important and concise information in a fraction of the time it took me.

"If no one is going to talk, I'll tell you what I have so far," she said after taking a long sip of coffee.

"Did you find out who's been sending me the DM's?" Nikki asked.

"I've been working on it. So far I've been able to track that specific Twitter account through five different countries, ending in Georgia—the country, not the US state." She looked up from her tablet, blinking slowly at Manny. "Wanna hear how I did this, handsome?"

"Don't start with me, supermodel. Just tell us what you got."

"Sadly, this was all I got." Her hand fleetingly touched the back of her neck. People were inclined to do this when they were hiding something. "I have a few more ideas on how to track this guy. Just give me time. I'll get him."

"Bloody hell. You are hacking Twitter or doing something equally illegal, aren't you?" Manny must have also noticed Francine's deception cue.

"Me? Hacking? Why, my dear handsome agent, I would never do such a thing." She blew him a kiss and started swiping and tapping on her tablet's screen again.

I was about to share with them the new information I had gathered on Minister Savreux when Colin walked into the team room. One look at his face and I spoke before I thought. "You found something exciting."

Colin closed his eyes briefly, a blocking gesture our limbic brain employed when we wanted to avoid something. He looked at the pastries on the table and smiled. "Breakfast. Great. I'm really hungry. Vin, can I have some coffee, please?"

"Frey." Manny's voice was low with warning. "Where have you been and what did you learn?"

Colin took his time placing a blueberry muffin and a croissant on a plate and accepting a mug of coffee from Vinnie before he settled in the chair to my right. He looked at me and sighed. "If only you didn't see so much and speak so fast."

"I'm not sorry, but I feel like I should apologise."

"It's okay, Jenny." He glared at Manny. "I was going to share my discovery in any case."

"Well, then. Don't make us wait any longer." Manny moved his hand in a rolling gesture to hasten Colin.

"When Nikki showed me the DM about the Flinck, she also showed me the first DM about the Vermeer. Since we knew what happened in Savreux's place, I thought it might be a good idea to check out the first address as well."

"You broke into another house?" The *supratrochlear* artery on Manny's forehead was becoming prominent. "What kind of cockamamie thing is that to do? If you are arrested for illegally entering a house, there is nothing I can do for you, Frey."

"Oh, keep your hair on." Colin tilted his head and smiled. It wasn't a sincere smile. "Oh, wait. You don't have much hair."

"Colin." Whenever Phillip used this tone, clients always calmed down. So did Colin. "Tell us what you found in this new place that is so significant."

Colin took a sip of coffee and immediately put the mug down, his lips drawn sideways into a sneer. He was, by his own admission, a coffee snob. "I must be honest that there are very few things in life that can manage to shock me these days. But I surely was not prepared to find Vermeer's The Concert in that house. Nor was I ready for the revelation of whose house it is."

"The Concert of Vermeer?" Phillip had half-risen out of his chair, his eyes wide and his mouth slightly open. "Are you sure? Is it the original? Oh, dear lord."

"What the hell is this Concert and why is this so shocking?" Manny asked, his head swivelling from Phillip to Colin and back.

Phillip sat back down, but looked shaken. "It is one of thirteen works of art that were stolen from a museum in Boston in 1990. It is one of the biggest art heist mysteries in recent history."

"And the value of those paintings together is over five hundred million dollars," Colin said quietly.

There were gasps and shocked exclamations around the table. Though I worked daily with articles insured for incredible amounts, this amount was staggering, even for me.

"Let me give you the complete picture." Colin leaned back in his chair. "It was our lucky day. No one was home and the security system is really below par. It was no fun breaking in. Imagine my surprise when I saw egotistical photos of René Motte all over the house. His walls are covered in photos of his exploits around the world. Whatever wall space is not covered with his face has a few pricey paintings, but not the kind of stuff that would make it worthwhile for an art thief to break in. The street value of all of it on the black market might, and I'm emphasising might, get you one million euro."

"That sounds like it is worthwhile to me," Manny said. "One million euro can get one quite far."

"Nope." Colin shook his head. "It would mean you have to carry out at least fifty paintings, nine statues and other little ornaments to reach that amount. This is not a stealthy operation, and would require time and the unwanted risk of being noticed by the neighbours. It is for small-time crooks and they almost never steal art."

"So the Vermeer wasn't on the walls." I wanted to know more about the painting that was causing Colin's hands to have slight tremors of excitement. "Where did you find it?"

"In a preservation room on the ground floor."

"Wait." Manny scowled. "What is a preservation room?"

Phillip looked at Colin, and nodded when Colin gestured with an open hand for Phillip to continue. "True art collectors understand the delicate nature of the pieces they own. A preservation room is set up to control the temperature, humidity and light to a level that will preserve the artwork in the best possible environment. Some people turn this into an elaborate office or library. Others purely set it up as a store room with rows and rows of shelves, holding the most valuable pieces they have collected."

"I would rather do the library-office thing," Nikki said. "At least I can sit and look at all the beautiful stuff I spent so much money on."

"I'm with you on that one, punk. Why bother buying all these crazy expensive stuff if you're never going to appreciate having it?"

"For investment," Phillip said.

"Oh, don't even try, Phillip." Colin looked at Vinnie with disapproval. "Vin and I have had this argument many times. He understands that art gives an even better return on investment than property and playing on the stock market, but he doesn't think that pretty pictures is the same as having cold hard cash—"

"—hidden in a safe place." Vinnie glared at Colin.

"Can we return to the topic?" I hated when conversations got derailed. "What did you find in the preservation room?"

"A lock that was easy to pick, and security worthy of a few minor artworks, not the pieces I found in there. René Motte should be arrested simply for having inferior security. Okay, okay." Colin patted the air with his palms down to placate me. I was shifting in my chair. "Motte had his preservation room set up as a display room, with a swivel chair in the centre. On the one wall were shelves with Modigliani sculptures, Incan masks and Ancient Egyptian artefacts. On the other walls were quite a few Picasso paintings and sketches, but it was the Vermeer that had central stage. He had obviously decorated the room to give that painting the most prominent place."

"Which means it has the greatest value to him," I said. "It could be the monetary value or the ownership value."

"I think it might be both. Owning a stolen piece of art that not only is that valuable, but comes from a heist that has had many law enforcement agencies scratching their heads for almost a quarter of a century is quite a coup."

"What do we know about this Mud guy?" Manny asked.

"Motte. René Motte." Francine rolled her eyes and waved her tablet. "He has his own Wikipedia page. He's also listed by Forbes as one of the five hundred richest people in the world. He got some money from inheritance, but smartly invested in oil companies and that was where he hit... well, black gold."

"An oligarch." Vinnie put his croissant on his plate, his mouth pulled in an expression as if he had tasted something unpleasant. I assumed it wasn't the pastry. "Most of the oligarchs are Russian and we know that they are all thieving bastards."

"Says the pot calling the kettle black."

I ignored Manny's provocation. I also decided not to question Vinnie's certainty that the Russian oligarchs were thieves. It would mean digressing. Again. "What is Motte doing now?"

"He's been CEO of a few companies, but the last decade or so, he's been sitting on several boards as a member, and is also part of a think tank for the Democratic Platform party."

"Isn't that the president's party?" Nikki asked.

"Yes, it is," Francine said, still swiping her tablet screen.

"Can you find any connection between him and Minister Savreux?" I leaned forward. We might be getting somewhere.

"Not from Wikipedia, no."

I frowned. "I thought you said to never believe anything from Wikipedia. That it is all propaganda and lies."

"Of course it is." She sucked in her cheeks, and flipped her hair over her shoulder in a jerky movement. "I sometimes use it as a starting point. It's already given me a few links to reputable websites with credible information on Motte. Soon I'll tell you what he eats for breakfast."

"Why would he own a painting stolen in Boston twenty-four years ago?" Phillip asked. "Francine, in your research, also look for any connection Motte has with Boston."

"Here's another thought." The tone in Colin's voice got

everyone's attention. "Thirteen works of art were stolen from the Isabella Steward Gardner museum in Boston. This Vermeer, two Rembrandts, drawings by Degas, a Manet and Govaert Flinck's Landscape with an Obelisk."

"Oh, bloody hell." Manny rubbed his hand over his face. "And you think that is the painting you were directed to in Savreux's house?"

"I think it is a safe conclusion taking the latest developments into consideration." The muscles around Colin's eyes and mouth contracted into a genuine smile. "I think we are in the process of solving a twenty-four-year-old crime."

"Don't get too cocky, Frey. We're still far from solving anything. Tell me more about this heist in Boston. Did the locals have any suspects?"

"Me! Me!" Francine's enthusiastic answer startled me, especially when she waved her right hand above her head. "I recently read that the FBI said they knew exactly who had stolen the art, but didn't name the suspects, because the statutes of limitation have run out. Since all the art is still missing, they didn't want to shoot themselves in the foot, but rather look for the works. Anyhoo, that got me interested and I looked into it. There are some really cool theories about who was responsible for that heist."

"Um, maybe later you can add that to your research report, Francine." Phillip was a master in diplomacy and negotiation. "Let's hear from Colin what he knows about it."

"Since Frey is the expert on stealing art, I agree with Phillip on this one, supermodel." He grunted when Francine winked at him. "At least Frey won't have theories that include alien invasions."

"You might be as sexy as hell, but you're a real spoilsport, Manny." Even though Francine's mouth was pulled into an unhappy pout, her eyes communicated merriment. After all this time, I still didn't fully comprehend the pleasure she took in pestering Manny.

He ignored her and turned to Colin. "So? What happened?"

"Two men walked into the Isabella Stewart Gardner Museum, tied up the guards and eighty-one minutes later walked out with thirteen works of art to today's value of five hundred million dollars."

"Bloody hell."

"You can say that again. These guys disguised themselves as policemen and entered through the side entrance of the museum. They buzzed the intercom and demanded to get in, saying they had received reports of a disturbance inside. There were only two guards securing the entire four-storey building, so it was easy to overpower them. They tricked the first guard, who was sitting behind the main security desk, by telling him they had an outstanding arrest warrant for him. He stepped away from the desk and the alarm button that he could've used to call the real police, and they duct-taped him.

"They tied up the other guard as well, disabled an alarm when it went off and took their sweet time stealing the art. It took them less than an hour and a half. Two trips to their car and voila! They had half a billion dollars' worth of hot art."

"That easy?"

"Making it look easy isn't always that easy." Nikki shrugged when everyone looked at her. "What? Doc G makes reading people look easy, but I know she studied very long to be able to do that. Francine makes hacking look easy, but it took her a long time and a lot of practice to get to that level."

Concern tightened my chest. I turned to Nikki. "Your expression tells me that you admire Francine…"

"I have no plans to start hacking anything, Doc G. I also

don't plan to steal anything or to intimidate anyone, but I still think Colin and Vinnie are cool."

"Thanks, punk." Vinnie shook his index finger at her. "But you better not get any criminal ideas. We will spot you coming from a mile away."

I exhaled loudly. There were too many personalities seated around the table. This caused every conversation to be derailed at least five times. In the beginning, I had kept count of the distractions, but found that knowledge useless. Manny was now mocking Colin and Vinnie's sincerity because of their criminal pasts. From experience, I knew that it would require anger from my side to bring the conversation back on track. I didn't desire expending energy on such a doomed ambition, so I closed my eyes and went over the numerous bits of unconnected information.

Was Minister Claude Savreux's death connected to the Boston heist? If so, how was it connected? Most importantly, who was sending Nikki those direct messages? How did he know of her connection to us and where did he get his information? Was he connected to the Boston heist? There were many unanswered questions requiring attention, yet the arguments around the table continued.

Chapter FOUR

It was the sudden silence in the team room that had me opening my eyes. The reason was leaning against the doorway to the corridor. Dressed in an immaculate suit, dress shirt without a tie and the top button undone, Henri Fabron communicated careless style. He was the president's aide and was supposed to work closely with us on any case the president sent our way. In the year we had been working under the president, I had only seen him twice. Today was the second time.

After our first meeting, he had insisted on meeting only with Manny, claiming that the rest of us were inconsequential since we had no law enforcement training. He had told Manny our intellect aside, he was not convinced that any of us would understand the intricacies of politics. He hadn't met any of the others, but had told Manny he didn't trust our team. I didn't trust him.

"Good morning, Manny." Henri stepped into the room, his focus on Manny as if he was the only person in the room.

"Sorry, boss." Tim walked around Henri towards Phillip, his facial muscles tense. "I told Monsieur Fabron there was a meeting, but he insisted on coming in."

"No problem, Tim." Phillip stood up and held out his hand. "Henri, welcome. Please join us."

"I'll get a chair from the other room." Tim started walking to my viewing room.

"No!" I jumped out of my chair, reaching out as if to stop

him. Tim's whole body jerked and he slowly turned around. I lowered my hands and cleared my throat when I realised all eyes were on me. "Please don't take anything from my viewing room."

"He can have my desk chair," Francine said as she walked to her desk and rolled her chair to the round table. She stopped in front of Henri and smiled. It was not a genuine smile, but a smile I had come to recognise whenever Francine was planning something. "Hi. I'm Francine. Who are you?"

"Henri Fabron." He held out his hand to shake hers. The contraction of the muscles around his eyes and the dilation of his pupils was a clear indication of his attraction to Francine. She often elicited this response from men.

"Henri is from the president's office," Phillip said, his eyes moving between Henri and Francine. His expression didn't reveal his thoughts, but his pursed lips indicated displeasure. "We don't see you often enough, Henri."

"I see him more than enough." The change in Manny's posture was miniscule, but the effect large. He hunched his shoulders and adjusted his body language to appear disinterested, even bored.

"Please join us." Phillip gestured at Francine's chair.

"Thank you, Phillip." Henri sat down. In the first and only meeting with me, Henri had also insisted on first names. He inhaled to say something else, but stopped when Colin's smartphone started ringing.

"Sorry." Colin didn't look contrite as he took his phone out of his pocket. He glanced at the screen and his eyes widened very slightly before he controlled his expression. He looked at me. "I have to take this. Be back in a second."

I nodded while trying my best not to confront him about

his irrational mention of time. It was going to take him at least three seconds to leave the room. What he had said was physically impossible.

"I hear you were at the scene of a murder last night." Henri looked around the table, but studiously avoided looking at me. This had also happened at our first meeting. His attempt at sounding nonchalant about Minister Savreux's murder was noble, but he failed. Curious. "Care to fill me in?"

Manny shrugged. "One of my CI's got an anonymous tip about some noises and a possible body in a house filled with valuable art, so I reached out to my contact at GIPN to meet me there and the rest I'm sure you know. Have you not read the report?"

Manny did not often lie. He was too impatient for that. The few times he had told an untruth had left me in awe of his smooth ability to do so. It was fortuitous that Henri was avoiding eye contact with me, else he might have seen my quick smile at Manny's expert delivery of the lie. Were I not a top expert in nonverbal communication, I would've been prone to believe Manny. He had just told the most exceptional lie.

"I've read the report. I also spoke to Officer Daniel Cassel. He tells the same story." Henri straightened in his chair to give himself more height. "As I told Officer Cassel, this case will be investigated by a special team that has been assembled for Minister Savreux's unfortunate death. You are to hand over all information to me and move on to the next case."

Observing everyone in the room was a fascinating study. Nikki had made herself as small as possible, hugging her coffee mug to her chest. I knew she would not say a word. Francine was pouting and playing with the pendant of her necklace, drawing attention to her cleavage. Why she was trying to distract Henri, I did not know. Vinnie was leaning back in his chair, watching Manny and Henri through narrowed eyes, and Phillip was his usual professional self. From the body language around the table, it was clear something important was taking place. Something that Manny was taking control of, and everyone was allowing Manny to lead. I was not going to interfere. It was far too educational to watch.

Colin came back into the room and sat down next to me. He looked at Manny, as if to start an argument, but changed his mind and looked at Vinnie. The gesture was subtle, but Vinnie rubbed his index finger vertically over his lips, telling Colin not to speak.

"Why should we just sit back on this investigation?" Manny said with adequate conviction, presenting the requisite protest at having a case taken away from him. "As you know, we are still looking for Dukwicz, so it's not like we're lying on our laurels all day here. But since there aren't any new leads in Dukwicz's case, we might as well take this one."

"This is a direct order, Manny."

"From who?"

"Whom," I said before I could stop myself. Manny glared at me.

"Who gave that order, Henri? President Godard? You know that we only answer to him."

"And you know that just like you work in a team here, we also work in a team. The president has full knowledge of any and all meetings I have with you, as well as the meetings you have with Antoine Lefebvre."

Antoine Lefebvre was the Minister of Justice. Because he presided over the running of the court system, and also supervised the prosecution service, Manny'd had a few meetings with him. I had never met him, but had heard that he was an exceptionally intelligent man. Other words used to describe him were shrewd, cunning and unflappable. He was one of the few officials to ever be involved in our cases. He took an interest since the majority of our cases were at a level most prosecutors didn't function at. He had been a great support, making sure to appoint the best prosecutor to each of our cases. He was also a friend of President Godard's.

"You still haven't answered my question," Manny said.

"This order comes from President Godard at the request of Monsieur Lefebvre. Another, much more important, event has taken place that will need your attention and expertise." Henri paused. People did that to build anticipation towards the apex of their anecdote or announcement. "This morning at seventeen minutes past five, a thief broke into the Jean Monnet Museum and stole art to the value of thirteen million euro."

"What museum is that?" Vinnie asked.

Henri raised his chin a bit higher to look down at Vinnie. "Jean Omer Marie Gabriel Monnet is considered to be one of the founding fathers of the European Union. He was a political economist and diplomat, regarded by many as the chief architect of unity in Europe. This museum was founded in his memory for the great things he'd done for France and Europe."

"You're shitting me. With a name like that?" Vinnie chuckled. "Poor sucker."

"What did they steal?" Phillip asked. The corners of his mouth were turned down, as it was every time he heard of an art heist. He called it a nightmare to even think about this happening.

"A Caravaggio, a Renoir, a Klimt and a Picasso. They

always go for the Picassos. All in all there were six pieces stolen. Not the biggest heist in history, but it happened on our front door. Since you guys are the art theft experts, the president would like for you to take this case."

"What's the president's interest in this museum? Why would he want us to take the case?" I asked.

"The president's wife, Madame Godard, is one of the patrons of this museum, not that it really matters. You exist as a team at the president's request. If the leader of this country asks you to look into a case, you should not question it. You should just do it."

His disparaging tone and the disgust on his face elicited immediate responses. Everyone shifted in their chairs to more alert positions. Everyone except Manny. He waved his hands in a dismissive gesture. "Fine, we'll look into this heist. We don't have any file open on Minister Savreux's death yet, so there's nothing to give to you. We were actually having a team meeting to brainstorm how to tackle this when you came in. Good thing too, else we would've wasted time on a dead politician. No offense, of course."

"None taken." Purposefully, Henri looked around the table, making eye contact with everyone but me. I registered every micro-expression he exhibited when he looked at the team, especially when he looked at Nikki. He was schooling his expression, controlling it to reveal only contempt and disrespect. A few contradictory micro-expressions gave me pause. I needed to process what I was observing. Finally, his gaze fell on Manny. "I want to know that you will put your everything into finding not only the thieves, but especially the artwork stolen this morning. Can I count on you?"

A lot of insincere mumbles rose from the table and I watched in amazement as Henri accepted this. When I had met him a year ago, I had thought of him as astute. Now I thought of him as cunning. He appeared mollified with the lies Manny had told him and the feigned assurances the team had given him. It was in the relaxed muscles in his face as he got up and wished us happy hunting. Very suspicious.

Phillip got up with him and closed the door behind Henri when he left for the elevator. There was a moment of stunned silence before everyone started speaking at the same time.

"Quiet!" Manny stood up, his shoulders straight. "Be quiet for a second."

Francine inhaled to say something, but stopped at Manny's glare.

"What is the latest we have on Dukwicz?" Manny asked.

His sudden change of subjects confused not only me. Everyone was staring at him.

"I spoke to a contact that told me he's in town again," Vinnie said. "Do you think he's responsible for this morning's—"

"—heist?" Manny interrupted. "It's a possibility I'm considering given his track record of breaking and entering. That bastard has been able to get past extremely good security systems with worrying ease. I'm also wondering if supermodel has been diligent in checking our systems for bugs."

Manny's voice dropped half a tone, the micro-expressions around his eyes and mouth revealing a hidden message behind his sentences. I wasn't good at guessing, but it seemed like the others were. Both Colin and Vinnie's body language went from confusion to alertness.

Francine's nonverbal cues told me she too understood Manny's innuendo. She jumped up and dragged her chair back to her computer station. "I check the computers every morning, so I know there's nothing here, but I haven't checked the rooms for possible bugs. I'll get to it right now. Vinnie will help me. Nikki can supervise. We can't have Dukwicz know what we're up to."

Finally I understood the nuances being communicated, but I was struggling to interpret all the pointed looks Francine was giving Manny and Vinnie. Turning to Colin, I lifted my shoulders and hands in an inquiring gesture. He mouthed the word 'later' and winked.

"While supermodel is checking to make sure Dukwicz has not breached our security, we will go to the museum and check out this art theft. Come on, Frey. Since you're the expert, you can tell us how they did it."

Colin and I got in his SUV and followed Manny for twenty-three blocks to the Jean Monnet Museum. Colin had given me a warning look that I understood to mean that the car was also not a safe place to talk. From Colin's music selection, I chose Mozart's Clarinet Concerto in A major and sat back to listen to the soothing sounds for the twelve-minute drive to the city centre.

We parked behind Manny's ten-year-old sedan. It was curious that we had found parking so easily at half past ten in the morning. Not only was the museum located in the city centre, but it was in the tourist area that saw a lot of foot and vehicle traffic. Despite the month and the lack of tourists, this part of the city was always busy and packed during workdays and weekends alike. This led me to wonder if the police had cleared the area of traffic and parked cars.

I got out of the SUV and pulled my scarf higher over my chin. It was cold. On the opposite side of the street, pedestrians were slowing down their pace to gawk at the police cars haphazardly parked in front of the museum.

The entrance to the museum was blocked, a police officer standing there, his posture lacking any welcoming cues. It deterred any curious onlookers from crossing the street and asking questions.

Manny waited for us to join him after he spoke to the officer to let us through. The museum was housed in an older building which was well maintained to retain its old-worldly look. This building housed the museum, a boutique and a framing business. Taking up almost two-thirds of the building and using all four floors, the museum was large enough to have a permanent exhibition and host a few temporary exhibitions every year. I had been here when they had a display of Leonardo da Vinci's sketches.

A portly man rushed towards us. "Are you the specialised team? Are you the people who will find these... these barbarians? Why would they break into my museum and steal my art?"

"Did those paintings belong to you?" Why had Henri Fabron not told us this?

When the short man huffed, his stomach jounced. "All the paintings, all the art in my museum get treated as if they were mine."

"And you are?" Manny had on his disinterest persona.

"Rémy Bonfils, the curator of this museum." He dismissed Manny after a quick glance at Manny's oversized and wrinkled coat, and turned to Colin. "What are you doing to get my art back?"

"I'm Sydney Goddphin. Pleased to meet you." Colin took a step closer to Monsieur Bonfils and shook the curator's hand. The curator evaluated Colin's dark winter slacks, his designer coat and expensive Italian boots. I supposed Colin's attire qualified him better as an art theft investigator than

Manny's. People's irrational prejudices amused me. Colin blinked twice at me and stepped away with the curator. "I can guarantee you that my team is doing everything in our power to solve this heinous crime as soon as possible. Now if you could be so kind as to tell me exactly what happened."

Manny watched Colin lead the man to the far side of the room. I didn't observe any animosity. Only calculation. "That Frey is a dangerous player."

"Colin doesn't take part in any sports, except for jogging and some body-building."

"I mean he is a dangerously good liar, Doc." Manny turned to me. "At least we can now walk through this ark and see what happened."

"Firstly, this is not an ark. And secondly, you are also an exceptional liar, Manny. Your skills with Henri Fabron impressed me."

"Don't make too much of it, Doc. I just wanted to get him off our backs. That little wet-behind-the-ears twerp has been riding my arse since the day the president got this team together." Manny only ever lapsed into metaphors when he was distracted or extremely angry.

"Why are you distracted?"

"What makes you... never mind." He nodded to the staircase. "Let's go look where the thief entered and took Monsieur Bonfils' paintings."

The foot of the staircase was almost in the centre of the room, leading up to the first floor. A wide balcony ran along three sides, with views onto the floor below. From the balcony, doors led into separate rooms, each holding different parts of the exhibitions. The second and third floors were accessed by a different staircase.

"Have you been here before, Doc?"

"I was here seven months ago." I reached the top of the staircase and looked around. "Everything looks the same so far."

"Tell me if you see something out of place." Manny waved over a police officer who had come out of one of the rooms. "Where is the scene of the crime?"

"Upstairs, sir." The officer pointed to the ceiling. "It is the room closest to the street."

"Thanks." Manny and I walked to the beautiful staircase. It was grandiose and appealed to my sense of the aesthetic. The stairs were covered in thick red carpeting, the edges showing slight wear from the many people who had gone to the next floor. We reached the next level and it was easy to see where the crime scene was. People were milling around, some dressed in white disposable coveralls, everyone wearing gloves.

After establishing that the crime scene investigators had released the scene, we entered the room to the right of the landing. Close to the windows, three men were in a deep discussion, but stopped the moment they saw us.

"Do you have permission to be here? Who are you?" The largest of the men walked towards us, his chest puffed out, his arms away from his body and his hands fisted.

"Agent Manfred Millard and this is my associate Doctor Genevieve Lenard. We are here to assist in this case." Even though Manny's shoulders were still hunched over, the *masseter* muscles in his jaw tensed and he huffed softly.

"Oh, thank God." The man turned back to his colleagues. "Let's get out of here, guys."

Manny lifted one hand to stop them. "We need to know what you know before you hand over the scene."

"Of course. We're just really keen to get back to our weekend." The large man closed his eyes for a second. He looked tired. "I have nineteen open cases on my desk at the moment and am very happy to hand this one over to someone else."

"Okay, so fill me in." The authority in Manny's tone left no freedom for arguments.

"It seems like he came through the back door, the one from the alley."

One of the other men walked closer, his body language less fatigued. "He picked the lock so well that only tiny scratches are visible. We don't know yet how he managed to disable the alarm system, but the system shows he did it in twenty-three seconds. We're thinking he is a professional."

"Is there any security video footage?" This was my forte and I was curious to see if everyone was correct in their assumptions that the thief was a man. Statistically, the probability was high.

"We're waiting for the curator to copy it now. We haven't looked at it yet."

"So you also don't know the route he took through the museum." I was surprised at their confused expressions and had to remind myself that not everyone had the thinking patterns I did. "If he—and we are all working on a gross assumption that it is a man—came directly to this room, took the paintings and left, it would indicate that he knew what he wanted to steal and where it was. If I could look at the footage, I would be able to tell whether he was conflicted about his loot, whether he wanted to take more, but couldn't. I really need to see that footage."

"Ah, you're *that* Doctor Lenard," the large man said, smiling. "The one who can tell your future by just looking at your wrinkles."

"That's absurd. No one can predict the future, much less

by analysing—"

"Doc, he's joking." This was one of the select few times the *zygomaticus* muscles around Manny's mouth twitched. Manny didn't smile often. I didn't understand why he was amused. "The doc is right though. We need that video. We can determine height and weight at the least, and at best Doc here can tell his future."

I sucked my lips in between my teeth and bit down to refrain from correcting Manny. It was clear he was bantering with the other men, building rapport. I tried. I really did, but after twelve seconds, I simply couldn't hold it in any more. "I cannot tell anyone's future. It is impossible. People who believe that are naïve and ignorant."

"I know, Doc." Manny surprised me by winking at me.

It took me a millisecond to decipher his behaviour. "You were teasing me."

"I'll make a detective of you yet." Manny turned back to the men who were shifting from one foot to the next. They were impatient to leave. A few questions later, I realised they had nothing more of value to add and I walked to the centre of the room.

Across the doorway was the longest wall with the most paintings. Except now there were three paintings missing. The wall to my right had two empty spaces, and directly next to the doorway was another obvious gap in the exhibition. The remaining paintings were from masters like Van Gogh, Rembrandt and Botticelli. Surely the thief would've done well taking those paintings as well.

Soft footsteps stopped next to me and I glanced to my side. Colin was staring at the same empty spaces.

"Why choose those specific paintings?" I asked. "Are they more valuable than these hanging here?"

"All of these are valuable. They could've taken any six paintings from these walls and it would've been a nice day's work."

"Then why those six?"

"A good question, Jenny." Colin's shrug was slight. "It could mean something. Or it could mean nothing."

"You're right. Speculating about it is a waste of time. We should get the video footage and get back to the office so I can analyse it." I turned to face him, took note of his expression and leaned closer to him. "What do you know?"

He closed his eyes, huffing a small laugh. When he looked at me, it was with affection. "You really see too much, love. And I mean this in the most positive way possible."

"I didn't think it was negative."

"Of course you didn't." He smiled. "To answer your question, I have a strong suspicion, but I know how you feel about speculation. I suggest we get back to your viewing room to check out those videos. Maybe then I can confirm my suspicions and tell you."

I leaned a bit closer and spoke quietly, respecting Colin's need for confidentiality. "Does this have something to do with the phone call you received?"

"Yes and no."

"That is not an answer." I hated it when he didn't give me clear answers. His expression told me I was not going to get anything better than that. "Do you know this thief?"

He sighed. "Maybe. A few things the curator said and especially the method of entry sounds like someone I know."

"Well then, let's stop faffing about and get back," Manny said from a few feet away. I hadn't heard him come closer. "And you better tell me every bloody thing you know, Frey."

Chapter FIVE

Manny walked into the foyer of Rousseau & Rousseau, looking back to make sure we were following him. His strides were long and purposeful, his face conveying his disapproval. He was grumbling about Colin not sharing everything he knew as he learned it.

We followed Manny into the team room and walked over to the round table where Vinnie and Nikki were sitting. Manny, however, didn't stop until he stood in front of Francine's desk. She was, as usual, working on the three computers she had running simultaneously. She glanced up and immediately returned to her computers when she saw Manny glaring at her. The *orbicularis oculi* muscles around her eyes and the muscles around her mouth told me that she was having fun at Manny's expense.

A full minute passed while Francine worked on the computers, her face and body relaxed. Manny's posture was becoming increasingly rigid, his breathing louder through flared nostrils. Vinnie and Colin had once watched a movie with a scene where two cars were racing towards each other as if planning a head-on collision. Vinnie had called it playing chicken. This situation between Manny and Francine was reminding me of that scene and I wondered who was going to concede first.

"For Pete's sake, supermodel!" Manny slammed both hands down on Francine's desk and leaned closer to her. "Talk to me."

Francine finished typing something, clicked with the mouse a few times before she slowly lifted her eyes to meet Manny's. "Hey, sexy. What do you want to talk about?"

"I want you to talk about the security in this room." Tension was causing Manny's throat to constrict, making the words sound strangled.

"All the computers are secure." Her voice had the same tone she used when she was flirting with the waiter at her favourite wine bar. I had visited that establishment with her on two occasions. She lowered her eyelashes and slowly lifted them again, a typical nonverbal flirtation indicator. "I double-checked all the computers as soon as you guys left. Nothing managed to get past my supergeek security."

"And do the walls have ears, little girl?" Manny only resorted to this name-calling when he was really annoyed with her.

Francine's eyes widened and she threw her hands up, feigning sudden recall. "Oh my, how did I forget about that? Hah! Gotcha. We checked and found three bugs in this room."

Manny straightened and looked down at Francine, the corners of his mouth turned down. "Stop screwing around with me. Tell me exactly what you found."

"We found the bugs in all the places that weird man was," Nikki said as she stood up. She walked over to Manny and put her arm through his. "You make it too easy for Francine to tease you."

Manny turned to Nikki, none of the annoyance present on his face. "You helped them look for the bugs?"

"I found one." Her shoulders pulled back and her chin lifted. "Vinnie said I would make a great spy."

"But she's never going to be one. Right, punk?"

"Sure, Vin. I don't want to stress like you guys do." Nikki

pulled Manny's arm and led him to the table. "Let Francine finish what she's doing. I'll tell you about the bugs. We found one on the doorframe where Weirdo was leaning, one under the table where he was sitting and one under Francine's chair."

"The chair he was sitting on," Manny said. "Bastard."

"That's what Vinnie also said." Nikki glanced at Vinnie. "And a few other things."

When Nikki had first come into our lives, Francine had been very strict about the use of language. She didn't want curse words used around Nikki. Her intent had been noble, but realistically it was impractical to expect of these men to eliminate swearing. I had noticed their efforts in toning down the use of strong language.

"Well? Did you disable all the bugs?" Manny asked.

"I crushed them," Vinnie said with a cruel smile.

"Okay, listen carefully." Manny turned back to Francine. "You too, supermodel."

"I'm listening, handsome. I'm very good at multitasking."

"Hmph. From now on we must be careful what we say, where we say it, and which computers we use for what. Supermodel will make sure that these two rooms and Doc's apartment are clear of any electronic surveillance at all times." Manny waited for Francine to nod before he continued. "This means that until we solve these cases, we only discuss it in here and at Doc's apartment."

"What about our cars?" I discussed a few of my ideas with Colin whenever we were travelling together.

"Too big a risk," Francine said. "It's easier to control access to buildings, but the moment you park your car on the street, an innocent-looking pedestrian can easily place a magnetised bug somewhere on the car. We'd have to sweep the cars all the time. Too impractical."

I saw the logic in Francine's argument. "I will refrain from talking in the car."

"Supermodel will tell you which computers you can use for research, but use your Interpol access only from one computer and be very careful what you look for on the Interpol system."

Francine got up and slowly walked to Manny. She was wearing a brown leather skirt stopping mid-thigh, dark brown tights and high-heeled boots that covered her knees. Her cream silk shirt was more costly than the last three first-edition collector's books I had bought combined. I had been with her when she had chosen that shirt. But it wasn't her outfit, her exotic looks or her beautiful hair that caught my attention. It was the way she walked towards Manny. On the National Geographic channel, I had witnessed it numerous times when predators stalked their prey.

"Manny." She stopped in front of him and ran a manicured nail down the collar of his jacket. Her voice was husky, her mouth a slight pout. "You know just how to turn me on. Please tell me why we are playing little computer games with Interpol. Or even better, tell me that we are going to screw over one of the Big Brothers like the NSA."

"Get off me, Delilah." Manny pushed her hand away, but she brought up her other hand and played with his earlobe.

"Come on, you sexy animal. That's not what you said last night."

"Bloody hell, woman." His face flushed, Manny grabbed both her hands and pushed her until she had to take a step back to regain her balance. "Stay away from me, you evil siren."

"Look at you flirting with me." Francine failed to control her enjoyment and laughed. "Nikki is right, you know. You make this too easy. Now could you please tell us why we should be so careful? I mean, we all know the government is constantly spying on us with huge dragnets, but you've never been paranoid like this. Am I bringing you over to my side?"

Manny sat down at the round table and gestured at the empty seats with both hands. He waited until everyone was seated. "Henri Fabron is toying with me. I don't like when someone thinks he can dupe me. His visit and those bloody bugs prove to me that he is trying to hide something about Savreux. He's really stupid if he thinks his orders are going to get us to stay away from looking into Savreux's death."

"Is that why you didn't tell him about Nikki's direct messages?" I asked.

"That's one of the reasons, yes." Manny was all business now. There was no fake slouch, no pretend ignorance. "I also don't want him to as much as glance in Nikki's direction. He's a politician—"

"And we don't trust politicians," Francine said.

"—and they always look for easy scapegoats," Manny said, glaring at Francine. He looked at me. "Doc?"

"I know what a scapegoat is."

"Good." Manny nodded. "Since we still don't know anything about who's sending those bloody direct email messages, and why they are sending it, I think it is better that little Henri doesn't know about it. Once we have enough information, we will take it to the president."

"Do you trust him in this?" I asked.

"I don't trust anyone, Doc." He scowled when I inhaled to point out his lie. "With the exception of you and Nikki."

"You trust me?" The lightness in Nikki's tone indicated her surprise and pleasure.

"Yes, I do. More than I trust these criminals."

I could see that everyone knew Manny was lying. Manny knew everyone was aware of his untruth. These people were so strongly opposed to being clear and honest with their emotions. I considered life much less complicated with honesty.

"Supermodel?" Manny waited until Francine looked at him. "Stop painting your nails and find out who the bleeding hell is sending Nikki those email thingies."

Francine raised one eyebrow. "Even with wet nails, I can do more on a computer than you."

"Then do it. Back to your question, Doc. Up to now, the president has not given us any reason to distrust him. Henri Fabron has given me more than enough reason to wait before I include him in any discoveries."

"So, do you want us to look into Savreux's death or today's art theft?" Colin asked.

"We are going to do it all." Manny leaned forward and started counting on his fingers. "We are going to find out everything about Savreux so we can figure out why he was murdered. We are going to figure out who murdered him. We are going to find out everything we can about the 1990 Gardner museum heist and figure out if and how it fits in with Savreux and today's heist. We are also going to look into today's heist. My gut tells me that they are all connected if we look closely enough."

"What about little Henri?" Vinnie asked. "Want me to see what he's up to? And Lefebvre? He's also pushing hard with his prosecutors and stuff. Should I check him out too?"

Manny leaned slightly back, his eyes briefly shifting up and to the right. He shook his head. "No. Not yet. Let's first see what this will bring us. Then you can contact some of your goons and check those two out."

"Just say when." Vinnie reclined deeper in his chair, satisfied.

"Now let's start with those direct messages. Nikki." Gone was the gentle affection Manny had shown towards the student earlier. "The next time you receive anything suspicious, you come directly to me. Am I clear?"

Nikki's face had lost colour at Manny's tone, but she didn't hunch her shoulders and cross her arms in a full-body hug like she had done when she first came to us. "I told you that I didn't think anything of it until the last DM."

"And you went to Frey."

"He was sitting right next to me on the sofa." She crossed her arms. It wasn't a full-body hug. It was a blocking gesture. "You weren't there."

"My number is in your phone. I was there."

"Colin was closer."

"Stop badgering her, Millard. She did what she thought best at that moment."

"And then you went off to go and check it out without telling anyone about this. Was that what you thought best at that moment?" Manny had a valid point, but I didn't want to exacerbate an already tense situation by taking Manny's side. The last seven weeks' tension returned in full force. I wished Phillip wasn't in a meeting elsewhere. He would've effortlessly calmed everyone down.

"This is not a productive conversation," I said. "Instead of wasting time talking about what should've been done, can we rather talk about what *can* be done?"

"It is productive, Doc." Manny took a deep breath and continued in a calmer tone. "You people need to understand that I cannot help you if I don't know what is happening. Nikki, I cannot protect you if you don't tell me things."

"Sorry, Manny. I'll tell you next time." She lowered her head and mumbled, "After I tell Colin who will be sitting next to me on the sofa."

"Point made, young lady. As long as you tell me. Now can someone give me more information on Savreux? What do we know about him?"

"Before we had our team meeting this morning, I got more information on Savreux's personal life," I said. "How detailed do you want this to be?"

"A broad overview and only the points you think might be relevant to our cases." Often Manny became extremely frustrated when he asked me to tell him everything and I did. We had agreed on starting reports by first inquiring about the depth of the information needed.

"Understood. A quick overview is that Claude Savreux was born in 1952 in Lyon, France to middle-class parents. He went to public schools, but proved that he was an exceptional student. His parents sent him to the best university they could afford, but soon didn't have to pay since he got scholarships. He studied Economics and International Politics, but changed to law later on, and graduated in the top of his classes every time.

"His first job was as a legal intern in one of the top legal companies in Paris. They had recruited him from university. Very quickly, he worked his way up. He was working there for two years when he met his wife. They got married after eighteen months and had their first child a year later. It was their only child and he died at the age of nine in an accident at school. It was winter when he and his friends were playing around on the ice on the school grounds. He slipped and hit his head hard against a step and died."

"That's really sad," Nikki said.

"It is." Francine sighed. "I don't know how anyone can recover from the death of a child."

"I don't think Savreux and his wife did," I said. "According to the newspaper articles and few magazine articles I read, Minister Savreux's wife said that she was never able to accept the death of her child. He lost himself in his work and left her to deal with this alone. For almost a decade after the child's death, he spent most of his time at work. He had just started rebuilding his relationship with his wife when she was diagnosed with cancer. She died sixteen years ago." I took a deep breath when I realised that I was giving too much irrelevant information. "Minister Savreux never remarried, but has been in relationships with numerous models, celebrities and prominent businesswomen."

"You make it sound like he had a lot of women."

"If I go with the information from articles and interviews, I counted seventeen women in the years after his wife's death. But I have to make it clear that I don't trust the credibility of all these reports."

"I know you more than double-checked this info, Doc." Manny exhaled loudly in an almost snort. "Seventeen is quite a lot of women to go through. And here we thought he was a civic-minded philanthropist."

"A real dog." Vinnie's top lip curled. "Typical politician."

"Not all politicians are bad." I had proof of a handful of politicians in every country who dedicated themselves to improving the lives of their constituents.

"Only ninety-nine point nine percent of them are bad." Francine's expression warned me of what was to come. I had spent a few unfortunate lunches arguing with her about this. "Those few honest politicians are as scarce as hen's teeth."

"Hens don't have teeth." Why did I always have to point this out to her?

"I know, right? That is why it is so rare."

I held up my hand to stop her. "You are digressing from the topic, Francine."

"Sorry." She didn't look contrite, especially not when she winked at me.

"What else did you learn about Savreux, Doc?"

"He hasn't been connected to any woman in the last two years. Taking his history into account, I thought this might be significant."

"How?" Colin asked.

"I don't know yet. Something happened two years ago that caused Savreux to slow down or stop his philandering. It could be important or not."

"Look into it, Doc."

"I will. I also want to find more information on his professional life. Without any of Francine's conspiracy theories, there is a large probability that his death is related to his profession. We know that politicians make many deals with each other to build their networks. Maybe he made a deal with the wrong person."

"The work he was busy with at the moment was pushing for the treatment of PTSD and fighting the president on this No Secrets law." Colin steepled his fingers. "We need to know more about this law. From the little I know, his death will give the president a definite advantage."

"Making the president a prime suspect." Francine's eyes were bright with emotion.

"That is leaping to conclusions, Francine."

"Aw, come on, girlfriend. A political scandal? This is so up my alley and far too much fun to not go there."

"Doc is right. We need more information. What do we know about this No Secrets law nonsense?"

"It is to stop government officials from embezzling money." Francine was up to date with most political developments. She had to be to build her elaborate conspiracy theories. "President Godard has been after this since he got serious about politics."

"That was ten years ago."

"Right you are, handsome man." Francine winked at Manny. "He didn't want a repeat of all those politicians in the seventies and eighties using their positions to steal gazillions from the government and from taxpayers. When he became president two years ago, a lot of people got really nervous that he now had the power to force officials to be more accountable and trustworthy."

"And this is actually about to happen?" Manny shook his head. "I'm yet to see a transparent government."

"Ooh, I really hope President Godard gets his way. The scandals coming out will be more delicious than those in the nineties." Francine shivered with excitement. "I love that the president's wife is pushing for this as well. She's my hero. Smart and beautiful. She still practices as a neurosurgeon, she helps her husband in her official capacity and she's a patron of the Libreville Dignity Foundation."

"I know that name. Wait a moment." I looked through my notes until I found the relevant page. I straightened in my chair and blinked a few times. "Minister Claude Savreux was one of the founders of this charity."

"Bloody hell. Is this a coincidence? What do you know about this charity, supermodel?"

"Not much. I only know about the president's wife's involvement. She became a patron of this charity nine years ago. They have done some amazing work, especially for Gabonese women in France and the local women in Gabon. They're especially involved in education and health, helping these women to get the basics of both."

It was silent in the team room for a few seconds. Manny looked at Colin. "Would you care to enlighten us now about your mystery phone call and whatever the curator told you that made you think you know who stole the art this morning?"

"Dude!" Vinnie punched Colin on the arm. "You know who did this?"

"I have a suspicion, and I think it's better if I show you. Do we have the security videos from the Jean Monnet Museum yet?"

"I'll check," Francine went to her computer and smiled after a few seconds. "It's on the system."

"Good. Give me a few minutes." Colin ignored Manny's complaints and walked to Francine. "I'm going to need your help finding another video as well."

After five minutes I realised it was going to take longer than another one of Colin's inaccurate estimations of a 'few minutes'. I went to my viewing room to organise my thoughts on my notepad. Writing things down helped me to process information.

Chapter SIX

"Jenny?" It was only when Colin touched my arm that I looked up. "Are you okay?"

I followed his glance to the paper on my desk and frowned. Instead of writing down notes about the case, I had taken out empty music sheets and had started writing Mozart's Clarinet Quintet in A major. The need to write music occurred mostly when I was severely stressed, hence my surprise. I didn't consider myself particularly troubled at present. But I had to admit the disorganised state of these cases could very well be the cause of my mental distress.

I had only written a page and a half. It would've taken me around twenty minutes. I looked back up at Colin. "Why did you take so long?"

"It took Francine a bit longer than expected to find the other video." Colin was sitting next to me in his desk chair. I hadn't heard him pull it closer. A week after everyone had moved into the team room, he had moved his workstation into my viewing room. His reason was his inability to share space with Manny for extended periods. "The videos are up in the team room, but we can watch it here if you want to."

"No, I'd rather not have everyone in my space."

"Are you okay?" he asked again.

"There are too many bits of information and I don't know if it is connected, or what is connected to what, or how it is connected."

"We'll figure this out. We always do." He squeezed my arm. "Shall we?"

I gave a single nod and followed him to the team room. Everyone was sitting at the round table, fresh coffee and muffins in the centre. Phillip was also present, Manny telling him that Colin had received a mysterious phone call.

"And he's going to tell us about it now, right, Frey?"

Colin sat down and took a muffin. "The call was from one of my fences. He told me that he had heard of some very hot merchandise on the market. Since he knew I was into high-end art, he thought I might know more about it."

"I assume he wants to be the one selling those artworks," Phillip said.

"Most definitely, yes. He wants in on the action. We are talking large sums here, not a little sketch selling for a couple of hundred thousand. These works are worth millions on the black market and he wants part of that." Colin took a bite of the muffin and reached for a mug of coffee. "It was the artwork he mentioned that got my attention."

"From the Gardner heist or today's?" I asked.

"Today's heist. It's always better to sell the art immediately or you'll have to wait months before moving it." He gave Manny an insincere smile. "Law enforcement is always slow in getting the word out after an art heist like this. If you can shift the art within twenty-four hours, you're golden. After that, all kinds of alerts are out and travelling with it might become more complicated. Not impossible, just more complicated."

"I would like to know how this fence already knows about this morning's theft." Manny paused for a moment, thinking. "You received that phone call four hours after the heist took place, at exactly the same time we were informed about it. How the bleeding hell did he hear about it so fast?"

"Good question. And no, I'm not going to ask him. It will make him suspicious and right now I need him to be desperate for my business, not questioning my loyalty because I ask too many questions."

"Pity. If you don't value him too much, we can find something to arrest him for and then interview him while he's in custody."

"A ham-handed approach that won't work, Millard. For this you will need finesse, something you are clearly not familiar with."

"The video." The two words came out a bit louder than I had intended. I had come into the team room for that purpose and didn't want to listen to another digression.

"Firstly, a bit of interesting information." Francine's idea of interesting information could be of true interest or it could be a theory about some new world order controlling all the governments and manipulating industry. Hoping it was the former, I waited for her to continue. "Our thief was very smart. He cut the whole block's electricity. Not many people would notice this at five o'clock in the morning. It also disabled quite a few security cameras in the area that had no battery backup. Really shocking how outdated some systems are."

"What's the point of security if it can't function without electricity?" Vinnie exhaled loudly through his nose. "Amateurs."

"This Monnet Museum was quite a bit more prepared." Francine smiled. "Their cameras have good battery backup that enables recording for twelve hours before it needs to be recharged. It is supposed to immediately upload footage from all the videos to their cloud account, but our clever thief scrambled the wireless systems. Also something unlikely to be noticed at that hour of the day."

I was fast becoming impatient. "Do we have a video or not?"

"We do." Francine gave her tablet to Colin. "You can do the honours. You know what you are looking for."

"What are you looking for, Frey?"

"Wait and watch." Colin's lips twitched when Manny called him a very unflattering name. He tapped twice on the tablet screen and the large screen against the wall came to life.

"Let me get the lights." Phillip got up and turned off the lights.

"Just a bit of extra info," Francine said in an almost whisper. "The museum uses really cool cameras that record with night vision at night and HD colour during the day."

I decided to not ask her why she was whispering and focussed on the screen. It was divided into six different screens, presumably from different cameras throughout the Museum. Colin fast-forwarded the video until the screen went dark.

"Here is when the building lost power. Give it another second and the batteries will kick in." Colin was wrong. It took two seconds before the six images filled the screen again. On the second screen in the top row, I spotted movement.

"Stop the video," Manny demanded. "Now, Frey. Stop this video."

Colin tapped on the tablet screen and all movement stopped.

"Enlarge the second camera."

"What about the magic word, Millard?"

"Now, Frey," Manny said again. Colin smiled, tapped on

the tablet and the second image filled the screen. "Holy hell! It's a woman."

The silhouette was undeniably female. She was of average height, with a more than average curvaceous figure. She was wearing yoga pants, soft-soled shoes, a tight-fitting jacket with a hoodie, and a balaclava, all in black. Her body language communicated confidence and stealth simul-taneously. She wasn't crouching, arms tightly tucked against her sides as could be observed with most thieves. Her limbs were loose and relaxed, her movements sure. She knew where she was going and knew she was safe.

"A friend of yours, Frey?"

"I can't be sure, but I suspect it is Sue." Colin exhaled loudly when he saw Manny's disbelieving expression. "Can *you* see her face? Well, neither can I. She's wearing a mask and a hoodie, so how the hell am I supposed to be one hundred percent sure it's Sue?"

"Have you seen the whole video?" I asked.

"No, just the first few minutes."

"Maybe she reveals her identity later on. Let's continue watching." I seldom made direct eye contact with people. It was an excruciating discomfort for me, but I understood the impact it had. For this reason, I looked at Manny until he lifted an eyebrow at me. "Please don't interrupt again. I find it much more efficient to watch the whole video to get an initial impression before studying it frame by frame."

"Yes, ma'am."

Vinnie and Francine's snorts indicated Manny was being sarcastic, which meant that he was angry. I didn't care. The video was more important than his good humour.

I turned to the screen and watched Sue walk deeper into the museum. She had the sure-footedness of specially trained operational officers. Despite her poise, there was an underlying tension in her muscles, similar to those of soldiers always prepared for action, always on alert.

She moved off screen and Colin changed to the next security camera to follow her journey through the museum. Not once did she stop anywhere to look at the valuable pieces of art she was passing, but walked directly to the room facing the street. Again Colin changed cameras to give us the view into the room.

She walked straight to the Klimt, looked at it for a second before carefully feeling around the back of the frame. The *trapezius* muscle in her back tensed and lifted her shoulders slightly when her fingers made contact with whatever she had been looking for.

"She's disabling the magnetic contact alarm," Colin said. "It is usually set up as a completely separate alarm that screams like hell when the painting is removed from the wall and the contact is broken. The curator told me this morning all the paintings in the Monnet Museum are fitted with these alarms."

I couldn't see what Sue did, but her shoulders relaxed and she lifted the painting from the wall. From her small backpack, she took out a folded canvas bag, shook it out and placed the painting in it. We watched her repeat the process with the other five paintings, each time placing the artwork in the bag. The paintings were all of similar size, small enough to make it easy to carry together. She zipped the bag up and carefully hooked her arms through the two thin straps that turned it into an uncomfortable-looking backpack. She walked out of the room with the same relaxed self-assurance. We followed her as she retraced her steps until she disappeared from view.

The room was silent while everyone continued looking at the now unchanging screen.

"What do you think, Doc?"

I thought about what I had seen. "Not once did she check her watch, glance at the cameras, windows or exhibit any form of nervous nonverbal behaviour. She was completely confident in her time frame and the disabled security. Either she had someone there watching out for her safety or she knew that she was not going to be caught. The confidence in her behaviour is congruent with what Colin said." I looked at him. "Do you still think it's Sue?"

"Yeah, I'm pretty sure it's her." The muscles around his eyes contracted the way they did when he was deliberating different possibilities. "I've known her for more than a decade. She only ever does work she considers worthy and only if it's a specific order. She's never done any work for herself."

"Why does this worry you?"

"If this theft is connected to the Gardner heist, and if these two are somehow connected to Savreux's death, I have great difficulty imagining her being involved in this."

"Why?" Phillip asked. "Does she like you only steal back stolen goods?"

"Yes and no." Colin smiled at me, knowing how much I hated it when he gave that non-answer. "As far as I know she has never been involved in anything violent. Her thefts have mostly been retrieval of photos, videos and other evidence used to blackmail her clients. She's stolen back jewellery, paintings and other valuables when the police were useless in finding or claiming back her clients' property. But she's always refused to do any kind of espionage work, outright theft or anything that would violate her ethics."

"Ethics?" My eyebrows shot up. Then I sighed. Why was I still shocked to hear that thieves worked according to some code of honour and ethics? After eighteen months with Colin, Vinnie and Francine in my life, this should no longer surprise me. I shook my head to stop Colin when he leaned towards me. "Please, don't explain. Rather tell me where we could find Sue."

"I don't know, but I'm going to find her, don't you worry."

"I'm not worried."

He smiled and returned his attention to the tablet. He swiped a few times at the screen and a different image filled the large screen. "I got this for you, Jenny. This is footage of a theft four years ago. There was no proof this was Sue, but in this case I knew it was her. I thought if you saw this, you would also agree that it could've been Sue this morning."

He tapped the tablet screen and the security video started playing. It looked like a library in a private home. Tall bookshelves covered three walls, the fourth hidden by heavy curtains, most likely covering floor-to-ceiling windows. A slight movement in the curtains drew my attention a second before a figure stepped out from behind it. Dressed in tight-fitting black clothes, the woman walked to a bookshelf and removed a few large leather-bound volumes.

"It's her." I didn't need to watch and analyse hours of this footage. The way she held her body, her movements and even the way her shoulders tensed when she uncovered the hidden safe, left no doubt in my mind. "It is the same woman from this morning's heist."

Colin stopped the video, looking more concerned than before.

"We need her, Frey. Not only to get those paintings back, but to find out who she is working for."

"You are working on the assumption that she's working for someone." I didn't like conjecture, but I was more distracted by Manny's incorrect use of 'who'.

"It's a pretty safe conclusion, Jenny." Colin was convinced of this. "I've never known Sue to steal for herself. In this second video, she was getting back the last will and testament of her client's deceased father. The client's brother had forged another will to make him the sole heir and she had no other way of proving that it was not her father's last will. Sue only steals for other people."

"Why?"

"Because she's really good at it, because of the challenge, because she can help someone get back what was taken from them. She has her own reasons for doing this."

"Find her, Frey."

"Not if you're going to arrest her, Millard."

"Oh, for the love of all that is holy!" Manny put his mug down so quickly some of his milky tea spilled. I swallowed away my need to clean it. "Did you not just see her steal six paintings to the value of thirteen million euro? And break into a private home?"

Colin's whole body went still. He was proficient at hiding his emotions behind neutral, but amicable facial expressions. It was when his expression lost its friendly quality that I knew his emotions were getting stronger. "I'll make a deal with you, Millard. If it really is Sue in those videos, I'll get those paintings back. If, and only if, she agrees, we'll speak to her, but you'll let her go."

Manny was shaking his head while Colin was speaking. "No can do. She's a wanted thief. We have the proof here."

"What you have here is what looks like a woman, dressed in black, leaving no fingerprints, no trace, nothing. You can calculate her height and weight quite accurately, but that will be it. You can't guess her hair colour, her facial structure, her eye colour or if it really is a woman."

"It is a woman," I said softly. "Or an extremely effeminate man with abnormally large pectoral muscles, which I think unlikely."

Colin glared at me. "But it is a possibility."

"Yes, but it is also a possibility that it is Sue and she is stealing for herself."

"My point"—Colin looked back at Manny—"is that you have no concrete proof to arrest Sue. So let me get those paintings back and find out what is going on."

Manny's lips tightened as his face reddened. "I don't like this."

"I don't care."

"Gentlemen." Phillip sighed. "I agree with Colin on this one. I'm sure the museum and their insurance company will not complain if those paintings surface. Finding and arresting the thief is secondary to finding those masterpieces and returning them for the safekeeping of generations to come."

"Fine." Manny picked up his mug and took a sip. "I still don't like it."

"And I still don't care."

"I might have something to make you sexy man-beasts stop fighting." Francine tapped her fingernails on the table until she had everyone's attention. "I'm the queen of multitasking and need to be worshipped."

"I think you better tell us what you found before the old man has a stroke." Vinnie leaned a bit towards Manny. "He's looking very red in the face."

Francine laughed softly and held out her hand for Colin to give her the tablet. She took it, and after a few swipes and taps, a face appeared on the large screen against the wall. "This is René Motte."

"The dude with the Vermeer in his preservation room?" Vinnie asked.

"The one and only. I've been running a search on him while doing all these other things and got a bit more info on him. I haven't analysed it or summarised it, but I noticed—"

"What did you find?" People wasted so much time on their need for long introductions.

"Right to the point, girlfriend." Francine's smile was genuine. I was glad she was my friend. She didn't offend easily. "The highly respected René Motte is currently in Paris, but should return in the next few days for the parliamentary meeting. Even though he's on the think tank for the president's political party, he's another strong opponent of the No Secrets policy. You know what really pissed me off when I checked him out? He travelled the very short distance between Strasbourg and Paris by private plane, which in my opinion is a shocking abuse of public funds. This pissed me off so much that I looked into that some more and found that he used his own plane."

"That he can afford because he is an oligarch. Thought you had something interesting and new, supermodel."

"I do. The bastard was one of the politicians deeply involved with Elf." She ended her sentence with both hands thrown up and her tone indicating that it was a significant proclamation.

"Are you talking about the eighties TV show with that adorable alien?" Vinnie had the same tone as when he talked about his aunt Helen. "I loved that little guy. Hey, you promised not to give another alien conspiracy today."

"Not Alf, Vin. Elf. With an E." She looked around the

table, her facial expression changing from excited expectation to disappointment. "You really don't know? Did none of you follow that case?"

"Why don't you explain this to us dummies, supermodel?" Manny asked. "And for the love of Pete, keep it short and don't involve aliens and government conspiracies."

"Unfortunately I have to include the latter, Manny." There was no evidence in Francine's nonverbal cues that she was teasing. "This case truly involved the government on so many levels that it shocked the world."

"My God, are you talking about the Gabon oil company?" Manny's eyes widened.

"Technically, Elf wasn't a Gabonese oil company. It was an international oil company making gazillions in Gabon."

"Was?" I vaguely remembered this being in the headlines. "It no longer exists?"

"Nope. It was privatised in 1994 and later merged with one of the world's leading oil companies.

"How is that related to this case?" I hoped Francine wasn't on another flight of fancy.

"René Motte was appointed as the assistant to the Gabon–France liaison in 1985. He slowly worked his way up the ladder until he became one of the big shots at Elf. He had graduated from law school, worked for less than a year as a lowly lawyer, but lost his interest in that. He then finished his engineering degree and that's how he was perfect to become the head legal advisor of Elf. When he was appointed at the age of thirty, he was also the youngest in top management. The management of Elf was so powerful that they influenced Gabon elections and leadership. Elf also bankrolled quite a few French politicians' campaigns, and those politicians helped Elf gain more power in French territories."

"My question still remains." I raised both eyebrows. "How is this related to the case?"

"In 1988, Minister Savreux was in the military. He had also worked his way up the ladder, or should I say ranks, and had somehow landed himself on a committee dealing with the many problems in and around Africa. Of course, we're talking about those countries that were colonised by the French. Anyone wants to guess which country he was appointed to? Huh? Huh?"

"Gabon," Vinnie said, his voice bored.

"That's right! Later in 1988, René Motte and Savreux served on the same committee. The next year, France became the owner of Elf. Motte was pushed out of his position and returned to France. At exactly the same time, Savreux was passed over for promotion, and he was taken off that committee he had served on. After that, Savreux and René Motte had no more connection to Gabon. Not until they founded the Libreville Dignity Foundation more than a decade later."

"The same charity that President Godard's wife is a patron of? Very good work, Francine." I truly enjoyed it when Francine applied her considerable intellect to worthy pursuits instead of dreaming up unsubstantiated theories.

"Thanks, girlfriend." She lowered her voice and I sighed. "But this goes with that theory that in 1990, some French politicians organised the Gardner heist to fund a campaign they were still planning. It is very clear that the timing is suspicious. Around the same time Savreux stopped being involved in Gabon affairs, gazillions of dollars' worth of art is stolen in one foul swoop. See? It all makes sense now."

"No, it doesn't." My mind was racing with this new data.

"But I do agree with you about the dubious nature of René Motte and Savreux's connections."

"I'm not saying that I'm buying into Francine's theory, but finding the Vermeer in Motte's house and the possibility of the Flinck in Savreux's? That connects them to the Gardner heist as well as to each other on yet another level."

"Holy hell." Manny rubbed both hands over his face a few times. "Okay, people, we need clear information on all of these elements. Supermodel, are you listening? Clear information, not some nutcase conspiracy theory."

"Ooh, I like it when you go all alpha on me." She laughed when Manny exhibited all the cues for rage. "I'll get you your clear info, handsome. Don't you worry."

Chapter SEVEN

I felt refreshed and fully rested after a very hot shower. It had been a long afternoon and evening sifting through the vast amount of information. At nine o'clock, Nikki had insisted that she was bored and wanted to come home. I had continued refining my searches and organising the findings until Colin had closed my laptop over my fingers. That had resulted in a short argument that he had won and I'd gone to bed. It was now seventeen minutes after six and I was ready for this day.

One more glance around the bathroom reassured me that it was as spotless as before I'd had the shower. I walked into the bedroom to find Colin still in bed. He was sitting against the headboard, reading something on his tablet. Francine had been pestering me for months to buy a tablet. Or to use her word, 'invest'. I didn't see the need for it.

Colin looked up from the tablet and smiled. "Already dressed? You really want to get back to work, don't you?"

"You don't seem all that motivated. You're still naked in bed."

He looked down. "Not naked. I'm wearing pants."

"You're still in bed."

"Really?" He put the tablet on the bed. "You want to start arguing this early?"

"I'm not arguing." I saw the *zygomaticus* muscles lift the corner of his mouth. "Don't tease me before I've had coffee. You have me at a disadvantage."

"That's exactl—" Every muscle in his body went still. He tilted his head and lifted his index finger to stop me when I inhaled to ask him what he had heard. Then I also heard it. A soft knock at my front door.

Nobody knocked on my door. People needed to ring the intercom at the building entrance before they could come up to my apartment. When Manny or Phillip came around, they always rang the doorbell, which was next to my front door.

Colin jumped out of bed, not bothering with a robe or slippers. He reached into the bedside table on his side of the bed and came out with a handgun. Knowing about his deep dislike for force, I was taken aback by the familiarity with which he handled the weapon. If it weren't for the watchfulness on his face, and the strangeness of a knock on my front door at this hour, I would've confronted him over keeping a firearm in my bedroom. It wasn't even locked in a safe.

Moving with the stealth born from his career as a thief, he left the bedroom. I followed him, confident that my socked feet wouldn't make any sound on the solid wooden floors. I didn't know how he managed to move that fast, but by the time I entered the living area, Colin was a few feet from the front door. He held his gun loosely to his side, but his body language told me he was ready to use it at any moment. He would not be the only one using such deadly force. Vinnie was already at the front door, also in his pyjama pants, also holding a handgun.

A voice came from the other side of the door, but it was too soft for me to hear. It must have been someone Vinnie and Colin recognised, because the muscle tension in their bodies decreased significantly. Vinnie peeked through the peephole, straightened and nodded to Colin. Then they both lifted their shoulders, simultaneously communicating their confusion. Vinnie held out his hand, took Colin's gun and stood to the side.

The few seconds it took them to confirm the identity of our visitor was enough for me to reach their sides. Colin pushed me behind him as he opened the door. Vinnie stood a metre to my left, still ready with both guns.

"I hope you're not aiming any weapons at me," a familiar male voice said from the hallway. I stepped around Colin.

"Daniel." I was surprised to see the leader of the top GIPN team at my front door. He was wearing his uniform pants, but a thick ski-jacket with a fur-trimmed hood. The visible muscles on his face were tense. "What's wrong?"

"Good morning, Docto... Genevieve. I'm sorry to drop in unannounced, but I was hoping to speak to you."

He pushed the hood off his head and unzipped his jacket. His one foot shifted closer, his other nonverbal cues confirming his expectation to be invited in. I considered this. I knew Daniel only from the few times he and his team had assisted us in our cases. There was no reason he should come and visit me at home unless it was important. I took a step back and pushed Colin with my elbow to force him back as well.

"Come in." I decided to wait until he was seated before I questioned his unexpected visit.

He walked through the door and immediately turned to his right, facing Vinnie. "Two guns?"

"And my charm." Vinnie's smile wasn't friendly.

"You're going to need more than that to catch me, bub."

Vinnie's smile disappeared. "The name is Vinnie. Not bub."

Daniel took a step closer to Vinnie, not exhibiting any sign of being intimidated. He held out his gloved hand. "Daniel Cassel. Pleased to meet you, Vinnie."

It was clearly not what Vinnie had been expecting. His eyes widened slightly before narrowing. His stare went from Daniel's hand to his face and back to his hand again. After a considerable amount of time, Vinnie tucked one of the guns in the back of his pants and took Daniel's hand in what looked like a crushing grip. "Don't fuck with us."

I sighed. "As soon as you are finished posturing, Vinnie can make us coffee and you can tell us why you are here."

Daniel waited until Vinnie let go of his hand and turned to me. His glance went to Colin, but then settled on me. "Thanks, Genevieve. Coffee would be great. It's been a long night."

I pointed at the sofas to my right. "Let's sit down. Vinnie?"

"Coffee." He nodded once, gave Daniel a look that clearly carried a warning or a threat, depending on the individual's interpretation.

"I didn't know you were all living together." Daniel walked to the sofa facing the balcony and sat down.

Colin had been quiet this whole time, observing. In my opinion, it was this skill that made him such an exceptional thief. He took his time learning everything he could about his target or, in this case, his possible adversary before taking action. Without looking at him, I knew his face was in a neutral expression, his eyes absorbing every small detail. We sat down on the other sofa.

"I never considered you naïve, Daniel," I said. "You know my profession, you know that I can read your nonverbal communication cues and yet you lie. Frankly, I feel insulted."

Daniel laughed. "I've been trying to hone my skills. Obviously, I'm failing miserably. I knew you were all living here. What I didn't know was that there were so many weapons in this apartment."

I also hadn't known this, but that I could only blame on my lack of experience in and awareness of such matters. I shouldn't have been surprised that Colin had a weapon at his immediate disposal. Not with all the physical danger we had faced in the last year and a half. Vinnie? Some of the people he called friends were arms dealers, so again I should have expected this. Sometimes my single-minded focus on the case at hand disabled my larger observation skills.

"Jenny." Colin touched my arm and I realised that I had lost the thread of the conversation. "I'm going to get dressed. I won't be longer than five minutes, so wait before you get Daniel to tell you all his secrets."

"I don't want to know all his secrets."

"I know, love." He squeezed my arm. "But please wait with your questions until I'm back."

Colin looked towards the kitchen and I knew that Vinnie was going to join us to protect me from Daniel while Colin got dressed. "Daniel won't hurt me. He's here because he trusts me, but he doesn't trust you."

"Good." Colin got up and looked at Daniel. "I don't trust you either, so keep that in mind. Five minutes."

I didn't watch him walk to the bedroom, nor did I pay attention to Vinnie and his threatening body language as he fell into the far end of the sofa Daniel was sitting on.

"How do you know I trust you, Genevieve?"

"Logic." I shrugged. "If you didn't trust me, you wouldn't be here. You are an intelligent man and have already calculated all the risks involved in being here. This leads me to presume that you are willing to trust Vinnie and Colin simply because I trust them. You wouldn't be here otherwise."

"Very astute."

"I know."

Daniel turned to Vinnie. "Don't you want to get dressed?"

"Why? Do my scars offend you?"

It wasn't often that I saw Vinnie's naked torso and the many scars chronicling his violent past.

"Not at all. I've just never found the elastic in my pyjama pants to be a good holster for my weapons." Daniel's open body language and straightforwardness encouraged reciprocity. It was effective. Vinnie no longer looked ready to jump into action at the slightest provocation. Instead, he leaned deeper into the sofa.

We sat in silence for a while. Daniel didn't appear uncomfortable while I studied him. I estimated his age to be early forties, but physically he was likely to be fitter than most twenty-year-olds. He held himself with the confidence of someone who had excelled at his job for a long enough period to eliminate any need to prove himself. From previous encounters, I knew he not only had received training in interpreting micro-expressions and other nonverbal cues, but he was adept at this.

There was nothing exceptional in his looks—medium height, cropped brown hair and brown eyes. I imagined it served him well when handling situations where he had to calm down a victim or even the perpetrator. He seemed harmless, most likely an image he had worked hard to perfect and project. I didn't need the past experiences to know that Daniel was as dangerous as Vinnie, Colin and Manny.

We were still quietly observing each other when Colin returned, dressed in dark colours. He sat down next to me and took my hand. I didn't know if this public display of affection was for comfort or a show of possession. Either way, it annoyed me and I pulled my hand out of his.

"Why are you here?" I asked Daniel.

"For all the reasons you already stated, but mostly I'm here about Savreux's death."

"It's no longer our case." Colin's lie was well executed.

"Hmm. You are a much better liar than me." Daniel looked at me. "Genevieve? Are you still looking into this case?"

I swallowed. "We've been ordered not to."

"That is not my question."

"Why are you here, flatfoot?" Vinnie leaned forward. "No more answering questions with questions."

Daniel smiled at Vinnie, but turned back to me. "This is not something I'm comfortable doing and therefore I need some reassurance from you."

"I don't know what you are not comfortable doing, so I cannot give you any reassurance. You know me by reputation and we have worked together for short periods in the past. If you cannot trust me on that alone, I can't convince you otherwise."

He took a deep breath, unzipped a pocket on the side of his uniform pants, and took out a flash drive. "This is everything the police have on Savreux's case at the moment. The lead investigator on this case was a rookie with me a million years ago. He's one of my best friends and one of the best detectives I know. He asked me to give this to you."

"Why?" I didn't take the flash drive even though Daniel was holding it out to me.

"He believes that there is much more to the case than the higher-ups want them to believe. Every time he starts asking any detailed questions, he gets stonewalled. The powers that be pretty much want him to find a suspect so they can bury this. He wants to know why." Daniel shook the flash drive. "This has all the crime scene photos, all his notes, everything he has so far. He knows that you guys were first on the scene, and he also knows your reputation. That was why he asked me to give this to you."

"But we were ordered not to look into this case." All the warnings from Francine and Manny about surveillance and about being careful with this case made me wary of taking that drive. I wasn't sure if I wanted to commit myself to cooperating with someone I didn't know. The few times we'd worked together had given me no inclination to trust Daniel. Especially not if it included my whole team, and not if it included Nikki's safety.

"You might have been ordered not to look into this case, but I'm sure you have been looking into it. I bet you are suspicious of not only the circumstances of Savreux's death, but also why you were ordered away from it." He held out the flash drive to me again. "I know you have no reason to trust me, but consider this from a different perspective. Giving you this flash drive goes against a direct order. It puts not only my career, but my friend's career at risk. Everyone is putting a lot on the line here, but we have more to lose than you guys. You work directly for the president. I don't. By including you in the investigation, my friend is going against all police protocol, as am I. We have entire careers, our pensions and even our freedom to lose by giving this to you. In my mind, that should give you reason to trust me enough to just look at what is on this drive."

Nobody spoke and I was grateful for the silence in which I could contemplate his well-presented argument. It didn't take me long. I took the small device from his hands and acknowledged the instant relief on his face with a nod. "I will look at this, but you know I can't promise anything."

"I know. Thank you." He exhaled with a puff of his cheeks. "There is something big going on here. My friend doesn't want to know what you guys find out unless it affects him personally. He would rather you unravel this mystery."

"Why?" I asked.

"You are under the president's protection. Not him. It would be easy to make him disappear." He smiled when I frowned. "I didn't mean they'll kill him. He would lose his reputation, his rank and be stuck on foot patrol or something similar. It would be easier to dispute his findings and opinion than yours."

"Okey-dokey." Vinnie got up. "I'll get the coffee while you guys look at that thingie."

"I'm not looking at it," Daniel said. "I only brought it for you to look at."

"You've already looked at it, formed opinions and have insight that will help us. Why are you being coy?" This was the first time Colin spoke and his assessment was accurate. Daniel's reaction confirmed this. Colin lifted one eyebrow. "You are here. Why not help us?"

"Because I have never gone against a direct order of this magnitude."

"What does that mean?" How could one direct order be larger than another?

"I think"—Colin rested his elbows on his knees, his hands dangling loosely—"that Daniel has never received an order from someone so high up the food chain."

Again Daniel's reaction proved Colin's suspicion to be true.

"This is why I agreed to bring this drive here. We've had high-profile crimes before. We've had politicians murdered before. Why is Savreux so important that the president's aide,

Henri Fabron, told my boss that we should leave the crime scene? And why is he keeping tabs on this investigation?" Daniel shook his head. "I've never seen anything like this. Fabron has never even been in law enforcement. What gives him the right to interfere with this investigation?"

"Is he really interfering?" The tone in Colin's voice indicated he was asking a different question, but I didn't know what. Apparently, Daniel understood. His eyes widened and he leaned back in the sofa.

"No, he didn't do anything that could be seen as outright interference. The bastard knows it would look suspicious and he might even be arrested for doing that."

"How has he been handling this?" Colin asked.

"He's been using the president's connection to Minister Lefebvre. He told my friend's boss that the Minister of Justice requested they close the case as quickly and quietly as possible. They didn't want this to become a scandal-laced investigation, or a witch-hunt. He said that the Minister would get his best prosecutor to get this to go away. I think Fabron said at least ten times they didn't want a scandal."

"Typical politician." Vinnie placed a tray on the dining room table. He had changed into dark brown cargo pants and a long-sleeved black t-shirt. "Here's your coffee. I'm making breakfast, so you might as well move the party to the table."

As we walked to the dining area, I wondered about everything Daniel had said. We sat down and Vinnie served coffee. I watched Daniel stir sugar into his coffee and decided I was right. "There is more to your suspicion. What?"

"The crime scene." Daniel took a sip of his coffee and sighed. "There was something off."

"What?" Colin asked.

"The working theory is that Savreux was murdered by an intruder, most likely a burglar he had surprised. I get the feeling that this is the story Fabron and his ilk would like everyone to believe. I don't buy it. I've been to enough crime scenes to know that if this one was a burglary gone wrong, it is one of the cleanest burglaries I've seen."

"Were they able to ascertain that nothing was stolen?" I asked.

Daniel looked at the flash drive I had placed on the table. "According to the reports, nothing was out of place, nothing was stolen."

"Nothing they knew about," Colin said. "I can think of at least one thing that wasn't there."

"And what is that?"

"A Flinck painting."

I was surprised that Colin had decided to trust Daniel with this information. He was also treating Daniel with much more courtesy than he'd been showing Manny lately. I placed this in the back of my mind for later analysis. The curiosity about what was on the drive was becoming too great for me. I got up and retrieved my computer from its bag on one of the dining room chairs.

Colin was telling Daniel that an anonymous tip had led him to Savreux's house. I sat down at the dining room table, turned on my computer and glanced at Daniel. He wasn't convinced of Colin's explanation, but didn't appear annoyed by the untruth. Colin was sitting to my left and Daniel sat down to my right. Vinnie was standing behind me. I swallowed down my discomfort at the feeling of being surrounded and inserted the flash drive into the computer.

There were seventeen folders organising the content.

Going through all this information was going to require time. I also would prefer doing it in my viewing room, not at my dining room table with three men hovering around me. With an internal sigh, I realised that I had that many people and more hovering around me at the office, but there I could close the door even if it were a glass door.

"Have you gone through this?" I asked Daniel.

He nodded.

"What were your impressions?"

"I'm not a detective."

"But you are trained in reading people and situations in order to make split-second decisions. You were also at the crime scene and I'm sure you have impressions about that. I would like to hear those."

Daniel took a moment before he spoke. "You'll see this on the medical examiner's report. I thought Savreux had about a dozen stab wounds, but I was wrong. Whoever killed him stabbed him twenty-five times."

"Oh my." Involuntarily my hand covered my suprasternal notch, the hollow just above the breastbone. A self-soothing gesture typical to women. "That is an immense emotional display."

"Or it is made to look like it."

"Why do you say that?"

"The stabbing was done post-mortem. First, the killer garrotted Savreux and, when he was dead on the floor, stabbed him to make it look like a crime of passion. The angle of the bruising left by the garrotte indicates that it had to be a person of at least one hundred and ninety centimetres in height."

"What is that in American?" Vinnie asked as he walked

back to the kitchen. The smell of toast was stimulating my appetite.

"American isn't a language, Vinnie." No matter how many times I told him this, he still insisted on having height, weight and distance translated into this non-existent language.

"That would be around six-two, six-three," Daniel answered. "There is evidence that Savreux put up a struggle as he was being garrotted. That means the killer had to be strong enough to subdue Savreux and keep the garrotte in place until he died."

"It was a tall, strong man," I said.

"Footprints around the house also supports that theory. The crime scene guys had their work cut out to get all the evidence and sift through it in such a short time, but there is a lot of pressure on everyone to close this case. At least the footprints were simple. Our boots were fast to eliminate, so it left Colin and the killer's footprints in the snow around the house. Colin's winter boots were easy to track with their generic tread. It's the killer who was dumb enough to wear Russian-style military boots."

My heart rate increased, yet my hands felt cold. "Is your friend changing the profile of the killer according to this information?"

"He tried, but his boss wouldn't let him. The boss insists that it was a burglary committed by some dissatisfied constituent. We all know there are people out there hating politicians who have old money but do nothing to improve the lives of the everyday citizen. That is who they would like to hang this on even though it doesn't make sense. Savreux had a reputation for his philanthropic work, which makes the egoistic rich politician an unlikely theory."

"What other observations did you make?" I was impressed with his acumen.

"Savreux had not been home for long. When we got there, his car's engine was warm enough to indicate that he had arrived less than an hour before."

"From the time I phoned Jenny to the time you went into the house was about forty minutes," Colin said. "When I got into the room, I was sure that he had died less than ten minutes before."

"So the killer could still have been in the house." I took a calming breath, but failed. "You shouldn't have gone in there. It could've been you."

Colin took my hand and pressed it hard against his chest. "I know, love. Believe me, I also don't like that thought. This is not my kind of thing. I'm no James Bond."

"I don't see how that is relevant." For a change, I knew one of the many film characters Colin and Vinnie frequently referred to. "Please don't do this again."

"Aw, Jenny. You know I can't promise that."

Daniel cleared his throat. "As a law enforcement officer, I'm not sure I should be hearing this."

"You chose to come here, dude." Vinnie put a stack of plates in front of Daniel and started setting the table. "If you want our help, you're going to have to develop selective hearing. It seems to work for the old man."

"He's talking about Manny. And he's right." I rearranged the plate in front of me to be equidistant from all the corners of the placemat. This small activity was helping me sort through the other questions I had. "But that is of lesser importance now. Who exactly has been in contact with whom about this case?"

"As far as I know, it's only been Henri Fabron who has been phoning around. He was the one who phoned my boss' boss to order us off the scene. He also phoned the *Commissaire Divisionnaire*, who in turn phoned my friend's supervisor. This is how it has been filtering down."

Any further questions were interrupted by a crash coming from Colin's side of the apartment, followed by a very unladylike expletive. Two seconds later Nikki rushed into the living area, dressed in her pyjamas, her hair in a messy ponytail.

"Oh good, you're all here." She looked at Daniel. "Who are you? Oh wait, I know you from somewhere. Or do I know you? Oh, I don't know if I know—"

"Nikki, what's wrong?" I often became frustrated with her adolescent behaviour, but this was not typical for her. She was prone to believing she knew better than us, but she was not prone to being flustered.

"I, um"—she glanced at Daniel again and lowered her voice—"I got another DM."

Chapter EIGHT

The doors to my viewing room whooshed open and Manny walked in with long, urgent strides. He barely glanced at me before his eyes fell on Nikki. She was sitting in her usual place in my viewing room—on the floor in the space between the second and third filing cabinet. It was becoming a common scene. Now more than ever, Nikki would come into my room without saying a word, put on her headphones and start drawing. Since the beginning of the academic year at the university, heavy textbooks sometimes replaced her sketchpad. Today she was drawing.

Manny stopped in front of her and took off her headphones. "Are you okay?"

"Me? Sure. Why wouldn't I be okay?" Her eyes widened. "Oh, you're worried about that DM. Doc G and Francine have that under control, so that's sorted. My house arrest still sucks."

"You're not under house arrest. We are trying to keep you safe."

"You guys are all paranoid and overprotective. If this continues, I'll never have a sex life."

Manny took a step back. "I really don't want to hear about that."

Nikki laughed and looked at her headphones. "May I have those back? Doc's music is not quite my thing."

Manny handed her the headphones and turned to me. "Meeting in five minutes. I need tea."

He left without waiting for a response from me. I was glad Manny had returned from his meeting with his Interpol bosses. As soon as Nikki had shown us the direct message, I had phoned him, but he'd already been on his way to the meeting. We had agreed to come to the office and he had joined us as soon as he was done. It had given Francine time to do more work on tracking the direct messages, and me time to look through the files Daniel had brought us.

Our breakfast had been cut short with Nikki's announcement. Daniel had stayed for a few slices of toast and a healthy helping of scrambled eggs after we'd told him Nikki was the anonymous source who had given Colin the information on Savreux. We had all agreed that it would raise suspicion if he were seen visiting the apartment or Rousseau & Rousseau. He'd left immediately after breakfast, the fur-trimmed hood pulled low over his eyes, his large jacket further hiding his identity. This was becoming the kind of covert investigation I despised and Francine revelled in.

I took my notebook, unplugged my laptop and took it to the team room. Vinnie and Colin were already seated at the table, and Tim was unloading a tray filled with coffee mugs and pastries. I didn't know how he did it, but we were never served the same types of pastries within a period of two weeks. He was good with supplying a variety of baked goods, but seldom a healthy alternative.

"Good, we're all here." Manny sat down and placed his milky tea in front of him. "Let's start with those blasted direct messages. Supermodel, get your butt over here and tell us what you've found."

"Look at you talking sexy to me." Francine came to the table, tablet in hand. Today she was wearing a dark grey knitted dress, light grey tights and black ankle boots. Her nails were painted in the exact same shade of grey as her dress. I wondered where she found the time for all this grooming while she did so much work on her computers in the office and at home. "We're not going to find this guy in the usual ways. He's extremely smart in covering his tracks."

"I thought you could find anyone." Manny took a sip of his tea.

"I'll tell you why I won't find him through his digital footprint." This was the tone Francine used every time someone challenged her skill set. "He—I'm assuming it is a he—buys a cheap smartphone. He goes to some shopping mall or café and sets up an email account with one of the popular free email service providers. Using that email address, he then sets up a Twitter account with a handle that's just a bunch of numbers, and sends that one DM to Nikki. As soon as that is done, the Twitter account goes dormant and the phone is turned off. For each of the three DM's Nikki received, he used a different phone, a different email address and different Twitter account, and connected from different places in Strasbourg. He also managed to get it to look like he connected from Georgia."

"But he is in Strasbourg?" Manny asked.

"The phones he used were, so it's safe to say he was here too."

"But you can't find him."

"I'm going to try and trace the phones to the sales points and maybe I'll get lucky with security camera footage of this guy in the shop or on a street close to the shop. Other than that, he's quite smart not reusing any of the accounts or phones. And before you ask, I tried to remotely turn those phones on, but it seems he's removed the batteries, completely disabling the phones. There is no signal for me to track its location or anything like that."

Instead of being frustrated, Francine appeared excited by this challenge. While she was talking, admiration was clear in her expression and tone.

"Who the bleeding hell is this guy?" Manny looked at me. "Doc, what do you make of his blasted direct emails? Can you read some psychobabble in there?"

"If you are asking me to profile this person, I refuse. These messages consist of so few words, written in the shortest way possible, that I don't think creating a profile based on this could be accurate. Nikki has been telling me about the Twitter-type language people use to communicate. Words are shortened, articles and prepositions are left out since there is a limit on the number of characters one can use for a tweet."

"Ridiculous," Manny muttered. I agreed. I felt uncomfortable using these words outside of the context of birds.

"However, this wasn't a tweet. All three messages were direct messages, which allows the author to write more words. This person didn't. He stayed within the limits, which most likely influenced the way he wrote this message. I can't even comment on his spelling, vocabulary or grammar, since the sample is too small. I will not speculate." I shook my head even before I finished my sentence. I had seen Manny's expression. "There is too little to work with."

Manny glared at me for a few seconds, and then nodded. "You've got a point, Doc. But what do you make of this last direct message?"

"It's so short. *'Only 10 days. PLEASE!'* didn't tell me anything. "In ten days a lot of things could happen, Manny. It is senseless to start guessing."

"It could be something to do with the president speaking to parliament," Francine said.

"Or it could be numerous other things, Francine." I was bored with baseless theories. I wanted to find real connections, real evidence. "The third message is a warning, but it was the second direct message that led us to Savreux's house, where we found him murdered. Let's focus on that. How does the Flinck, Motte's Vermeer and the Gardner heist connect to Savreux?"

"Didn't you find any leads from the files Daniel gave you?" Manny asked.

"Not connecting Savreux to any of the artwork from the Boston heist, no. I did find a lot of other interesting information. Most crimes can be solved by looking at the person's finances. Savreux's finances are a fascinating case study."

"Why?" Vinnie asked. "Spending money on booze and women is not really fascinating."

"He didn't spend money on booze and women. At least not money that can be traced. His credit card use is very average: expensive restaurants, clothes, shoes, and a lot of books. He seemed to favour one specific bookstore."

"Is that relevant, Doc?"

"Oh. No, it isn't." I had found that interesting though. "Basically, his finances are exactly what one would expect from a person of his standing and income."

"Still not fascinating, Jen-girl."

"Going back three years, I couldn't find anything in his finances indicating the purchases of any of the finer artworks in his house." I opened my computer and connected it to the system so I could display what I was looking at on the large screen against the wall. "If you look at these crime scene photos of his entrance, you'll see a Yulia Brodskaya artwork. This specific paper illustration was done two years ago. I have no record of that illustration bought with one of Savreux's credit cards or even a bank transfer."

"It could've been a gift," Colin said. "Politicians often receive bribes under the guise of gifts."

"I considered that possibility, but there are too many other examples in the house to make this a coincidence." I changed to the different photos as I gave the examples. "There is this Louis Gossin bronze sculpture that was paid for in cash by an anonymous buyer at an auction last year. This watch is one of only fifty made by Bremont. It is a limited edition that came out three years ago. Francine phoned the company and managed to confirm that Savreux bought one of these watches. He paid cash."

Manny's head swung to Francine. "How did you...? Hell. No, actually I don't want to know."

"I've not gone through all the crime scene photos, but so far I've calculated around seven million euro's worth of goods not paid for with the money in Savreux's accounts. Money that he had come by honestly."

"What about this inheritance from his wife's estate, or investments or something like that?" Manny asked.

"I checked it, but will admit that I didn't have a lot of time to do a thorough check. As far as I could see, his investments have been untouched for years. He's only taken a modest amount from the interest every month. That shows in his financial statements and also in his tax return forms. If it weren't for the content of his house, I would never have become suspicious of his finances."

"Were there any cash recovered from the house?"

"Ten thousand"—I looked at my notes—"three hundred

and sixty euros. There were also five hundred dollars and a few loose coins of various currencies, but that was all the cash they found in the house."

"Not enough to buy any of those watches, ornaments or paintings," Colin said.

"Also not enough to explain his chartered plane to Ibiza and the luxury accommodation he lived in for ten days last month." Francine had found this information and I hadn't asked how. She was tapping her grey nails on the table as she continued. "It also doesn't explain the new Porsche in his garage that was also paid in cash."

"Bleeding hell. Who walks around with that much cash?"

"What about his insurance?" Colin asked.

"Good question," I said. The direction of his thinking was evidence Colin was spending a lot of time looking into insurance fraud as well as other art crimes. "I would like to get his insurance forms, but the other company is likely to claim confidentiality."

"I'll get onto that," Manny said. "Having a badge does come in handy at times."

"Is that a good idea?"

As soon as I asked the question, the understanding showed on Manny's face. "Bloody hell. No. Of course not. We're not supposed to be looking into this at all." His eyes narrowed. "Maybe Phillip can help us with this. Where is he?"

"I don't know."

"He's meeting with some rich old lady." Francine crossed her arms when we looked at her. "What? With that jewellery dripping off her, she is definitely rich. And even Botox can't hide her oldness."

"Oldness is not a word." No sooner had I started speaking than Francine smiled.

"Gotcha. God, you make it so easy."

In the beginning, their teasing used to offend me, sometimes more than others. Now I knew that teasing was endemic in close friendships and I tried to see it as such. It still irritated me. I turned my focus back to the crime scene photos and clicked on the next photo. It was the inside of the home office where Savreux was murdered. There were a few works of art in there I wanted Colin's opinion on.

"Hold up." Colin stiffened and leaned towards the large screen. "Go back to the previous photo."

"This one?" It was of the wall separating the room from the hallway. A beautiful dark wooden wall unit covered half of the wall. It was a unit displaying not only books, but also ornaments, statues and other beautiful pieces.

"Zoom in on the clock," Colin said softly. The body language of everyone around the table changed instantaneously. The coldness I had experienced this morning when Daniel had mentioned Russian-style military boots returned to my hands. I zoomed in on the clock, but Colin wanted an even closer view. He seemed particularly drawn to the centre of the clock face.

"I didn't see that blasted clock," Manny said.

I wasn't familiar with different clocks, but this one looked like an early Benjamin Lautier. It looked in working order, showing the time to be fifteen minutes past four. It could have been taken yesterday morning at that time.

"Of course you didn't see the clock. You were looking at the dead body. Zoom out again, love." I did and Colin leaned in. "That clock has been moved. I didn't notice this when we were there, but now it's clear."

"How would you know that, Frey?"

Colin pulled my computer closer, ignoring my and Manny's

complaints. He opened a search engine and soon had another photo on the large screen. "While you were doing all your research yesterday, I was bored and looked for articles on Savreux. I found this one. It was published a few months ago, talking a lot about Savreux's work with the charity and whatnot. The interview was done in Savreux's house and the photos taken in that room. Look at the clock here."

He zoomed in on the wall unit until the clock was in the centre. Then he split the screens to put the crime scene photo next to the article photo. "See? Everything else is still the same, except for the clock."

"I don't know, Frey." Manny tilted his head. "It's only been moved to the left and forward. You really think that is significant? Maybe the cleaning lady moved it."

"Then why is everything else in the exact same place? Why would the cleaning lady put everything back to its original position, but not the clock?" Colin pushed the computer back in front of me, shrugged and leaned back in his chair. If I weren't glaring at him for taking my computer, I might not have seen his micro-expressions. I didn't think anyone else had noticed it. Colin was planning something.

"Since we are looking for Dukwicz and his thing is stealing clocks, maybe it might be worth looking into," Francine said.

Not only did Dukwicz collect clocks and watches from his victims, he had also stolen three clocks from me five months ago. And he was known to wear Russian-style military boots.

"We can't go back to Savreux's house." Manny pinched the bridge of his nose with his thumb and index finger. "That crime scene is sealed and we are most definitely not allowed to go in there. Do you think Dukwicz did this, Doc?"

"He fits the physical requirements and the profile." I

clenched my fists on my lap. They were freezing. I would never forget my personal experiences with the international assassin. "He is tall and strong enough to have done this."

"Hmm. This is an interesting addition to an already frigging nightmare. How are we supposed to follow up on that lead?"

"Well, we know it wasn't Dukwicz who broke into the museum, but maybe he has a connection to Sue." Francine turned to Colin. "Any ideas?"

"I don't know her that well. And I didn't know about Dukwicz until my—our—unfortunate introduction to him when he kidnapped us."

"What did you find out about Sue?" I asked him. "Did you contact her? Is she the one who stole those paintings?"

"It wasn't as hard as I thought it would be," he said. "Through a mutual friend, I got a message to her. I'm expecting her to contact me today. She has my phone number."

"Can you track it, supermodel? Maybe we can locate her and arrest her."

"I thought we talked about this, Millard." Colin straightened. "If you want my help retrieving those paintings, stay away from Sue. I'll handle her."

Colin's body language had become protective. Since Sue allegedly only stole back works that were already stolen, he possibly felt a kinship with her.

"You do that, Frey. As soon as we have those paintings back, I can get those dogs off my heels."

"What dogs?" I knew he was using a euphemism, but I didn't know about whom or what he was talking.

"My two-hour meeting this morning? That was my

Interpol bosses wanting us to close this case post haste. Bloody Henri Fabron has been phoning them, pressuring them into getting our full attention on this heist. What really tipped the scales was a personal call from Minister Antoine Lefebvre."

"Oh, come on!" Francine slapped her hands on the table. "This is too much. Why the craziness to turn us away from Savreux's case and solve this silly theft?"

"A silly theft worth thirteen million euro." Manny grunted. "Frey, get those bleeding paintings."

"I'll do my best for you, Millard." Colin's tone and words communicated sincerity. His expression not.

"Doc, supermodel, did you find anything more on the Libreville Dignity Foundation?"

"At a cursory glance we found two interesting bits of information." Francine and I had focussed on different aspects and it had proven fruitful. "Firstly, President Mariam Boussombo of Gabon is currently in Strasbourg. She is one of the few politicians in Gabon fighting against corruption. She's also a patron of the Libreville Dignity Foundation. She's brought a lot of attention to the plight of women in Gabon."

"It's one of the worst countries when it comes to government corruption," Francine said. "As a matter of fact, Gabon was ranked number hundred and two for government transparency on the list of a hundred and seventy-four countries in the world in 2011. France was twenty-second on that list. Not too bad, all things considering. I still think it will be better if government officials are more accountable to the public with all things financial."

"Returning to the topic of Gabon." Sometimes it felt like I was fighting a losing battle in my attempts to stay on topic.

"Gabon is not a poor country. Its economy is dominated by oil. More than eighty percent of its exports are oil-related. On top of that, it has a low population density and healthy foreign private investments, making it one of the richest sub-Saharan countries. A disturbing fact is the incredibly huge socioeconomic divide. The financially well-off citizens account for less than twenty percent of the population and they receive more than ninety percent of the money in this country. Almost all these people are connected to the oil industry—"

"—like the oil company Motte worked for. Elf," Francine added.

"Yes. Because of the big divide, few people are willing to stand up for the poor majority and risk losing either their high social standing or, if they are of the lower eighty percent, their lives. Mariam Boussombo has been one of the select few vocal in not only fighting corruption in the government, but also fighting for women's rights. By law, women in Gabon should have equal rights to men in most areas. Yet in numerous cases wives have to provide written permission from their husbands if they are to open a bank account or qualify for a loan. President Boussombo's been fighting that. She is here to bring attention to the Libreville Dignity Foundation, and to her work in Gabon."

"A brave woman," Vinnie said.

"The interesting discovery I made was that LDF is located on the same block as the Jean Monnet Museum." Francine sounded proud of herself.

"LDF?"

"It's shorter than saying Libreville Dignity Foundation every time, isn't it? Well, the LDF is almost next door to the Museum."

Almost as one, the people around the table moved a fraction back. People did that when surprised. That movement could sometimes be strong enough to resemble being punched in the face.

"The bigger implication of this discovery is rather dire," I said. "We know that when the electricity was cut for the heist, it affected the whole neighbourhood. That means it also left the Libreville Dignity Foundation's offices without electricity, security and vulnerable to a break-in."

"Did someone break in there?" Manny asked.

"Yes." I had been impressed with how quickly Francine had given me this information. "Because of the attention the museum heist was receiving, the police took a long time to get to the charity. According to the person Francine spoke to, they were missing a few computers and some petty cash, but nothing serious. She said the computers had nothing valuable on it, only administration stuff."

"In other words, it has everyone involved in the charity, all their events, all their fundraising efforts, all their finances." Francine snorted. "Nothing valuable, my ass."

"They have all their data backed up, so nothing is lost to them," I said. "Francine said it's easy to access their system, so she'll—"

"Don't tell me." Manny shook his head. "Just see if there is anything on those computers that is connected to Savreux and to the heist."

"Not for nothing, but that heist could've been just a diversion." Vinnie put the last pastry on his plate. I was sure he had eaten most of them. He had made a valid observation and while Francine started talking about international conspiracies and spies, I allowed my mind to wander. I still had the rest of Savreux's case to analyse. As soon as Francine accessed the Foundation's system, we would have to look through that to search for links as well. There was a lot of work to do. If Nikki's latest direct message was to be believed, we didn't have a lot of time.

Chapter NINE

It was the incessant ringing of Colin's smartphone that woke me. Despite researching late into the evening, I had not found any satisfactory connections between the heists, the direct messages and the people involved in this case. I had gone to bed frustrated and exhausted. That was why I was uncharacteristically irritated when I had to reach over Colin's empty side of the bed to grab his phone from the bedside table.

One glance at the screen told me it was twenty minutes past two in the morning and it was Vinnie calling. I uttered an annoyed grunt at Colin for not being here to answer his own phone. Normally I would never do something like this, but taking the time and the person calling into account, I swiped the screen and lifted the phone to my ear. I wasn't given any time to answer or to ask Vinnie why he was phoning Colin at this hour.

A cacophony of sounds came over the phone so loudly that I held the device away from my ear. It sounded like Vinnie was in a club, but the yelling seemed unusual for a dance club. "Dude! Yo, bro, can you hear me? I can't hear shit! Listen up. I think I've been led into a trap. I'm about to leave Club X, but I'm sure I'm going to need backup. I'm being followed and these mean motherfuckers don't want to dance with me. Fuck it! Dude! Hurry! I don't even have my fucking truck here. I'm going try and shake them, and get to Chilli Park. Meet me there. Chilli Park! Oh, fuck!"

Before I could tell Vinnie that it was me he was speaking to, not Colin, the call was disconnected. With shaky fingers, I tapped the screen to call Vinnie back. It went directly to his voicemail. I tried once more before I lowered the phone and stared at it. My breathing sounded loud in the room and the darkness of impending panic was working its way into my peripheral vision. I felt ill-equipped to deal with situations such as this. My forte was in things cerebral, not physical altercations, my self-defence training notwithstanding.

More severe than my aversion to physical violence, was my fear for Vinnie's safety. He had phoned Colin in good faith, believing that his friend would come to his aid. I had no doubt in my mind that Vinnie had been truthful. The tension in his voice had been too real, and his last expletive filled with too much anger. He needed help, which meant I had to find Colin. I jumped out of bed, put on my nightgown and slippers, and went through my side of the joined apartment and then Colin's side, not finding him anywhere.

The next logical option was going to enrage both Colin and Vinnie, but I didn't care. I ran back to my bedroom, took my smartphone from its designated place on my bedside table and phoned Manny. When he didn't answer on the fourth ring, I started tapping my foot. The call went to voicemail and I phoned him again, wondering why, on the night I really needed people to answer their phones, they didn't. After the third attempt, I accepted the fact that Manny was not available. I left him a terse message to call me immediately.

My hands were still shaking and my concern for Vinnie's wellbeing was increasing by the second. I had run out of options bar one. I closed my eyes, convinced that this idea would not end well, but seeing no other alternative. For a few seconds, I allowed a Mozart symphony to calm me as

I tried to build up the courage to do what was necessary. When I opened my eyes, I felt less panicked and more focussed, yet unconvinced that I was making the right decision.

Colin once said that overthinking often impedes effective action. With this in my mind, I walked to Nikki's room. I didn't even knock, but opened her door and turned on the light as I entered her chaotic space. She groaned loudly and hid her face under the covers.

"Nikki." I touched her shoulder. "We have a problem and I need you to wake up."

Gone were her typical age-appropriate reactions, which normally included rolling her eyes. She pulled the covers down, squinting against the light, but alert. "What's wrong this time?"

"Colin isn't here and Vinnie needs help. I'm going to go there, but I need you to stay here and be safe."

"Yeah, I know, I know. Go to your room, lock myself in and don't leave until I hear one of you." She got up, took her smartphone and looked at me. "Please be careful."

"Of course." This was a repetition of two nights ago and I was strangely less concerned with having her stay in my room this time. I followed her to my room and only when I heard the third lock of the reinforced door to my bedroom click in place did I run to Vinnie's room. My earlier naivety was gone. Logic dictated that Vinnie would have weapons in his room. I just had to find them. If I were to leave the safety of my apartment to help my friend, I was going to need something much stronger than my IQ.

A few months ago, I had gone into his room looking for him only to find him going through a large case. He had shut it and pushed it under his bed the moment he had seen me. I hoped the content of that case was what I now suspected. I might need it. I knelt next to his bed and pulled the case from under it, only briefly worrying about scuffing the floors. Relief flooded me when I found the case without any locks, and I opened it.

Inside were at least twenty different handguns, teargas grenades, flash grenades, stun guns and a few other weapons. I took the revolver on the top and exhaled loudly when I saw bullets in the cylinder. I abhorred violence, and guns were the ultimate expression of it. I dropped the gun back into the case and looked around Vinnie's room. Next to his bed was the dark blue backpack he sometimes used. I grabbed it and filled it with anything but handguns. I was desperate to help my friend, acutely aware of my incompetence in executing such aid. A millisecond before I got up, I grabbed the revolver and dropped it in the backpack.

Cognitive dissonance made my mind feel like it was split in two. On the one hand, I was shaky with concern for Vinnie and on the verge of dark panic. On the other, I was rationally analysing every step I was taking. That included grabbing the keys to Vinnie's pickup truck. My little city car was great for manoeuvring through the small European streets and for parking. It was not the type of vehicle to use when entering an unknown, possibly dangerous, situation. A powerful truck was a much better alternative.

I looked down at my nightgown and slippers, closed my eyes and sighed. Getting dressed would take another five minutes—time I didn't want to waste. For the first time in my adult life, I was going out into public wearing my pyjamas.

After setting the alarm and locking all five locks to my apartment, it took me only two minutes to pull into the street. At this hour Strasbourg was asleep, which made it easier for me to race through the streets. I knew the exact location that Vinnie had given and estimated the journey to take around fifteen minutes with traffic. Six minutes after I left my apartment building, I slowed down on the corner Vinnie had said he was going to meet Colin.

For four months last year, there had been a chilli dog vendor, selling his unhealthy and unappetising wares from a small and very unhygienic stand. French palates had not appreciated the greasy food as much as Vinnie did and it had closed down. By then Vinnie had dubbed this street corner Chilli Park. I didn't see him and continued on to the club he had mentioned. It was only a few blocks away.

There were numerous narrow side streets and I tried to look into each one as I passed them. It was looking into one of those that made it feel as if my heart stopped beating and dropped from my chest. Three men were kicking and beating somebody lying on the ground. I slammed my foot down on the brake pedal and brought the truck to a stop. It was impossible to positively identify the victim, but I had recognised that jacket. Francine had given it to Vinnie for Christmas.

I had to get to my friend before they killed him. I reversed, took a deep breath and pressed my foot down hard on the accelerator. I nearly clipped a building when I turned into the street at a reckless speed.

Vinnie was curled in a foetal position in the middle of the street. The thugs didn't stop kicking and punching him when I stopped a few metres from where they were. They briefly looked up at the truck, the rumble of the large engine loud in the night. The one kicking Vinnie's back said something and two of the men's body language changed. I knew they were going to attack me if I didn't leave. I couldn't do that.

I reached in to the backpack on the passenger seat and felt around until my hand closed around a flash grenade. Once I had experienced the effect of this weapon and it had not been pleasant. It produced an extremely bright light, blinding a person for a few seconds. The loud bang accompanying the light caused temporary hearing loss, and could even result in a loss of balance with its effect on inner ear fluid. I had not enjoyed that experience at all. I felt around for a second grenade.

Lacking the time to analyse my options and actions, I pulled the pin of one grenade out with my teeth while I opened the window. The moment it had lowered sufficiently, I threw the flash grenade at the approaching men. Immediately I repeated this with the second grenade and fell into the passenger seat. I closed my eyes and covered my head with my arms while counting the seconds. A man shouted and another was rattling the car door when a loud bang rocked the car accompanied by a bright flash that lit up the street. I saw this even through my closed eyes protected by my arms. A second later, another loud bang sounded.

I had a very short time to act. From the bag, I grabbed a canister and jumped out of the truck. A few feet away, a large man was on the ground shaking his head. I aimed the canister at him and sprayed pepper spray directly into his face. He screamed and instinctively rubbed his eyes. It worsened the effects and gave me the opportunity to aim the canister at the second man, who was pushing himself into a crouching position. His eyes widened in shock and I depressed the actuator button for two seconds.

As soon as the irritant took effect, I looked up to search for the third man. He was gone. I looked deeper into the street and saw his receding figure. I ran to Vinnie and dropped onto my knees next to him. He was lying very still. It took all my rational strength to push away the dark panic threatening to take me away from this moment.

"Vinnie? Vinnie!" I shook his shoulder, and tears filled my eyes when he groaned and opened his eyes. I pulled on his arm. "We don't have a lot of time before they recover. Come on!"

One of his eyes was already swollen and most likely would be completely shut by the time we reached the apartment. His face had numerous lacerations and there was blood all over his clothes. He was as strongly affected by the flash grenade as the other men and could clearly not hear me. I suspected he'd had his eyes closed when the grenade had gone off, enabling him to see me. I mouthed 'come' and pulled at his sleeve again. It took a very long thirty seconds to help the hundred-and-ten-kilogramme man to his feet.

A few glances towards his attackers reassured me the inflammation and swelling of their eyes, mouth and nose was causing them great discomfort. It also gave us a time advantage, but I didn't want to linger and test their resilience.

Vinnie and I were both breathing hard by the time he was on his feet, swaying. I put his arm around my shoulders and focussed on the adrenaline pumping through my body. I could not think about his blood transferring to my nightgown and pyjamas, or the street dirt on my knees, or the danger these men still posed. I kept my mind on getting Vinnie into his truck, and grunted under his weight. He was hunched over as if he had received a lot of punches and kicks to his torso. I hoped he didn't have any internal injuries.

It felt like I had done two hours of weight training when we reached the passenger door twenty seconds later. The muscles in my legs were burning, but I wasn't breathing as hard as Vinnie. This concerned me and I briefly considered taking him to the hospital. That thought lost importance when I opened the passenger door and swiped the backpack from the seat. It took some time and a lot of effort to get Vinnie in the truck, but soon I ran around the front and jumped over the man writhing on the ground and pushing his hands hard against his eyes. I made sure he wasn't close to the tires before I got in and put the truck in gear.

It required a lot of concentration to back the wide truck out of the narrow street. Not because I wasn't a confident driver, but because every muscle in my body was trembling. Whether it was from stress or from the strain of helping Vinnie didn't matter. It made me feel weak and I loathed that feeling. It wasn't as bad as the darkness calling me to its warm safety. I didn't want to risk focussing on Mozart in case I shut down completely.

Vinnie grunted something and I glanced at him. He was slumped against the door. Again I lauded my decision to take his truck. At least I wouldn't have to wash his blood from my car seats and door.

"Jen-girl."

"I'm here, Vinnie."

"Jen-girl?" This time he raised his voice, loud enough to hear if I had been on the other side of the street.

I realised he couldn't hear me. With a sigh and a suppressed shudder, I touched his knee and squeezed.

"No hospitals. Don't want hospital."

I wasn't going to enter into an argument with a man who couldn't hear what I was saying. I was taking him to a hospital and I didn't care about his preferences. He was clearly in pain and I was concerned about internal injuries. I turned into the road that would take us to the closest hospital.

"Can you also not hear?" Vinnie shouted. "I said no hospitals. Take me home."

I was considering shouting back at him when my mobile phone rang. I recognised the ringtone and uttered a sound of relief. I took the phone from my coat pocket and swiped the screen. "Manny."

"What's wrong, Doc?"

"Vinnie's been attacked. I'm taking him to the hospital."

"What happened?"

It was against the law to speak on one's phone while driving, but I considered these extenuating circumstances, and told Manny what had taken place.

"You went there on your own?" His voice reached the same decibels as Vinnie's had earlier. "What the bleeding hell were you thinking?"

"I phoned you and you didn't answer."

He was silent for a few seconds. "Take Vinnie to your apartment. I'll get a medic I trust to come check him out. If there is the slightest concern, we'll get the criminal to a hospital. Go home and wait for me. I'm going to phone Daniel and see if his team can get to those guys while they're still down."

We argued for a few more minutes before Manny convinced me that taking Vinnie home was the best course of action at the moment. Any hospital I was going to take him to would have to report Vinnie's injuries. Police would come and this could become something we didn't want it to be. I hated that Manny had presented such a reasonable argument, but I conceded. With great reluctance. I did not like the situation. Vinnie's silence concerned me more than I liked.

As I turned into our street, Vinnie pushed himself up in his seat. "Where's Colin? Why did you come?"

"Can you hear me?" I didn't want to shout.

"If you can speak just a bit louder, I'll hear you just fine. The ringing in my ears sucks monkey balls."

"Colin wasn't home when you phoned." I chose to ignore the reprehensible visual image he had created. The parking space I had left thirty minutes ago was still available and I manoeuvred the truck into it. "I don't know where he is and I couldn't leave you without any help."

"You are a stupid, brave woman." He turned to me and waited until I pulled the key from the ignition and looked at him. "Thank you, Jen-girl. You're a kick-ass friend."

"Is that a compliment?" I couldn't accurately read his facial expressions, not with the amount of swelling.

"The best kind." He tried to smile, but winced when his lip started bleeding again. "You rock."

"Okay." Sometimes Vinnie would start with his slang and euphemisms, and would continue until I left the room. "Let's get inside the apartment and wait for Manny."

I got out and walked around the truck to help Vinnie, but he was already outside, leaning heavily against the side of the vehicle. At a loss on how to act in such a situation, I stood motionless. I had learned that men were very sensitive about portraying their strength. I didn't know if Vinnie would be offended if I offered to help him again.

"I don't think my legs are going to hold, Jen-girl. I just need to lean a bit on you for balance." He lifted one arm as if to give me a one-sided hug and I moved in under his arm. He wasn't ashamed of admitting his need for assistance. I focussed on my breathing to help me to deal with the panic that threatened to overwhelm me.

Feeling as if I was physically surrounded by Vinnie when he put his arm around my shoulders and leaned on me was definitely a trigger that needed Mozart. Yet I knew that I would shut down the moment I focussed on the usually calming music. Vinnie still needed me. He seemed stronger than in the side street though and we arrived at my front door in due time. While I unlocked the door, Vinnie leaned against the hallway wall. A glance at him told me he was struggling to hide his pain and to remain conscious.

"You really should go to a hospital." I opened the door and walked to the small panel disguised as a key holder to turn off the alarm.

"They will phone the cops and I don't want to talk to those idiots tonight," he said a bit too loudly. He walked into the apartment. "It's just a few bruises, Jen-girl. I'll be fine."

"Vinnie!" Nikki ran from my room and stopped in front of Vinnie. Without hesitation, she pulled his arm around her slender shoulders. He towered over her, dwarfing her slight frame in what looked more like a hug than a young woman assisting a muscular man into one of the dining room chairs. "What happened to you?"

"You should've stayed in my room, Nikki."

"I heard it was you when you came in, Doc G. I was worried." She leaned in to look at Vinnie's swollen eye. "We have to get some ice on that."

This was not the first time I had an injured person in my apartment. It appeared that I was not becoming desensitised. The sight of the blood on Vinnie's face and his badly bruised and bloody knuckles bother me even more than it would have a year ago. Was it the blood itself, or my emotional connection to this man? Annoyed with myself for even asking this inane question, I went to the guest bathroom to get the first-aid kit. That was another addition to my apartment I had never considered essential before.

When I came back with the large bag filled with more than the basic home first-aid kit, Vinnie was leaning his head back, holding one of my dishtowels to his eye. I assumed it was filled with ice. Fortunately, I replaced my dishtowels every three months. This one would just be disposed of much sooner, together with everything I was wearing.

I put the black bag on a thick towel on the dining room table and unzipped it. As I reached for the disinfectant, the doorbell rang and Vinnie's body tensed. He lowered the bag and started pushing himself out of the chair. "Are you expecting anyone?"

"It must be Manny." No sooner had I said it than Manny impatiently called for me to open the bloody door. I waved Vinnie back to the chair. "I won't open it unless I'm sure it's Manny."

A quick look through the peephole confirmed to whom the voice and insistent knock belonged. I opened the door and let Manny in.

"What the bleeding hell are you people up to?" He walked to Vinnie and took a moment to inspect him. "Nah, you'll live. Who did this?"

"Three men," I said.

"I didn't ask you, missy." Manny turned to me. "The next time you leave this bloody criminal to fight his own battles. No more driving in on your white horse."

"You can't drive a horse. It doesn't have an engine."

Manny's face turned red. "You wilfully enter a dangerous situation and now you are correcting my grammar?"

"Not your grammar. An illog—"

"I don't want to hear it. You should've phoned the police.

Holy hell, the more I think about it, the angrier I get at both of you."

"I told you exactly what happened, Manny. What would you have done differently?" I welcomed the anger. It pushed away the panic just enough to make it manageable. "I have seven years of self-defence training, but I know that I am not faster than a bullet. That was why I took the flash grenades. And the pepper spray."

"That's another thing. Where the hell did you get those things from? It's illegal for civilians to have them."

"Shut up, old man." Vinnie sat up, but immediately leaned forward with a grunt. "You're speaking so loudly that I have no problem hearing you. Give Jen-girl a break. She most likely saved my life and I think she rocks. Those flash grenades were mine. And I'm not telling you anything else."

Manny glared at Vinnie, turned to me and glared for a few seconds. Then he walked towards the front door, turned around and walked back to us. He repeated this a few times until he stopped in front of me, a bit calmer. "Doctor Face-reader, I don't want anything bad to happen to you. When you do things like this, it drives me crazy with worry. I most likely would've done the same you did, but it doesn't mean I like that you were in danger."

"I wasn't really in danger. I had enough flash grenades, stun guns and pepper spray with me to incapacitate ten large men. And I didn't leave the car until they were on the ground."

"You're going to be the death of me, Doc." Manny sighed and rubbed his hand hard over his face. He shook his head at me and looked back at Vinnie. "Who attacked you?"

"I don't know. Really, I don't. I got a call from a contact that he had some info on Dukwicz and that I was to meet him at Club X. When I walked into the place, I got a bad feeling, man. I didn't wait around, but they jumped me as soon as I left."

"Do you have any suspects?"

"Dukwicz?" Vinnie lifted one shoulder. "Seriously, man, I don't know. All I know is those guys were military trained. Their moves were too practiced for them to be street fighters."

"Daniel is sending his team there, but I'm not holding my breath that we'll have someone to interrogate."

"Oh, they're long gone." Vinnie accepted another dishtowel filled with ice from Nikki and placed it on his eye.

"Did you get anything from them? Description, height, nationality?"

"Dude, they were beating the fucking shit out of me. I wasn't taking down notes." Vinnie looked at Nikki. "Sorry, punk."

Nikki rolled her eyes.

"Daniel should be here soon." Manny pulled a chair out and sat down. "He told me that he's bringing a medic and he's also got a surprise for us."

"I don't like surprises." Actually, I despised surprises. The thought of it brought back the panic. That made me angry and I grabbed onto the anger, hoping it would keep me from shutting down.

"I know, Doc. I'm not too fond of them either." He looked around the apartment. "Where the bleeding hell is Frey?"

Vinnie shifted and I glanced at him. Because of the swelling in his face, I couldn't be sure, but I thought I had seen guilt. Just as I wanted to confront him, the doorbell rang again. In two seconds Manny went from slumping in the chair to standing, his gun in his hand and his body in combat alertness. "Stay here."

He walked to the door, peered through the peephole, his whole body tensing as if he had seen something shocking. He leaned back, shook his head and looked through the peephole again. I could only see his body language from behind and didn't know how to interpret the strange stiffness I saw as he opened the door. He was blocking the view and I got up to see who was causing this behaviour. What I didn't expect was Manny bursting out in laughter.

I realised that in the eighteen months I had known Manny, I had never heard him laugh. A few times he had smiled, but never what could be defined as a grin. He sometimes chuckled, but it was short-lived and never as joyful as this. He was not a man with a great sense of humour.

His belly laughter made me therefore even more curious to see who was at the door. I walked closer, captivated by Manny bending at the waist, his one hand pressed against his stomach, the other one hanging to his side loosely holding his gun. His laughter was so contagious that I was smiling when I reached the door. When I saw what had triggered Manny's uncharacteristic mirth, a frown replaced my smile.

Chapter TEN

In the hallway, Daniel was standing next to Colin, their body language a thrill to read. The *zygomaticus* muscles around Daniel's mouth caused his lips to twitch in combinations of enjoyment and victory. His posture was relaxed despite the strong grip he had on Colin's elbow. It was Colin's situation causing Manny's continued laughter and Daniel's nonverbal cues of triumph.

Appearing unperturbed, Colin looked at Manny wiping tears from his cheeks. Colin lifted his handcuffed hands. "You better enjoy this moment, Millard. You might never see it again."

"I…it…oh…" Manny shook his head and started laughing all over again.

Despite Colin's outward appearance, I could see he was livid. I didn't know whether it was because he was in handcuffs, because Daniel was clearly in control of this situation or because of Manny's laughter. Combining my nonverbal analytical skills and my intimate knowledge of Colin, I knew the situation was very close to escalating into something much worse than the last seven weeks' animosity.

I pulled on Manny's sleeve and he easily moved out of the way. "Come in."

I stood to the side and waited for Colin and Daniel to enter. A tall man was standing to the left of the front door, observing us. He was dressed in the same uniform as Daniel, the GIPN badge an additional clue that he had come with

Daniel. This was yet another situation that I knew Phillip with his exceptional mediation skills would've handled much better than me. Especially with my own state of mind being volatile after what had just occurred.

Self-awareness alerted me that I was seconds away from shutting down, so I centred all my energy on analysing the stranger's nonverbal cues. I studied the tall man until he lifted both eyebrows. There was nothing indicating malicious intent or that he posed a danger. Yet I didn't want this outsider in my home. I felt too vulnerable at present. But the last eighteen months have taught me that there were other needs aside from my own. I sighed. "Please come in."

He nodded his thanks with a smile and walked past me. I took note of his lack of discomfort at the strange situation. He didn't seem concerned at all as he stopped just inside the apartment and readjusted a large black bag slung over his shoulder. The red and white cross on it explained his presence in the room. He was the paramedic. Colin in handcuffs was the surprise. I closed and locked the door.

"Dude!" In normal circumstances, I was sure Vinnie would have spoken louder than usual seeing Colin in cuffs. With his ears still affected by the flash grenade, he was shouting. "What the fuck is going on?"

Daniel and Colin had not moved deep into the apartment when Colin held out his hands. "You made your point. Take these things off."

"Please don't," Manny managed to say through his chuckles. "This is too enjoyable."

"Enough, Manny." I made sure my voice carried enough authority and annoyance for Manny to pay attention. "Daniel, unless you plan to put Colin in jail, I suggest you take those cuffs off right now."

Colin shook his hands at Daniel, lifting his eyebrows. The flush on Colin's skin, the tremors in his hands and his tight fists were unlike anything I had observed in him before. He had never exhibited such rage.

Daniel must have noticed the lack of humour in my tone and face. His eyes narrowed briefly and he looked at Colin. It took him only two seconds to reach a decision and he uncuffed Colin, much to Manny's disappointment. Fortunately, the older man was calming down. He sighed happily. "Daniel, my friend. You've just given me the best gift ever. For that I thank you."

Colin rubbed his wrists, took the backpack from his back and walked to me. He stared at the blood on my nightgown, his face losing colour. "Are you okay?"

"I'm not hurt. It's not my blood." I suppressed the overwhelming desire to rip off my nightclothes and scrub my skin under a hot shower. "Vinnie was attacked."

His eyes widened and he walked the dining room table. "Vin, you look like shit. What happened?"

"What does it look like? I got the crap kicked out of me. Why didn't you have your phone with you?"

Colin shook his head. "I forgot it. I actually forgot to take my phone with me.'

"Your turn." Vinnie pointed his chin towards Daniel. "What happened?"

Daniel and Manny started talking at the same time Vinnie and Colin continued their conversation. This was too much for me. "Stop!"

Instant silence filled my apartment. I closed my eyes and inhaled deeply as I sought to control the numerous emotions attacking me. Three breaths later, I opened my eyes to find everyone still looking at me. "We all need to know what happened to each other. I suggest we sit down at the table and debrief while the man with the large medical bag takes care of Vinnie."

As one, everyone turned to the front door where the tall man was watching us, amusement around his eyes and mouth. His gaze turned to me and understanding replaced his relaxed expression. "Of course. Yes. I'll take care of the injured man."

"Vinnie, his name is Vinnie," I said. "Who are you?"

"Martin Proulx." He walked towards me with his hand out, but dropped it to his side when I crossed my arms.

"Martin's part of my team." Daniel walked to the table and sat down at the far end. "He transferred in a few months ago. I've known him for more than eleven years and I trust him implicitly. Nothing said here will ever leave this room."

Martin winked at Daniel, leaned over until he was eye-level with Vinnie and started asking him questions about his injuries. I was grateful that no one continued conversations or argued with me. Within a minute we were all seated at the table, Martin was tending to Vinnie's injuries and Nikki was making coffee. I didn't wait for anyone to take charge of the discussion, but immediately gave a concise report on what had taken place before Colin had returned. Taking control like this was helping me.

"What are you thinking, Vin?" Colin asked when I finished.

Vinnie winced as Martin cleaned another cut on his face. "Dude, you have to speak up. My hearing is still not right."

Colin repeated his question, a bit louder.

"I'm thinking it's Dukwicz. He knows me from my days with Hawk." Vinnie had considered Nikki's criminal father a close associate, if not a friend. I had seen how Hawk's death had affected Vinnie. "What bothers the hell out of me is not that I got beaten up, but that they didn't kill me."

"How could that bother you?" My voice shook and my fists tightened on my lap.

"Jen-girl, I got jumped by three big-ass dudes. They could've killed me seconds after I left the club. They didn't. Someone had given them orders to hurt me, maybe even put me in a coma, but not to kill me."

"A message," Martin said. He put a second butterfly bandage on the long cut on Vinnie's temple and nodded to himself.

"Who is sending what message?" Manny asked.

Vinnie sighed and pushed Martin's hand away from his face. He straightened in his chair. "I have a feeling that someone has spread the word that I'm a rat."

"What makes you think that?" Colin asked.

"A rat?" I knew Vinnie didn't mean this literally, but I hadn't come across this euphemism before.

"An informant for the police, Jen-girl. Don't ask me how I know this, but I've been suspecting this for a few days now."

"And you think that is why Dukwicz got you beaten up?"

"Shit, I don't know."

I was glad Vinnie admitted not knowing, else I would've felt compelled to point out the numerous weaknesses in his argument.

"Your turn, dude." Vinnie sat back and nodded to Martin to continue tending to his face. "How did you get made?"

Colin looked at Daniel. "Some smart bastard followed me. I didn't see him, not until I left the house."

"Back up, Frey. What house and what were you doing there?"

The fleeting expression on Colin's face warned me that he

was about to say something that would infuriate Manny. Colin looked happy about it. "I broke into Savreux's house to get that clock."

"You what?" Manny shot out of his chair, walked to the kitchen, glared at Nikki, walked back to his chair and walked away again. Nikki placed the last coffee mug on a tray and brought it to the table. When she had seen Manny's anger the first time, she had reacted with fear. Now there was only a marginal increase in her muscle tension. She left the tray on the table, excused herself and went to her room. She was smart enough to know when her presence might hinder the freedom of our discussions.

Manny walked back to his chair and fell into it. He glowered at Colin. "Why on this bleeding, frigging, damned earth would you do something so moronic?"

"I had a gut feeling it might give us a break in this case."

I looked at Daniel. "You are good at reading body language. Did you see something in Colin's nonverbal cues when we were looking at the crime scene photos?"

Daniel nodded. "I knew he had seen something and I had a feeling that he was going to follow up on it. So I tailed him. I know this case is a forest of mirrors, and I thought it might be a good thing to let Colin do what he was doing. Something is very wrong with Henri Fabron ordering us off the case. I've never liked politicians or cover-ups. And I'm all for exposing the truth of whatever sensitive situation the bigwigs want to keep under wraps. I wanted to make sure nothing went wrong while Colin did the heavy lifting."

"Why did you arrest me then?" Colin's jaw and neck muscles were tight with tension.

"I didn't arrest you. I just handcuffed you. Big difference. You have some serious skills. I almost lost you a few times.

If you hadn't gone to Savreux's house, I would've lost you two streets before. When I saw your car pulling into the next street, I assumed that was your destination. I was convinced that I'd got to the house before you, but I never saw you go in. It was pure luck that I caught you coming down the wall."

"He came down the wall?" Manny asked.

"Like a spider." Daniel's face revealed his admiration as he looked at Colin. "You and I have to go rock climbing one day. Even better, do it with my team to teach them some humility."

A slight frown drew Colin's eyebrows together. I had to admit that I was also not clear on how a law enforcement officer could be so approving of Colin's criminal skill set.

"Yet you felt the need to slap cuffs on me." There was a particular reason this action disturbed Colin. I wasn't one hundred percent sure, but in context and processing Colin's micro-expressions, it seemed like he felt betrayed.

"I know your history with Manny and incidentally agree with him that you take too many chances." Daniel shrugged. "Thought it would give Manny a kick and make a point with you at the same time."

Colin's lips tightened. "That was above and beyond just to make a point."

"But it gave me such joy, Frey. Would you please tell me now why you broke into a sealed crime scene and stole evidence?"

Ignoring Manny, Colin lifted his backpack from next to his chair onto his lap and unzipped it. He opened it as wide as possible and carefully lifted a form out of it. He removed the soft cloth covering it to reveal the clock we had seen on the crime scene photos.

"Why didn't you tell me you were going to steal the clock?" I asked softly. My breath stuttered at everything the clock represented, at the person this clock implicated.

He looked away from the timepiece, giving me one of his uncompromising stares. "What would you have done if I had told you?"

I thought about this. "I would've phoned Manny."

"And that is why I didn't tell you." There was no anger or censure, just his observation.

"That's a good girl, Doc."

"Don't be smug about this, Manny. I wouldn't have told you in order for you to stop Colin. You had said that you cannot protect us if you don't know what we are doing. I would've phoned you to help Colin."

Both men took exceptional offence at my words. There were so many conflicting messages in their expressions that I felt lost. Generally, I felt that I had a good understanding of the people in my life. Times like these proved how erroneous I was in this presumption.

"We can discuss this later, Jenny." Colin's tone was sharp. I bit down on the insides of my lips to prevent the many questions causing turbulence in my mind from escaping. My compulsive need to understand was difficult to suppress in favour of maintaining a certain level of equanimity around the table.

"Frey." Manny waited until Colin looked at him. "You know this was borderline stupid, right?"

"There is something about this clock, Millard. You would never have agreed to let me get it."

"You sure about that?"

I studied Manny's expression, wondering if he would've helped Colin if I had phoned him. Manny's career in law enforcement, interviewing suspects and dealing with political issues had honed his deception skills. Eighteen months of observing him gave me an advantage in reading his expression. I smiled. "He might have agreed, Colin."

"Don't read me, Doc. Oh hell, what am I saying? Of course you're going to read me." He leaned towards me. "Then I hope you can read how pissed off I am."

"You were," I corrected him. "You are quick to anger and quick to calm down. You're mostly calm again."

Manny's lip curled and he leaned back in his chair. "Next time you have another cockamamie idea, tell me about it, Frey."

"Sure." Colin's smile didn't even lift the corners of his mouth. "I'll tell you while we braid each other's hair."

Manny's returning anger was interrupted when Vinnie uttered a loud expletive. Martin was examining his torso, pressing along his ribs. "Dude, that hurt."

"That makes three badly bruised ribs. Those are the ones I can feel. I'm not even a hundred percent sure they are only bruised. You might need to get x-rays done."

"I'm fine. Tape me up. They'll heal."

Colin wasn't listening to his best friend convincing the paramedic that three bruised ribs were nothing for him. All of Colin's attention was on the clock as he carefully placed it on the cloth on the table. Not once did he touch it with his bare hands. He got up, went to the kitchen, and came back stretching a disposable latex glove over his left hand. His right hand was already gloved. No one spoke. Vinnie grunted a few more times as Martin examined his torso. There were many angry bruises already forming, but no discolouration indicating internal injuries. Colin sat down and gently felt around the clock with his fingertips.

"What are you looking for?" I asked after watching him for a minute. Colin didn't answer me. I saw no indicators of anger. He was concentrating. A slight widening in his eyes told me he had found what he was looking for. With his fingernail, he pressed against the side of the clock until we heard a click. A panel at the back of the clock opened and Colin carefully pulled it wider, peering in.

"Careful, Frey. Having this bloody thing here is bad enough. I don't want to explain why evidence was destroyed."

"Put a sock in it, Millard." Colin didn't look up. He leaned closer and tilted his head, examining the inside of the clock. "Well, as I live and breathe."

"What?" I was becoming impatient. The satisfaction and triumph on Colin's face created suspense. I didn't like it. "What did you find?"

Colin reached into the clock with his thumb and index finger, twisted something a few times before a genuine smile lifted his cheeks and caused wrinkles next to his eyes. He pulled out an electronic device and held it in the air. "A nanny cam."

I've heard of these before. "Aren't they usually found in teddy bears or children's rooms?"

"That is not a nanny cam." Daniel took a glove from Martin's medical kit, put it on and held out his hand. "That is a pinhole surveillance camera with a wireless receiver. Top of the range in spy cameras."

"How the hell did you know it was there, Frey?" Manny's jaw was slack.

"A trained eye, Millard." Colin laughed softly when Manny swore again. "Okay, I thought I saw a tiny lens in the clock on those crime scene photos, but I wasn't sure."

"So you tried to convince me to get it because it was *moved?*"

"Hey, it was a good argument. I still hold to it. You agreed that it was the only thing out of its usual place."

"Hmph." Manny looked away and mumbled, "Good work."

"Say what?" Surprise was clear in Colin's tone and on his face.

"Where are the recordings?" That was the only thing I was really interested in. I wasn't interested in Manny and Colin starting an argument. Nor did I care about the little camera, an apparent technological marvel that had them making noises of wonderment. "Are they stored inside the clock?"

"No. See this?" Daniel pointed to what looked like a mini-antenna on the camera. "This transmits the footage to a nearby recording device."

"Which would be somewhere in Savreux's house," Manny said.

"Manny is right," Daniel said. "It will only be able to transmit up to a maximum of ninety metres. The good news is that it limits the radius to Savreux's property."

"The bad news?" Colin asked.

"The bad news is that nowadays it is common to wirelessly upload all the recordings to the user's cloud account. It's not like the old days when it was saved on a disk, a tape or a computer file. The convenience of this is that the cloud is controlled by the user. It can also be accessed by the user from absolutely anywhere."

"You are saying cloud and I'm thinking weather." Manny scratched his stubbled cheek, his brows drawn down. "Speak English."

Daniel laughed. "A cloud is an internet storage system. There is a lot of debate around the security of these systems, but they're becoming more and more popular. I'll get my guy onto this."

"I don't think so." Manny pointed to the device and then to the table. "Put that down. My gal will figure this out. You should not be here, you should not be involved at all."

"Um. You phoned me, remember?"

"That was before I knew you were following Frey and digging yourself deeper into this case. This is going to hell in a handbasket." Manny sighed. "We need to limit your involvement. Let my team handle the cloudy thingie and you watch your back."

My apartment grew quiet for a few minutes, everyone busy with their own thoughts. My mind was returning to the narrow street, the violence I had been part of and the dirt on my clothes. I pulled my pyjama pants away from my legs, concentrating on not giving voice to the keening I felt in the back of my throat. Colin's hand closed over mine in a firm grip. His touch anchored me.

"If I may?" Martin's quiet question gave me something to fix my mind on. "Who's the kid?"

"What kid?" Had I missed an important bit of information?

"The one who made us coffee."

"She's not a kid." I frowned at Manny and Colin's immediate disapproval of my statement. "She's not. Three months ago, she turned eighteen and is legally an adult."

"And still a kid, Doc."

"She's a kid, Jenny."

I strongly disagreed with them. Despite Nikki's seemingly blithe approach to life, she had grown up in the shadow of a criminal father. Her father had sent her to America for her high-school education, which had led to her feeling socially and emotionally detached. Her father's death had finalised her discontentment with her sense of displacement. She had insisted on returning to France and for unknown reasons had pleaded to stay with us. At first, her attachment to me had been disconcerting, to say the least.

Her interest in art had built an immediate rapport with Colin and he had grown very fond of her. Part of her petition to move in with me until she came of age had been her promise to disrupt my privacy, routines and life as little as possible. I had thought it impossible and had told her so. She had been taking great pleasure in proving me wrong and reminding me about it whenever I expressed my surprise to find her quietly sitting in my viewing room or my living room, not intruding at all.

It was her quiet strength and her determination to move out from under her late father's notorious reputation that had won my respect and trust. Lately, we had spent a few afternoons discussing her past and how she was dealing with being the daughter of a legendary European arms dealer. Her pragmatism and maturity had not only impressed me, but had also assuaged my concerns. This was the main reason for my refusal to call her a child. She had shown wisdom, insight and self-awareness far beyond her biological age.

"Seriously?" Surprise raised the pitch in Martin's voice and it caught my attention. My mind had drifted off and I had missed part of the conversation. "She doesn't even look like him."

"She's his kid and she's nothing like him." Manny's nonverbal cues communicated his protective attitude. "She's young, but she's smart. When she was small, Hawk used to let her sit in on all his deals. She's used to keeping secrets."

"You really trust her?" Martin exhibited every indicator of disbelief.

"More than I trust you." Manny's expression didn't change when Martin and Daniel laughed.

"Touché."

Vinnie shifted in his chair and groaned. His pallor was an unhealthy grey, bringing his attack back to overwhelm my thoughts. I needed to be alone. I needed Mozart. "If there is nothing more to discuss, you should leave."

Everyone looked at me in surprise. After a moment, Daniel and Manny got up with a nod. Martin's expression told me that he didn't know how to interpret my harsh demand.

"Get some sleep, Doc. We'll take this up at nine." Manny glanced at his watch. "At least we'll get another three hours or so of rest."

Martin followed their lead and soon only Vinnie, Colin and I were in my apartment. I double-checked the locks on the front door, walked back to the table and stood in front of Vinnie. My whole body felt stiff, but I had to reassure myself about him first. He started to sigh under my scrutiny, but grunted and held his hand to his ribs. "Son of a whore."

"Look at me."

"Yes, Jen-girl." He looked up and allowed me to study his badly beaten face. There was a lot of swelling and that one long cut on his temple, but nothing looked grave.

"I can't read your expression, so please be honest with me. Do you need to go to the hospital?"

"Nah. My cousins once beat me up worse than this. Then it took me three weeks to recover. I bet the swelling will be down by tomorrow evening and I'll look like my old handsome self by Sunday." His nonchalant statement brought only marginal relief.

I straightened. "I want your word that you will get medical help the moment you notice something is wrong."

"You have it, Jen-girl."

I nodded and walked rigidly to my bedroom. The need to

scrub my skin and hair clean was becoming harder to resist. I knew it was my imagination, but it felt like my skin was burning in all the places where Vinnie had touched me, where his blood might have made contact—even if it was only with my pyjamas. I needed to dispose of these pieces of clothing, but first I had to change the bedding. I would never be able to sleep knowing that Nikki had slept on the same sheets.

I stripped the bed with trembling hands, holding tightly onto my control. I heard Colin helping Vinnie to his room as I put fresh linen on the bed and walked to the bathroom. In automated movements, I undressed, put everything I wore in a plastic bag and turned on the shower. I didn't allow myself to think or feel, or to even look at the water swirling down the drain.

The water didn't feel hot enough and I turned up the heat. My skin was turning red from the vigorous scrubbing and the scorching water. Yet I didn't feel clean. I continued rubbing my soaped sponge over my skin with increasing desperation.

At first I thought it was water running down my cheeks, but the salty taste shocked me. I never cried. I had shut downs and very infrequently melt downs, but not tears. Impatiently, I wiped my cheeks with the back of my hands. It didn't help. A loud sob escaped from my chest and I slapped my hand over my mouth.

Colin putting his life in danger by going back to the house where someone had been killed and Vinnie's attack came bearing down on me with a force I could not fight. It felt like someone punched me in my stomach and I folded double, struggling to breathe. When Colin found me, I was sitting on the shower floor, clutching my knees to my chest and keening loudly. I couldn't stop to tell him how much his actions had affected me.

"Shh." He turned off the water and put a large towel around my shoulders. "I'm here, Jenny. Vin's going to be okay. We're okay."

I shook my head. I wasn't okay. I didn't feel okay. I wanted to stop feeling like this, so I slowly sank into Mozart's Piano Sonata no. 16 in B flat Major. I knew Colin would take care of me. Being naked on the shower floor, not going through my usual pre-sleep routine was much less important than the warm safety I felt while the music flushed out the horror of the last two hours. I trusted the man who was picking me up from the floor to take care of my body while I tried to put my mind back in order.

Chapter ELEVEN

The irritation in Manny's voice drew my attention away from Francine's computer monitor for the third time. I had woken up completely rested, but had to spend a total of eleven minutes convincing Colin that I was no longer distressed. The extreme concern I had observed in his nonverbal cues had revealed the depth of his emotional investment in me. Once he had been placated, we had come into the office.

My first priority had been to find the cloud where Savreux stored the recordings from his home office. Francine was the best person for this particular task, and I was sitting next to her at her desk. We had been trying to locate that cloud when Manny had received a phone call. It had taken only two sentences to determine that it was Henri Fabron on the other side of the call.

"Of course we are making progress on finding those paintings." Manny's lie sounded convincing, but also conveyed his irritation. His grip on his phone was so tight, I wondered if a man could crush a phone with his bare hands. "I will send you a written report by the end of the day."

"Maybe we should work in my room," I said to Francine.

The mostly one-sided conversation had been going on for more than fifteen minutes now and I was finding it very distracting. The first ten minutes Manny had handled the call with indifference. But then Henri must have said something that had breached Manny's professional control. His voice had since raised a few decibels and his face was a deep red.

"Why don't you go to your room?" Francine said. "I'm used to his blustering. I promise you will be the first one to know the moment I find the footage."

I went to my viewing room and was immensely grateful when the glass doors sealed to close off Manny's arguments. I sat down and stared at the ten monitors in front of me, displaying different parts of this case. I needed to organise my thoughts regarding the various elements in this case.

Clockwise the monitors showed the Boston heist of 1990, Flinck's Landscape with an Obelisk, Nikki's three direct messages, the crime scene photos at Savreux's house, the heist of two days ago and Motte's Wikipedia page. I tilted my head, thought about it some more and moved Motte's page between the Flinck painting and Nikki's direct messages. Had there not been so many seemingly coincidental links between these different elements, I would easily have dismissed this as fanciful imagination.

I wanted to show Colin the monitors and ask for his input, but he wasn't here. He had excused himself after receiving a text message almost an hour ago and I had not seen him since. I folded my legs under me, leaned back in my chair and closed my eyes. I needed to find the one link that connected all of the pieces.

I emptied my mind and called up a clear music sheet. The lines bundled in sets of five were a work of art that never failed to calm me. Mentally, I drew the G-clef in one movement, enjoying the beauty of the curls and lines. Only the C-clef came close to the elegance of the G-clef. On another inhale, I drew the set of sharps, preparing the staff for a Mozart concerto.

My eyes shot open after the second page. I glanced at the clock on my computer and relaxed when I saw only thirty minutes had passed. I needed to confirm the suspicions that had blasted into my thinking brain when I had drawn the staccato sign.

I pulled up a few more files and soon lost myself in the data. It was Colin's angry tone that drew my attention away from the monitors. I turned towards the glass doors and immediately regretted the move. Pain shot up through my hips, my back muscles and even my shoulders.

"I can't believe they left you like this, Jenny." Colin rushed into the room and sat in the chair next to me. "Are you okay?"

"My legs are numb. Why are you angry?"

Colin helped me lower my legs to the floor. I winced at the aching in my joints and muscles, and his frown deepened. "Tim said you came in here this morning and you haven't been out."

"This morning? How long have I been here?" Surely I hadn't been looking at these files for more than a couple of hours.

"It's just after five, love. Have you eaten anything?"

"Hmm? No." I had been sitting in the same position for seven hours. My physical discomfort now made sense. The blood was beginning to circulate through my lower extremities again, making the pins and needles not just unpleasant, but painful. "Where have you been?"

"I'll tell you later. First, you need to eat something."

"I'm not hungry."

"You are. You just don't know it yet." This was always his argument when he didn't like my answers. He squeezed my hand and got up. "I'll get you some water and something to eat from the kitchen. Don't leave again."

I knew he didn't mean that I wasn't to leave the room.

When I became hyper-focussed, I lost all interest in the world outside of my mind. Colin said I left and went into my head. I had given him literature on this particular behaviour feature of autism. He had read it and told me that even though he understood it, he wasn't comfortable with me disappearing like that for long periods. We had reached a compromise that I would not fight him when he enforced breaks every two hours. It had not been easy. He made sure to remind me every time of my promise while he insisted that I drank and ate something.

I turned back to the monitors, looking at the new links I had formed when I noticed an inaccuracy. I reached for my keyboard, but my hands froze mid-air as Colin said, "Don't touch that. It will be another hour before I get you to eat something."

My fingers curled in to form fists before I pulled my arms back. He put a tray with two bottles of water, a glass of fresh juice and a rye sandwich next to my keyboard. "Eat."

I stared at the tray for a few seconds before I looked at him. "Thank you."

"My pleasure." He opened a bottle of water and took a long sip. "And don't go overanalysing this again. I've told you before I don't mind looking out for you. Drink your water and eat something while I tell you what I've been up to."

"Does it have something to do with that large canvas bag in front of your desk?" I opened the bottle of water and drank half before I took a breath. Having insight into my behaviour did not necessarily help managing it. I had spent many years learning to control my autistic behavioural patterns, but sometimes my control slipped and I would work on a project for sixty nearly uninterrupted hours. At least today it had been only seven hours.

Colin waited until I finished the rest of the water. He handed me the juice with a smile of approval. "It definitely has something to do with that bag."

"What bag?" Manny walked into my room. "Where have you been, Frey?"

"I can ask you the same question, Millard. Tim says you left this morning and have been out all day."

"I've been calming little Henri Fabron down. This heist is causing all kinds of political flack."

"What political flack?" I asked.

Manny looked at me and narrowed his eyes. "Have you been here all day?"

"Yes." I didn't want to elaborate.

"Sitting in that chair? The whole time? Where's supermodel?"

I closed my eyes, trying to remember. "She left at eleven. I wasn't listening to her, but I think she said something about looking for the source."

Manny grunted. "That sounds like she's looking for some alien spaceship. I hope she's not wasting time on one of her fairy tales. I have just lost a day of my life listening to people who think they're important go on and on and on and on."

"Then I will make you a happy man, Millard." Colin stood up.

"What? You're going to handcuff yourself?" Manny chuckled at himself. "That was the second best day of my life."

"What was the first?" I was sure I knew, but didn't like assuming anything.

"The day *I* arrested Frey." Manny had never said anything about it, but Colin had told me about the day he and Vinnie had broken into a museum to steal back an artwork. A security guard had made an unscheduled check and upon seeing Vinnie had gotten such a large fright he'd had a heart attack. Colin had sent Vinnie away, phoned Manny and tried to keep the man alive with CPR. He had died and Manny had arrested Colin. A few hours later, Interpol had recruited Colin in a top-level secret position, and Manny had lost his arrest. That had been a long time ago.

"You might want to let that one go, Millard." Colin picked up the large square bag from where it was leaning against his desk. "This will not only be the best of your career, but you'll get to throw this in Henri Fabron's face."

"You didn't!" Manny looked from the bag to Colin and back to the bag. Genuine happiness crinkled the corners of his eyes. "You bastard."

"Happy birthday, Millard." Colin handed Manny the bag. "They're all there."

Manny took it and aimed for my desk.

"Not here. Take it to the team room." I didn't even tolerate it when Colin left a stray pen on my desk. I was not about to accept the unknown contents of that bag littering my uncluttered desk.

Without as much as a frown or sigh, Manny walked to the team room. I got to my feet and stood for a few seconds to ensure my legs were going to hold me up.

"Okay?" Colin asked me, but was looking into the team room. He seemed to be enjoying Manny's reaction.

I nodded and followed Colin into the next room. I was intrigued by the contents of the bag. With his right hand covered in his winter glove, Manny was unpacking the bag, leaning paintings on the chairs around the table. I recognised the Renoir as one of the paintings stolen from the Jean Monnet Museum two days ago.

"Sue gave you these paintings?" I had thought such an

action highly improbable. "Why would she give away millions of euro's worth of artwork?"

"She didn't want these pieces. At first she considered selling them, but changed her mind."

Manny put the last painting on a chair. "Are these the six original paintings, Frey? Not some brilliantly forged copies to replace the real ones and fool idiots like me?"

"Those are the real McCoy, Millard. Untouched, undamaged, not sold on the black market."

"Help me understand. You had some tea, a little natter and this Sue gave you six paintings worth thirteen million euro?" Manny stood back from the table, still staring at the paintings. "I have a hard time believing this, Frey. Why would she change her mind about selling these pieces?"

I agreed with Manny. It was most unusual.

"Where's your friend, Frey? We need to bring her in and question her."

Colin was shaking his head before Manny finished. "There is no way she's coming in. Something is seriously off and she won't set a foot here."

"Did you ask her to come in?"

Colin snorted. "I tried, but she didn't even let me finish my question."

"Is that what I think it is?" Phillip stepped into the room, his eyes wide. His micro-expressions communicated reverence and the kind of joy seen on people's faces when they looked at their new-born child for the first time. Phillip took his time slowly walking around the table, leaning in to study each painting.

"I'm waiting, Frey."

"And I told you she's not coming in. She gave the paintings to me and asked me to never connect her to this heist." This was one of the few times Colin was not baiting Manny or being insolent. He sat down in Francine's chair. "You want more? Okay, this is what happened. I made contact with Sue a few hours after the theft. The situation was still too hot for her to meet with me, so we agreed to meet today. I've known her to be careful, but never as neurotic as today. She made me jump through a million hoops to eventually get to the meeting place. It was like going on a treasure hunt, something she obviously did to make sure I wasn't followed."

"Were you?"

"No. Not even Daniel would've recognised me." Colin was a master in disguising himself. "It took me three hours to get to her. Something scared her into being this paranoid."

"Did she tell you what?"

"No, but I actually think it isn't a what that scared her, but rather a who. Sue has never been caught. Outside of a small community, very few people know she exists. She has a day job, a family, drives a Ford sedan. She lives an ordinary life."

"And then she goes and steals art worth millions. Yes, very ordinary life, Frey."

"That is how she maintains her cover." Colin crossed one leg over the other, resting his left hand on his right thigh. Strong blocking behaviour. "She didn't tell me how she got to do this job. Jenny, you should've been there. I'm sure you would've seen a lot more than I did, but the fear in her eyes was clear as day. She's terrified. I thought I was going to have to deal or negotiate with her, but as soon as I said I would like to take the paintings, she handed them over."

"Just like that." Manny's tone and expression implied disbelief.

"Just like that." The *corrugator supercilii* muscle drew Colin's brow down and medially, producing vertical lines between his eyebrows. "She said she never wanted to take the job, but she wasn't given an option. Whoever had ordered her to steal the works told her to make sure she got maximum worth, but was in and out of the museum in minimum time. She had scoped out the place earlier and knew what to take and where to take it. She chose these six paintings because of their worth, but also because of their size. Put together in that bag, she didn't have any problems moving around with it. And she left with an extremely valuable loot. She treated this like any other job, with the difference of not receiving any payment."

"Did they threaten her?" I thought of possible reasons she would do this and not get paid. "Was she blackmailed?"

"She wouldn't tell me. Whatever they had on her is big enough to keep her quiet as well. She refused to tell me who they were, she wouldn't even tell me if it was a man, a woman or a group. Whoever ordered the job was not interested in the paintings at all. They told her they would do all the prep work, she just had to go in and steal at a specified time. They were going to cut the power to make it easier for her getting past the security system. After the heist, she could sell the paintings and it would be her payment. She didn't want anything more to do with this job and handed me the paintings."

"At least this lays the museum heist to rest," Phillip said.

"As far as Henri Fabron and those other arseholes are concerned, yes." Manny scratched the stubble on his chin. "But this is far from finished. There are too many loose ends."

"Who would order the theft of millions and not want it?" This was only one of the many questions I had. "I would like to know what the ulterior motive was and whether it can be traced back to Gabon and the No Secrets law."

Everyone turned to me with different expressions of confusion. It annoyed me when I forgot that other people were not part of my thought process. I couldn't just announce the conclusions I had come to. I was going to have to explain the findings I had made while in that hyper-focussed state.

"Come with me." I walked to my viewing room without waiting to see if they were following. The minute it took for Phillip, Manny and Colin to stand behind my chair gave me sufficient time to order my thoughts. I pointed to the first monitor with a photo of President Godard and his wife. "They add complications to my theory. I know they are connected to the case, but I'm not sure how. Not yet."

"Tell us first how all these connect to Gabon." Colin sat down next to me. "We can get to the president and his wife later."

"To date we have three direct messages sent to Nikki. The first one places a Vermeer in Motte's house. The second direct message places a Flinck in Savreux's house. Both the Vermeer and the Flinck point back to the 1990 heist. Motte and Savreux are connected through their individual work in Gabon—Minister Savreux while in the military, René Motte working for Elf. Then later on they founded the Libreville Dignity Foundation, connecting them to Gabon again. What I've also discovered is that even though René Motte was pushed out of Elf in 1989 when the French government became the oil company's owners, he still had money invested there. It had brought him a significant return."

"How do you know about his investment in Elf?" Manny asked.

"His riches made him famous enough to have a very public profile. I found numerous articles and interviews with him. There were some conflicting facts, but this I am sure of. During the Elf investigation and trial in the late nineties and early 2000s, his association was scrutinised and his finances made public. Out of his involvement with Elf from 1983 until now, he accrued over ninety million dollars."

"Bloody hellfire."

"He's a smart businessman and used that money to make more money. René Motte is now worth just under three billion dollars."

All three men uttered crude expletives.

"If he has so much money, why the hell does he have a stolen Vermeer in his house?" Manny asked.

"The psychology behind owning stolen masterpieces is of special interest to us as insurance companies," Phillip said. "There are numerous reasons accomplished, wealthy individuals want to own something they could easily afford."

"Some artwork is not for sale," Colin said.

"True. That is another set of reasons for owning something no one else can own. There is something about the excitement of forbidden fruit that applies here." Phillip pointed at the monitors. "Genevieve, how does the rest of this lead to the No Secrets law?"

I counted off on my fingers. "Savreux is connected to Gabon. René Motte is connected to Gabon and the Boston heist in 1990. If we were to believe the direct message Nikki got about the Flinck, Savreux is also connected to the Boston heist. Both of them are connected to the Libreville Dignity Foundation. This charity, obviously connected to Gabon, was targeted while Sue stole the paintings which are now in the team room.

"The president of Gabon, Mariam Boussombo, is connected to the Foundation and is in Strasbourg. I looked into her visit and noticed that she's to address the Senate in favour of President Godard's No Secrets law. She's been actively campaigning for something similar in Gabon."

I took a deep breath. "President Godard is set to speak to Parliament next week about this law. It's speculated that this law has a strong possibility of being passed—politicians are about to lose a lot of privacy rights and some of their immunity. If Minister Savreux had not been killed, he would've lost his office. He had publicly vowed to resign if that law got passed. He had a television interview scheduled for Sunday evening to reiterate his reasons for being against this law."

"This is a nice summary with some extra information, Doc. But it doesn't really blow my hair back." Manny winced. "There's no exciting new discoveries."

"Of the next part I'm not sure, but I read it on enough independent and trustworthy news websites to warrant attention. There have been rumours that Minister Savreux was going to give some kind of exposé to prove his stance against the No Secrets law. The rumours went on to say that it was going to be some private information about the president Minister Savreux was going to share. I didn't find any official confirmation of any of this."

Manny's eyebrow rose high on his forehead. "Holy saints, Doc. Do you realise what you are saying?"

"I'm saying it, which in itself should make it clear I know what I'm saying."

Manny shook his index finger at the first monitor. "You are saying that Savreux was going to hang out the president's dirty laundry to prove that privacy is needed. That means that the president had motivation for killing Savreux. Bloody hell. Just exactly what was Savreux going to reveal? Does it have something to do with Gabon as well?"

"Firstly, I did not once say or even imply that the president had motivation for killing Minister Savreux. Or that Minister Savreux was going to reveal any of the president's secrets." My voice was low and void of emotion. "Secondly, I have President Godard's photo up because he is involved in this case, but that is the part I have not worked out yet. His wife, on the other hand, has a much clearer connection. We know that Mrs Isabelle Godard is an active patron of Libreville Dignity Foundation. Thus she has a strong connection to Gabon, to Motte and to Savreux."

"Doc, you need to do your magic Mozarting thing and connect these bleeding dots. We can't have the president or his wife implicated in a murder case."

The information on the monitors was drawing me in again. The elusive factor connecting it all was buried in there.

"What's that, Jenny?" Colin touched my arm and pointed at the far right monitor.

"Oh, that is the Foundation's financial information." My subconscious was telling me the key to understanding it all was not in those spreadsheets.

"Jenny?" Colin squeezed my arm. "Why do you have the Foundation's finances up with everything else?"

"Because I suspect the charity is a front for money laundering." I frowned.

Manny inhaled so fast, he started coughing. "Doc, you're killing me. Explain."

"Colin said that Sue was ordered to steal paintings. Any paintings as long as they were of the highest value possible, right?" I waited until Colin nodded. "I posit that the theft was indeed a distraction. Whoever had hired her, needed her to steal at a specific time, during which the whole block's electricity was out. They were able to gain access to the charity without drawing attention since the focus was obviously on the stolen paintings worth millions."

"As opposed to a little burglary in a charity office," Manny said.

"Exactly. This brings forth three important questions. The first would be, why did they need physical access to the Foundation? The second question is, what didn't they want investigators to see? And the third, why did they change the financial data on the Foundation's system?"

"Wait. What are you talking about, Doc?"

Whenever in a hyper-focussed state, hours, even days, melted into one. It wasn't always easy to remember what discoveries I had made when. Or whether I had shared all these discoveries. I closed my eyes for a second to sift through my thoughts, and looked at Colin. "Before Francine left this morning, she found out that the computer data the Libreville Dignity Foundation had thought was backed up had been compromised. At a first glance, all the financial data appeared intact, but it isn't. During the heist somebody replaced the financial data on the Foundation's system."

"Replaced it with what?" Colin asked.

"Slightly altered data."

Manny rubbed his hand over his mouth. "Now what?"

"Francine spoke to the accountant at the Foundation. She gave us good news. She's only been working there for six months and felt out of her depth. In order to familiarise herself with the Foundation's financial history, she copied everything on an external drive to take home and study." I pointed at my computer. "She brought it in a few hours ago and I've been looking at some of it."

Manny appeared overwhelmed at my explanation. I thought I had been rather succinct.

"Hellfire, Doc. What did you find in those financials?"

"Two years ago, Libreville Dignity Foundation ran out of funds. It was unable to pay its staff and I found emails between the staff discussing dissolving the charity. A few weeks later, their bank account received an infusion of seven hundred thousand euro. This was from an unnamed donor. I'm not as good as Francine, so I could only trace the bank account number to a bank in Samoa."

"One of the few go-to tax havens left for the rich and criminal," Colin said.

"This account and three others from different banks, all located in Samoa, have deposited into the Foundation's account the combined sum of ten million three hundred thousand euro over the last nine years." I purposefully called them deposits. That amount of money in this context no longer looked like donations.

"Is all that money accounted for? Spent on charitable work?" Manny leaned forward, squinting at the monitor. He wasn't going to see the answer on that particular spreadsheet, so I changed it to the appropriate one.

"I still have to work through the expenditures, but at a first glance it looks as if only a small percentage went to charity." I highlighted a line on the spreadsheet. "Five months ago, there was eight hundred thousand euro in the account. All but thirty thousand euro have been withdrawn since."

"Who has access to this account?"

"The old and new accountants, the managing director of the charity and the chairman."

"Bloody René Motte. The bloody chairman." Manny leaned back. "Gabon, Boston and these idiot politicians are all somehow connected. Where did that ten million come from though? I would really like to know that."

"My time would be better spent looking through Savreux's finances," I said. "Francine would be much faster and more efficient finding the source of that ten million."

"Could that be the source she was talking about this morning?" Colin asked.

"I doubt it. I only found those anomalies this afternoon, after she had left."

"Back up for a second." The look Manny gave me was filled with emotions usually reserved for Colin or Vinnie. "What do you mean looking through Savreux's finances?"

"Francine emailed the files this afternoon." I realised I should've mentioned it to Manny, but until he had looked at me as if I was a criminal, I had put it out of my mind as non-essential information. I held up both hands. "I'm sorry I didn't tell you earlier. Francine didn't say anything in her email about where she was or what she was doing. She only sent a hyperbolic victorious email with attachments. They are terribly disorganised and will take me some time to set in order before I analyse it. None of the entries seems to be organised according to any system. The dates are in completely random order. I can't yet see which entries are expenses and which are income."

Whenever Manny's one eyebrow raised slowly, and his eyes lost their focus, I knew I was sharing too much detail. I bit down on the insides of my lips, immediately releasing them again. I didn't want to start another nervous habit. "I will analyse Minister Savreux's finances and Francine can locate the origin of the ten million euro."

"Not today." Phillip pushed his shoulders back and stood taller. He did this when, in his own words, he was laying down the law. "It is time for everyone to go home and rest. I'm sure Vinnie and Nikki will appreciate a break from each other by now."

"Oh, my." For a while, I'd completely forgotten about them. "Are they okay? Did something happen?"

Phillip shook his head. "I should've have chosen different words. I spoke to Nikki this afternoon and they are well. Apparently, Vinnie is grumpy and has been cooking for hours. That means you should go home, have a good home-cooked meal and rest. Minister Savreux's financial analysis can hold until tomorrow."

He waited until I nodded. I did so with reluctance. I respected Phillip too much to lie to him and the words rushed out of my mouth before I could stop it. "I'm going to take my computer home and organise the files. I can promise to not analyse the data, but I won't be able to sleep with the state those attachments are in."

To my utter consternation, the three men's body language relaxed and their expressions warmed. I had thought my confession would have irritated them, yet they were looking at me with affection. I didn't understand this.

Colin took my hand and pulled lightly. "Manny and Phillip can take care of the paintings and take all the credit for that while we go home."

I studied Colin's expression and noticed only his usual derision when speaking to Manny. There was no annoyance at my insistence on organising the files. Fully intending to ask him to explain this inconsistent behaviour, I agreed and got ready to go home.

Chapter TWELVE

"When did she say she'll be back?" I was relieved that we had heard from Francine. Colin and I had left several messages for her to return our calls or at the very least send an email that she was well. We had not heard from her last night, nor this morning. Not until she had phoned Colin a few minutes ago.

"She said she'll be back as soon as she gets the source." Colin sighed. "She sounded a bit out of it, displaced."

"What does that mean?"

"You know how she gets when she thinks she has a brilliant theory and she starts losing touch with reality? Well, she sounded like that."

"She also sounds like that when she's working on a solution to a complex computer or internet security problem." I didn't consider her absentmindedness strange. Maybe because I had a personal understanding of losing myself in my work.

"She said you should look at your emails. She sent you something."

Colin and I were in my viewing room, working through Minister Savreux's finances, scrutinising the folders for anything suspicious. After five hours, we hadn't found anything that merited a deeper look. Minister Savreux had worked wisely, albeit conservatively, with his finances. The data portrayed him as a man living within his means, regularly donating to a few charities as well as an animal shelter.

I turned to my computer and opened my email programme. Three new emails were in my inbox, one from Francine. I clicked on it, read the single sentence telling me the attachment contained more financial information on Savreux, and downloaded the attachment.

Before I could open the new files, Colin frowned and leaned towards the monitors displaying several spreadsheets. "Do we know Savreux's mother's name?"

I changed windows and scrolled through the numerous pages of personal information we had on Minister Claude Savreux. I found what I was looking for and put the article on one of the other monitors. "Odette Savreux is his mother. She has Alzheimer's and was declared mentally unfit six years ago. The court appointed Savreux to take care of her finances and wellbeing. In this interview, he talked about the lack of decent care for the elderly, not only in France, but in most of Europe. He said that he considered himself immensely fortunate that he had the financial means to put his mother in a fantastic care centre, but he was concerned about those without the finances to do so."

"A typical politician thing to say," Vinnie said from the door. I turned and was pleased to see the large man's posture almost back to normal. It was no surprise that he still favoured his left side ever so slightly. That side had all the bruised ribs. Most of the swelling on his face had gone down, leaving dark bruises behind. I had to admit I was impressed with how quickly he was recovering.

"What are you doing here?" I asked.

"Aw, Jen-girl. You always make me feel so welcome." He started to laugh softly, but grunted and folded into himself. "Son of a cheap, ugly gun. This hurts."

"Your ribs were bruised. It will still take three to four weeks to heal. You should take care to not do anything strenuous. That includes laughing." I had done some research since Vinnie continued to insist on not going to the hospital.

"Such a ray of sunshine you are, Jen-girl." Vinnie walked in and sat down carefully in the third chair in my room. "I cannot stay cooped up at home for another day. And I know you guys are doing all sorts of interesting things, so I thought I'd come in and lend you my expertise."

"Do you know if they found the men who attacked you?"

He shook his head. "Nope. The old man said they were gone when Daniel's team got to that little street. There was no trace of them."

I wasn't surprised. Dukwicz had been exceptionally elusive. If those men were associated with him, it stood to reason they had a similar skill set. Another concern entered my mind. "Where's Nikki?"

"In Phillip's office. She's helping Tim with some something that I really don't care about." He nodded at the monitors. "What are you up to?"

Colin gave Vinnie an update while I opened the first of the five files Francine had attached. It was Savreux's mother's finances. I saw nothing out of the ordinary. It seemed she was quite a wealthy woman. If he'd had full access to her money for the last few years, he had been dealing very responsibly with it.

"Everything we have indicates that Savreux was a respectable man." I wasn't pleased with this conclusion, but I couldn't refute the evidence in front of me. "There is so far nothing to make me suspicious of him. Not even that direct message to Nikki suffices, since we never found the Flinck in his house. On paper he appears to have been an average man with a rather conservative lifestyle."

"But?" Colin asked.

"But it doesn't explain the expensive items found in his house."

"Just say it, Jen-girl." Vinnie smiled. "You have a gut feeling."

I ignored him and opened another file. This spreadsheet triggered my curiosity. Colin complained for the nineteenth time this morning that I was changing windows too quickly. Unlike the other times, I didn't slow down.

The numbers flowed as streams through my mind, connecting and separating at certain points. It started connecting to numbers from different files I had earlier looked at. The light this new data shone on all the numbers turned the previously innocuous information into something different altogether.

I closed my eyes and focussed on Mozart's Violin Concerto in E flat major. Having the soothing concerto in the background of my mind helped me sift through this new information to get to that one element which would provide the key to understanding if and how the different finances were connected.

"Jenny?" Colin's firm touch on my arm brought me back. Thirty-five minutes had passed. "Phillip's brought us Chinese takeout for lunch."

"Later." I lifted both hands when he frowned. "No. You will want to see this. I promise I will eat after I show you."

"Show us what, Doc?" Manny was in the doorway, a fast food box in his one hand, chopsticks in the other. "This better be good, because I'm hungry and this food smells delicious."

"I think I know where the Flinck is."

"You what?" Manny handed his food to Nikki, who was peering around him, and walked into the viewing room. "Where is it?"

I turned to Colin. "Preservation rooms are used for old and valuable artworks, right?"

"Right."

"Quite a few of our clients have preservation rooms." Phillip was now standing next to Manny. "As insurers, we prefer that above expensive pieces hanging around the house. Not only does it protect the art inside a controlled environment, it adds another layer of security."

"But there is no preservation room in Savreux's house," Manny said.

"A preservation room needs strict climate control, right?" When both Colin and Phillip nodded, I pointed at the last file I had opened. "Would a wine cellar do?"

Phillip's facial muscles revealed his thought process from doubtful to thoughtful to agreement. "Absolutely."

"I see I have to repeat myself." Manny was losing patience. "There is also no cellar in Savreux's house."

"No, but he leased a wine storage unit in some self-storage warehouse." It took me less than a minute to locate the storage service's website and display it on one of the monitors. On the home page they had links to their numerous services. On offer were lockers for those with smaller wine collections, or rooms for those with extensive collections. "They advertise their high-end service as uniquely designed spaces for each wine collector's individual needs."

"Bloody hell," Manny said when I clicked on the link that took us to the page with photos of specially designed rooms.

"Look at those cellars. The place looks like a bloody five-star hotel."

"Just like art, there are collectors who buy wine as an investment," Phillip said. "These rooms are extraordinary."

"Did Savreux have a room like this, Doctor Face-reader?"

"Yes. It was registered in the name of Odette Roche, but I believe that he was the one who rented it." I briefly explained about Minister Savreux's mother and his control over her estate. "There are a few bank accounts in her name, and three in the name of Odette Roche. It was easy enough to check and confirm that Roche was his mother's maiden name. It is impossible that she opened the three accounts, as it was done after she was declared mentally incompetent."

"Devious," Manny said.

"These three accounts have had the biggest amounts deposited and withdrawn. Both as cash and electronic transactions. Of those electronic transfers, I recognised two external account numbers that I had seen in the Libreville Dignity Foundation's finances. The same two accounts sending and receiving money from Odette Roche also transferred a combined seven hundred thousand euro to the Foundation two years ago when they were about to go bankrupt."

Manny rubbed his hands hard over his face. "So Savreux used his mother to launder his money. Bastard. I suppose we will find transfers to and from Samoan bank accounts."

"You suppose correctly." There were many corresponding account numbers between the Foundation's financial records and all of Savreux's financial data.

"We need to get into that storage unit," Colin said.

Before I could comment on his nonverbal cues, Manny shook his index finger at Colin. "No, you don't. Don't even think about it, Frey. You are not breaking in there."

"Then you better find a legal way for us to enter."

"We cannot be seen anywhere near Savreux's case. The moment a search warrant traces back to me, every single one of us will be knee-deep in crap. And we might lose any advantage we have at the moment."

"What about asking Daniel to get his friend to organise a search warrant?"

Manny thought about it. "No. His friend already took a huge risk in sharing the investigation with us. He's too low in the hierarchy to make this happen and survive the aftermath."

"That leaves my option." Colin's chin lifted and his shoulders pulled back, signs of confidence or in some cases arrogance.

"Forget about that, Frey." Manny rubbed his face again. "I have a few people owing me favours. I'll see what I can make happen."

I considered this topic closed and moved on to the next one. "From the three accounts in Odette Roche's name, he's been paying very high monthly premiums to GCFS."

"What's GCFS?" Manny asked.

"It's an insurance company similar to Rousseau & Rousseau," I said.

"That's Alfred La Ruche's company." Phillip frowned.

"Aw, dammit. I haven't even asked you to check out Savreux's insurance." Manny lifted his eyes to the ceiling and shook his head, then looked at Phillip. "Seems like we have it now. How well do you know this Alfred? Does he provide services to criminals?"

"I consider him quite a good professional friend. As far as I know, he doesn't have anyone who deals in anything illegal on his client list." There were small but distinct indicators of doubt on Phillip's face.

"Is it possible that he never told you about that side of his business?"

"Anything is possible in this business." His smile was sad. "Money is a powerful friend and enemy. Everyone has a price. Tempt somebody with the right amount or other motivator, and they will compromise their personal principles."

"I don't think Jen-girl has a price." Vinnie winked at me. "She's the only one I know with iron-cast principles."

Manny scowled at Vinnie. I wondered if it was because Vinnie had, by implication, told Manny that he would compromise his principles. One of the traits I respected most in Manny was his strong belief in right and wrong. In the last eighteen months, I'd had to adjust the previously immovable position I'd held on the black and white divide I had judged everyone by. Colin, Vinnie and Francine had made me realise that there was no one rule that applied to everyone equally.

"I'll set up a meeting with Alfred today," Phillip said. "I hope he will prove me right that he doesn't know of Savreux's illegal activities. I'll ask him about this insurance account. What were the monthly payments?"

I highlighted those payments on the spreadsheet. "As you can see, it increased a few times over the past three years."

"That would happen if something of high value is added to the inventory. It would push up the monthly payments." Phillip tilted his head. "These are incredibly high payments."

"Could this be for the content of Savreux's house?" Manny asked.

"Most definitely not. Not even with the expensive watches

and other items Genevieve had catalogued. This kind of payment is what my clients pay when they have artwork or collectables worth more than fifty million euro."

Vinnie whistled. "That's... that's... no, that's just wrong."

"When you speak to Alfred, ask him if it possible to give us a copy of the inventory," Manny said. "It would be helpful info. What else do you have, Doc?"

"That's it for now." I stretched my neck to the side. My back and neck muscles were tight from tension and lack of movement.

"Let's have lunch then. Maybe the food will still be warm enough to eat."

We moved to the team room and found the round table empty.

"Where is my food?" Manny looked at Colin. "I was hungry."

"What are you looking at me for?" Colin leaned back. "I didn't steal your food."

Manny snorted. "But you did go and steal that clock."

"It was to help this case." Colin shook his head once and stepped closer to Manny. "You know what? I've had enough of your distrust and your disrespect, Millard."

The subtle changes in the body language of both men made me realise there was much more going on here. I thought back over the last seven weeks, once again berating myself for not having paid close enough attention. Also for hoping they would sort this out themselves. The more I thought about the body language I'd observed in them, the more I recalled Manny's discomfort hidden under layers of annoyance.

"Manny, what did you do?"

"Why do you think I did something?" Manny didn't back away from Colin, but he was not his usual confrontational self.

Colin laughed after two tense seconds. There was no humour in his short laughter. "You're not going to tell her, are you? You're a coward, Millard. Scared that your precious Doc is going to lose respect for you because of what you did."

The anger in Colin's tone and on his face was unfamiliar. I surprised myself by stepping closer to Colin and putting my shoulder in front of him, putting myself between him and Manny. I studied the older man for only a few seconds to see the contrition on his face. "Oh, Manny. What did you do?"

Colin's chest pushed against my shoulder. "Yes, tell her, Millard."

Manny rubbed the back of his neck. "I placed listening devices in Frey's car and in his phone."

"You what?" Vinnie stood up from where he was sitting and stepped into Manny's personal space. He looked at Colin. "Why didn't you tell me about this?"

"Because Francine asked. She knew you would've beaten Millard up and that would upset Jenny. She, we, didn't want that."

"She's in on this?" Vinnie's voice raised a few tones.

"She was the one who found those bugs."

"Why would you do that?" I asked Manny. Watching the anger and true distrust between these people I had come to care for felt like something was strangling my heart. I sought for calm and rationality.

"To find something to arrest me. What else do you think, Jenny?" Colin's tone was heavy with rage, his body trembling slightly from controlling his temper. "When Francine found those things, I took them to him, threw them on his table and asked him to explain. He didn't. No explanation, no apology, nothing. After all this time, the arsehole still wants to put me in jail."

Manny's micro-expression belied that assumption.

"No, he doesn't. There's more to this situation. Tell us, Manny."

The room was unnaturally quiet. Nobody moved and everyone's body language was hyper-alert, ready for action. Phillip was quietly observing, but even his body language had changed. He was frequently glancing at me, concern around his eyes.

Despite Manny's deception abilities, I could see the decision-making process in his micro-expressions. Finally, he stood taller and pulled his shoulders back. He looked Colin in the eye, unflinching and open. "Have you ever given thought to why it was so easy to find those bugs, Frey? I've been in this game a long time. It would've been easy for me find out all your dirty little secrets without you ever knowing that I was listening or watching."

Colin couldn't control his slight jerk of surprise.

"Manny?" I lowered my voice in the same way I did when I tried to calm Nikki. "I can see that there is a lot of nuance happening here, but I'm not able to catch it. Please explain this to me."

Manny closed his eyes for a second and shook his head. There was regret in his downturned mouth and in his eyes when he looked at me. "I'm sorry about this, Doc. I also didn't want you upset."

I raised both eyebrows, my mouth slightly agape. "You argue with me all the time. You upset me all the time. How is this different?"

"Because this is not work, this is friendship." Phillip looked at Manny. "Explain yourself."

"Apart from the president and a few top people at Interpol, no one else is supposed to know Frey is working for the good guys." Manny had let go of his usual slouching and deceptive behaviour. His nonverbal cues were open and genuine. "I don't know how or why they got this intel, but a task force at Interpol knew of my association with Frey. They asked me if I could get some dirt on him and everyone he came in contact with. I told them that he's my confidential informant and that I wasn't going to spy on him, but they got their boss to order me to do this. I went to the top guys and they told me to do this. They needed it to look as if Frey was still on the wrong side of the law.

"I told the task force that Frey's team is the best and whatever surveillance we planted, they'd find it and it would warn them that someone was watching. These idiots were willing to take the risk and that's when I put those bugs in the most obvious hidden places possible."

"How long were they there for?" I asked.

Manny snorted. "Seven hours. All they got was Frey talking sweet to some woman. That would be you, Doc. They also got Frey ordering some old books. At first they thought it was a theft or some code, but then realised it—"

"—was none of their business," Colin interrupted. "Why didn't you just talk to me about this? You could've explained to me when I brought you those bugs."

"How did you know they were mine?" Manny lowered his chin and looked at Colin from under his brow.

"I didn't. I had a suspicion and your reaction when I confronted you confirmed it. God, I was livid. I still am."

"No, you're not." I turned to Colin. "Your skin is no longer flushed, your vocal cords are relaxed, making your voice… You don't want me to continue."

Colin closed his eyes and sighed. When he opened his eyes, he looked resigned. He took my hand in his and squeezed. "You're like the un-secret keeper."

"That doesn't make sense." I turned back to Manny. "You're a liar. And you have double standards."

"I beg your pardon?"

"I said, you're a lia—"

"I heard you the first time, missy. Explain."

"You expect of us to not make decisions without consulting you first. We're not allowed to take any action unless you know about everything at all times. A concept I find ludicrous in its impracticality." I leaned a bit closer towards Manny. "Yet you never consult with us. You make executive decisions and expect us to follow blindly. I've been reading up on teamwork a lot since we started working together. You're not a team player. You're also not a team leader. You are a dictator, according to my books."

There was a moment of silence before laughter filled the room, breaking most of the tension. Manny didn't laugh. He looked insulted.

"She's got you there, old man." Vinnie chuckled as he returned to his seat at the table. "Dictator. Hah."

Manny was glaring at me and I returned his stare without flinching. I waited, knowing Manny needed time to process what was happening. Soon enough contrition flitted across his face. "You really think I'm a dictator, Doc?"

"No, I don't. It was an extreme statement to make you think about your behaviour. Nikki often uses hyperbolic speech and I thought I'd try that. It worked." I cleared my throat to return to the topic. "I do, however, think that you have double standards by expecting our trust, but not returning it. I know you trust us, but you really should show more faith in Colin, Vinnie and Francine. Nobody will think less of you when you consult or even ask advice from people who are often involved in criminal acts."

Manny shifted and rolled his shoulders. "Point taken, Doc. Now I think we should eat."

"Well, then," Phillip said and turned to the door. "Sit down, I'll find the food."

We sat down and after a third deep breath, Manny straightened in his chair. "I really got your point about the teamwork, Doc. I'll try."

"Aw." Vinnie leaned closer to Manny, wincing at the movement. "Wanna hug it out, old man?"

"Don't push it, criminal. I'll break all your other ribs." He looked at Colin. "Next time I'll speak to you. And maybe supermodel. She can help us set something up for those task force idiots."

Colin nodded. "She would love putting one over on them."

I wasn't naïve enough to believe that all was forgiven and forgotten. Or that Vinnie was as amicable as he tried to appear. I knew Colin was going to take time to trust Manny again. But this was a good start. A few minutes later, Phillip returned with Tim. Both were carrying trays laden with steaming plates of food. Chinese food was one of my few indulgences. I had a hard time rationalising how I was so obsessive about never eating in restaurants, yet this one Chinese restaurant was acceptable to me. Not only did their kitchen pass my frequent inspection, but the owner was a rude Chinese woman who didn't tolerate mistakes, not on her menus, services, food or delivery. A few times I had seen waitresses in tears.

"I hope you guys don't mind that I took the food while you were working." Tim placed plates in front of each person, impressing me with his memory of everyone's specific order. Mine was still in its box. Only once had he erred by not allowing me to inspect the box and content before dishing it up. With a smile, he put the box in front of me and a white plate to the side. "I thought you would be busy for some time and that I'd heat it up when you were done. You were faster than I'd thought."

"Thanks, Tim." Phillip sat down and waited until the younger man left with both the trays. "*Bon appétit.*"

The small talk during our meal bored me and I thought about the case. I wondered where Francine was and what information she was going to bring back.

"Doc?" Manny put his knife and fork loudly on his empty plate. Everyone had finished. I looked down at my plate and sighed. I had no recollection of eating all my food. I also placed my cutlery on my plate and waited for Manny to continue. He was frowning. "Have you by any chance been able to trace the ten million euro from the Dignity Foundation's accounts?"

"I've been busy with Savreux's finances. I told you yesterday Francine would be better at tracking that money."

"But she's not here, is she? I need to know how Savreux, Motte, that ten million and the Foundation all fit together. But I really want to know where that ten million came from."

"That's quite a long list of things you want to know, handsome," Francine said as she walked into the room. Despite her corrective makeup, the tiredness around her eyes was evident. "You know you just have to ask and I'll give you everything your heart desires."

There was something more to her banter. I stilled and studied her. She was in exceptional good humour. Maybe she had found that source she had mentioned earlier. I wondered if she had slept at all in the last twenty-four hours.

"Where have you been, supermodel? You should've helped Doc find out where all this money came from." He nodded at my viewing room.

"What money?" She walked to the open seat next to me and sat down.

"I found anomalies in the Libreville Dignity Foundation's finances. There are significant deposits that we should trace."

"I'll get on it later." She took an excited breath, her shoulders shuddering. "We are so going to celebrate later on, girlfriend. I've found treasures. Loads of treasures."

She took her tablet out of her buttery soft brown leather bag and connected it to the system. "Today was a good day, my friends. My favourite lipstick was on sale, I flirted with a police officer, then I flirted with her partner—who was a man—and I hit pay dirt."

"There is so much wrong with what you just said, I don't even know where to begin," Manny said.

"Begin with telling me how much you adore me." She straightened and dramatically waved at the large screen against the wall. "Ladies and gentlemen. I present to you Minister Claude Savreux's home videos."

Chapter THIRTEEN

I never went to the cinema. Knowing that cinema seats hosted not only staph and diphtheria, but also colonies of faecal matter, was not conducive to relaxing and enjoying a film. But there was more to my intense dislike for cinema theatres. A cinema custom I found both an auditory and olfactory offence was popcorn. The smell clung to one's clothes like smoke in a club. The sound of hands seeking for more popcorn in the box, followed by loud crunching had resulted in a very short first and only cinema experience for me. I had gone home, washed my clothes on the longest cycle possible and had taken a hot, disinfecting shower while listening to Mozart.

At present I was seated in the team room at the round table with four people each holding a large bowl of popcorn. Upon hearing that Francine had located and accessed the cloud account where Minister Savreux had been storing the footage recorded from the clock camera, Vinnie had run out to find Tim. As if Phillip's assistant didn't have enough work-related tasks to do, Vinnie had convinced Tim to order popcorn from a nearby independent movie theatre. I pressed my fists into my thighs as Vinnie forced another handful of popcorn into his mouth. We'd just had lunch. Where did they find the appetite?

Their micro-expressions of genuine pleasure were the singular reason I was restraining myself from putting a stop to this utterly inappropriate and unprofessional behaviour.

Vinnie, Francine and Colin's lives were complicated. They moved in circles where they had to be on full alert at all times. It was seldom that I saw them partaking in a simple activity that gave them such pleasure. Most often it was Colin and Vinnie watching wrestling matches on my large-screen television. The earlier tension and confrontation was no longer present. Even Manny was happily eating the popcorn Tim had handed him. The young assistant had quickly pulled back the bowl of popcorn offered when he had seen my expression.

"Where shall we start?" Francine asked. She wasn't going to share with us where and how she'd located the files. Manny'd accepted that it was more important that we had these recordings. As soon as Francine had found them, she'd only looked at a few clips to confirm that these were the video files we wanted. Without looking any further, she'd rushed to the office, knowing we would want to see it straightaway. There had been hundreds of files in no particular order. While Vinnie had ordered the popcorn, Francine and I had organised the recordings according to date.

"We should start with the last entry." I thought that made the most sense. "We might be able to see who killed Minister Savreux."

"Good idea, Doc."

I bit down on the insides of my lips not to reprimand Manny for talking with a mouth full of popcorn. I wished they'd hated popcorn as much as I did. I sighed, dismissed my fanciful hopes and focussed on the video that was starting on the screen.

The video gave a surprisingly wide view of Minister Savreux's home office. I estimated that only fifty or so centimetres from the door into the room were not visible. The areas directly in front of the shelves where the clock had been were also not visible, but I didn't think it was more than twenty centimetres. The room looked exactly like it had when we had been there, with the exception that Minister Savreux wasn't lying on the floor dead.

"Pause it, Francine." I leaned forward. Something had registered in my mind, but had not yet worked its way to my cerebral cortex, the thinking brain. I had an exceptional memory and having studied the crime scene photos had solidified the exact decor of this room in my mind. Then I saw it. I jumped in my seat and reached for Francine's tablet. "Can I have that, please?"

Francine handed me her tablet. It had been a pleasant discovery that Francine and I used the same viewing software. It made it easy for both of us to work on footage that the other provided. I ignored the questions asked past the popcorn and zoomed in on the wall above the fireplace. It was the wall to the right of the camera and it was at an angle awkward enough to complicate the viewing. I wasn't interested in the ornaments on the mantelpiece. It was the painting above the mantelpiece that had caught my attention. I zoomed in on that and knew I had been right.

"Oh my God, Jenny! You found it." Colin put his bowl of popcorn on the table and walked to the screen against the wall. "Can you do anything with the angle?"

"What are we looking at?" Manny also put his popcorn on the table. "What is it with the painting?"

"It's not the painting that was there when we entered the house." I cropped the image of the painting and started manipulating it to alter the angle.

"That painting was a Rembrandt." Colin didn't take his

eyes off the screen. "As I've told you before, Flinck's paintings were so close in style that plenty a scholar had confused his work with Rembrandt's. The painting that was above the fireplace when I got there was a Rembrandt. Not a Flinck."

"Is this a Flinck?" Vinnie asked. He didn't put down his bowl of popcorn.

I finished manipulating the image and used a few basic tools to sharpen the image.

"Not *a* Flinck, Vin." Colin stared at the screen, his mouth slightly agape. "This is *the* Flinck. This is Flinck's Landscape with an Obelisk that he painted in 1638."

I found a clearer photo of this painting on the internet and placed it juxtaposed to the manipulated screenshot from the video. It was a dramatic landscape typical of that era. The intensely lit obelisk was under swirling clouds, the strong contrast in light and shadow adding to its atmosphere. In front of the trees on the right was a figure on a horse, talking to another person. A stream separated them from the obelisk, a small bridge crossing to the other side.

"This is the bloody painting stolen in Boston?" Manny straightened in his chair. "Where is it then? Why wasn't it there when we got there? Doc, start playing that video, so we can see what happened to it."

I closed the photo manipulation programme and tapped on the tablet screen to resume the video. Colin sat down next to me, leaning towards the screen. Three seconds later, Minister Savreux walked into the room. His shoulders were slightly lower than they should have been. When tired or upon receiving bad news, our shoulders and heads usually drooped. The opposite could also be seen whenever people received good news. Whether Minister Savreux's posture was from being tired or having had a particular problem, we would never know.

He walked straight to the serving table with the liquor in crystal bottles and poured himself a generous amount of alcohol in a tumbler. He finished all of it and immediately poured another liberal helping. While walking to one of the chairs, he pulled his tie away from his collar and undid the top button. He rolled his neck and sat down heavily on the chair facing the door.

For a few minutes he did nothing but stare into space and sip from his glass. Then he shuddered and turned his gaze on the Flinck. The *orbicularis oculi* muscles around his eyes contracted. He shook his head, put the glass on the coffee table next to his chair and rolled up his sleeves. From one second to the next, his relaxed posture changed to caution and finally to fear. He did not move from his position on the chair, but every muscle in his body was tensed as if ready to jump to action.

"What are you doing here?" Savreux was looking at the door. The intruder must have been standing in the doorway.

"You know why I'm here." That voice. I would recognise it anywhere. I shuddered and tapped on the pause button.

"It's Dukwicz." The contract killer we had been spending months looking for was right there on this video.

"Thought so too." Manny's lips were in thin lines, his brow lowered and in deep wrinkles. "Good thing there's sound. We might get a lot from this. Play on, Doc."

I tapped the touch screen. The fear intensified on Savreux's face.

"Why? At least tell me why."

"You of all people should know I'm not interested in the

why. I agree to the contract and execute the job. That's it." A small chuckle sounded. "Pun intended."

"Is there any way I could persuade you to not do this?" Savreux swallowed a few times, his voice at a higher pitch. "I have a lot of money. I can give you millions of euros. You'll never have to work again. You can have anything you want."

Dukwicz's laugh was loud and cruel. "The money is only a bonus for me. I'm doing this because I enjoy it, not because it pays well. And it gives me such great street status. Anywhere you mention my name, people are scared. Do you really think I'm going to risk the reputation of going soft? For money?"

He laughed again and walked deeper into the room. The camera caught him at a diagonal angle from behind. I could see one side of his face, not enough to accurately read his facial expressions. But it was enough to make a positive identification.

Minister Savreux jumped from the sofa and ran to his desk. A logical conclusion would be that he had a weapon in his desk that he was trying to reach. Dukwicz was faster than him. He reached Savreux in three long steps, brought a garrotte over the minister's head and jerked the shorter man against his chest with the thin cable to his throat.

Minister Savreux reached for his neck and tried to get his fingers under the garrotte. In the struggle, he scratched open his skin, but didn't stop. It took forty seconds before his struggles became more sluggish. It felt like hours. All this time Dukwicz balanced himself on both legs, his physical strength clear as he easily kept control over Savreux.

I knew I wasn't going to watch this particular part of the video again. The genuine smile that lifted Dukwicz's cheeks and formed wrinkles in the corners of his eyes was very disturbing. Here was a man who found joy—real joy—in killing another human being. Minister Savreux eventually went slack and Dukwicz lowered him to the floor, his tongue between his lips. People did that when they felt they had been victorious. Or that they had gotten away with a deception or manipulative action. Dukwicz was getting away with murder.

"Holy hell." Manny's soft whisper was the only sound in the team room.

From the crime scene I knew what was going to come next, and decided I didn't want to watch it too closely. I looked at my fisted hands on my lap and concentrated on relaxing my fingers until my hands were resting flat on my thighs. I glanced up to see Dukwicz raising a medium-sized knife and plunging it into Savreux's chest. Immediately I dropped my eyes to my hands again, but the wide-open eyes, dilated pupils and the smile on Dukwicz's face were imprinted on my mind.

Belief in religion, myths, unseen elements and Francine's aliens was not based on rational thinking. I didn't believe in good and evil. Each person was the result of a complex set of elements, including their gender, upbringing, psychological makeup, brain chemistry and numerous other influential factors. The people sitting around the table had taught me more about emotions than my many years at university studying psychology. They had taught me that not everything could be quantified. This was giving me the freedom right now to mentally categorise Dukwicz as evil.

"It's done." Colin took one of my hands in his and squeezed it gently. I looked up and watched Dukwicz wipe the blade on Savreux's shirt before putting it into a scabbard on his belt. He took a deep breath, smiled and looked around the room. As his eyes moved towards the camera, the clock, I waited for the change. I wasn't disappointed. The moment he saw the clock, his eyes flashed open and his mouth opened slightly. It was pure pleasure from looking at an indulgence that gave him great contentment.

He stepped over Minister Savreux's body and walked towards the camera, not taking his eyes off his goal. On his way across the room, he pulled off his bloody gloves, pushed them into his pants pocket and from the other pocket took out a new set of gloves. He put on the gloves and stopped in front of the clock, his expression similar to the simple joy on Vinnie's face when he saw Francine after a weekend away from her. The image on the screen became distorted when he stood in front of the clock, too close for the camera's auto-focus to function properly. The image shook and shifted, indicating that he picked up the clock and turned it this way and that to look at his one weakness.

The erratic movements stopped and slowly turned. Then we saw the room again as before, with a minor adjustment to the left when Dukwicz didn't replace the clock in its exact original position. He stepped towards the door, his brow lowered and his head tilted slightly to the side as if he was straining to listen. He must have heard something, because his facial expression changed again to one of sadness as he looked at the clock with longing.

Dukwicz moved in utter silence to the door, disappeared for a second and returned with a large backpack. From it, he took a painting and rested it on the sofa.

"Bleeding hell, it's the Rembrandt." Manny again spoke softly as if to not disrupt the viewing.

In economical and sure movements, Dukwicz took the Flinck from the wall, replaced it with the Rembrandt, put the

Flinck in the backpack and rushed to the curtain-covered windows. He pulled one curtain just enough to allow him to step behind the heavy drapery. It was a slow and measured movement, and the curtain settled in two seconds, completely hiding Dukwicz from view.

Three seconds later Colin stepped into the room. I took a sharp, involuntary breath, horrified at how close he had been to that evil man.

Colin's movements mimicked those of the GIPN officers when they approached a building or room with stealth. He was light on his feet, careful where he stepped and what sound he made. Dukwicz had to have exceptional hearing to have heard Colin's entrance to the house.

To push away the black panic threatening to overwhelm me, I reminded myself that Colin was sitting next to me, unharmed. I watched as he took a few steps into the room, his eyes roving around as if sweeping the room for a safety overview. He was standing at an angle that afforded me a good enough view of his features. The moment he noticed Minister Savreux lying on the ground, the *procerus* muscle drew his eyebrows down and together. He looked around again, I supposed to ensure the killer was not in the room, and took a step closer. The wince marring his features told me he had seen the excessive stabbing and must have come to the conclusion Minister Savreux was dead.

He took his phone from his coat pocket, swiped the screen a few times and put the device to his ear. Not once did he take his eyes off the dead body on the floor.

"Jenny, you need—"

We listened to the short conversation he'd had with me, the horror of who was behind the curtains bringing the panic back to my peripheral view. I was clutching Colin's hand with both of mine, watching as, onscreen, he put the phone back in his pocket. With even more care and stealth, he left the room, not sparing another glance at the walls or display shelves. He disappeared out of view. A minute later, the curtain moved ever so slightly before it settled again. I paused the video.

"He must have left through a window or door behind those curtains." Colin's voice was rougher than usual. Strong emotions affected the muscles around our throat, resulting in a change of breathing, but also in more tension on the vocal cords.

"Dude, that was fucked-up." Vinnie put his bowl of popcorn on the table. He had stopped eating the moment Colin had entered the room on-screen. No one was eating any more. I looked more closely and saw that everyone had lost some colour in their faces. I'm sure my expression mirrored those I was looking at.

"That was a close call." Francine rubbed the space just under her throat, the suprasternal notch. "Too close, Colin. This was too close."

"Before you all pile onto me about this, I know that this was too close for comfort." Colin folded his arms, blocking further discussion. "Okay, so what did we learn from this video?"

"Dukwicz is a sick fuck." Vinnie leaned back in his chair, the *levator labii superioris* muscle pulling his top lip up.

Manny huffed, ignored Vinnie and started counting on his fingers. "We know that the Boston Flinck was there before Colin went in. That means the direct message Nikki received had been correct."

"But where is that Flinck now?" Colin asked. "I don't think it is in Savreux's wine cellar like Jenny thought. I'm willing to bet that the person who ordered Savreux's murder is now looking at it and gloating."

"Are we even sure it is the original?" I asked.

"There's no way to be sure, Jenny. Not without looking at it up close."

"I'm still counting here." Manny shook his raised index finger. "We can worry about authenticity later. What else do we know? We know that Dukwicz killed Savreux, but didn't kill Frey."

"Why not?" I asked. Francine looked at me with horror in every muscle on her face. "I'm trying to ask rational questions here."

"Doc is right. Why didn't Dukwicz kill Frey?"

"I would venture that he is not the type of personality to commit a crime of opportunity. This would've been too easy for him." I tightened my hold on Colin's hand. "From what he said, he enjoys the hunt, the planning, executing the plan. I don't think he would kill in a rage or just because the opportunity presents itself."

"What do you call the stabbing then?" Francine asked.

"Strategic." I shrugged when she raised her eyebrows. "I didn't watch the stabbing too closely, but the body language I saw indicated that he enjoyed the garrotting much more than the stabbing."

"He could've done the stabbing to throw us off," Manny said. "Crazy overkill like that usually comes from a crime of passion. Someone with a lot of pent-up rage against the victim. That would've kept us looking for someone in Savreux's closer circles—someone Savreux might have wronged in some way."

"And Dukwicz never kills for himself. He kills for money." Colin sounded more like himself now. "Whoever had ordered this hit might have also requested him to set up the crime scene like this."

"Which brings us to the next question. Who ordered this hit?"

"And why did they want Minister Savreux dead?" I didn't know if my question was more important than Manny's. "Is this also connected to Gabon? To the Libreville Dignity Foundation? How is any of this connected to the President? To his wife?"

"For the love of Pete, stop." Manny lifted both hands, palms up. "It's not like we don't have enough questions already. Why don't we stick to what we do have?"

"We know that the person sending Nikki direct messages believes we have limited time. What we don't know is what this deadline entails." I sighed. "What we don't know is a lot more than what we do know."

"Then it's time we find out more so we can answer all our questions. Doc, will you go through these videos and see if there is something that could help us? I will get this bunch to help me look into the Boston heist."

"You plan to solve that, Millard?" Colin laughed softly. "It's become the Holy Grail to some of the best detectives, but they've never solved it."

"Well, they're not me." Manny stood up. "And they didn't have you. Doc, are you okay with watching this?"

I thought about it and nodded. "As long as Savreux didn't kill anyone in his home office, I think I will be able to watch the footage."

Chapter FOURTEEN

I watched as yet another politician waited on the sofa in Minister Savreux's office. For the last two days, I had been alternating watching the footage with analysing all the other data. The footage was organised in reverse chronological order, from the most recent date to the earliest. The event on the monitor had taken place two weeks ago. In the two weeks after this, Minister Savreux had ushered eighteen different middle-aged men into his office. Every time he would prepare them a drink and tell them to wait. A few minutes later, a woman would enter. It was never the same woman.

The man currently on the monitor in my viewing room sat up when an overweight woman entered. At university, I had done a semester in abnormal sexual psychology. Part of the course dealt with fetishes. The extreme differences in the women made me think that Savreux had in some way catered to his peers' fantasies, providing them with the type of women they desired.

When I had talked about this last night at dinner, Vinnie had called Minister Savreux a pimp. I knew that word and found it a very appropriate description. The overweight woman swayed her ample hips from side to side as she walked to the sofa. Most times their sexual acts were in full view of the camera. Not once did I closely watch any of these men living out their fantasies on that sofa. I had fast-forwarded over those scenes until the women had left and

Minister Savreux had entered the room to enquire about his guest's satisfaction.

It fascinated me—this emotionless, and rather professional, arrangement Minister Savreux had had with these men. Afterwards, they would share a drink and discuss contracts, politics, negotiations and a next fantasy session. Minister Savreux never sat on the sex sofa.

Before Colin, for me sex had been about physical satisfaction. Even then, it had never been emotionless. I had always chosen men I had found reasonably likeable and we'd had some shared interests.

For the last year, I had been sharing my bed with Colin and the experience had taken on a completely different meaning. Involving an emotional connection in something that had been purely physical had changed it from having sex to making love. The intensity of our intimacy had increased significantly. I didn't think I could go back to having sex merely for a physical release.

How Savreux and these men could use and discard these women without a caring word revealed a lot about their characters. Most of these men I had seen at one or another time on some of the news programmes I favoured. From the little I knew about them, I'd had the impression that they were respected public figures. They presented themselves as family men with high moral and ethical standing on most issues. As I fast-forwarded through another sex scene, I wondered what would happen to these men's careers were any of these videos ever to be made public. If President Godard's No Secrets law was passed.

The post-copulating conversation between Savreux and this businessman was inconsequential and I moved to the next clip. It had taken place fifteen days ago at half past four in the afternoon. At this time of the year, the light was already giving way to the winter evening and the room was cast in shadows. Minister Savreux was alone in his office, sitting on the chair facing the door, when a man stepped into the room. Only his leg and foot were within the camera's viewing range. A subtle change in Savreux's body language made me narrow my eyes and lean a little closer to the monitors.

"What are you watching?" Colin's voice right next to my ear caused me to utter a sound closely resembling one of Nikki's screams when she was watching a horror movie with Vinnie. I placed my hand over my heart, breathed deeply a few times, and glared at Colin as he laughed. "Sorry, Jenny. I didn't mean to give you such a big fright."

I waved my index finger in front of his face. "That is not an expression of contrition."

He laughed again. "I'm sorry, but it was quite funny to see you jump in your chair."

"It didn't feel funny." I looked at the chair by his desk. "Bring your chair and watch this with me."

"What are we watching? Another porn tape?" He brought his chair over and sat down.

"You just missed it. This time it was with an overweight woman."

"Like one of those really huge women?"

"No, I would estimate her to be only around twenty kilograms overweight."

"So she was plump."

I thought about this. Body types were difficult to describe accurately. "I would rather say she was voluptuous. Oh, what are we talking about? We're wasting time."

"If you say so." His tone and the relaxed muscles on his face indicated he was teasing me.

"Focus on the work, Colin." I turned my attention back to the video, which had continued playing. I took it back to a second before the man entered the room. "This is different from the other videos. Minister Savreux never sat in his office and waited for anyone. He met these men somewhere in his house, presumably the front door, and showed them into the room. See how relaxed he is sitting there? Now watch this."

I clicked on the button to continue playing the video. I slowed it down for my own benefit and saw how the *platysma* muscles in Savreux's neck tensed, pulling the corners of his mouth even further down. I resumed playing the video at normal speed.

"What are you doing here?" Savreux leaned back in the chair and tried to appear relaxed. "How did you get in?"

The man took a small step into the room until just his left shoulder, arm and hand were visible. If he moved his head, we might be able to see his ear, but not enough of his jaw line to attempt a description.

"I own you, remember? Since I own you, I also own this house." The man's voice was thick and nasal as if he had a terrible cold. "Your security is worthless, Savreux. I got in through the garage. You left the garage door unlocked and the door to the house is also not locked. Not very smart when you have your private little parties going on here."

Savreux blanched. "What private parties?"

"Oh, that's how you want to play it? Pretend as if you don't hire your house out as a brothel? You're an idiot. You better not screw anything up."

It took Savreux a few seconds to make a decision. When he did, his shoulders moved back and his head lifted. "These parties are my private affairs. You of all people should know how good I am at compartmentalising. This is completely separate from our deal."

"Is everything in place?" The man's hand disappeared into his jacket pocket and came out with a handkerchief. He sneezed and blew his nose. "Did you do what I asked?"

"It's done. I spoke to Motte. He's ready. I also made a big fuss when a reporter caught me on the street in front of my office. I said that I would not support something that only acts as a witch-hunt, and does nothing to focus on where help is really needed, like in the employment-creation sector or more help with PTSD. You know, the normal political BS."

"Good. We need to surprise him with the info you have."

"Oh, he'll be surprised, all right. It will give me a hard-on to watch him change his tune because he has no other viable option."

"Don't gloat, Savreux." He pushed the handkerchief in his pocket and dropped his hand to his side. "You need to pay attention to what you're doing and saying. Overconfidence will have you make mistakes and destroy everything we've worked on for decades. I won't tolerate arrogance. Too much is riding on this."

"Don't worry. I'm well aware of our desired outcome. But I'll order champagne all the same."

The other man didn't answer, but only stood there and, I assumed, stared at Minister Savreux until he lost his confident posture. His shoulders lowered a few millimetres, his chin also dropping. It was all the mysterious alpha male needed to know he had Minister Savreux's submission. With a grunt, he turned and left the room, not once revealing his face to the camera.

I clicked on the pause button and stared at my keyboard. My brain was processing the wealth of information it had just absorbed, and I was trying to make sense of it all. Colin sat quietly next to me, most likely also thinking about what we had just witnessed. I closed my eyes and started mentally writing Mozart's Flute Concerto No. 1 in G Major. I only needed three bars of the Adaggio non troppo before the realisation hit me.

"Oh, my. Oh, my." I knew my eyes were stretched when I turned to Colin. "Savreux wasn't the one who put that camera in the clock. It was this man. He put it in. He knew exactly where the angles were and avoided being caught by it. Now it makes more sense. I was wondering why Minister Savreux would be so foolish to record his illegal conversations and these sex parties when it could incriminate him."

"And this guy said that he owns Savreux. That is most likely why he put that camera there. To see if Savreux was doing as he was told. He was keeping tabs on him."

I thought back to the last part of the conversation. "What do you think they were planning to celebrate?"

"I have a theory, but it is speculation." Colin smiled. "Want to hear it?"

I valued Colin's insights. When he hypothesised, it was nothing like Francine's outlandish ideas. "Tell me."

"I think that those rumours you read were true. It sounds like Savreux was planning to surprise someone with some heavy information. It also sounds like they were hoping it would change that person's opinion about something. I'm thinking Savreux had real secrets on the president he was going to reveal."

"Their conversation can definitely be interpreted as such. But it's still conjecture." I leaned towards the monitors. "Who is this man? Why did he say he owns Minister Savreux? How can a person own another person if not through slavery?"

"Are you seriously asking this?" Colin frowned.

"Have I ever asked something and wasn't serious about the answer?"

"True." He tilted his head and looked at the ceiling for a few seconds. Lately, he'd taken to doing that when he was planning how he would explain something to me. "It's like *guanxi*."

"The Chinese form of networking?"

"Exactly."

I knew that this was not pertinent to our discussion, but I simply couldn't allow for such misinformation. "*Guanxi* is not about owning people. In the Chinese culture, it is important to cultivate connections with people in case one needs assistance of any sort. This assistance could be in the form of physical help, advice or influence."

"Which sounds like manipulation to me."

"Granted. In modern society, the more corrupt elements of the community have been using this to manipulate people through fear of revealing some ill-gained personal secrets."

"In other words, they own that person." Colin lifted both brows and looked at me while I considered his reasoning.

"I can see how you reached that conclusion. I don't like it, but I will acquiesce."

"Um. Thank you." He smiled and pointed to the monitor. "This man very likely owned Savreux because he had evidence strong enough to completely destroy Savreux's career, maybe even put him in jail for a long time."

"Minister Savreux would not easily have surrendered to blackmail. Not according to the psychological profile I've created on him."

"Which means that whatever this man had on Savreux was huge."

"Could these tapes be it?"

Colin thought about this for a moment. "No, I don't think so. I think he put this camera in there to keep an eye on Savreux, not to gather incriminating evidence."

We sat in silence for a few minutes. More disconnected pieces were being added to this mystery, but I knew that it would require another Mozart concerto or a keyword that would cause it all to fall into place and make sense to me.

"Did you hear what he said about Motte?" Colin asked.

"Savreux had talked to him."

"See if you can find footage with Motte on it. If we can get that conversation, we might know what it is that Savreux had been planning and what is supposed to happen." He got up and kissed me on my cheek. "I'm going to check on Francine."

"Are you making progress in solving the Boston heist?"

"Not as fast as Manny wants, but we're getting closer. Francine thinks she has a lead that one of her people found. I'm going to see if it is worth looking into."

I stared at him. It took immense control to not get out of my chair and insist on going with him into the team room. This was not the first time we worked separately, but for some inexplicable reason, a negative feeling dominated whenever I thought about them working on the Boston heist.

"What's wrong?" Colin sat back down and swivelled my chair to face him.

"I don't know."

He waited for a few seconds and smiled when I didn't elaborate. "Want to try and explain it to me?"

"I have a negative feeling about you working on the Boston heist."

"A negative feeling as in a bad feeling? A bad feeling like an ominous foreboding?"

"You know I don't believe in that nonsense."

"Okay, so what kind of bad feeling is it?"

In my head, I went through the list of negative and even dark emotions to see which one fitted with what I was currently experiencing. Even though I had applied myself from a very young age to not only understand other people, but also being able to recognise and identify my own emotions, it still didn't come easily to me. I tilted my head and was rather embarrassed when I identified my emotion.

"What is it?" Colin took my hand in his.

"I feel left out." I pulled my hand from his and exhaled angrily. "This is ridiculous. I've never had a need to belong anywhere. Why would I suddenly need to be part of an investigation that would only rob my time? It might be a meaningless hunt while I could much more efficiently use my time doing what I'm currently doing."

"Hey, I think it's cool that you want to be with us."

"I think it is immature and shows a preposterous lack of rationality."

He laughed softly and leaned forward until our lips almost touched. "I really love you, you know?"

"I know." I swallowed. It still wasn't easy to verbally express my vulnerability. "I love you too."

He laughed again and kissed me before pulling back. "You don't have to sound so spooked about it."

"Go away." I turned my chair, so I was facing the monitors again. "I need to work."

He left, still laughing. I didn't understand what humour he had seen in my words and actions, but I had seen the nonverbal cues communicating his affection and enjoyment. It was enough for me. It had been a hard lesson, but I had learned that I didn't need to understand everything. Colin and the others had taught me to sometimes just accept.

Like flipping a light switch, I closed off all thoughts of my private life and started looking through the myriad video files, hoping to come across René Motte's meeting with Savreux. Many different people were on these clips. Whenever an unknown person appeared on my monitor, I listened for a name. The names I got from the onscreen conversations, I immediately researched on the internet, familiarising myself not only with as much information on them as possible, but also with as many photos as I could find. I needed to know whom I was looking for in case one of these people became more than only a person of interest. I didn't have to search far into the past videos to find the short, almost petite man. He had met with Minister Savreux two days before the mysterious man had paid the minister a visit.

I started the video and, like I did every time, looked for any changes in the room. It was the same. Minister Savreux was sitting at his desk when Motte entered. The minister got up, a social smile wide enough to show his white teeth. "René, come in, come in."

He held out his hand to indicate the sofas. He led Motte to the sex sofa, a smirk closely resembling a social smile on his face when he turned to pour some drinks. "What can I get you?"

"Scotch would be good. On the rocks, thank you." Motte's voice didn't match his frame—it was deep and authoritative.

Minister Savreux prepared the beverages and sat down in his usual chair. For the next ten minutes, I listened to them talk about their disgust at legalising brothels. Minister Savreux agreed with Motte's outrage that prostitutes were even allowed to work in France. As far as he was concerned, these women, and men, should be sent to prison for violating the moral purity of society.

Again I was captivated by Claude Savreux's nonverbal communication. Unless someone had exceptional observation skills, they would never have noticed his deception cues. He was uncanny in his sincerity and agreement that sexual activity should only ever take place in the sanctity of marriage. I wondered if his reason for leading Motte to the sex sofa was because he was internally mocking the smaller man.

"Is everything in place?" Motte lowered his chin, the expression in his eyes conveying a hidden meaning. "I'm leaving for the Caribbean the day after tomorrow and will not be reachable."

"Not at all?"

Just as Motte was about to answer, a ringtone filled the room. Motte took his smartphone from his jacket pocket and glanced at the screen. "We'll have to talk tomorrow. Contact me so we can arrange the where. I have to take this."

Without waiting for Minister Savreux's response, he got up and started whispering into his phone as he left the room. Minister Savreux didn't get out of the chair, slowly relaxing while sipping his drink. After some time, he shook his head and muttered, "Sanctimonious midget."

The video stopped and I sat back. How was it possible that these videos started and stopped at certain points without the help of a human at the controls? If the camera had been triggered by motion sensors, it would have started the moment someone crossed one of the sensors, not a few seconds before like on most of the videos. All of them also stopped a few seconds after an important meeting, never in the middle or an extended time later. Someone had edited these recordings into the clips that I had been watching.

The mysterious man with flu had exhibited such suspicious behaviour that I was considered it within reason to suspect he had been the one to either give the clock to Savreux as a gift, or place the camera in the clock. Before I watched the video featuring him again, I needed to make sure that I didn't miss anything. Motte had told Savreux to meet with him the next day. It was most inconvenient that their meeting had been cut short. It might have supplied needed answers. I double-checked, but could find no footage of a meeting between the two of them, not the next day or any day thereafter.

I reached the clip of Savreux and the mysterious man and watched it another three times. The first time, my attention was solely on Savreux—his expressions, his words, his tone, everything. The second time, I focussed on the interaction—the length of time between questions and answers, the changes in both men's tones as the conversation progressed. It was the third time that I found something very valuable.

Focussing my attention completely on the mystery man was not very informative. The angle provided me with very little body language to read and not one single facial expression. I hated phone conversations for that reason. Without the context body language lent to tone and words, I more often than not misunderstood the true message.

That was why I was searching for the smallest nonverbal cue from the mystery man as he talked. I needed context. That came the moment he put his handkerchief back in his pocket and dropped his hand to his side. A second before he spoke, he touched the tip of his little finger to the tip of his thumb. He repeated this conscious action three more times before he left. For some reason he was using an anchor. This was most interesting and might help to build a better profile of this man. I couldn't wait to share this with Colin and Manny.

I knew they were busy and didn't want to interfere, especially now that Colin knew I wanted to be part of their investigation. These were new emotions that I was going to have to work through. The hardest part of friendship had been the constant sense of vulnerability. Colin had told me it would get better the more I trusted them. Thus far, it had not proven true.

To avoid any more pesky emotional thoughts, I continued my perusal of the video clips. On the notepad in front of my keyboard, I neatly wrote down the details of each clip. I had the names of around eighty percent of the visitors. Some I had recognised, others' names had led me to their profiles. For those unidentified, I wrote a brief description and their purpose of visit. I loved making lists. There was something very calming in putting down one's thoughts, chores, or in this case, suspects, in neat columns. It also helped me organise potential theories and ideas.

I lost myself in the process of analysing the nonverbal cues, listening for important information, noting down the details and fast-forwarding scenes I did not care for. Each filename was the date and time of the recording. That meant there were recordings as far back as five months ago. Even though I was curious to see the very first recording, I could not bring myself to disregard my compulsive need to follow the numbers. The thought of skipping to the first clip increased my heart rate and left my hands cold and sweaty. I took a deep breath and played the next clip in the cue. I had a lot of footage to get through if I wanted to reach the first one.

Chapter FIFTEEN

"Jenny?" Colin soft touch on my shoulder startled me and my fingers tingled from the minor surge of adrenaline.

I had been fully immersed in my viewing and resented being pulled out of it. I paused the video and turned to him, annoyed. "I had lunch two hours ago. It can't possibly be time to eat or drink or sleep again."

He smiled. "I have something better."

"What can be better than leaving me alone to work?"

His expression lost its light-heartedness and he turned his head slightly to the right. I had learned that this sideways look came when I was being particularly rude. I considered this and sighed. "I'm sorry. I'm getting very close to the first clip recorded in Minister Savreux's home office and I am very curious what can be learned from it."

"Apology accepted." He nodded to the door. "Come with me. What I have might just trump your first video."

The excitement on his face caught my interest. Only a few things energised Colin this much. The top of the list was stolen art. I narrowed my eyes. "Did you steal something? Did you break into Motte's preservation room and steal that Vermeer?"

He laughed as he grabbed my hand and pulled me from my chair. "No, I didn't steal anything. Not this time, anyway. We got it the legal way."

"What is it?" I had become trapped by Colin's enthusiasm. I walked faster than usual, following him through the team room into the hallway, growing more curious by the second. "Where are we going?"

"The large conference room. We've got it set up there."

A year ago, Phillip had extended one of the conference rooms to be large enough to host a small exhibition. Whatever Colin was currently excited about had to be large enough to require being displayed in that room.

At the door of the conference room, Colin stood aside to let me enter first. I walked in, only to stop after two steps. Vinnie and Manny bustled around the room, but it was the many paintings on the walls—more paintings than in some smaller galleries here in Strasbourg—that held my interest. The conference table covered with one of the expensive linen tablecloths Phillip had bought also caught my attention. Not much of the cream cloth was visible under all of the statues, clocks, Fabergé eggs, masks and other artworks carefully displayed there.

"Where did this come from?" I didn't intend to whisper, but that was the result of being confounded by what I was looking at.

"Oh, Doc. You're here." Manny came from the other side of the long conference table and waved his hand around the room. "What do you think?"

I cleared my throat. "Where did this come from?"

Colin walked past me and lovingly touched a small marble sculpture that looked distinctly Renaissance in style. "All of this was in Savreux's cellar."

"He had stored all of this in that wine cellar he rented? Oh, my."

"Millard came through with a search warrant and this is what we found."

"Genevieve." Phillip walked into the room, his cheeks flushed. He was a self-possessed man, always in control of his emotions. The pleasure of having these artworks in his company's conference room was clearly overpowering his usual composure. "Isn't this wonderful? Look at all of these works. We are busy inventorying it, but so far we are looking at hundreds of millions of euro's worth of artwork here."

"Plenty of these pieces are on different stolen art registries, including the FBI and Interpol's registries." Colin picked up a fragile-looking bottle with a lid. "This is a glass water bottle from the Ottoman period. It was stolen in Turkey a few months ago. Look at these gilded motifs. Such incredible fine work." He walked deeper into the room, pointing out various paintings and other works. "See this watercolour? It's a nineteenth-century Pissarro, the Rue a Macon. This oil painting is a Paul Grim. A Paul Grim! See how he catches the light on the side of the mountains? That's why he called it the Sunkissed Slopes. God, this really upsets me."

I didn't know how to respond to this, so I merely nodded. How did this fit into all the previous information I had learned about Minister Savreux and the rest of this case? I stopped in front of a painting of the cubist artist, Juan Gris, and quickly turned away. It brought back unpleasant memories of our last case.

"It makes sense that Minister Savreux wouldn't want these paintings on display in his home," I said. "In the videos I have been watching, Minister Savreux didn't just use his office as a brothel, he had a number of professional meetings with other politicians and economists there. From the conversations and body language, these visitors had no illegal connection to the Minister."

"There is also the possibility that one of these gentlemen would've asked questions about the works if they were hanging on his walls," Phillip said.

"Someone did ask him about the Flinck above the mantelpiece. He told the gentleman that it was a reproduction he had made. Savreux was a more than adequate liar."

"And that is why I would never call a politician a gentleman, but that's just me." Manny was standing next to the table, leaning towards a small wooden chest. His arm closest to the chest was slightly away from his body, his fingers uncharacteristically fidgety.

"What is in the chest?" From his body language, I knew Manny considered it valuable.

"The secrets to the universe." His expression was filled with expectation as if he had delivered the punch line of a joke. When I didn't react, he grunted and opened the lid. "Loads of files on different people and different cases. Some of these almost read like biographies or non-fiction books."

"Have you read them?" How long had they been looking at these artworks and other findings?

"No, I skimmed through it. There are also a few computer things, which might tell us a few secrets as well. Supermodel is already checking those out." He tilted his head to where Francine was sitting with her laptop on her lap before he lifted a handful of CD's from the chest. "These are neatly marked videos. They have dates and names on them."

"But that's not all." Vinnie's dramatic delivery of the sentence brought smiles to everyone's faces. He lifted a large gym bag, his arm muscles bulging from the weight of the content. "Here we have about a million dollars in dollar bills, pounds, euros, Australian dollars, Canadian dollars and even yen. In the old man's treasure chest there on the table are passports for these countries for different names, but Savreux's photo is in each one of them."

"There isn't a Japanese passport though." Manny lifted a few passports from the chest and shook them. "It would be too suspicious to have a European face with a Japanese passport."

"Why would he need aliases?" I asked Colin. I had met him when I had uncovered the numerous aliases he had been using. He was the best qualified to answer this question.

"Never for a legal reason, Doc."

Colin nodded his agreement. "The photos in the passports are definitely him, but with subtle changes. He might have wanted to travel incognito or he didn't want his trip, his flight to be public record. If a crime was committed in a few countries and he was present in all those countries at those times, it would lead to the obvious conclusion that he was somehow involved. There are many other reasons, but like Millard said, none of them could be honest."

"At a glance, none of these passports has been used in the last two years." Manny threw the passports back in the chest. "What happened two years ago that got this man to become so careful?"

It was a question I had been asking myself, but was yet to find an answer. I looked around the room. "And the art? Do you think he stole it?"

"Not all these pieces are reported stolen." Phillip looked up from the tablet in his hand. He was inputting information on it, most likely completing the list of everything in the room.

"The big news here is that we have all five of the Degas drawings from the Boston heist. Look." Colin pointed at the wall to Francine's right. Five drawings were next to each other.

"Is there any damage?" I asked.

"Nothing. They're pristine." Colin's voice shook with emotion. "Do you know what this means, Jenny?"

"Minister Savreux was somehow involved in the 1990 theft from the Gardner museum in Boston."

"He might have been the one who orchestrated it," Colin said.

"Are you sure those works are authentic?"

"I'm convinced these are the Degas drawings from the Gardner, but there is always a margin of error."

"One of my trusted colleagues will come today to look at these," Phillip said. "He is one of the top art experts who does authentication, and is also a friend. I know I can trust him with this."

"You better be sure about him, Phillip." Stress lines framed Manny's mouth. "Until we know what all of this means, we cannot let any of this reach the public."

"It won't." Phillip's tone was confident.

I pulled out a chair and sat down. "How can we find out what role Minister Savreux played in the Boston heist?"

"Ooh, I found something!" Francine bounced in her chair, but didn't look away from her laptop screen. "I don't know what I found, but it looks delicious."

"What do you mean delicious, supermodel?" Manny walked around the table towards Francine.

"Numbers, lots and lots of numbers. Big numbers. The kind of big numbers you get in big scandals."

"Francine, you're not making sense." I often wished she would forego the dramatics and just say what was needed.

"Let me show you." She stood up, frowned and looked

around the room. "Hmm. Give me a moment to get the projector connected."

It took her more than two minutes to wirelessly connect her computer to the projector hanging from the ceiling, and to lower the white screen hanging a few centimetres from the far wall. The first image that filled the screen wasn't clear because of the lighting in the room. Phillip was closest to the door and turned the lights down.

"See? Loads of numbers?" Francine was right. On the screen were two pages, side by side, filled with strings of numbers. Even though all the numbers were neatly separated into columns, there was nothing indicating what any of the numbers represented.

"What do you think, Doc?" Manny looked at the screen for a few seconds, but showed cues of boredom. "Is this important?"

"If Savreux had this secretly locked away in a room filled with stolen artwork, he must have considered it of value." I got up and walked closer to the screen. "This looks like it could fit on a spreadsheet."

"I think so too," Francine said. "Why on earth it is in a Word document, I really don't know. Who on earth does their finances in Word?"

"I do mine in Word. Something wrong with that?"

Francine stared at Manny, her jaw slack. "Seriously, handsome? You could not be more of a Luddite if you tried. You've just lost a few brownie points with me."

"Oh, how devastating." Manny's expression didn't look like he was devastated.

I turned back to the numbers. "There aren't any dates to show when the transactions took place. That is assuming that these are transactions."

"Do you think that the last column might be a date, but coded?" Francine highlighted the last column. In each row were twelve numbers, too many to indicate day, month and year. The usual numbers were either six or eight digits for dates.

"I think it's possible. These numbers are following each other in chronological order. We'll have to decode it, but you might be right."

"I think this is from many years ago." Francine sounded so sure that I turned around to look at her.

"Why do you think that?"

"For starters, the whole Word thing. Seriously. Secondly, the date the document was saved on this disk is easy to find."

"When was this document saved on that CD?" I asked.

"In 1996. It doesn't mean that was when the document was created, but it was when this disk was burned."

"Interesting." I wondered what happened in 1996 that Savreux had felt compelled to save this information. "I would offer to help you decoding this file, but I know that you are quite capable of doing this yourself."

"Why, thank you, girlfriend."

"I will take those." I pointed to the recordings in the chest. "As soon as I'm finished with Savreux's videos, I will go through those."

"We've left you with those videos the whole day. Have you found something useful, Doc?"

"Why are you looking so apologetic?" It was most unlike Manny to display cues of contrition.

"I…um…I'm not apologetic. I just think watching videos is boring and you've been doing this the whole day."

"I've been doing this for the last three days, Manny. It's not boring. As a matter of fact, I have found a few useful bits of information. I have a list of Savreux's visitors and their activities. Not all of them went there to live out their sexual fantasies." The expression on Manny's face gave me pause. "You were feeling guilty that I had to watch all those sex tapes."

"Oh, Doc. Don't call it that."

"It's exactly what it is, Millard." Colin smiled. "Who knew you were such a prude."

"Not a prude, Frey. Just not into that kind of weird stuff."

"But how would you know if you've never tried any of it, handsome?" Francine winked at Manny, her lips pouting.

"And how would you know that I haven't tried any of it, supermodel?"

"Kabam!" Vinnie burst out laughing. "The old man got you good, girl. He got you good."

"Oh, shut up." Francine threw a pen at Vinnie and turned back to Manny. "You have me very curious now."

"And so you shall remain."

"Jenny, you said earlier that you wanted to get to the first clip." Colin's change of topic was most welcome. "Why?"

"I suspect that if the first clip is indeed the very first video that was recorded, it might give us some clues about that mysterious man. It is just a suspicion that I would like to confirm by finishing the other two and watching the first one." I got up and took the CD's from Manny. "I will return to Minister Savreux's recordings now. When I'm done, I'll go through these."

Twelve minutes later, I reached the last clip. The preceding two had been of politicians I'd held in high regard. I was aware that public figures worked hard at the image they presented. Even though, I found myself quite disillusioned.

Francine's mindset of extreme cynicism was becoming an easy trap to fall into.

"May I join you?" Colin dragged his chair closer and sat down.

"That was a rhetorical question, right?"

He had never asked permission before, and he was already seated. His answer to my question was a genuine smile. He was in a good mood and I was certain it was because of the art in the conference room. "Have you watched the last video yet? Or is it the first?"

"It is last on the list, but was first to be recorded. I was just about to start watching it."

"Good. I'm very interested to know what's going to come from it."

"I would've thought you would rather be in the conference room."

"Millard is beginning to annoy me. I'll wait until he's no longer there to pollute all that beauty with his presence."

I was very proud of myself for being able to refrain from commenting. My control was not absolute though and I knew if I opened my mouth, those words might slip out. So I pressed my lips tightly together and turned my attention to the footage. I clicked on the play button and picked up my pencil to take notes.

Minister Savreux was sitting on the sofa, a tall black man on the sex sofa. This was one of the few clips that didn't start before anyone entered the room. As in the other clips, nothing in the room had changed, the Flinck hanging above the mantelpiece. Both men held whiskey glasses in their hands, not drinking.

"I'm reaching my limits, Savreux." The African man spoke French, but had an accent—the type of accent found in

African countries with French history. "My country is getting out of control. *She* is getting out of control."

"What do you mean, Paul?"

I wrote the name on my notepad.

"Do you know who that is?" Colin asked.

"No."

"Hmm. Paul is a very common name, but let's do a quick search in any case." Colin leaned closer and reached for my keyboard. I put my arm out to prevent him from taking over my workspace, and paused the video.

"I will do it." I ignored his chuckle and searched for an African politician or leader with Paul as a first name. The search engine gave me over two million hits within one point eight seconds. It was far too generic. Following the preceding evidence in this case, I narrowed the search to Gabonese politicians with Paul as a first name. One point two seconds later, there were more than one million hits. I checked the images and found him in the first row of photos. The image was linked to an article. I clicked on the link and waited for the BBC news article to open.

"Paul Ngondet from Gabon." Colin whistled softly. "Gabon again. This place is definitely a key player here. We need to know more about it."

"Later." I scanned the article, but it merely reported a diplomatic meeting between Paul Ngondet and the British prime minister to discuss aid for Gabon. It did, however, give me a name and a position. Paul Ngondet had been the CEO of a large international company before he was elected as the Minister of Trade and Industry in Gabon. Not only was he a politician, he was a very prominent politician.

I entered his full name in the search engine and one point three seconds later had numerous articles on him, including a

Wikipedia page dedicated to this man. I opened a Gabonese government website that had Paul Ngondet's profile listed.

"So he is a strong opponent to the president of Gabon?" Colin was reading as fast as I was. "He has also been in politics for the last thirty years. How old is this guy?"

I pointed to the date of birth on the monitor. "He is fifty-nine years old. Some politicians remain in public office well past the usual retirement age, which makes him still young."

"I think you should go to the Wikipedia page."

"Why? Those articles are notoriously inaccurate."

"But they have all the good gossip. You can confirm any facts later, but Wikipedia always gives a better place to start from. On this government site, we're only going to get their PR crap."

He was right, both about the state website and about Wikipedia. The latter site had improved the quality of their articles, but I was reluctant to believe anything from an open source site. I went back to the search results and a click later, we were looking at a much more detailed profile of Paul Ngondet.

"Aha!" Colin pointed to the bottom of the monitor. "Look there. See! There it says that he has been actively campaigning against President Mariam Boussombo. He wants Gabon to go back to its roots, not influenced by Western culture with their customs of giving women the right to destroy men's masculinity. He appears to have quite a following. Hmm."

I returned to the clip. One click, and Minister Paul Ngondet answered Minister Savreux's question.

"I mean that she is now insisting on an independent commission to look into alleged corruption. She doesn't even want to have any control over or connection to this commission. And you know what's going to happen if this is approved."

"It's going to turn into a witch hunt." Minister Savreux took a sip from his glass. "A lot of countries that went through a regime change established these commissions. South Africa had the Truth and Reconciliation Commission to address wrongs committed during the apartheid regime. Poland has the Institute of National Remembrance investigating crimes committed during the Second World War and the later Communist rule. The one in Poland especially turned into a witch hunt, destroying people."

"She will destroy us, Savreux. All of us." Distress was exhibited on Paul Ngondet's face through the *corrugator supercilii* muscles pulling his eyebrows down and together. "I—we—cannot allow that."

"What do you propose?" There was caution in Minister Savreux's tone.

"Something that will benefit all of us." Paul Ngondet leaned forward. "If she was to, let's say, dance her last dance, her little group of do-gooders will be lost without her. I hate saying this, but she is a good leader. People like her and like to follow her."

"Which makes it even more complicated to get her to dance that last dance."

"My friend, we've come a long way." Paul Ngondet shifted closer to the edge of the sofa. He was reaching out to Minister Savreux, unconsciously revealing his desperation. "You and I were a dynamic team back in the eighties and nineties. We got things done. Not like today where leaders give their uneducated, uncivilised citizens rights to make decisions. We had a long-term vision and could make decisions that would get us there. These little people see nothing but their own hunger and poverty. They don't know what we know, what we have already forgotten. It kills me to see how she is destroying my country, my traditions."

They sat in silence for a minute. The view of Minister Savreux was not as clear as of Paul Ngondet. I could only clearly see two thirds of the minister's face, enough to know he was deceiving Ngondet. Throughout Ngondet's speech, he had nodded sagely, barely hiding his elation. I waited to find out what he was so happy about.

Savreux coughed lightly into his hand. "I might have a solution."

"You do? What is it, my friend? Anything you need, I will give you."

"Let's hope it will not come to that." Savreux gently swirled the alcohol around in his glass, taking his time to continue. "There is already a plan in play. A plan I'm part of. And I think there might be a place for you at the table. Of course, I will first have to speak to the other players before I tell you anything more and you have to know from the very beginning that it will cost you."

"Anything. You know I have endless resources. Money is not an object."

"Good. Good." Savreux nodded slowly. "I'll meet with them post haste and be in contact with you before the end of day tomorrow. You are staying in Strasbourg for some time, no?"

"I'll be here until my work is done. There is no reason for me to rush back to Gabon."

They returned to speaking about inconsequential things and three minutes later, Minister Savreux ushered Paul Ngondet out of the room. He came back and sat in one of the chairs. The video continued to play and I wondered what else could have been recorded. Then a slight movement in the right-hand corner of the screen caught my eye. There was a man standing in the door, just outside the camera view.

"Did he fall for it?" This time the voice was not as obscured by a cold and he was speaking too softly to make his voice identifiable, but I was sure it was the same mysterious man from earlier.

"Hook, line and sinker. We've got him."

"Good. We've worked hard to get to this point. Make sure you have all the other people set up for this. No mistakes, Claude."

"There will be no mistakes…" The video cut out.

"No." My tone was plaintive. The person who had edited this video had cut out his name. Irrationally, I took it back two seconds and played again with the same results. "We still don't have his name."

"Who is this guy?"

"He had a cold in the first video. Here he is speaking very softly, but it is the same man. Look here." I told Colin about my earlier discovery and played the current video from where the mysterious man came to the door. I waited a few seconds before I paused. On another monitor, I opened the other video with him in it and took it to the exact moment the man touched his little finger to his thumb. "This is his anchor."

"His what?"

I turned my chair to face Colin. "Do you know what NLP is?"

"Neuro-linguistic programming. I know about it."

"They use a method which can be compared to Pavlov's theory on conditioning. Anchoring is an external trigger used to access an internal response." I sighed when I saw Colin's expression and took a few moments to organise my thoughts. "When dealing with a certain issue, for example impatience, the theory is to reprogram yourself, your thinking, in order to control your response. While in the process of reprogramming, you need to choose an anchor. It is usually a small gesture like touching your ear, or in this case touching his two fingers.

"When practicing your new patience, you would use your anchor every time, reinforcing the new programming. The next time you are faced with a challenging situation in real life, you could use this anchor to trigger the mind programming to control your response or behaviour."

"So I'm trying to not get angry and I touch my little finger to my thumb and I'm all zen? This really works?"

"It's much more complex than this, but yes, the brain is programmable in most cases."

"Cool." He looked back at the monitors. "You think Anchor Man studied NLP? Could he be a psychologist?"

"I think no such thing. He could be an executive who read one of the numerous self-help NLP books available on the market."

"How would that help us find him?"

My shoulders slumped. "It won't. It could, however, assist in recognising him as a possible suspect if I spoke to him."

"But you would need to speak to him."

"That is true." This clip had given me additional information to process. "What do you think he meant by 'dancing her last dance'? His nonverbal cues indicated that it wasn't about dancing at all."

Colin tilted his head back for a moment, thinking. When he looked at me, I saw concern. "It could be a euphemism for destroying this woman's career."

"Or not. I don't want to speculate." Earlier I had been so

thrilled with this discovery. Now it seemed moot. I reached for the CD's on my desk.

"No, Jenny. We're going home." He looked at his watch. "It's way past seven and Vinnie's already left to make dinner. Let's go home. We can watch these tomorrow."

It had been a long day and the thought of dinner, a hot bath and an early night sounded good. Tomorrow I would continue to go through the increasing amount of evidence.

Chapter SIXTEEN

"Dude!" Vinnie's voice boomed through the combined apartments. The urgency in his tone sent adrenaline rushing through my system, destroying the relaxed mindset I'd had when Colin and I had settled into bed after a filling dinner.

Colin jumped out of bed, grabbing the gun from his bedside table. "Stay here."

As he ran out the door, I heard Vinnie call for Colin again, this time following up with a string of curse words I had never heard him say. I opened my bedside table drawer and took the weapon Vinnie had given me two nights ago. Armed with pepper spray, I carefully followed Colin. I had no desire to become involved in another physical altercation, but Nikki was in my home. Her safety overwhelmed my thoughts to the point of obsession.

"How the fuck did he get in?" This was one of the very few times I ever heard Colin swear. In his tone I heard anger, but nothing else that warned me of an intruder. Instead of turning to Nikki's room, I walked to Vinnie's.

"I don't know, dude. I cleaned up the kitchen, had a shower and didn't pay attention until I took out clean boxers." Vinnie looked at me as I entered his bedroom. "Jen-girl."

Colin swung around and glared at me. "I told you to stay in our room."

How could I justify my decision to protect Nikki with a

little canister filled with a lachrymatory agent? I ignored his question. "What happened?"

"Jenny!" Colin took two long strides until he was in front of me. In my personal space. "I told you to stay in our room. Why didn't you listen?"

I weakly lifted the pepper spray and closed my eyes. "I know it doesn't make sense, but I was going to stand in front of Nikki's room to protect her."

"Jenny, look at me," Colin said after a few seconds.

It took a lot of effort for me to open my eyes.

"What do you see?"

"You're angry. Very angry."

He shook his head. "What else?"

I took a deep breath and looked past the embarrassment of my ridiculously irrational action. "You're worried."

"About you and Nikki." He lowered his head. "You need to use your analytical brain to prevent yourself from doing things that can put your life in danger, love."

"I have seven years of self-defence training."

"And I would like for you to not have to use that. Not in our home." He sighed heavily and stepped aside for me to see where Vinnie was standing next to his chest of drawers. Dressed only in a large towel wrapped around his hips, he looked ready to enter a battle. The top drawer next to him was pulled half open, but that was not what caught my attention. It was the three clocks arranged on top of the chest of drawers. My three clocks.

It felt like I was falling from an incredible height. Increasing dizziness reminded me to breathe. I looked away from the clocks and blinked a few times, trying very hard to not lose the tenuous grip I had on my control. "Dukwicz was here? In your room?"

"These are your clocks, right?" Vinnie pointed at the three timepieces. "The ones he stole six months ago?"

I nodded.

"How did he get in, Vin?"

"The window." Vinnie's lips tightened to thin lines, the scar on his face becoming more prominent as anger affected his skin tone. "Windows are always a weak spot. They are often the easiest to open. The latches are not made for security, but for locking out the wind or cold. We're up on the top floor, which makes the windows easier to reach from the roof, but also more difficult because access to the roof is not that simple."

"It was easy enough for you," I said to Colin. The first few weeks of our acquaintance, he had refused to use my front door, always breaking in.

"I think by now it is safe to say Dukwicz is good at getting into very secure locations." Colin looked at the windows. "Vin—"

"I'm on it, dude. Tomorrow, I'll re-secure the windows. They will be as secure as a nuclear bunker. I hate saying this, but that scumbag has to be good to have gotten past the security I'd set up here. I swear, I'm gonna lock it down like Fort frigging Knox."

"He's mocking us." I stepped closer to the clocks. "It's like a cat playing with its prey. He wants to terrorise us with these clocks. That knowledge will give him great pleasure."

"It's not terrorising me, Jen-girl. It's making me want to fu… It's making me angry." He scowled at the clocks. "Do you want these things?"

"No, thank you." I was shaking my head excessively to make my point. I doubted I would ever be tempted to buy another antique clock.

"Jenny's right, Vin. He's laughing at us, proving that he can get to us without even trying."

"It's also significant that he chose Vinnie's room," I said. "He picked the room of the physically strongest in the house. That way he can really prove his dominance."

"Dominance, my ass." Vinnie grabbed a backpack from his closet and threw the clocks in it. I didn't even cringe at the sound of the valuable pieces breaking. It felt cathartic. Especially when Vinnie flung the zipped backpack into his closet and closed the doors. "I'll take the night shift. Try to get some sleep. When I sort out these windows tomorrow, you better solve this case and find this asshole."

After four more minutes, I concluded that nothing worthwhile could be added to our conversation. Vinnie and Colin went from speculation to discussing security, and I decided it was best to return to bed. Knowing that Dukwicz had been in my home made me clutch the pepper spray tightly in my hand as I walked back to my room. I wondered why Nikki didn't wake up amidst all the noise. It was highly likely that she'd gone to sleep with her headphones on.

That assumption did nothing to assuage my concerns and I gave in to my need to check on her. I opened her door, took a step into her room and squinted against the dark, checking the bed for her sleeping form. Her room was as messy as always, but it didn't matter. I stared at her sprawled figure on the bed, headphones on her ears, the light from the hallway revealing the soft expression on her face. A tightness in my chest I didn't even know had been there loosened up.

"She's safe, Jenny," Colin said softly behind me. He kissed the top of my head and pulled me against his chest. "Let's go to bed. Hopefully we'll get some sleep."

It took only a few minutes to settle back into bed. But it

took me much longer to still the frantic activity in my mind. In the end, I didn't sleep well. Or enough. At five o'clock, I gave up attempting to sleep and got ready for the office. Colin woke up when I came out of the shower, but didn't say anything about me getting dressed. He just smiled and picked up his tablet.

I left him reading, and met Vinnie in the kitchen. He insisted on driving me to the office and I immediately agreed. I didn't need to be convinced and was actually relieved to sit next to the large man in his freshly cleaned truck. He even walked me into my viewing room. As I got ready to watch the footage from Minister Savreux's rented preservation room, he left the room, but I didn't think he left the building.

It empowered me to be working and not agonise over the break-in. I clicked on the first clip and picked up my pen. Forty-seven video clips later, I had nothing. I supposed it wasn't nothing per se. These videos contained incriminating evidence that could cost people their careers and, for a few, their freedom. Some videos were conversations Minister Savreux had recorded while discussing sensitive business and political negotiations. He had been extremely careful to never say anything that could be used against him in court.

These videos had to have been taken with a camera attached to Minister Savreux's tie or shirt buttons. It was at a lower angle, sometimes cutting off the top of the other person's head. But it was enough to use in some way to control that person. Colin's earlier mention of *guanxi* combined with these videos now made me suspicious that Minister Savreux had achieved his success not through hard work, but by manipulating others through ill-gained information. It was the worst form of *guanxi* in action. This ethical violation was shocking to observe.

A deep disappointment came from my inability to find anything useful or relevant to our case. I also had not found any meeting Minister Savreux had had with Motte. I had hoped to find a recording that might have told me what plan these men were plotting. There had been a worrying malice in how pleased they had looked with themselves. It didn't bode well.

"Doc?" Nikki's voice broke into my thoughts. I turned and saw her standing at the door with a tray. "Okay if I bug you? Colin sent me with food."

I glanced at my clock and saw it was eighteen minutes past ten. I hadn't heard anyone arrive or work in the team room.

"Come in." I looked into the tray. "What did you bring?"

"Colin told me to bring coffee, water and snacks." She put the tray on the desk next to my keyboard. I would move it later.

"So you brought me enough food to feed five people?" The coffee mug and water bottle took up less than a quarter of the large tray. Three ceramic bowls filled the rest of the space, all three overflowing. One with fruit, one with chocolates and one with pastries.

"I knew this would be too much, but I didn't know what you would prefer, so I thought I'd rather bring too much than too little." She chose a chocolate and unwrapped it. "I know that I need a lot of energy food when I'm studying."

"I'm not studying."

She snorted. "You might as well be. This is such brainiac work that my little brain would fry in the first five minutes. Nah, I'd rather paint or sketch."

I was unsure how to reply to her statement. Or whether I should reply. Instead I took the coffee and enjoyed the aroma as I brought the mug to my mouth. The coffee was perfect and exactly what I needed. Nikki didn't seem in a rush to leave, taking another chocolate and unwrapping it.

I searched for an appropriate conversation starter. I didn't imagine she would be interested in the intriguing political complexities of this case. I chose personal interest. "What are you busy with?"

"I'm helping Tim. We are checking the provenance of some of the art in the conference room. It's totes cool. Did you know that when the Mona Lisa was stolen from the Louvre in 1911, they thought Pablo Picasso was guilty? They like arrested him and everything. They even arrested his friend, some poet, as well. Another fun fact, it took them two years to get the painting back. In that time, more than six reproductions were sold as the original. Isn't that cool? Oh, and they let Picasso and the poet go quite quickly. Must have been embarrassing to arrest the wrong people." She smiled and unwrapped another chocolate.

It was good to see her relaxed and enjoying something. When she had come into my life, it had been under a lot of hardship and anxiety. She had a radiant character, an innocence I did not often come across. For me it was a novelty and an uncommon thrill to be a witness to this personality. She continued to tell me about the two paintings she and Tim had been researching, but I wasn't paying attention to her words. As I often did, I simply enjoyed her zest.

"You're doing it again." Her hands were on her hips. "You're looking at me in that strange way. What did I do now?"

"Nothing, and that is why I am looking at you. It is refreshing to look at someone so open and guileless."

"Oh." She frowned. "Okay. I think."

She was uncomfortable and I didn't want that. I didn't

know how to change that, so I asked the question that had been in the back of my mind. "Where's Colin?"

"He's helping Phillip and Mister Manny solve that big art theft." Whenever Manny was being particularly difficult or rude, she stopped calling him by his first name.

"He's helping Manny? Are they arguing?"

"All the time." She laughed and rested her buttocks on my desk. I bit down on my jaw. I didn't want most of my communication with Nikki to be telling her what she couldn't do when she was with me. It was hard. She didn't notice my distress. "Francine is not really helping, either. She's pouring fuel on that fire. Why does she tease Mister Manny like that?"

"I don't know. She seems to enjoy it immensely."

"Maybe she likes him."

"Of course she likes him."

"No. I mean, likes him." She drew out the 'like' and widened her eyes in a meaningful way. I didn't know what that meaning was.

"Could you please ask her to come here?" I needed her expertise with the Libreville Dignity Foundation's banking statements. Those files were on display on the other monitors. Since I'd finished with the video clips, I was going to work on the finances next. I'd made some interesting discoveries and I wanted Francine's input.

Nikki gave me a genuine smile and winked at me before she grabbed three more chocolates and left with a very light step. Meeting Nikki had once made me wonder what it would've been like to live a carefree life. The thought of such a lifestyle had sent me into an intense panic. It had taken a full Mozart concerto and an additional étude before I had felt in control again.

I turned to my computer to organise my thoughts. Explaining my reasoning to other people always required forethought and energy. I had just opened another spreadsheet when the jingling of Francine's bracelets came closer.

"What's up, girlfriend?" She pulled Colin's chair closer and sat down next to me. "Ooh, chocolates! Can I have some?" She immediately started searching through the colourfully wrapped pralines.

"Why do you even ask?"

Her eyes widened when she saw a specific wrapping. "To be polite. But I knew you would say yes. You don't like chocolates."

"That's only partially true. I do like chocolate, but not these."

"You're such a snob." She sat back and bit half of the praline. Some of the liqueur centre dripped on her fingers and she sucked it off. "Hmm. These are really good."

I wasn't going to get into another debate about chocolate. The last time we had been in a restaurant, Francine had taken great offence when I had pointed out that normal milk chocolate often contained sixty or more insect fragments per hundred grams, the majority being cockroach fragments. She'd avoided me for two days after that.

"The Foundation's finances." I pointed to the monitors. "I've seen the finances of Rousseau & Rousseau's clients, so I know the average annual donations given to charities. Very few individuals would donate substantial amounts. Usually the amounts are just enough to impress their peers."

"Or for a tax deduction." She put the other half of the chocolate in her mouth.

"That too. These donations to the Libreville Dignity

Foundation were made by individuals and companies. I haven't looked into the companies yet, so I can't say whether those were legitimate donations or not."

"How big were these donations?"

"Hundreds of thousands, millions and in one case seven million euro."

"Oh, my God. That's lots of money. What did the charity do with it?"

"See that?" I highlighted an amount. "This was transferred to an offshore account."

Francine leaned back, her eyes narrowed. "Don't tell me. Samoa?"

"Yes. So far, I've isolated thirteen account numbers that had frequent transactions to and from the Foundation's account. It includes the accounts I had before. But I have no names for the owners of those accounts. There's another thing."

"What?" she asked when I took too long changing windows. I opened the statement I was looking for.

"What do you see?" It had taken a Mozart minuet before my mind had registered what was now on the screen. I highlighted the key numbers to help Francine.

She jumped out of her chair, her hand on her mouth.

"Oh, my God." She repeated this phrase a few times as she stared at the screen. "How did we not see this before?"

"It's hidden in a sub-account, made to look unimportant. It's made to look like anything but a transaction."

She shook her index finger at the monitor. "Eighty-nine million euro is not unimportant."

"That's true. I looked at it and all that money came from those thirteen accounts. These were the files that were deleted from the Foundation's financial folders. They left no trace of the sub-account and its transactions."

"I'm going to find out who owns those accounts." Her lips were set in determined lines. "I need to list their names."

Her statement reminded me that I had made a list of the people who had made donations to The Foundation. In the more benign income and expenses columns of the Foundations spreadsheets, the donors' names were listed next to the amounts. I grabbed the notepad lying in front of my keyboard and paged through it.

"What? What are you looking for?" Francine leaned closer to look at my notes. I moved away from her and tilted my notepad to afford only me a view.

"I recognise some of the names." My voice tapered off as I got the two different pages I was looking for. My memory was serving me well. "Here they are. Francois Bonhomme, Gilles Comtois, Serge Perreault and Thierry St Martin. All of them have donated significant amounts to the Foundation and they have also been Minister Savreux's guests. It doesn't mean they own one of the thirteen accounts, but it is worth looking into."

"Those guys had kinky sex in Savreux office? Definitely not a coincidence. I wonder if Savreux was blackmailing them. Or it could've been the price they had to pay for their fetish."

"I find that hard to believe. Who would pay four hundred thousand dollars for a sexual fantasy?"

"Plenty of men. If they have that kind of money." A deep frown appeared on her face. "Please, please, please tell me none of those girls were underage."

"I don't believe so. There were a few who looked in their early twenties, but most women looked older."

"Makeup can do that, you know."

"I was looking at their nonverbal cues, Francine. Those women wanted to be there. Their motivation might have been money and not pleasure, but not once did I notice cues that were worrisome. A few were less than pleased with the way the men looked, but never indicated the desire to leave. They also didn't appear under the influence of a narcotic." I didn't think I could have watched such footage.

"Did you watch all of those videos closely?"

"No, I didn't, but I didn't need to. The time before they started doing anything sexual was enough to get an accurate reading on both parties."

She exhaled loudly and stared at the monitors again. "Okay. If you are sure."

"I'm sure." I found it fascinating that someone with morals and ethics as dubious as Minister Savreux's could play host to sexual fantasies without any underaged girls. This dichotomy was what made us such as psychological beings an interesting study.

"Wait. I've seen those account numbers before." Francine leaned forward to get a closer look at the thirteen numbers from the sub-account. After a few seconds, she turned her head and smiled at me. "Look at us, you remember names and I remember account numbers I've seen before. Aren't we just a sexy memory bank?"

Countless times I didn't know how to respond to something Francine had said. It was better to stay on topic. "Where did you see those account numbers before?"

"I'll show you." She got up. "Give me a sec. I need to get my laptop. I'll be back in a flash."

I watch her run out of my viewing room on ten-centimetre-high heels. Even running, Francine looked elegant and would attract the attention of every man she passed. She must have left her laptop in the conference room since it took her much longer than a 'flash' to be back.

"Got it. Look here." She walked back into my room with long strides, sat down and frowned at my desk. She moved the tray with snacks out of the way and put her laptop there. "These are the numbers from the wine cellar files and those Word tables. There are amazing amounts."

"Which numbers look the same?" I was losing patience with her explanation.

Using my computer, she scrolled around until she found what she was looking for and pointed at the Foundation's sub-account. "Look there. On the thirteenth of August 2002, the Foundation received eight hundred and sixty thousand euro from an account with these numbers." She turned her laptop until I could see the screen, and highlighted a row of numbers. "This Word document has only numbers, but the account number is there and the amount too."

"It doesn't mean much."

"It wouldn't if it were the only number. But look here." She showed me on her laptop six more account numbers with corresponding amounts that coincided with those that had given donations to the Foundation. "I'm sure there will be more if I actually start looking for it."

"The improbability of this being coincidental far outweighs its alternative." I leaned back in my chair. "We have account numbers."

"Ooh! This will help. Give me a moment and I will break this code to give us names and more details. I was just about to crack this puppy wide open when Nikki told me you were looking for me."

Through experience, I had learned not to take any of those words literally. Especially not anything time-related. People said a moment, but it often resulted in many minutes, even hours. I left Francine to work on both computers to solve the code. I drank the last of my coffee and focussed on Mozart's Violin Concerto in E flat major.

"Who's your daddy? Huh? Huh?" Francine's triumphant statement drew me out of the concerto. She had adopted a few words and expressions from Vinnie's lexicon.

"Did you decode it?" I dropped my feet to the floor. I couldn't remember folding my legs under me.

"I did. Here." She pushed her laptop towards me, the rubber feet under it squeaking on my desk. I knew the look I gave her was not friendly when I picked up the laptop and placed it parallel to my keyboard. Francine didn't say anything about my need to have things in a certain way, at a specific angle. It made her more than merely tolerable as a friend, despite her frequent lapses into irrational theories.

I was impressed with how much she had done in the forty minutes I had been listening to Mozart in my head. The numbers that had previously been in the Word document from Minister Savreux's wine cellar were now neatly arranged in a spreadsheet. Not only were there dates next to the transactions, but she had also found a way to decode the names.

"All of these transactions were made prior to 1990," I said.

"Actually all the transactions were between 1983 and 1989."

"We need to identify this company." The last forty minutes had not gone to waste. Separate bits of information I had collected were starting to fuse together to create a better view of this case. "Look for international companies in Gabon that would have had this kind of turnover in the years between 1983 and 1989."

"Gabon?" She pulled her laptop back, put it at a distracting angle and started working. "Well, what do you know? We have fifteen international companies in Gabon that fit that bill."

She turned her laptop so I could see the screen. I wasn't surprised when I recognised the third name on the list. "It is Elf. All of this has some connection to Elf."

"The oil company that no longer exists?"

"It still exists, but merged with another company, putting it under different management and control." I thought about this some more. "I suppose it could be argued that technically it no longer exists."

"Um, what do you think Elf has to do with Savreux's murder and the art in the conference room?"

"I don't know yet. I have more important questions. Why did Minister Savreux have Elf's financial data in an encrypted form hidden in his rented wine cellar? Who transferred that money into the thirteen accounts? And who did those accounts belong to? Was it a person working for Elf?"

"Are you sure these financials are Elf's?"

"It is highly unlikely that it would be any other company's. Not one of the fourteen other companies on your list ever came up in our investigation. Savreux has a strong connection to Motte. I have them on video, discussing some plan." I sucked in a breath. "René Motte worked for Elf from 1983, became head legal advisor in 1985 and left in early 1989."

"The exact time frame of these encoded finances."

We fell quiet for a few seconds.

"But that doesn't help us with knowing who killed Savreux," Francine said.

"Dukwicz did." Had she not watched that video?

"I know. I know. What I mean is, who ordered Dukwicz to kill Savreux. And why."

"We don't have evidence that is not circumstantial to link all this information." I closed my eyes and thought about it a little more. When I opened my eyes, Francine was no longer sitting next to me. Colin had taken her place and was eating one of the pastries Nikki had brought. Francine was sitting on Colin's desk, Vinnie standing in the door and Manny leaning against one of my cabinets. When he saw me looking at him, he straightened.

"Supermodel's just told us what you two have been up to." Manny blinked a few times. "Eighty-nine million bloody euro."

"I need to see the president of Gabon." I knew she would have answers to some of my questions.

"Whoa there, Doctor Face-reader. Why on Pete's earth would you want to see the president of Gabon?"

Having spent the last twenty minutes in my head made it difficult to return to communicating with others. It always took me a while to move out of my head into my surroundings. I breathed deeply a few times while doing that. When I knew I would be able to express myself without drawing Manny's ire, I cleared my throat.

"We know that President Mariam Boussombo is in Strasbourg at the moment. She was one of the biggest supporters of an investigation into Elf's activities in Gabon and the corruption surrounding it. All these separate elements indicate that her presence in Strasbourg has something to do with this." I waved my hand at the monitors. "She's here to speak at the headquarters of the International Institute of Human Rights, and to speak to the Senate in favour of the No Secrets law. She also has a few meetings with charity organisations, including the Libreville Dignity Foundation. I want to speak to her."

"And say what, Doc?"

I crossed my arms, realised what I had done and uncrossed them. "Don't look at me like that, Manny. You know that I can be diplomatic and phrase my questions and statements carefully to not give offense."

"I know that, but we can't just knock on the president's hotel door and have a little natter with her. There is protocol to deal with."

"Then deal with it." I was convinced she was the key to understanding and interpreting all the evidence we'd gathered up to now. "I want to speak to her as soon as possible. Tonight even."

"Not asking for much, now are you?" Manny grumbled, but I knew he was already thinking how to arrange a meeting with President Mariam Boussombo. "Why do you want to speak to her?"

"I think her life is in danger. Remember I told you about the Gabonese politician, Minister Paul Ngondet, visiting Minister Savreux? He was talking about a woman who was insisting on an independent commission to look into corruption. He also said that it would benefit everyone if she were to 'dance her last dance'. I googled that phase to see what different interpretations it might have, and I saw a very disturbing meaning. What if they were planning her assassination?"

"Holy hell, Doc." Manny put both hands on his head. "Now we're adding a bloody hit on a president to the list of current disastrous situations?"

Francine was looking at her nails, stretching her fingers. "Do you want to know what I think?"

"No!" Vinnie, Manny and Colin spoke at the same time. I smiled at the men's solidarity in this odd issue, and Francine's unconvincing anger at their reaction.

"Doc, we're going to have to be careful with this."

"I know. Just because I am not naturally charming or manipulative doesn't mean that I don't understand the strong undercurrents of international politics."

Manny nodded, his eyes losing focus as he rubbed his hands over his head a few times. I had full confidence that he was going to organise a meeting with Gabon's president within a few hours. I turned back to my monitors. I also needed to strategise if I wanted to be prepared for a diplomatic meeting with a president.

"Doc G! Doc G!" Nikki ran into the room, her breathing erratic. "Oh good. Everyone's here. I got another DM."

Chapter SEVENTEEN

Nikki shoved her phone at me. "Take it. I don't want this. I think I'm buying a new phone after this stupid case."

Colin took the phone before Manny could grab it. I wanted to ask Nikki about her reasoning behind getting a new phone, but knew the latest direct message took precedence.

"Well, Frey? What does it say?" Manny moved from one foot to the other.

"It's another address." Colin tilted the phone. "*Manet @ 381 Rue Danielle. High five, low rectitude.*"

"The address is all good and dandy. What the bleeding hell does the rest mean? What is 'rectitude'?"

"Moral virtue," I said absently. "Also rightness in principle or conduct."

"If anyone is interested?" Colin waited until he had everyone's attention. "Manet's Chez Tortini was also stolen from the Gardner museum in Boston. Anyone want to bet that this is the Chez Tortini?"

"It's too obvious, dude. I'm not the brains in this outfit, but even I know that it will be the Chaz Tortellini."

Colin smiled at Vinnie's many incorrect statements. The tall man didn't have my IQ, but he was not dim-witted. He had the type of intelligence that Francine called street smarts. I would unquestioningly accept Vinnie's advice about situations outside of my expertise. He knew how to deal with dangerous people, violent situations and even how to make friends with a chilli dog vendor. Those were innate skills I sorely lacked.

"Jenny?"

I looked up to see everyone watching me. "What?"

"What do you think about the last sentence?"

I played with the four words in my mind. "Nothing. It's simply too little to go by. At least in that other case we had, the professor sent us decent cryptic clues. These are just a few words, no context, and we're expected to make assumptions. It almost appears as if this person is trying to sound intelligent or cryptic just to gain our attention. I don't even know what to make of the high five."

Vinnie and Nikki looked at each other, smiled and slapped each other's palms high in the air.

"That's a high five, Jen-girl." Vinnie nudged Nikki with his shoulder. "A lower high five for me, because punk is so short."

"I'm not short. You're freakishly tall." She punched him on his shoulder. Vinnie smiled.

"We need to know who owns this house." My mind was working at top speed now. "The last two addresses gave us Minister Claude Savreux and René Motte. We've been able to connect them to the Libreville Dignity Foundation, Elf and Gabon. This next person might be another connection to these two men and all the other elements in this case. It might help us find the nucleus of this case—what, or who, everything is revolving around."

"And what these idiots are planning," Manny said. He rubbed his stubbly cheek for a few seconds and looked at me. "To show you just how trusting I am, I'm going to let Frey handle this one."

"Rock on, handsome." Francine kissed her fingertips and blew over it towards Manny.

He rolled his eyes. "I've been getting calls from little Henri all day. Apparently he now wants to meet with me at Minister Antoine Lefebvre's offices. I've got to handle this to keep them off our backs. Frey, you go to this address. Take the criminal with you. Do not, I repeat, do not get caught. That task force has it in for you and I don't know why yet. If you get caught, I don't know what the top brass will do to get you out of their clutches."

"Oh, keep your panties on, Millard. I'm not going to get caught." Even though Colin attempted annoyance, the acceptance of Manny's trust was there on his face. I wondered why he wasn't more concerned about the task force. "Vin will back me up. We'll be in and out before you can say, 'bloody hell'."

Everyone laughed, except Manny. "Watch your back, Frey. You too, criminal."

"Aw, old man. Look at you caring about us."

Manny ignored Vinnie. "Doc, I'm going to do my best to get you your meeting with the president of Gabon. I don't promise anything, but I'll try. For now, I want you to stay here. You don't leave. Neither does Nikki. Supermodel, you also stay here. I don't want to worry about you gals."

I shut out Francine's weak arguments against Manny's chauvinism, expecting the little women to stay in the kitchen and cook. She wasn't making sense and I wanted to get back to my computers. Manny's orders had been rational and I had seen no reason to dispute his decisions.

"Jenny, will you be okay here?"

I studied Colin's expression. "Why are you asking me when

you know I'll be safe and content working in my viewing room?"

"Double-checking."

I turned towards my computers. "I can see that you are comfortable leaving me here. You should trust that. Go and find out whose house is at 381 Rue Danielle."

"Yes, ma'am." His tone was light.

I looked back at him until all his lightness turned serious. "Please be safe."

He leaned closer to me until our noses touched. "I'll make sure to come back to you in one piece, love."

"I'll make super sure of it, Jen-girl," Vinnie said from the door. "I've got my man's back."

A few more unnecessary reassurances were given before the three men left. Nikki settled herself between the two filing cabinets with a sketchpad and Francine returned to her computers to find the names of the thirteen account holders. I sat back in my chair, crossed my legs and allowed Mozart's Clarinet Concerto in A major to organise my thoughts. The different threads of this case were beginning to untangle as we discovered more pertinent information. I hoped that Colin and Vinnie would return with even more information to help infuse more sense and connect the unconnected elements of this case.

"Love, we're back." Colin's soft touch and relaxed tone pulled me out of the concerto. He was sitting next to me, dressed in black, a genuine smile lifting his cheeks. "It was a quick in and out. The maid was home, but Vin kept her busy."

"She wants to meet me for coffee later this week." Vinnie was leaning against the doorway. "Poor thing is going to be heartbroken when I don't show up."

I took my time studying first Vinnie and then Colin. Both were unharmed from this recent breaking and entering. I was annoyed at the intense relief I felt. "Was the painting there?"

"Oh, yes." Colin took out his smartphone and swiped the screen a few times. He handed it to me. "Hanging as large as life above the bed in the master bedroom. I got a nice close look while Vinnie was flirting. It's the original Manet, Jenny. The real thing."

The picture of the painting was small, but clear enough for me to see the man dressed in a black coat and top hat, sitting at a desk, writing something. Next to his hand holding the pen was a glass, and he was looking directly at the painter. It was simple and beautiful.

"This dude has some serious dough... er, money. Another rich asshole." Vinnie folded his arms. "Poor people commit crimes out of desperation. I get that. These rich idiots who commit crimes for the fun of it? They're bad seed, man."

I inhaled, but Colin stopped me with his hand on my arm. "Don't. You've had this argument with him before and it went around in circles for hours, remember?"

I remembered. Vinnie couldn't see how his crimes fell in the same category as the ones he despised. For more than a year, I had suspected that Vinnie was committing crimes without any moral motivation, unlike Colin. Reappropriating art was Colin's forte. He stole back property that was taken from their rightful owners. Vinnie never talked about his activities, but the more we worked together, the more I realised he had a strict moral code. He seemed to take great pleasure in betraying the trust of his criminal friends to other criminals in order to damage reputations, product quality and even lead them to be arrested. He had been successful in doing this while maintaining the appearance of a ruthless criminal.

"Jenny?"

"I'm listening. Vinnie is wasting time talking about all the expensive electronics in the house. Whose house is that?"

"A Monsieur J.L. Legrange."

"J.L.?"

"There were a few certificates in his home office for that name."

"I don't know why people use initials for names," Vinnie said. "Are they ashamed of their names or something?"

"Sometimes." I'd had a classmate at university whose name was initials. It had triggered a bout of research. "For others it creates gender obscurity. For a writer, it is sometimes better to not have a gender attached to their name if they write in certain genres. Men writing romance novels, women writing thrillers. What is this J.L. Legrange's profession?"

"Those certificates were all legal stuff, so I reckon he's a lawyer."

"I've got him here." Francine walked into the viewing room, holding her laptop in front of her. She sat down on the third chair in my room and settled the computer on her lap. "As soon as the guys got in, I started checking out the name. His full name is Jean Louis Legrange. Maybe he felt too average with every Tom, Dick and Harry in France being named Jean Louis."

"Why would…"

"Ooh, sorry, girlfriend. That's just a silly saying. Ignore that. I've got juicier stuff here." She pointed with both hands to her computer screen. "Our J.L. was René Motte's lawyer during the Elf trials."

"René Motte was prosecuted?" Colin asked.

"Yes." I frowned. Had I not told him this? "Even though he left the oil company before France took ownership, he had brokered quite a few deals between the French government, Elf and the Gabonese government. Because of that, he was included in the investigations, indicted on a few crimes and tried. I hadn't thought to check who represented him during the trial."

"You can't think of everything, Jenny."

"I should." I put aside my self-aimed annoyance and focussed on what I had learned. "The case against René Motte was quite strong, but it was not because of his actions. It was the deals he had brokered and the people he had been connected to. The prosecutor had built her case entirely on those facts, because she couldn't find anything in his financial history, in his correspondence or anywhere else that incriminated him."

"So it was mostly circumstantial evidence."

"Yes, and that was why he was acquitted."

"By the one and only J.L." Francine tapped her nails on her computer. "Want to hear what other dirt I have on J.L.?"

"Shoot," Vinnie said. He used this word often enough that I had early on surmised its meaning from the context.

"Like the other two men, he also studied law. But he's quite a bit older than Savreux and Motte, so by the time they got their first internships, he was already working his way up to top lawyer in his company."

"Where?" I asked.

"In Paris. It's one of those fancy legal companies that only work for the rich and famous. And sometimes they come down from their thrones to do a pro bono case for the poor people so they can look good." She waved her hand and her bracelets jingled. "Anyhoo, in 1995, he became one of the top guys in another legal firm, the one that represented quite a few of the forty executives, politicians and intermediaries prosecuted during the Elf trials. Motte was only one of his clients, but he won most of the other cases too. He has a very good reputation as a white-collar criminal lawyer."

I thought about this while Vinnie complained about rich people. He was very opinionated today, the affluent his focus. Next time, it might be another demographic.

"What do these three men have in common other than stolen paintings from the Gardner heist?" I asked.

"They studied law. Ooh, let me quickly check." Francine typed faster than I did and soon her nose crinkled. "They didn't all study at the same university. Wait. Wait. Oh, my God."

All of us leaned towards Francine, waiting for her to continue.

"All three of these men worked at FGMB in Paris. It is that top legal company I mentioned earlier, and it's the place where they all began. Hmm. Let me just make sure." She clicked around on her computer a few times. "Yup. Savreux and Motte started there as interns in 1980. At that time, J.L. was already working there. I don't know what position he held, or if he even worked with the other two, but that puts them in the same company more than thirty years ago. As we know, Motte didn't go for the lawyer thing. He left FGMB after only seven months in the company, went into engineering and onto the fertile fields of Elf."

While Francine was talking, I looked for their photos and put it up on the three centre monitors. I tilted my head and studied these men who shared a history that stretched over thirty years. Colin shifted in his chair and I glanced at him. His expression caught my attention. "What do you see?"

"This." He took his smartphone from my lap where I had absentmindedly put it. Four swipes later he handed it back to me. "I took a few photos while I was in J.L.'s house. This photo was in his home office in an obscure place. It looked like J.L. wanted to have this photo around, but not allow anyone else to see it. He had it pushed deep in between books, almost unnoticeable to any visitor."

I looked at the photo on the small screen.

"Let me put this on one of the monitors." Francine held out her hand and I gave her the phone. A few seconds later, she clicked around on my computer. The monitor below the three with the men's photos filled with a portrait of four men in their early twenties in an obvious gay mood. Their hairstyles and clothing indicated that the photo was taken a few decades ago. Possible the late seventies, early eighties.

Two of the young men had their arms around each other's shoulders, one was holding up two fingers behind another's head, and the fourth was almost folded double, laughing and pointing at the camera.

"The guy laughing looks like Savreux." Francine lifted one eyebrow. "He was quite a stunner. Look at those legs."

They were all dressed in shorts and t-shirts, next to a lake somewhere. The area looked isolated, perfect for young student men looking to spend holidays away from the crowds.

"The one making the rabbit ears looks like J.L. and the smaller guy laughing could be Motte." Vinnie was standing behind me. "Those bastards have been friends for a long time. Who's the other guy?"

"We'll have to find out. That makes it four men who might be in on this conspiracy," Francine said. For once I didn't correct her when she mentioned a conspiracy. This far-reaching case now had all the earmarks qualifying it as one of her favourite topics.

"It makes five people, Francine. Not four. The fifth is most likely also a man." I zoomed in on the young man laughing. Motte. "He knows the photographer. They all know the photographer. The familiarity in their postures, the easy laughter, and Motte pointing at the camera like that? They know this person."

"This means we need two more names."

Something I had said triggered another thought, but it was hovering just outside of my grasp. I closed my eyes and ignored Francine's suggestions on how to find the other two men. Mozart's Piano Sonata no. 16 in B Flat Major just started playing in my mind when I made the connection. "*High five, low rectitude.*' These might be the five that direct message was talking about."

"My God, you are right." Francine straightened in her chair. "The three men we know all hold very high positions. It stands to reason that the unidentified man in this picture is also some VIP, as well as Mister Mystery Photographer."

Francine's silly name brought to mind the mystery man in two of Minister Savreux's home office videos. I wasn't going to voice it in fear of Francine's enthusiastic hypothesising, but I wondered if he could be the same man as the photographer in the thirty-something-year-old photo.

Another thought surfaced from my subconscious with such force that I gasped. I ignored Colin and Francine's questions and frantically paged through my notes. I found the page and turned to Francine. "Can you trace national identity numbers without anyone noticing?"

"Is the Pope Catholic?"

"Yes, he is."

Francine's smile was wide and genuine. Her fingers

hovered above the laptop's keyboard. "Give me the numbers, girlfriend."

When I gave her the second number, Nikki got up and stood next to Vinnie. "You're the coolest, Doc G."

It took another three minutes before we had confirmation. Francine leaned back in her chair. "Would you believe that. Those numbers used as Twitter handles were actually ID numbers. Good catch, girlfriend. Four twitter handles and four names."

"It gives us one new name, Remi Dubois. I should've seen this earlier. We could've had these names much earlier and possibly have made more progress by now." I was furious with myself. One of my greatest strengths had been noticing anomalous data, recognising patterns and fitting seemingly disconnected pieces together. Was I losing my focus?

"Are you one hundred percent sure that we would've solved this case by now if we'd had those names?" Colin leaned back in his chair, his arms folded.

I thought about this. "No."

"Well, then. Stop blaming yourself." He uncrossed his arms and lowered his chin, making sure I could read his expressions. "Francine works daily with people's ID numbers. Why didn't she see it? Why didn't I or Millard see this? You're not in this alone, Jenny."

The relief at hearing his reasoning was overwhelming. My life had been rife with challenges, one of the largest allowing myself to not be perfect. It was hard. I swallowed and nodded. "Thank you."

"Okay, now let's find out who this Remi Dubois is," Colin said

"He was the bank manager for a few banks in Paris and

later in Strasbourg. He died three years ago from a stroke. He was only fifty-eight when he died. That's really young for a stroke." Francine scrolled down the page she was looking at. "Ah, ladies and gentlemen, guess where he worked in his first job?"

"FGMB? The same as the other three?" I asked.

"The one and only, my pretty." She tapped the monitor with her index fingernail. "He studied finance and worked in FGMB's accounting department, at exactly the same time as our other three bad men worked there."

"What are their more recent connections?" Colin asked.

"This might take a while." Francine's fingers were already flying over the keys. I turned to my computer and started researching my line of thought. From the corner of my eye, I saw Colin get up and take his chair to this desk. For more than an hour the three of us were working on our computers, speaking very little. Vinnie and Nikki had left after mumbling something about food.

"Oh, my God." Francine's soft exclamation drew my attention away from my search.

"What?" Colin asked from his desk.

"President Godard also worked at FGMB."

"At the same time as the others?"

"No. Much later. The others all left before 1990. He started working there in 1991."

"Can we work on a timeline?" I tired when people jumped from one thought to another. The same applied to conversations about time. "It would be easier if we can develop some pattern in their behaviour. We need to find pivotal events in their lives, their personal and private lives."

"Cool." Francine shifted in her chair. "I'll start. We already know the four bad guys started working at FGMB in 1980."

"We've been over this." I loathed repetition. "Let's start in the later eighties, after René Motte was already working in Elf."

"Okay. The only thing I have here on any of them before Motte lost his job in 1989 was that J.L. divorced his third wife. You'll call it petty gossip, I know."

"Maybe not." I leaned my head back. "If we work on the hypothesis that these men were involved in the Boston heist, we need to look for a motive. In the year 1989, we have Minister Savreux being passed over for promotion, René Motte losing his job and J.L. Legrange's divorce. Those three events could be motive enough for them to combine their energies to commit such a crime."

"If they sold some of those paintings, it definitely would've helped with J.L.'s divorce settlement. That woman took him to the cleaners."

"What does that mean?"

"She took almost all of J.L.'s money." Francine's smile was malicious. "I wonder if he deserved it. If he's lost three wives to divorces, one has to wonder what kind of arsehole husband he is."

"What do you have on the bank manager, Francine?" Colin rolled his chair closer. "I didn't find anything interesting on him. He was a workaholic with nothing interesting on the internet. He seemed to keep to himself."

"That's what I got as well. But I didn't really look hard. I'm too shocked by the president's connection to FGMB."

"It's a tenuous connection." I couldn't see negative implications. "If it is such a prestigious company, one could safely assume that any young lawyer would like to start his career there. President Godard had no contact with those men while working there."

"You sound very sure."

"I'm only as sure as my research. I looked through the numerous articles on the president and could find no early connections. Later on, Minister Savreux obviously had contact with the president due to their political careers. René Motte's connection is also obvious, being on the president's political party think tank." Something was bothering me. "What about more recent links between these four men? Do we have any?"

"Nope. Not until Savreux and Motte started the Foundation."

"We need to look into this. There might be more that could help us solve this. I also need to know exactly what connection Minster Paul Ngondet from Gabon has to any and all of them."

"I'll get onto that, girlfriend." She pointed at the team room with her chin. "I've got a programme running to get those thirteen names."

"What thirteen names?" Colin asked. Francine explained to him about the offshore bank accounts receiving money from Elf, and the many transactions between those accounts and the Libreville Dignity Foundation's sub-account.

The annoying song about a poker face coming from my smartphone interrupted the conversation. I took my phone from its place next to my keyboard and swiped the screen.

"Hello, Manny."

"Doc. Get ready. We're going to see your president."

"I don't have a president."

A grunt sounded over the phone. "The president of

Gabon, missy. I'm picking you up in fifteen minutes. Don't come downstairs. I'll come get you. And tell Frey that neither he nor the criminal can come with. I had to cash in a lot of favours to get this done."

The call disconnected before I could comment or argue. In light of this new information, I wondered what added questions I could ask President Mariam Boussombo.

Chapter EIGHTEEN

After a distressing twenty minutes with the security detail outside the hotel suite of Gabon's president, I was thoroughly unnerved. They had insisted on frisking me and I had refused. I didn't care that I would be fully dressed while they patted me down. I was not going to have a stranger touch me to ensure someone's safety, not when I had the trust of the president of France and his wife. My practiced diplomacy had lasted one full minute. Manny had interfered after my second explanation had still confused these people. I had been about to comment on the deficiency in their vocabulary and comprehension, but Manny had interrupted and had used impressive finesse to convince the four men and one woman at the door that I was harmless.

I was now seated in the living area of the modest but elegant suite and Manny was walking around, attempting not to appear restless. The president of Gabon was still in a meeting in the office to our left, but we had been informed that she would not be long. Manny stopped in front of the large windows overlooking the river, his back to me.

"Doc, you're going to have to try more diplomacy."

"With the president, of course I will."

He turned around. "Why not with the guards outside? They could have easily prevented us from meeting with President Boussombo."

"Don't be silly. You would never have allowed that. Daniel and his team are far better trained than those five people.

Their inability to take note of your deception cues was deplorable. If they are to protect an important person effectively, they need to be more competent in their understanding of nonverbal communication, but also of verbal communication. They didn't even understand 'incursion of my rights and privacy'."

"Doc, *I* don't understand 'incursion'."

"You're lying. You might fool most people, but not me. Firstly, I am the best in my field and secondly, I know you. Combined, it leaves you at a great disadvantage if you attempt to deceive me."

"I can't believe I'm having this argument with you." He turned back to the window. "You are impossible."

"Without seeing your expression, I'm not sure, but your tone is telling me you approve of my impossibility."

Manny shook his head and snorted. The heavy office door opened and I stood up as two women entered the living room.

"Genevieve, what a pleasure to see you." Isabelle Godard, the first lady of France, came to me with her arms open. In her early fifties, she looked much younger and had a natural beauty many women spent fortunes to obtain. Her dark slacks and stylish rust-coloured sweater emphasised her athletic figure. She stopped two feet in front of me, dropped her arms and kissed the air as if it were my cheeks. This was the tenth time I'd seen her this year. She had greeted me like this the last nine times. The delight expressed on her face mirrored my feelings at meeting her here. I liked her. She respected my non-neurotypical idiosyncrasies.

"Isabelle, I did not expect to see you here. It is good to see you."

"And I you, my dear." She turned to the African woman

behind her with a genuine smile. "Madame Mariam Boussombo, this is my highly esteemed colleague, Doctor Genevieve Lenard. Genevieve, this is President Mariam Boussombo."

The slightly overweight woman stepped closer, curiosity in every muscle on her face. When she didn't extend her hand to greet me, I knew Isabelle had told her about me. I didn't study her as obtrusively as I did Colin or Manny, but I took a moment to assess her nonverbal cues. There was nothing indicating deception or discomfort. Her facial muscles were relaxed, her smile genuine and her posture open.

"Doctor Lenard, it really is a pleasure to meet you. Isabelle has told me so much about you."

"Only good things, of course." Isabelle looked excited about this introduction. I didn't know why she felt it important to reassure me about what she had told Mariam Boussombo. I didn't care.

"It's a pleasure to meet you too, President Boussombo. Thank you for making the time to meet with us." I gestured to Manny who had stepped closer. "This is my colleague, Colonel Manfred Millard."

The change in President Mariam Boussombo was immediate. Her open curiosity was shut down with a skill that I'd observed in the best poker players. I was witnessing all the markers of social politeness as Mariam Boussombo held out her hand and went through the formal introductions with Manny. It was astounding to see the change in this woman, and I knew it wasn't Manny who had caused it. It was his gender. Something had happened in this woman's life to have made her overly cautious around men. This going to be problematic.

"Manny, you have to leave."

Manny swung around and stared at me. "I beg your pardon?"

"You have to leave."

He closed his eyes and his lips thinned even though they were trembling slightly. When he looked at me, he was communicating a warning, his voice low. "Doc, remember what we talked about."

"Of course I remember. President Boussombo doesn't feel comfortable with you here, which means she won't trust us with any information and our visit here will be a waste of time. You have to leave."

Manny glanced at the two women standing across from me. We were standing in a triangle, Manny was on the outside. Our body positioning had already excluded him.

"Doc." This was one of the very few times Manny spoke to me through his teeth. His face was turning red and the *supratrochlear* artery on his forehead was becoming more visible. He stared at me for long enough that even I considered it impolite. I stared back. His bottom jaw protruded and he lowered his head to look at me from under his eyebrows. "I will be right outside that door with the other security. Be diplomatic."

He greeted the other two women with a nod and stalked to the door. All three of us were watching his angry strides and the controlled manner with which he closed the door. I had known Manny long enough to be well aware of the fact that I was going to receive a long lecture when we left. The moment the door closed behind him, Isabelle and President Mariam Boussombo burst out laughing. They turned to me with expectation. When I didn't respond in the manner they had expected, they laughed harder.

Isabelle was the first to quieten down. Her brow was

showing cues of concern. "Genevieve, you know that we weren't laughing at you, right?"

"No, I don't. I have no idea what you were laughing at."

"Oh, Doctor Lenard, you are such a delight." Mariam Boussombo dabbed at the moisture under her eyes and waved at the sofas. "Let's sit."

"Manny was sure I had offended you." I sat down on the far end of the sofa, Isabelle on the other end. President Mariam Boussombo took the deep armchair across from us. "Your behaviour indicates that I didn't. It hadn't been my intention."

"Please be assured that you did not offend me at all." Her African accent was light and lent a charming roundness to her speech. "In my line of work, I almost never come across such sincere honesty, but that wasn't what made me laugh. It was the look on Colonel Millard's face. You are in deep trouble."

"I'm always in deep trouble with him."

This made them laugh again. It gave me an odd pleasure that my honesty brought genuine enjoyment to a woman I highly respected, and a woman who had spent her life fighting to ensure better conditions for her country.

"Can I offer you something to drink?" President Boussombo shifted in her chair as if to get up.

"No, thank you."

"Isabelle?"

"Not for me, thanks Mariam."

President Boussombo settled back in her chair. "Isabelle told me you are on the spectrum. I have a twelve-year-old niece who also has autism. I think it is a great thing that you're helping Isabelle bring more awareness to the public."

Isabelle put her hand on the sofa next to me and leaned a

bit closer, but still keeping her distance. "I told her how you've spoken at six different events this year, telling people how anyone with a disability can succeed and live full lives. You're always so good when you give one of your speeches. Inspirational."

"People need to know more about autism." The corners of President Boussombo's mouth turned down. "There is so much ignorance going around and hurting people. That is one of our largest struggles in Africa. Because of our tradition, so many people believe that those with autism are possessed by demons, cursed by a witch doctor or some other superstition. My sister is now forcing my niece to go to a witch doctor to fix her autism."

"That's absurd." I scoffed at this folly. "Antiquated beliefs and superstitious rituals won't have any effect on developmental disorders or on how the brain functions."

President Boussombo laughed softly. "You're just like my niece, Linda. She tells her mom this, but my sister wants a normal daughter."

"There is no such thing as normal. Neurotypical, yes. Normal is a term that is subjective to each subculture and even smaller communities within."

"I like you." President Boussombo sat up. Her expression spoke of acceptance and trust. "Please call me Mariam."

"I'm Genevieve." I understood the social significance of what had just taken place. Once again, this reinforced my belief that there were indeed people who responded to sincere truth much better than polite dishonesty.

"So Genevieve, what can I do for you?"

"I have information that has led me to believe someone wants to kill you."

Isabelle gasped and pulled her hand back, but Mariam

laughed again. She appeared to laugh a lot. The lines next to her eyes attested to that. "My dear girl, someone's been wanting to kill me for the last twenty-seven years."

"Who?" How could she live with that level of threat all the time? And why wasn't this person caught?

"Many who's, my dear. Not just one person." She sighed. "I've made a lot of enemies on the way to where I am today. I was one of those outspoken and hated individuals who brought attention to the abuse of power in our government. That was in the eighties and early nineties. The men who were in power from the fifties to the eighties lived like kings while all the others were starving. There was little to no money spent on developing the country's economy, infrastructure and especially education and healthcare. Women were living in fear all the time, children being used as slaves or exported to neighbouring countries as soldiers. Those were horrid days."

"Mariam was part of a small group of women who stood up to those powerful men." Admiration was clear in Isabelle's tone and expression. "But she was smart. She knew that she needed international backing if she wanted to succeed."

"And we found allies in the same place we had found abusers and corruptors. Here in France were a lot of people who didn't like what their country was doing in Africa. They also wanted to aid our group in our ventures to educate women and protect children."

"That was when we became involved in a local charity organisation. It came from those days."

"Is that how long you have known each other?" More bits of information were flowing into one large stream.

"Yes, Mariam and I have been friends since long before we have been Madames."

They laughed and I saw the easy friendship between them. It was the same between Vinnie, Colin and Francine. I knew I had a bond with my three friends, even with Manny, but it wasn't easy. Not like with these two women.

I turned to Isabelle, my expression one that Manny called unsettling. "Do you trust Mariam?"

"With my life." There was no hesitation or rush to answer. It was the truth. "Why?"

"I don't think Manny would want me to share everything I know with you."

"What do you think?" Mariam asked.

I looked at her and studied her for a few moments while weighing up my options. "I think that Isabelle's trust is not easily given. I don't know you and therefore I don't trust you, but will entrust this information to you based on your friendship with Isabelle."

Her smile was genuine and warm. "Just like my lovely niece."

"Tell me how you met." Somewhere in their history I might find an important link.

"Isabelle helped us set up a local charity and it helped many women and children." She sighed. "Those early days were hard. Our main focus then was basic healthcare and we started a small health centre. The clinic was young and didn't get a lot of support. We didn't have large donations, but every little bit helped."

"When exactly was that?" I asked.

"The late nineties. We worked hard to get that clinic off the ground."

"Before Raymond went into politics ten years ago, we

discovered a charity here in Strasbourg that helps Gabonese women and children," Isabelle said.

I looked at her and saw only honesty. "You are talking about the Libreville Dignity Foundation."

"You know about this then." Still Isabelle had no deception cues. I also didn't see any suspicious micro-expressions on Mariam. "We approached them for financial aid and they took the clinic as one of their main projects. The Foundation was only a few years old then and still small. They didn't have much money to give, but they helped us as much as they could."

"They had a lot of money." I was purposefully provocative. "From the opening of the Foundation until now, eighty-nine million euro has been deposited into their accounts."

I watched their reactions and wasn't disappointed. Isabelle's *masseter* muscles lost their strength and her bottom jaw went slack, leaving her mouth open. Mariam touched her hand to her suprasternal notch, gently rubbing where her throat met her sternum.

"Where did you get those figures, Genevieve?" Isabelle asked softly.

"From Libreville Dignity Foundation's system."

It was time for me to trust the two women looking at me in shock. Before we had arrived, I had mentally prepared an abridged version of our case, and what we had learned so far. I took a deep breath and started talking. It was a challenge to not give into the compulsion to go into detail, but I managed to give them the most important points. I told them that we were breaking orders to look into Minister Savreux's death and that we believed it was connected to the 1990 Boston heist and this week's heist.

"And why do you think someone wants to kill Mariam?"

"Because I have a video of Minister Ngondet meeting with Minister Claude Savreux, saying that it would benefit everyone if she dances her last dance."

"Paul Ngondet? He said that?" Mariam's voice raised a pitch.

"Yes, exactly those words. Not once did he use your name, but logic dictates that there is no other 'her' ordering an independent commission looking into corruption."

"Where did you get that video? What else did he say?" She looked at Isabelle, her *corrugator supercilii* muscles contracting her forehead in and down. "If he prevents me from going to this meeting, he will destroy everything I have worked for."

"What meeting?" This might be the key. Both women looked at me and I saw their indecision. They wanted to trust me, but were wary.

"First tell me what else Ngondet said."

I told her word for word. "Nothing that gives us any clear idea what they are planning."

"Genevieve, what we're about to tell you is a very sensitive topic." Again Isabelle placed her hand on the sofa between us. I wondered about her need to touch me. "Very few people are privy to this information."

"My country, my continent are filled with wonderful people—people with good hearts, generous hearts." Mariam's voice was heavy with emotion, her affection for her country evident on her face. "Too many of these people live in terrible poverty, but they will give you their last chicken and their best chair if you are a guest in their house. Their strength lies in their closeness to nature, in their value for family, in their strong beliefs and their ability to laugh even when they have so little. They find joy in each other, not in what they own.

"Those are most of the people in Africa. A small minority exploit this. They abuse the power given to them and take as much as they can for themselves, callously leaving everyone else with next to nothing. If this power is not given to them freely, they take it by force. They use the country's resources to afford them a life of luxury while their people are living in inhumane conditions. In Gabon, we have difficulty reaching many villages with medical care. Education is often limited to only three years before the children are forced to work to help their families survive. If kids want an education, in certain areas they have to walk three, sometimes ten kilometres to school and back every day."

Mariam took a few deep breaths to calm herself. Her speech had gained momentum and volume as she had gone on. "As you can see, I feel deeply about this. Sadly, there are people in my country, in my government who are running a syndicate providing illegal services. To my disgust, I discovered that there are a few women involved as well. Together with the men, they take part in corrupt, unethical and horrid activities. Some of these people work with me. Every day."

Her voice broke and she looked away. I didn't need to see her expression to know she felt betrayed. That was obvious from the context. "Is that why you are here?"

She nodded. "Over the last sixteen months, I have gathered evidence of arms deals, human trafficking, art theft, slavery, and other unspeakable crimes, which I plan to give to the prosecutor of the International Criminal Court. I want these people to be prosecuted in an international court, not in Gabon. They have control over so many local law enforcement agencies and court officials that they might get a slap on the hand, at best. I want them to be in The Hague, tried in the ICC. I want the world to know what they are doing." Her voice softened. "I want my people to know that I am fighting for them."

"Is Minister Paul Ngondet one of those men?"

"Yes, he is. He doesn't know that I know about him."

"I disagree." I thought back to the video. "He knew that you had an important meeting that was going to cause him problems. What other meeting could you have to cause him difficulties?"

She thought about it. The *depressor anguli oris* muscles turned the corners of her mouth down. She looked at Isabelle. "This is a real problem. Our whole timeline has to move up."

Isabelle nodded and turned to me. "The plan was to use tomorrow's evening gala at the International Institute of Human Rights to hide Mariam's meeting with the ICC prosecutor. The meeting is set up for late tomorrow evening. Then she's going to present him with all the evidence she has gathered."

"Is there a reason why you didn't email this evidence to the head prosecutor? Do you think your emails and phones have been compromised?" I asked. "Is that why you didn't send him any of this electronically?"

"At this moment, I don't know who I can trust, Genevieve." Mariam's brow and eyes went from expressing concern to sadness. "As far as I'm concerned, only the people in this room can be trusted."

"That's good," a familiar deep voice said from the open office door. "Then you can hand all your evidence over to me."

As one, we turned to the man dressed all in black.

Dukwicz was tapping the broad side of a knife's blade on the palm of his hand. It looked like the knife he had used to stab Savreux twenty-five times. He lifted the knife and studied the blade. "And before any of you get the silly notion to start screaming like the bitches you are. Don't. I'm actually quite good at throwing knives, even if I have to say so myself."

Dark panic filled my vision. My breathing stuttered and an involuntary whimper sounded loudly in the room. I had seen what this man was capable of and it terrified me. My psychology background helped me understand how much he was enjoying my fear. I saw it around his eyes, his mouth and his dilated pupils. Other people's fear made him feel powerful, it fed his ill mind. I was giving him that pleasure.

To the other two women's credit, they didn't respond with fear. Mariam and Isabelle's breathing was even and no obvious signs of panic were evident. Yet I noticed the numerous micro-expressions indicating their alarm.

"Who are you?" Mariam asked, her voice strong and confident.

"Ask Doctor Lenard. She knows me well."

My chest tightened seeing the micro-expression of hurt and betrayal on Mariam's face. She thought I was working with Dukwicz. It was like a switch that turned off my panic and turned on my anger. I grabbed onto that emotion and allowed it to grow. Anger was a powerful driving force, something I desperately needed if I were to maintain control over my actions. I pulled my shoulders back, ignoring the panic still hovering in the back of my mind, ready to dominate my entire being.

"Dukwicz is a contract killer, an assassin. He's the one who killed Savreux." I took pleasure in seeing the widening of his eyes at my knowledge. "He is most likely here to kill you, or all of us."

"Smart as always, Doctor Lenard." He stepped closer.

"How did you get in?" Isabelle asked.

The smile he gave her held no humour, only cruel enjoyment. "They never secure the windows. That little balcony gave me quick access to the study. Windows are always the easiest to get through, aren't they, Doctor Lenard?"

Another whimper got stuck in my throat as I fought to keep my anger. I was not going to allow this man to intimidate me. Not again. I bit down hard and chose one area that always gave me control. I studied his nonverbal cues, a cause for great concern. He was about to take action and I knew I wasn't prepared for it. None of us were. Ignoring Isabelle and me on the sofa, he walked to Mariam Boussombo and pressed the tip of the knife against her cheek.

"Where is it? Where is the evidence?"

"Not here." She swallowed when the tip of the knife pressed deeper against her fleshy cheek, not yet breaking the skin.

"Please make this difficult for me. I will enjoy it so much more."

As I had done with so many other cases, I had compiled a profile on the target of our investigation. That profile dictated that Dukwicz would feel stronger the longer we resisted him, the longer we argued with him. There were two options. Either we gave him what he wanted immediately and be killed. Or we countered his attack without hesitation or delay. Knowing that he wouldn't respond like our previous suspect, Kubanov, to verbal sparring, I didn't waste any more time on analysing the situation. Instead, I did the most stupid thing of my life.

In one movement, I jumped out of my seat, over the small coffee table and tackled Dukwicz from the side, screaming loudly with the disgust of touching another person. I hoped Manny would hear me from the hallway. We fell to the floor in an inelegant heap, my arms tightly around Dukwicz's waist. Only the element of surprise had given me the advantage. From now on, it was going to be an unfair fight. I doubted my seven years of self-defence training and Vinnie's training in street fighting would help against a professional killer.

From the hotel door came the commotion of the security trying to enter, but I couldn't pay attention to that. I was still screaming and couldn't stop. Dukwicz punched me awkwardly on the side of my face, hard enough to disorient me and make me lose my hold on his waist. He turned and with an incredible force, pushed me away. I shook my head and sat up. The punch had been on my cheekbone, yet both my eyes were hurting. I stretched my eyes wide open to see Isabelle running to the front door, hopefully to let in Manny and men with many weapons.

Movement from my left caught my attention. I turned and saw Dukwicz raise his knife to stab Mariam. How and when she had come to be lying on the floor next to her chair I didn't know. With another scream, I jumped up and grabbed his arm as it came down, but I wasn't strong enough. The blade entered Mariam's side with shocking ease. Her eyes widened and tears filled them as she groaned loudly. The commotion at the door was becoming louder, and Dukwicz turned to look towards the door. He pulled his knife out of Mariam's flesh, simultaneously punching me with his other, weaker hand. That punch caught me on the same cheek and would've broken bones had it been his dominant hand.

In fluid movements, he got up and ran back to the office just as the front door burst open and armed men rushed into the room. I was still screaming uncontrollably, and pointed to the office. My behaviour wasn't a meltdown like some people experienced. The inability to stop saying the same word, singing the same song or, currently in my case, screaming, was behaviour that autistic people often manifested.

Repetitive behaviours were often a way for people on the spectrum to deal with overwhelming emotions. Sometimes it was to gain control of an unfamiliar situation. All of these applied to me as I continued yelling. I closed my eyes against the men running around the hotel suite, a security officer kneeling next to Mariam and pressing hard on her bloody side, and Manny ordering loudly into the phone that Colin should get to the hotel immediately. I didn't know how I was going to stop screaming.

Chapter **NINETEEN**

My throat felt raw, every inhale and scream burning against my vocal cords and swollen larynx. Still I could not stop. My voice had lost its strength and was becoming increasingly hoarse. I didn't want to open my eyes, knowing that those still in the hotel room would see the wild desperation I was feeling. This was one of the few times Mozart had failed to provide me with the meditation-like focus and serenity usually needed to regain control. The hard-won power I'd had over my autistic behaviour was so badly shattered that I didn't know how or if I could recover it.

"Jenny." Colin's voice was calm, but I could hear the concern. I still didn't open my eyes. Of all the people currently in my life, Colin had the most knowledge of my vulnerabilities. Having him witness this lapse made me feel even more powerless. Especially since I knew just how much I needed him. This became apparent at the calm that started flooding my brain the moment he touched my forearm. "Shh. I'm here. I've got you. Shh."

He stayed consistent in tone and touch, but it wasn't enough for me. I needed more in order to recover faster. Not knowing if it would work, I grabbed his hand as he rubbed my forearm and pulled him closer. His loud inhale told me I had surprised him with this action. Physical closeness was not something I ever encouraged. Outside our sexual intimacy, I had limited his physical closeness to a light, simple touch on my arm.

Not now. He shuffled closer on the floor until I was sitting between his legs. I was clutching onto his left hand and when he put his right hand on my free hand, I grabbed it and folded his arms securely around me. I was surrounded by him. My back was pressed against his chest, slowing the rocking I hadn't even been aware I was doing. I pulled his arms even tighter and took a shaky breath. It still came out as a scream, but I could feel my fragmented mind slowly mending as Colin continued to softly reassure me.

How long we sat like that I didn't know, but my last scream came out as a painful whisper. I had a coppery taste in my mouth and wondered if my throat was bleeding. Irrationally I thought how preferable shutdowns and meltdowns were to this. At least then I wasn't aware of my surroundings. The sounds of armed men searching the rooms and of paramedics asking Mariam questions had made it much harder to find the centre of my calm.

"Jenny?"

I nodded, my throat too sore to speak. I took a few more uneven breaths and opened my eyes. Someone was holding a bottle of water in front of me. I looked up at Isabelle sitting on the carpet, and tried to smile. I couldn't. It took a few seconds to get myself to let go of Colin's arm and accept the water. It wasn't opened and my fingers fumbled with the lid.

"Let me?" Isabelle held out her hand and I gave back the water. She opened it and handed it over. I took a few small sips, the liquid cooling the burning in my throat. The bustling in the room drew my attention. Three paramedics knelt next to President Boussombo, stabilising her. They were talking about getting her onto the gurney to rush her to the hospital. Next to Isabelle were two men—anger, frustration and vigilance in their nonverbal cues.

"How're you feeling?" Colin's voice rumbled against my back.

"My throat really hurts." Even whispering was painful.

"Would you let the paramedics look?" Isabelle leaned closer, but immediately moved back again. Her sensitivity was rare and notable.

"I'm not going anywhere," Colin said. "We can sit like that while they check out your cheek and your throat."

I considered this, felt the dark panic creeping closer and vigorously shook my head. Once started, I couldn't stop shaking my head. Tears of frustration formed in my eyes. This involuntary repetitive behaviour was most disconcerting. I turned my head, pressed my uninjured cheek against Colin's chest and brought his hand up to press my head tighter against him. Again he spoke in a low tone, reassuring me until I stopped the uncontrolled movement a few minutes later.

"Not yet," I whispered. Isabelle held out the bottle of water, and I wondered when she had taken it from me. I accepted it and took a few more sips.

"Doc?" Manny went down on his haunches next to Isabelle, concern dominating his face. "How're you doing?"

I nodded, and looked at President Mariam Boussombo as the paramedics carefully lifted her onto the gurney.

"How...?" I couldn't get further than that. It was too painful.

"You saved her life, Doc. When you grabbed Dukwicz's arm, you deflected the knife and what would've been a fatal injury became a flesh wound. The medics think the knife didn't get anything important, but they're taking her to the hospital now." He lowered his chin, his expression sombre. "How are you?"

I pointed to my throat and mouthed, "Painful."

"I can imagine. Who knew you could outdo an opera singer?"

I wished I had my voice to tell him opera singers didn't scream. Their singing was as skilful as a gymnast performing complex twists and turns with their bodies. It took years of training for opera singers to project their powerful voices in controlled use of their vocal cords to create flawless arias.

"You're arguing with me in your head, aren't you, Doc?" Manny's face relaxed, a small but genuine smile pulling at the corners of his mouth. "This is going to be interesting."

"Don't you have some law enforcement work to do, Millard?" Colin's arms tightened around me. I tapped on his arms, inhaled deeply and sat up. I didn't move out of his embrace.

"As a matter of fact I do. Doc, don't go anywhere until the medic checks you out."

"When you're ready," Colin said as Manny got up and walked to the other side of the room.

"Genevieve, I have to go." Isabelle's body language indicated that she didn't want to leave. She glanced at the two nervous men next to her. "I've been breaking protocol and scaring my security by not leaving immediately."

"She insisted on staying with you and President Boussombo," Colin said. "She even fought them off when they tried to physically remove her."

"I'm sure my overprotective husband is not going to be pleased, but I couldn't leave my friends." The look she gave one of the men spoke of indignation. "It's not like I'm one of the most important women in the world. For goodness' sake, I travelled to Africa all on my little ownsome and worked in rural clinics there."

"You're the wife of a world leader, Madame President," the man said with the familiarity of a brother.

"Bah! Don't Madame President me, Luc. I was the one who didn't tell your mother when you lost your car at university in a stupid bet with your friends." She got up and looked down at me. "Be well, Genevieve. I'll be in touch."

There was much more to her last statement than a mere greeting. Her tone had been light and polite, but the micro-expression around her eyes implied a nuance I didn't understand. No sooner had she uttered the cryptic greeting than Luc grabbed her elbow, the other man close to her other side, and walked her out of the room.

"How long...?" I hoped Colin understood the rest of my whispered question.

"It took me fifteen minutes to get here and you were like this for another ten minutes." He turned a bit to have a better view of my face. "It actually hurt to listen to you screaming your voice raw like that. I think you're going to be hoarse for some time."

I nodded.

"Wait, stop." Mariam Boussombo's voice drew my attention away from the distress on Colin's face. "Genevieve?"

"Yes?" I forced the sound out and winced at the stinging pain.

Strapped to the gurney, Mariam Boussombo looked at me. "Thank you. I will never forget what you did for me. Especially in your circumstances."

I nodded, unable to give her the reassuring smile people in this situation usually needed. Her expression told me she put a higher value on my action than she would've had I been a neurotypical person. It didn't make sense. She blinked twice, ending the emotional moment. The paramedics rolled the gurney out the room, but one stayed behind. He sat down on the coffee table, his eyes alert and interested.

Logic dictated it a wise course of action to have a medical professional examine the damage I had inflicted on my throat and vocal cords. I pulled Colin's arms tighter around me and nodded to the paramedic.

"Are you sure, Jenny?"

I nodded again. As long as I maintained this current position of safety, I could bear a stranger touching me. The fact that he took fresh gloves from a package and put those on his hands were even more reassuring.

"Hi, Jenny. My name is Arnaud."

"Genevie…" I started coughing, but forced myself to stop when tears filled my eyes.

"Her name is Doctor Genevieve Lenard," Colin said.

"Doctor Lenard," Arnaud said and knelt down in front of me. "I'm first going to check your cheek and then I'll check your throat."

I waved my hand to stop his explanation. I swallowed and slowly mouthed, "Just do it."

He smiled and leaned closer. I tightened my hands around Colin's arms, closed my eyes and forced Mozart's Piano Sonata no. 8 in A minor as loudly as possible into my mind. Ten anxiety-filled minutes later, the paramedic declared I had severely injured my vocal folds. My trachea and larynx were swollen and red from overuse. The painful prodding on my cheek had satisfied him that nothing was broken, but he still recommended I went to a hospital for x-rays. I knew I wasn't going to.

"I also recommend that you don't speak for a week. Your throat and vocal cords need time to heal." Arnaud put his instruments back in the large carry bag and stood up.

"Despite the hard hit to your head, it doesn't look like you've got a concussion. As a precaution—"

"I'll check on her every hour," Colin said. "It's okay if she sleeps, right?"

"Sure, but it will be better if you wake her up every hour, not just check her." Arnaud looked at me. "Get well soon, Doctor Lenard."

I nodded and leaned into Colin.

"Are you ready to go home?"

"She needs to give a statement to the police first, Frey." Manny sat down on the paramedic's place on the coffee table. "Are you up for it, Doc? Or should I tell them you'll give the report tomorrow?"

"Tomorrow." I mouthed the word and was relieved when Manny not only understood, but accepted it.

"They can come to us for that statement. I'll get right on it. Let Frey take you home. I'll be there soon." He got up and went back to the same man he'd been talking to most of the time.

"Do you want Millard to come to the flat?"

I turned in Colin's arms to give him full view of my mouth. I was going to heed the paramedic's advice, mostly because of the pain and the feeling that my throat was even more swollen now than before. I spoke with a combination of exaggerated lip movements and exhalation of air. It was the merest of whispers. "I don't mind. I predict everyone else is in my apartment now, right?"

"Most likely. You know how it is." He smiled gently. "Let's go."

The drive home was done in complete silence. Colin had put on Mozart's Clarinet Quintet in A Major after a quick phone call to Vinnie. Everyone was indeed in my apartment.

Vinnie was cooking and Francine was irritating him with her suggestions of trying out new spices. The quiet in the moving vehicle gave me time to think. It wasn't the case that was foremost in my mind. My latest autistic episode was causing me to reflect, something I seldom did for extended periods.

In the quiet and warmly lit hallway of our apartment building, I stopped Colin with my hand on his arm a moment before we reached the front door to my apartment. Before we went inside, surrounded by people and noise, I had questions that needed answers. He patiently waited for me.

"How do you know what I need?" I was still whispering and Colin leaned a bit closer, his eyes narrowing on my lips.

"You usually tell me. If not with words, with actions like you did tonight."

"You are not a typical male." Not according to the numerous textbooks I had studied at university, nor the men I had observed growing up.

"Um, thank you." He smiled.

"What do you get out of this?"

His smile disappeared and he tilted his head. "What do you mean?"

"People don't typically do things selflessly. There is always a return on any emotional or social investment. What do you get from this?" I moved my index finger between us.

"I get you, Jenny. Your unconditional acceptance of who I am, despite your lack of complete understanding and agreement of what I do, is more than I could ever have hoped for. You are real. I always know where I stand with you. I never have any doubts. What we have is more secure than ninety-nine point nine percent of relationships out there. It's invaluable to me." He moved in closer. "You are invaluable to me. You bring joy into my life."

I knew he was truthful. It wasn't just my trust in him, but his nonverbal cues spoke of complete honesty. It didn't make sense to me. I knew and understood my intellectual and professional value. I knew I was an asset to any case, to any company that would ever hire me, but personal relationships had me at a loss. No amount of rationalisation helped me find the value I added to anyone's life, especially Colin's.

"Aren't I emotionally taxing? I was told that I am too much hard work for people to want to be with me."

"It's their loss, Jenny. They don't know you like I do—like we do."

I closed my eyes briefly, reaching for courage. "You didn't mind picking me up from the shower?"

A soft smile replaced his frown. "I was wondering when or if you were going to bring that up."

"I was embarrassed."

"Of trusting me?" He lifted my hands and pressed them against his chest, over his heart. "It was the biggest compliment you could've given me, love. To know that you feel safe enough to let me take care of you? No, I didn't mind picking you up from the shower. I didn't mind at all."

I searched his face for any signs of deception.

"You're not going find anything but the truth on my face, love." He snorted softly and shook his head. "You really don't know, do you? You don't know how important you are to me. How much richer you've made my life. And Vinnie's, Francine's, Phillip's, Nikki's and even Millard's life. You make us better people. You." He rested his hand over my heart and I was surprised to feel tears form in my eyes.

The door behind Colin swung open and Vinnie stepped into the hallway. "Are you two going to stand here all night and play kissy-face or are you going to come in? The soup is getting cold."

Ignoring Vinnie's melodramatic declaration, Colin rested his forehead against mine. "I love you, Jenny. We all love you."

I looked into his eyes and whispered against his lips, "Thank you."

"Come on, dude. The soup. The soup."

Colin laughed and turned around. "Hey, Vin."

"Get your ass inside. I want to see my girl." Vinnie waited until I stood in front of him. He studied my cheek for a few seconds before looking into my eyes. He took a step back. "No hugging tonight, right?"

I nodded. "Thanks, Vinnie."

"Where's your voice? Dude! You didn't say she completely lost it." Vinnie followed me into the apartment and locked the door behind us.

"She kind of overused it. The paramedic says she shouldn't speak for at least a week."

"Girlfriend, what happened?" Francine got up from the sofa and left her laptop on the seat. "Are you okay?"

"Doc G." Nikki came running from Colin's part of the apartment. She was wearing the cartoon pyjamas Vinnie had given her for Christmas, her hair in a messy ponytail as if she had been sleeping. The acuity in her eyes proved she hadn't. She stopped next to Francine and stared at me. "Vinnie said you were attacked."

"Her voice is gone," Francine said.

It took about ten minutes for Colin to tell everyone what had happened. In that time, Vinnie had ordered us to the dining room table and had served a vegetable soup, not too thick or spicy. It soothed my sore throat. Francine had finished her soup and was working on her laptop. I knew she was listening, but the work she was busy with was causing her great concern.

The doorbell rang, interrupting the list of questions Vinnie was asking without waiting for an answer. Both him and Colin got up and walked to the door, their postures aggressive. Vinnie looked through the peephole and his shoulders lowered. "It's just the old man."

He opened the door and let Manny in. Francine looked up, and that was when I became concerned. There was none of the usual recognition and playful teasing evident on her face. She gave Manny an absent-minded smile and returned to the work on her computer. The tapping of her fingers on the keyboard had become more frantic, her lips gradually thinning.

Manny came to the table, looked at Vinnie and looked at the kitchen. "What's for dinner?"

"What do you think this is, old man? A restaurant?"

"Just bring me some food, criminal." Manny sat down heavily. "What a bloody night."

"How is President Boussombo?" I rapped my knuckles on the table to catch Manny's attention when he didn't hear my whispered question. "How's President Boussombo?"

"I haven't heard anything else, Doc. Sorry. I'll check just now if you want."

I nodded.

"Here's your soup." Vinnie placed the bowl down carefully in front of Manny, and threw down a spoon. Manny caught the spoon as it bounced and glared at Vinnie.

"Mrs Godard told us that Dukwicz was looking for

something. She refused to say what it was. What was she talking about, Doc?" Manny took a sip of the soup and groaned. "This is really good."

It made sense that Isabelle wouldn't have said anything in front of the paramedics and the numerous security personnel and police officers. I prepared myself to whisper my response. "President Boussombo has evidence against powerful officials in Gabon who are involved in high-level corruption. She was going to give this to the prosecutor of the ICC tomorrow evening. Isabelle has been helping her set up the meeting. We were talking about this when I noticed a look between Isabelle and Mariam."

"You're calling them by their first names?" Nikki asked. "That's so cool."

I ignored Nikki and closed my eyes for a second to recall those frightful moments. "I think Isabelle has this evidence with her. I don't know where, but it was not in Mariam's suite. I saw relief on both their faces when Dukwicz asked for the evidence. There had been no indicators that they had something valuable in the suite. As a matter of fact, Isabelle had a micro-smile. Yes. She has the evidence."

"You shouldn't speak so much, Jenny."

"I'm not speaking. I'm barely whispering." I could feel the strain on my throat, but couldn't stop speaking now. "Where is Dukwicz?"

"He jumped out the window." Manny put his spoon down. "The bastard rigged up ropes and repelled onto the balcony from the roof. That's how he got in. President Boussombo's security detail never thought anyone would gain access from the balcony and didn't secure it. When we came in, Dukwicz used the same ropes, but went to the street below. He was well-prepared. It took him only a few seconds before he was on the street and disappeared into the crowd."

A tremor of fear went through me. That man had been in my apartment, in Vinnie's bedroom just to make a point. Who knew what the next point was he would want to make? I didn't know if I could sleep tonight.

"We'll get him, Doc." Manny picked up his spoon and shook it. "We're going to get that son of a bitch."

"I rigged all the windows, Jen-girl. If a mosquito sneezes close to a window, I will know."

"I helped Vinnie put a whole new system up." Nikki looked proud. "All of your phones are connected to the alarm system and Vinnie has everything on the computer in his room. It kinda looks like a computer game."

"You're safe here, Jen-girl." Confidence was the dominant nonverbal cue on Vinnie's face. "You can relax in your own home."

I nodded, not sure if his reassurances were enough to help me sleep. I glanced at Francine glaring at her laptop, and frowned. "Francine, what is wrong?"

"Nothing." Her voice was two tones higher than normal.

"Francine." I waited until she focussed on me and I lifted my eyebrows. Her expression surprised me. I hadn't expected to see regret. "What did you find?"

"I don't know. I can't say for sure. I don't know what to make of this. It's all messed up. I haven't made any sense of it yet." She only rambled when the distress was from a close emotional connection.

Manny pushed his soup bowl aside and sat up. "Spit it out, supermodel."

"Firstly, I need to say what a huge fangirl I am of Mrs Isabelle Godard. I think she is smart, elegant, a good ambassador for woman's rights, a kind person, a loving mothe—"

"Supermodel!"

"In our previous case, we learned that Isabelle Godard used her maiden name, Lescot, until ten years ago. When her husband gave up his legal career and got serious about politics, she changed to using his surname to show her unconditional support. We also know that she used to go under Lili, short for Isabelle." She closed her eyes and spoke very fast, as if she didn't want to say the words. "Lili Lescot has an account in the same bank, same branch, as the Libreville Dignity Foundation. There have been lots of large amounts going in and out. I checked a few of those transactions in the last two years. The dates of the transactions coincided with reforms the president was pushing."

"Holy hell." Manny pressed his fists against his eyes. "What are you saying, supermodel?"

"This account was opened at the same time René Motte became the chairman of LDF. It was also the same year the president became serious about politics. Since then thirteen million euro has gone through that account."

"Oh, bleeding hell." Manny got up and walked to the kitchen. He turned around three times before coming back, but he didn't sit down. "Doc? What do you make of this?"

"It's clearly a setup," Francine said before I could formulate an answer. "Isabelle Godard is being framed for selling her husband's influence. I have to look farther back to see what she could also be set up for before the president became president, but I'm sure I'll find something. It's a setup, don't you see it?"

"Calm down, Francine." It was the third time ever I had heard Manny use Francine's first name. It was effective. She lifted her chin and straightened her shoulders. "Now, if you would give Doc a chance to answer."

Everyone looked at me. "I agree with Francine."

The reaction around the table was as I had expected. I seldom agreed with Francine's outrageous theories.

"Care to explain, Doc?"

"No." I saw the immediate irritation on Manny's face and thought it best to qualify my answer. "Unlike Francine, I first find proof for my theories before I freely share them."

"But you have a theory." Manny sat down. "For the love of all that is pure, please tell us."

"You know he's just going to nag like an old woman if you don't." Vinnie was enjoying this.

"No. I need to look at Francine's findings, compare it to my data and then I will share with you." I took a sip of water. Even whispering my answers were taxing. My throat was burning, I was exhausted and needed to shower. "I need to rest for a few hours. Then we can continue this."

Manny wanted to argue—it was clear in his protruding jaw and his flared nostrils. Thankfully, he didn't disagree. He gave a terse nod and got up. "I'll be here for breakfast. You better have something then, missy."

Breakfast was seven hours away. It was plenty of time for Francine and me to work.

"Go away, old man. Jen-girl will tell you when she's ready and not a moment sooner." Vinnie got up and herded Manny to the front door. "Breakfast will be served at eight. We eat later on Saturdays."

Manny turned and faced Vinnie as if the latter was not a head taller and more than a decade younger than him. "I'll be here when I'm here. I don't care about your little family schedule."

"This is so exciting." Nikki got up and took a few plates to the kitchen. "You guys have the craziest lives."

"You're one of us, punk. It's not like your life is normal either." Vinnie locked the door behind Manny and returned to the table. He took two empty soup bowls from Nikki, and pointed with his chin to the direction of her bedroom. "Go to bed, punk. We've got this."

"Thanks, big punk. Nighty night." She stood on her toes and kissed Vinnie on the cheek before turning to us. "I'm glad you're okay, Doc G. Sleep tight. See you in the morning."

I watched her walk to her bedroom with a light step. She was in my home and I felt responsible for her even though she was legally an adult and of no relation to me. How could I bring so much danger to a person so optimistic and open?

"I know that look." Colin took my hand and pulled me up. "Don't start thinking now, Jenny. Next up, you're going to try and save the whole world's problems, and you won't be able to do it tonight."

"That's absurd." I tugged, but he wouldn't let go of my hand. "I can't save the world's problems, but I need to speak to Francine."

"Tomorrow, girlfriend. Let me get all my ducks in a row tonight. When you get up tomorrow morning I will show you all the data I have on Mrs Isabelle Godard and you can help me make sense of it." Francine winked at me, dismissing my reproving frown.

I gave in to Colin's tugging and followed him to the bedroom. A shower and a few hours' sleep would by no means be enough to recover from the emotional turmoil I had experienced, but it might clear my mind sufficiently to look at Isabelle's financial history.

Chapter TWENTY

"I hate you." Nikki's words were uncharitable, but I detected no animosity in her tone as I walked out of my bedroom. I was surprised to find her in the kitchen. It was three minutes past five in the morning, and I had left Colin sleeping in bed. Despite being woken every hour, I'd slept enough and needed to work with Francine on Isabelle's financial information.

"Good morning, girlfriend." Francine was sitting at the dining room table, her laptop and tablet in front of her. "How's your throat? And your cheek?"

"Still hurts." I still could only manage a breathy whisper. I pointed to my swollen cheek. "This too."

"Good job with the makeup."

"You're lying. The swelling is very obvious, but that's not it." I sat down next to Francine and studied her expression. "You think my makeup doesn't hide anything."

She scrunched up her face and shook her head. "Sorry, but it really doesn't do anything. I'll help you later."

"Don't you think it's unfair, Doc G?" Nikki came to the table with two mugs of coffee, handed Francine one and me the other.

I wrapped my hands around the hot mug. "Thank you, Nikki. What is unfair?"

"That Francine looks so good after pulling an all-nighter. She had a shower, is wearing Vinnie's clothes and some of my makeup, and look at her." Nikki's expression indicated disgust and admiration. Curious.

I looked at Francine. She was wearing an oversized pair of black tracksuit pants and a t-shirt that I recognised as one that stretched tightly over Vinnie's muscular chest. On Francine, it hung loosely over her breasts, the V-neck revealing ample cleavage. Her necklace and many bracelets changed the masculine clothes into a sensual outfit. Her hair was perfectly styled, her makeup subtle.

"I don't see how you consider it unfair, but Francine does look good."

"Thanks, girlfriend."

"It's unfair, because she makes it look easy. It takes me hours to tame my hair." Nikki drew out the 'hours' for dramatic effect. It made me smile. She went back to the kitchen and picked up a mug and a plate with a sandwich. "I'm going to my room. You guys are going to talk boring numbers. I only want to hear about the scandals."

"It's the numbers that lead to the scandals." Francine flipped her hair over her shoulder. "Go to your room, you little wimp. Don't think because you let me borrow some of your makeup, I have to tolerate your insubordination."

"Whatever." Nikki rolled her eyes and left my part of the apartment.

"I like that little chica. She's a sweet thing."

I tried, but couldn't let it go. "You can't borrow makeup."

"Excuse me?"

"Borrow, by implication, means that you will return it. You cannot borrow something you can never return. Ergo you cannot borrow makeup."

"Did you just say ergo? To me? Me? Your bestest friend?" She pushed the back of her hand against her forehead and

I sighed. Francine was in one of her happy, playful moods. Days like this halved my understanding of anything she said or did.

"What did you find?" My throat was hurting and my head still aching from the beating it took last night. I needed to focus on something I could understand, something not emotional.

"Ooh, I found a lot of interesting stuff." She turned her laptop for me to see. "But you're going to have to help me make sense of all these insane numbers. You're the brains in this outfit that can connect all the dots. But I found loads of dots for you to connect."

She started showing her discoveries, but I had to stop her. Her presentation was without thought or structure. I told her as much and we both sighed. I asked politely for a more organised delivery and she complied. It took about twenty minutes for me to realise that we had both been right in our initial assumptions about Isabelle's financial detail. The next hour we spent finding evidence to affirm our suspicions. When applying herself, Francine was focussed and I only had to ask twice for her to clarify a statement.

"Working hard?" Colin rested his hand on my shoulder and I looked away from the bank statement Francine had just acquired illegally. He was freshly showered and dressed in a pair of designer jeans and a black knitted sweater. He frowned when he saw my expression. "What have you done? Why do you look so guilty?"

"I just hacked into a bank and Miss Goody-Two-Shoes is feeling flustered." Francine rolled her eyes.

He laughed softly and kissed me on my uninjured cheek. "Good morning."

"Good morning." I didn't feel guilty as much as extremely uncomfortable that I had condoned and, as a matter of fact, encouraged Francine to violate everything I believed in. We needed that information.

"Morning, dude. Ladies." Vinnie walked into the kitchen, but stopped when he looked at Francine. "Are those my clothes? Are you wearing my clothes?"

He walked closer, his stride aggressive. Francine lifted her eyebrows. "Now, look here, you overgrown Neanderthal. How many times have I helped you out of trouble? Picked you up from the shady side of town and saved your arse? Don't you think I deserve some support when I'm having an emergency?"

Vinnie's nostrils flared. "This is not an emergency, you spice-obsessed fashion doll. Why didn't you wear the clothes you had on last night? This is my lucky shirt. You're wearing my lucky shirt."

"Eeuw. I could never wear my outfit a second day. Only men lacking any sense of cooking and fashion would give their clothes the sniff test and wear them again."

I had become used to this. In the beginning I had found their arguing disconcerting, until Colin explained it was banter. The fun they had while insulting and calling each other names was indisputable, and I had realised it was a coping mechanism for both of them. As usual, I started shutting off, but the ringing of my doorbell brought me back to the present.

Colin and Vinnie's teamwork opening the door was becoming the norm, as was Manny's appearance and his dismissal of their lack of welcome. Manny walked straight to the table, sat down and snapped his fingers. "Criminal, breakfast. Doc, report."

"Fuck you, old man." Vinnie's brows lowered even more when Francine burst out laughing. He shook a finger at her.

"And you should know to never piss off the cook."

This made her laugh harder. Nikki came in, still wearing her pyjamas, but with an oversized hoodie zipped up to her throat. "What's funny? Did you find a scandal?"

"There'll be a scandal if those two continue." Vinnie walked into the kitchen, scowling. "Come help me, punk. These people are pissing me off."

"How're you feeling, Doc? Your cheek looks quite bad."

"Told ya," Francine mumbled.

"I'm mending." I didn't think it useful to explain in detail how my cheek was throbbing, the burning in my throat was gradually increasing as I was whispering more and my head felt, for the lack of a better word, sensitive.

"What do you have for me, Doc?"

"I think I should give the report, handsome," Francine said. "Genevieve has already talked too much this morning. She can add to it or correct me when I'm done. Is that okay, girlfriend?"

I nodded, thankful for her considerate gesture.

She cleared her throat. "Mrs Isabelle Godard's finances are all directly related to her husband's political career. Oh. No, wait. I'm going to start from the other side first. Her finances can be divided into two distinct parts, which are quite separate. The part we are not interested in is the three accounts that have daily activities in it. One savings account and two credit card accounts. Her salaries are paid into her savings account."

"Salaries?" Manny asked and moved back when Nikki put a placemat and cutlery in front of him.

"She receives a salary from her work as a neurosurgeon. There is also her income from her position as board member of three different boards. All of these are legit. This income is declared on her tax returns, she pays all the right taxes and spends quite a lot of money on perfume. I guess us girls all have a vice."

"What about the other part? The part we are interested in?"

"Well, that is where Genevieve and I spent most of our morning."

"She did most of the research work last night." I couldn't let Francine imply that I had done that work. At least I'd had a few hours of sleep, even though she looked more rested than I did.

"That is the Strasbourg Security Bank account that I talked about last night." Francine fiddled with her laptop's screen. "Eleven years ago, Mrs Godard became a very public patron of Libreville Dignity Foundation. The next year, René Motte became chairman. The very next week, LDF changed banks and opened an account in Strasbourg Security Bank. On the same day LDF opened their account there, Lili Lescot also opened her account there."

"We already know that from last night, supermodel."

"What you don't know, you impatient, but handsome man, is that there is no way Lili Lescot, aka Isabelle Godard, could've opened that account. She was on a volunteer mission in Gabon at that time. Eleven years ago, she still had a very strong neurosurgical career. She was considered one of the best in Europe. For two and half months, she went to Gabon and performed surgeries for free all over the country."

I rapped my knuckles lightly on the table to catch Francine's attention. "Mariam Boussombo."

"Yes. That volunteer mission was organised by Mrs Godard and Mariam Boussombo, not yet President

Boussombo. They were working together with a charity outreach programme in Gabon with the focus on children and women. That was what inspired them to get involved with LDF. Anyhoo, Mrs Godard was in Gabon from mid-May to the end of July that year. Lili Lescot's account in Strasbourg Security Bank was opened in June of that year."

"Could someone have acted as a proxy?" Manny asked.

"Nope." Francine turned her laptop around to show Manny the screen. "This is a scanned account application form. At the bottom of the form you will see Lili Lescot's signature. She signed for this account and it's written here that she opened it in person."

It was quiet for a few seconds. Vinnie and Nikki brought in trays of food and soon we all had a plate with one of Vinnie's delicious omelettes in front of us. I always marvelled at his ability to serve omelettes to so many people at the same time. I had only three pans.

"Which bank employee opened that account?" Colin asked. I had hoped someone would ask this question and wasn't surprised it was Colin.

"Ooh, this is where things get even more delicious." Francine stretched to get a fresh bread roll from the basket. She sat back down and dusted her fingers off. "Anyone wants to guess who the bank manager was? Huh? Huh?"

"It was Remi Dubois." I didn't have the patience for her games.

"Holy hellfire!" Manny threw his bread roll back on his plate. "The bloody fourth person in that photo."

"We found some more dirt on old Remi." Francine paused, widening her eyes dramatically, and intertwined her index and middle finger. "He was BFFs with René Motte. Yup, they were BFFs long before that photo was taken. They shared a flat when they studied and have always been allies. Cronies. You know, like in cronyism?"

"Oh, hell. This is turning into a total cataclysm."

Colin laid both his hands palms down on the table. "Someone is running a long con."

"What is that?" I asked.

"It's a long-term scheme to steal money from people." Nikki looked proud that she had shocked Francine. She smiled at Vinnie when he bumped her with his shoulder.

I was still not clear on the term and looked at Colin.

"Yeah, Frey." Manny leaned back in his chair and folded his arms. "Tell us exactly what a long con is."

"Something that would need more planning that you're capable of, Millard." Colin turned his back on Manny and looked at me. "A long con is a strategy to win the trust of the mark—the victim—in order to steal money or something else from him. It could also be a form of industrial espionage to steal information. It's not just limited to money or art. This usually happens over a period of a few days, weeks, sometimes months if the object is worth it. But I've honestly never heard of a long con stretching over decades."

"What is your conclusion?" I was interested in his theory, since he seldom hypothesized.

"Okay, let's say these five guys were all buds at university, Motte, Savreux, J.L. Legrange, Remi Dubois and the photographer." He looked up at the ceiling, a habit he had while mentally working through a problem. "They graduate, leave university and start their careers. They're friends, they help each other and that is how all of them landed up being involved with Elf in some capacity. They wanted to share the wealth with their buds or, more likely, wanted to keep the money in the family."

I ignored his many irrational conclusions and listened for the core of his theory.

"But then 1989 comes along and gives each of them a bad experience with jobs lost, divorces and passed-over promotions. They're pissed off and want to take revenge. Maybe because they've all been working hard at being part of this Elf embezzling scam. Now they're going to lose out on it so they want to get their own back.

"What better way to make loads of money quickly than a heist? Stealing cash involves a lot more danger than stealing art. Especially back then when security in most museums was insulting to the art. They get their plan together, fly off to Boston and walk away with art now worth nigh-on five hundred million dollars.

"They know the art is hot, so they need to store it. In comes Savreux with the clever idea of a wine cellar that could double up as a preservation room. He rents it in his mother's name… oh, wait. That doesn't work with our timeline, right?"

I shook my head. Even though Colin's theory sounded fictional, it was feasible.

"Oh well. At one point he rents it then. Back to my story. After the Boston heist, they don't immediately move the art, because it's too hot. A few years later, they move a piece or two, make shitloads of money and realise how easy it is. They start a whole art theft racket and that is where they get their large sums of money from. In order to clean that money, they start up the Libreville Dignity Foundation."

"Wait." I swallowed and continued whispering. "Mariam said one of the crimes she wanted the ICC to prosecute some Gabonese politicians for was art theft."

"I see where you're going with this," Colin said when I took a sip of water. "It is possible that these five guys collaborated with their Gabonese cronies to move that art. Hey, maybe they even facilitated the theft and fencing of other artworks as well. Who knows?"

"That's gross speculation." But I didn't dispute it.

"Can I continue the story? Can I?" Francine was bouncing in her chair and smiled widely when Colin nodded. "So when Raymond Godard became interested in politics right after the trial of the Elf politicians and executives, they got worried. He was young, dynamic and they knew him by reputation from their old legal company to always do everything by the book. They got particularly worried when he started talking about politicians being completely transparent in their finances. They knew that someone at some point was going to notice their finances didn't add up with their lifestyles. They needed to get rid of him. Barring assassination, what is the best way to destroy a politician? Damage his reputation. What better way to do it through his wife.

"They knew about her involvement in Gabon and saw an in. Ten years ago, they upped their involvement in LDF, knowing it would give them access to Isabelle Godard and a way to taint her. LDF's account and the account they opened in her name could be used to build a strong case against her and the not-yet president. But then they discovered exactly how useful the charity's account and Lili Lescot's account were. They could get their dirty money here without anyone noticing and continued to do so for ten years. Until something happened two years ago that made Savreux lose interest in all his girlfriends, and made them all desperate."

"What happened?" I asked. I was impressed that Francine remembered the change in Minister Savreux's behaviour two years ago. I was even more impressed that her theory was viable.

She thought for a moment. "I don't know."

"Two years ago, Raymond Godard became president," Colin said.

"Oh, my God. That would totally be it. With his policy for openness and honesty, his presidency would pose a vicious threat to their careers, all of their wealth, and all of their hidden secrets."

"How do Gabon and Paul Ngondet fit into this? Do you think he was their contact for their art theft ring in Gabon?" I asked, looking at Colin.

"Hmm. Don't know yet." Colin lifted both shoulders. "That's all I've got. Francine?"

"Nope. I've got nothing for Gabon and Ngondet. Unless you want to hear my other theories." She smiled when everyone shook their heads.

"Even though there is very little proof to support your theory, it could work."

"But it's useless without concrete evidence, I know." Colin smiled at me. "You'll find it."

"Sometimes it is useful to have a bunch of criminals helping on a case." Manny was serious, none of his usual derision on his face or in his tone. "That is a strong theory, Frey. If Doc can find us what we need, and also who the photographer is, we can put this baby to bed."

"There is much more we need to know." I rapped my knuckles on the table for emphasis. "This will not be enough to close this case, Manny."

"It will get us much closer, Doc."

I wanted to continue arguing, but the knock at the front door caused us to turn as one. It was most uncommon to have visitors apart from the people already in my apartment. The knocking made it even more worrisome. Manny, Vinnie and Colin walked to the door. I wondered if I would ever open my own front door again. Their postures relaxed when Manny opened the door and Daniel walked in.

"Good morning." His smile was genuine, but the lines around his mouth indicated strain. "Seems like I got everyone here. That's good."

"Do you also want food? This is not a restaurant, flatfoot." Vinnie didn't wait for Daniel to answer, but walked to the kitchen to prepare another omelette. Despite his complaining, I knew he enjoyed any excuse to be in the kitchen.

The rapport between Manny and Daniel was evident in their body language. There was mutual trust and respect. Manny invited Daniel to the table. It wasn't the first time almost all of the eight chairs at my large dining room table were occupied. I listened as Manny updated Daniel with our latest findings. At the mention of Isabelle Godard, Daniel's entire body tensed. It was slight and lasted less than a second, but I noticed.

Vinnie put a plate in front of Daniel and sat down again, glaring at the two law enforcement officers. Not being expected to speak had the delightful side effect of being able to observe everyone. In the twenty minutes Daniel had been at our table, I had seen enough to have reached a conclusion. He ate quickly and soon moved the last of his food on his plate around with his fork.

I rapped my knuckles on the table and waited until he looked at me. "Why are you here? What's wrong?"

Daniel pushed his plate away. "I'm here to arrest you."

"Me?" I pointed at my chest. "Why?"

"Not only you, Genevieve. Everyone."

An explosion of questions, outraged comments filled the air. I had to rap my knuckles hard on the table to get everyone to calm down. "Why?"

Daniel removed a folded document from the inside of his jacket and opened it. "For treason, conspiracy to commit mass crimes, terrorism, cyber-terrorism, and a few more. It's all listed here."

Francine started to say something, but I stopped her with a raised hand. I lifted both eyebrows and waited for Daniel to continue. His discomfort was not only in the muscle contractions around his mouth and eyes. He was also perspiring.

"One of you triggered an alert. Apparently someone googled something they shouldn't have. They were able to trace the online crime to this apartment."

"Impossible." Francine was shaking her head so vigorously, her hair was slapping into her face. "No one would've been able to trace me. It's simply not possible."

The shifting in the chair across from me caught my eye. I looked at Nikki. "What did you do?"

"I wanted to help, so googled Isabelle Godard's name in connection with Elf. I also looked for her connection to Savreux. That was it. I swear, Doc G." Stress caused the muscles in her throat to contract, raising the pitch of her voice. The *corrugator supercilii* muscles brought her brow in and down in deep furrows, but I knew she was truthful.

I nodded, but it didn't assuage her worries. Dealing with a young person was onerous at times. "Your actions caused problems, but your intentions were good. Those who care about you would be more concerned about your intentions."

"What are *you* concerned about?" Her question revealed more than she might have realised.

I knew the importance of this moment, yet the emotionality of it and the many people here made it most unpleasant. I made sure to exhibit all the right nonverbal cues. I leaned over the table, made eye contact with her and put my hands on the table as if reaching for her. I took a deep breath. "Nikki, I care about you. I'm only concerned about your intentions. We will deal with the unfortunate results of your actions together."

Colin squeezed my knee under the table and Nikki got tears in her eyes. "Thanks, Doc G. I'm really sorry."

"I still have to arrest everyone," Daniel said softly.

"That is ridiculous. How can they issue a blanket arrest warrant?" Manny took the document and read the contents. Of us all, he was most qualified to interpret it. He threw it on the table with a snort. "These are trumped-up charges and you know it, Daniel."

"Of course I know it. That is why I volunteered to come and arrest these horrible terrorists who pretend to be honest people and solve cases for the president. I have to protect the president, our nation and the world's right to freedom."

I leaned closer to Colin. "He doesn't make sense."

My comment broke the tension around the table as everyone laughed softly.

"Sorry, Genevieve. I was being sarcastic. This is just so ridiculous." Regret was around his mouth and eyes. "I still have to take someone in. If I don't, they're going to send in an entire team and then we're all screwed."

"Arrest me." Nikki lifted her hand as if she was answering a question in a school class.

"Over my dead body." Vinnie shifted his chair closer to Nikki's. "You're not going anywhere, punk."

"Why not? The government will look like witch hunters the moment the media finds out that they arrested a sweet, innocent little art student on terrorism charges. It's total discrimination, you know. Just because my daddy was a legendary criminal doesn't mean that I am following in his footsteps." Her voice took a tone as if she was speaking in public, appealing for their compassion and support. "What is happening to our freedom? To our ability to give young people a chance to cut their own path, to make their own way, to form their own identities."

"Okay, punk. You're making your point." Vinnie turned to Daniel, his top lip raised. "If you arrest her, you better fucking arrest me too. She's not going anywhere without me."

"That is what I was hoping you'd say." Daniel laughed at the deeper disgust on Vinnie's face. "I appreciate that this isn't easy for you, but at the moment you're not essential to the team."

"Well, ouch." Vinnie crossed his arms. "Throw in a bit of emotional torture, will ya."

"What I mean is that Manny has been keeping me in the loop with the case. At the moment, we need Francine, Genevieve, Colin and Manny on this case. They're the ones who will put this all together. The two of you can build some street cred in jail while these guys save the free world."

"Cool. Street cred. I have to go get dressed." Nikki jumped up and looked at Francine. "What does one wear to jail?"

Francine shrugged. "Once I had on this gorgeous red Armani mini dress, the other time it was a red, sleeveless Vera Wang. Do you have something like that?"

Nikki stared at her for a few seconds. "I hate you."

Francine laughed as Nikki stormed to her room. "She doesn't realise how much work it takes to look like this. She'll learn."

Chapter TWENTY-ONE

"I don't want to be here." I didn't say this to anyone specifically. The soundproof basement we were currently in was nothing like the safe environments I had created for myself. It was an unqualified violation of my need for a calm and organised space, the lack of street noise and other sounds notwithstanding.

"Are you in jail, missy?" Manny's tone was curt.

"Obviously not."

"Are you safe?"

We had all agreed that staying in my apartment or going to Rousseau & Rousseau might result in more arrests. Francine had not been overly enthusiastic, but this had been her surprising last-minute option. Our journey here had been covert, our entry into the basement unseen by anyone.

When we had entered this place, I had been relieved to see it was relatively clean. It even had a lived-in feeling. Heavy woven rugs covered the floor. Three of the four walls were covered in framed posters, adding to the atmosphere. With no natural light reaching the room, most of the lighting came from numerous floor lamps, creating a warm and homey ambience. It could have been a pleasant working space had it not been for overwhelming clutter. A tower of books stacked next to a leather sofa looked like it was about to fall over. My throat tightened, and it wasn't because of the damage sustained from my screaming.

A workstation was set up against the far wall. Not much of

the wall was visible under the many notes, articles, and other things tacked to it. Despite the panic-inducing disorder, there was thankfully no dust to be detected anywhere.

This basement was part of a building in an area of the city I had never been in. It was an old apartment building with small shops, a bistro and a dry-cleaner occupying the entire ground floor. I estimated the basement to take up at least half of the floor space. Francine had proudly stated that the room had been completely soundproofed, using the same methods some better nightclubs did.

I looked around. The underground room was large and in complete chaos. There seemed to be some sort of order, but the clutter was distracting me from finding a system in which it was organised. It appeared that all available surfaces to the left of the basement were covered in computer parts. Under those tables were boxes with more parts, wires hanging over the edges of the boxes. To the right were two long tables overflowing with maps, opened and unopened books, numerous notepads with curled pages, and a disturbing number of other loose papers.

"Yes, I'm safe." But my compulsive need to put this place into order was becoming stronger by the minute.

"Do you have everything you need here?"

"Yes."

"Then stop your whining about supermodel's dungeon and get to it."

Colin coughed and I was too slow to see if it had been a real cough or an attempt to hide another reaction. Francine wasn't hiding her reaction. She placed her hands on her hips, thumbs pointing to the back. She was going to argue.

"This is not a dungeon. It is my workspace and I don't want you here."

"Where can I sit?" I was clutching my computer bag to my chest. In it were my laptop, my notepad and three pens. I couldn't imagine putting anything down on these surfaces.

"Clear a space anywhere, girlfriend." She didn't look away from the four computers she was working on simultaneously. "Or let Colin do it."

"I can clear anywhere?" Colin asked.

"Sure. Just don't break anything."

Colin looked around and settled on a large wooden table to the right of the room. The top wasn't visible under the layers of paper, maps and books. He walked to the table, tilted his head, and swiped everything from the table. It landed in a disturbing heap on the floor, and I swallowed down my desire to rush over and organise the papers into neat, logical piles.

"Jenny?"

I nodded stiffly and within minutes had my laptop running and the notepad neatly aligned in front of it. My three pens were lined up to the right of my laptop.

Francine stood up and walked to me. "Give me a few seconds and I'll connect you to my network here. Then we'll be good to go. No one will trace us here."

I got out of the chair and clenched my hands into tight fists when she moved the computer to the left. Just as I exhaled a controlled breath, an alarm that sounded like an air-raid siren blared from her computer. I folded my arms tightly and stared at the red lights above her computer flickering on and off. "What's happening?"

"Oh, my God." She jumped up and ran to her computers. "Someone's breaching my security."

"Someone's hacking you?" Manny asked.

"No. Someone is physically breaching my security. Look

here." She sat down and pointed at one of the monitors. "There they are."

"Who is it? How did they know we are here? I thought you said we would be safe here." I didn't think they could hear my whispers above the siren. I took a step closer to Colin, irrationally moving away from the computer monitors. Had the police located us? The memory of spending a night in a police interrogation room flooded my mind, and the dark edges of panic filled my peripheral vision.

"We are safe." Manny leaned over Francine to get closer to the monitor. "It's Daniel."

I stepped closer and realised I was clutching Colin's hand. I let it go and held my hands in front of me. The video image on the monitor was of superb quality and it was easy to recognise Daniel. "He's not alone."

"How do they know where we are?" Francine said as Daniel lifted his fist and knocked on the basement door. The sound was loud not only on the monitor, but also seven meters from where we were standing.

Daniel looked around until he noticed the camera and looked directly into it. "Let us in."

"I told him where we are." Manny straightened. "I'll let him in."

Francine's face had lost colour. Her chin quivered as she stood and faced Manny. "How dare you? I brought you here as a show of trust. This is my place. My secret place. I've never had anyone in here before. I trusted you with my secret place and you invited Daniel? He's going to arrest me for all of these things."

Her arm swept in a wide arc to include the room. Manny took a step closer to her. He was the same height as her, and he looked her in the eye. "I know, supermodel. I know you trusted us. Now let me do my job with people *I* trust, so that we won't have to move into your dungeon forever."

Even though his words weren't diplomatic, his tone was gentle. They stared at each other for a few seconds until Francine nodded tightly. "So help me, Manny. If I land in jail, I'll find a way to make you suffer for it."

"Oh, I'm sure you will." Manny walked to the door and let the visitors in. While Manny and Francine had been in their visual power-struggle, I had studied the people waiting outside. That was why I wasn't surprised when Daniel was followed by Pink, Luc and Mrs Isabelle Godard, the president's wife.

Francine was right behind Manny, her posture confrontational. Her muscles stiffened when she saw Isabelle. Francine stopped and stared open-mouthed as the president's wife walked into the basement. Close up it was easy to identify her, despite the woollen hat pulled low over her brow and the oversized winter coat. Daniel was similarly disguised. Luc had pushed the large hood of his coat off his head when he stepped into the basement. He had a backpack slung over his shoulder and a leather briefcase in one hand.

"What a charming place." Isabelle looked at Manny. "We meet again, Colonel Millard."

"So we do, Madame Godard. A pity it is under such circumstances."

The shift in Luc's body language drew my attention. He exhaled angrily. "She should not be meeting you at all."

"Oh, pooh, Luc." Isabelle waved her hand towards the tall man. "He huffed and puffed all the way here."

Francine was still staring at Isabelle. She managed to school her features to something less awed, but she was unsuccessful in completely masking her wonderment.

Isabelle turned to Francine and extended her hand. "Hi. I'm Isabelle Godard."

Francine stared at Isabelle's hand for a few seconds before grabbing it and shaking it enthusiastically. "Hi! Oh, my God. You are Mrs Godard. I'm a huge fan. Like a really huge fan. I've been following your work for many years now. In a non-stalkerish way, of course. But you are just amazing. Oh, wow. Isabelle Godard."

Isabelle laughed lightly, not pulling her hand back. "I know who I am. Who are you?"

"Oh. Yes." Francine released Isabelle's hand and cradled her own as if she wanted to protect the hand with which she had touched the president's wife. "I'm Francine. This is my humble abode. Please come in. And please forgive the mess. I was not expecting guests."

Manny was looking at Francine as if seeing her for the first time. He shook his head in disbelief when the two women walked towards us.

"Are you sure it's safe here, Colonel?" Luc asked Manny.

"Just call me Manny. Everyone else does." Manny opened his jacket to reveal a gun holster attached to his hip. He nodded at the bulge under Luc's left arm and then nodded towards Daniel. "With all this firepower, we are safe. Unless you were followed here?"

"Definitely not." Daniel shook his head a few times. "We came here with Luc's niece's car. It's a tiny little thing that was easy to cut through traffic. We also left all our usual electronics at home in case they could track our GPS."

"They would not get you if you're down here." Francine turned back to the men. "I've got it set up to scramble signals of all sorts."

"Sweet." Pink looked around the basement, admiration

clear on his face. "You have a Scooby-Doo set-up here, girl. What system are you running?"

"Who are you?" Francine stood protectively in front of her computers.

"Pink. I'm the IT tech in Daniel's team. I hope to help if you would let me. I reckon two super-brains are better than one, right?"

Francine glared at him for a few more seconds.

"He's good stock, supermodel. Let him help."

"Supermodel?" Pink glanced at Manny and looked back at Francine with a wide smile. "It fits. You're gorgeous."

"I'll eat you for breakfast, little man," Francine said, looking up at Pink. She glared at him a moment longer, sat down and pointed towards the rest of the basement. "Find a chair. My name is Francine. Or you can call me your highness."

I was quietly watching this new development unfold in front of me. There were too many people talking for my whispers to be heard, so I did what I enjoyed most. I observed.

"Madame Godard, what are you doing here?" Manny didn't disguise his displeasure when he looked at Daniel. "I told you where we were in case of emergencies."

"Oh, don't fight with him, Colonel." She frowned. "May I call you Manny? Colonel is so formal. And please call me Isabelle. We're just a bunch of friends trying to sort out a looming disaster."

Manny stared at Isabelle.

"Aha. You're one of those. Yeah, Luc's like that too. I'm immune to staring, so you can stop. Just ask Luc. He's been trying that since we studied together."

"I tried to stop her from coming," Luc said. "Daniel and I

have cooperated a few times in the past. He contacted me a few hours ago and told me about your findings. I then made the huge mistake of telling her about it. Then she insisted on meeting you. When she starts, there's no changing her mind."

"I think I can help, Manny." Isabelle pointed to the backpack on Luc's back. "This might help you discover who wants you arrested and so prevent you from investigating Minister Savreux's death and everything connected to it."

Manny looked at Daniel. "Did you find out where the order for our arrests came from?"

"It filtered down so far through the chain of command that I didn't want to attract attention by asking too many questions."

"It's that little Henri Fabron." The intense dislike and disrespect accompanying Manny's words took me by surprise. "I don't know what that little shit is up to, but he's playing games."

I couldn't stay out of the conversation any longer. I stomped my foot on the floor until I had everyone's attention. "It's not Henri."

"Oh, Genevieve!" Isabelle's voice was high with concern as she walked to me. "You sound terrible. Is your voice terribly damaged?"

I shook my head.

"She's not supposed to be speaking at all." Colin offered his hand. He had met the president and his wife a year ago. "Colin Frey. Pleased to meet you again."

"Colin? Oh." She drew out the syllable and shook Colin's hand. "Genevieve talks about you a lot. Please call me Isabelle."

Colin managed to maintain his controlled expressions, but

I had seen the shock, followed by pleasure when Isabelle had said I talked about him. I *had* talked about him—about his expertise in the art world. I didn't understand why she had read more into that. Or what he was reading into it. Those had been purely professional observations about him and his knowledge.

"Have you been told about the photo?" I asked Isabelle. I didn't feel comfortable with the gentle look on Colin's face. I wanted our focus to be on emotionally safe topics.

"What photo?" Isabelle asked.

"Let me," Colin said. I was grateful to not have to speak. I was pleased with the fast and concise manner in which Colin briefed them on our findings of the previous day, including the photo of the four men.

"Now you know everything we know," Manny said to Daniel.

"They know everything too." Daniel looked at Luc and Isabelle.

I stomped my foot again. "Do you know who the fifth man is?"

"Can I see the photo?" Isabelle asked. "I have never met this Remi Dubois, and know the others mostly by name. Maybe I'll see something on the photo."

"Here it is." Francine pointed to the monitor in front of her. Pink was sitting next to her, working on a laptop in front of him. I assumed he had brought that with him.

Isabelle walked closer and leaned towards the monitor. She stared at the screen for a few seconds and straightened. "Sorry. I don't even recognise the men in that photo. They're so young there."

"We think the photo was taken in the late seventies, early eighties," Manny said.

"It certainly looks like it. That hair. I remember the bad hair of those days." She became quiet, her body shifting towards Luc. "Give me the files, please, Luc."

He handed over the backpack and she gave it to Francine. "Everything that is on paper is also on flash drives. They're in the little pocket in the front. You can open that."

Francine nodded, took the backpack and unzipped the front pocket. "Is this related to Savreux's murder?"

"Maybe." Isabelle sighed. "These are the files President Boussombo prepared for the ICC prosecutor."

"The files Dukwicz was looking for?" Manny asked.

"Yes. She gave it to me, knowing that there were a lot of people who didn't want her to hand this over to the ICC."

The content of the backpack was not as interesting as Isabelle's body language. I waved my hand lightly until she looked at me. "What else is worrying you?"

"Whispering is hard work, isn't it?" She sighed, walked to the closest chair and sat down. It was the chair in front of my laptop. "When Daniel told me what you guys have found, I just knew that everything must be related. Luc, tell them."

Luc's eyebrows lifted. "Sure?"

"Tell them."

"A month ago I started receiving SMS's. We tried to trace it, but every time it was sent from a different number."

"Let me guess," Francine said without looking away from her computer. "The phone was used only once and never turned on again. You couldn't trace it."

"Exactly. So far I've received three SMS's, but they stopped more than a week ago."

"What did they say?" I mouthed the words, but Luc saw it.

"All three warned about the president being in danger. Not life-threatening danger, but that something was going to happen that will destroy him. The sender said to be careful and watch the president's back. Those he considered allies were actually working toward his downfall."

"Do you suspect someone?" Colin asked.

"Henri Fabron." Luc lifted both shoulders. "Isab... Madame Godard disagrees with me, but he's the only one I can think of. He's been acting more awkward than usual around the president and Madame Go—"

"Oh, stop it, Luc," Isabelle said. "We've been friends since university and these people are also friends. No need to be so pretentious."

He rolled his eyes. "As I was saying, Henri's been acting more awkward than usual. He calls himself the president's biggest supporter. The SMS did say that it was someone the president considered an ally."

"Why are you taking these threats seriously?" Manny asked. "The president must be getting daily threats."

"Well, I wasn't taking them seriously at first. These SMS's weren't direct threats to the president. They were phrased as warnings, like telling me that I should look out for the president."

"Which is not his job," Isabelle said. "He's my personal detail, not Raymond's. And I don't think it's Henri."

"Neither do I." I tried to make my whisper louder, but it was too painful. I had been whispering too much.

"Girlfriend, be quiet for a moment. Let me sort something out here." Francine jumped up from her chair, walked over to my computer and clicked a few times with the mouse. Seconds later, she straightened. "I set up Word so it will convert the text to speech. You type very fast, so it won't be a problem to converse like that."

It was a brilliant solution. I knew of a few autistic people who were non-verbal, and communicated by using their computers in such a manner. Colin rolled another chair closer and I sat down with my computer on my lap, facing everyone.

"Isabelle, why don't you think Henri is the person behind this?" I typed and a female voice with a British accent asked.

"I have no proof, but I know it's not him. Henri has been with us for the last ten years, since Raymond got involved in politics. He's devoted himself to Raymond's career. Only recently did he start dating someone. I wish I knew who. Of course, he met her at some political function, but at least... Sorry, I digress. It is not Henri."

"I don't know, Isabelle." Luc folded his arms. "He's a little twerp and he's been more twerpy lately."

I thought of Henri's behaviour when he had come into the team room. His body language had been calculated. As usual I needed to analyse body language within its context and I didn't have enough context about Henri to correctly interpret the contradictory micro-expressions I had seen when he had tried to intimidate us.

"You know, now that I think about it..." Manny rubbed his jaw. "I met with Henri and Minister Lefebvre yesterday. He asked me at least three times if we were staying away from the Savreux case. The little shit seemed too eager. I told him that of course we were not looking into it at all. Doc knows that I can tell a whopper when I need to. Henri bought my lie and I really thought that I saw disappointment for a moment. I didn't think about it again until now, because Lefebvre came into the conference room."

I knocked on the arm of my chair until Manny looked at me. I started typing. "What happened to Henri's body language when Minister Lefebvre came in?"

Manny thought about it for a moment. "Hmm. He changed. You know, Luc was talking about his awkwardness. I saw that when he was with me, but not with Lefebvre. He was one hundred percent professional then. He glowed under Lefebvre's praise that we had found the Jean Monnet Museum paintings. Lefebvre would've preferred an arrest, but recovering the paintings had made a lot of important people happy, so he was happy. Bloody politician. Uh. Sorry, Madame Godard."

Isabelle laughed lightly. "I call my husband that at least twice a day, Manny."

"Do you think Henri is scared of Minister Lefebvre?" the British female asked as soon as I finished typing.

"I don't know, Doc. Maybe. Maybe that is why he was acting so kiss-arse."

"You can't possibly suspect Antoine Lefebvre." Isabelle's eyes were wide. "He's been a good friend to Raymond. His prosecutors are very excited about the No Secrets law. He's even warned Raymond that there might be quite a bit of backlash from this. He's meeting with Raymond later this evening to discuss this before Ray's big speech next week in front of the Senate."

I did a quick calculation.

"This could be the ten days we were warned about," the British voice said. "The second direct message came ten days before next Wednesday when the president is supposed to give his final appeal for the law to be passed."

"Ooh, girlfriend." Francine pointed frantically at her computer monitor. "I think I know why people want to stop President Godard from even dreaming about this No Secrets law. Looky here! Big, delicious scandals."

I put my laptop on the table and walked to Francine's desk.

Everyone else was standing close, but on Francine's other side.

"Are you familiar with this material?" Colin asked Isabelle.

"The basic situation, yes. I didn't know all of these details until three days ago. Mariam brought the human, drug and arms trafficking to my attention just after Ray became president. By then she had been looking into the case for a long time and had gathered some evidence, but nothing like this. When I looked through these files, I was horrified at the names, the amounts of money, and the shocking crimes outlined in it. Mariam has done an incredible job putting it together, but she told me that is would be useless if she didn't have our support.

"When Ray became president two years ago, she felt that we could put our powers together to deal with this. Two presidents working together are more effective than one president in a Third World country trying to stamp out corruption. She would have been ousted before she could email this evidence. A lot of the people named in these files are high ranking officials in Gabon. It would be easy for them to push her out. And if Ray went at this alone, he would be decried as a witch-hunter and they would find some scandal to bury him."

"Lili Lescot's bank account is the perfect scandal to destroy the honest president of France," Francine said, still focussed on the computer monitors.

Isabelle took a deep breath and nodded to Luc. "They have more than just that bank account."

Luc opened the briefcase and took out a painting. Colin tensed next to me a second before he sprang forward and took the painting from Luc.

"Oh God, Jenny. This is the Flinck. This is Flinck's Landscape with an Obelisk." He turned to Isabelle. "Where did you get this?"

"In the back of my closet. I was looking for a pair of winter shoes I had promised myself I would never wear again when I found this."

"Someone got into your bedroom? Into your closet?" Francine turned around, her lips slightly parted. "That's sacred ground."

"And should never have happened." Luc's insistence on not leaving Isabelle's side made more sense now.

"Oh, come on, Luc. You know how many people have access to our home. You security guys are in and out all the time." She pulled back her shoulders. "It's even worse here than in the residence in Paris. Here I'm supposed to feel like I'm home, but I have you guys all over my home all the time. There is security, yes, but if someone wants to get in, they can use the catering company, the cleaning company, the gardening company. Then there are the entourages that come with Raymond's guests. Last week, that billionaire came with his bodyguards and personal assistant. It's easy enough to sneak through my house if someone really wants to."

"It should not be possible at all."

"This could also suggest that the person is close to the president or close to you if they had access to your bedroom," Manny said.

I didn't want to think of the possibility that Dukwicz could have been in Isabelle's bedroom. Colin and Vinnie both had already reluctantly acknowledged Dukwicz's skill at breaking into seemingly impenetrable locations. I retuned my attention to Francine's computer monitor while Manny and Colin looked over the painting. The information was extremely well organised. The first page was a table of contents, giving an overview of the thousand-page document.

"Please go to chapter fifteen," I whispered. Fortunately, Francine heard and I was looking at the list of names implicated in the crimes Mariam Boussombo had been investigating. Next to each name were the crimes they could be accused of. I scanned the list, recognising many names. "These are not only Gabonese people."

"That's the biggest problem," Isabelle said. "France and Gabon are very closely connected in trade, industry and politics. When we had that huge scandal in the nineties—"

"The Elf scandal?" Francine asked.

"Yes. It did a lot of damage to the trust on both sides, but some of those people had kept contact. Mariam hadn't told me about these French politicians and executives until she handed me these files three days ago. She had told me that there were some French people involved, but she played this close to her vest, even with me."

I thought that it couldn't have been because Mariam didn't trust Isabelle. She had after all given her these files. I wondered about Mariam's motivation for not sharing this information earlier. Protecting Isabelle could have been one of her reasons.

"Let's have a look then, Doc." Manny leaned over Francine's shoulder and quietly read for a few seconds. "Holy hell! They're all here. Bloody Savreux, Motte, Legrange, even dead Dubois. Isabelle, does your husband know about this?"

Isabelle swallowed and straightened her shoulders. "I promised my friend total confidentiality. I hadn't told Raymond about this, but was going to tell him. Then I found the painting in my closet this morning, and Daniel told me about your discoveries, so I thought it might be better to first show it to you."

"Why?" I whispered.

"Because I'm terrified that if this situation is not handled correctly, it will destroy everything Raymond and I have been working for. It has taken us a decade to convince the leaders of this country to be more accountable to the people who have put them in those positions." Tears formed in her eyes. "Already Ray is worried about the speech on Wednesday. He's worried that something will happen to shift the majority support he currently has for this law. I didn't want to add to his worry. I thought you guys would help fix this."

"Raymond is going to have your hide for this, Lili." Luc's jaw was shifting from side to side, showing his anger. "How many more times are you going to be reprimanded for being too independently minded?"

It was clear Luc was at the beginning of a long diatribe. I put out my hand to stop him. It didn't matter that he was presenting a viable argument. There were more important matters. As clear as I could, I mouthed, "We need to speak to the president."

Chapter **TWENTY-TWO**

When the air-raid alarm went off this time, it didn't startle me as much as when Daniel and Isabelle had arrived. We'd been expecting the president. Using a phone Francine had taken from a hidden compartment under her desk, Isabelle had phoned her husband. After an initial conversation that had lasted only a minute, she'd given him five minutes to find privacy before she'd phoned again. The next thirty minutes she'd impressed me by giving him a chronological and succinct report of the chain of events that had led us to this basement. It had been easy to hear his displeasure at her subterfuge.

He'd agreed on the urgency of this matter and had cut a meeting short to rush to us. It had been hard for me to not inquire about his security and whether he would have been able to come here without his usual entourage. Instead I'd been working on my computer, looking through the files Francine had sent to my laptop—the files Mariam had given Isabelle.

Francine and Pink had also been working in an impressive show of team work. He had adjusted something in her programming and five minutes later we'd had the first name of the owners of the thirteen accounts in the Samoan bank. It hadn't surprised any of us that it was Remi Dubois. That account had been dormant for the last three years since his death. We still needed the other names. It was a general assumption that those would be Claude Savreux, René Motte and J.L. Legrange.

What we needed most was the fifth person, the name of the photographer. Colin was convinced that person would be the mystery man on Minister Savreux's home office videos. I thought it to be a valid assumption. All of these illuminating revelations and thoughts were now interrupted by the loud siren and the flashing red light.

I looked up from my computer, hoping Francine would put a stop to the horrid sound soon. Colin was next to me, admiring the Flinck he'd carefully placed on the table. He took a step closer to me.

"What the what?" Francine glared at her computer monitor. She clicked twice and silence filled the basement. "Who are all these people?"

Manny rushed from one of the sofas to the computer station. "What's wrong, supermodel?"

"He brought his whole staff with him." Francine threw her hands up in the air and swivelled her chair to face the door. "It was time to find a new place anyway."

Isabelle joined them, also looking at the computer monitor. After a quick glance at the computer, Daniel walked to the door, his weapon drawn, his body language alert and cautious. Luc stayed with Isabelle.

Manny's brow lowered and he leaned even closer to see the monitor. "He brought little Henri with him?"

A knock at the door took my attention away from Francine's ire. Manny walked to the door just as Daniel opened it. I got up to stand next to Colin, curious about the new guests, yet simultaneously dreading the growing number of people. Fortunately, Francine's basement was spacious. Cluttered, but spacious.

"Mister President." Daniel stood to the side to let the older man in. President Godard walked into the basement, confidence and authority in every non-verbal cue. He introduced himself to Daniel, whose reddened skin tone was the only clue to his emotions. Stepping away from Daniel, President Godard greeted Manny with a handshake speaking of familiarity and respect.

The president gave a cursory look around the basement until he noticed his wife. His nonverbal cues indicated relief, concern and deep affection. With long strides he walked to Isabelle and gave her a short but warm kiss. "You okay?"

"I'm fine." She looked around him towards the door. "What are they doing here?"

By the door stood Henri Fabron, Minister Antoine Lefebvre and a young woman I'd never seen before. Their body language was an interesting study. Henri exhibited cues of anxiety, frequently glancing at Minister Lefebvre and the young woman. She showed every indicator of fear, bordering on panic. Her eyes were wide, her pallor grey. Even with more than ten metres separating us, I could see the perspiration on her forehead.

Henri and the young woman walked deeper into the room, leaving Minister Lefebvre at the door with Daniel. The intense discomfort in the newcomers' body language sent a rush of adrenaline through my system and made me pay attention. I estimated her age about the same as Henri's. A few centimetres shorter than him, she was dark-skinned with her short hair tightly curled against her head. A pretty, albeit very nervous young woman.

The glances she sent Henri spoke of trust, her torso leaning towards him and away from everyone else. It only took a few more seconds of observation to convince me they were involved in a romantic relationship. This could be the woman Isabelle had been talking about earlier.

"Antoine was with me when you phoned," the president said. "Since he has a vested interest in both this week's art theft and Minister Savreux's murder, I thought we could do with his sharp mind."

He looked at me and smiled, his eyes widening slightly when he noticed the injury on my cheek. "Genevieve, always a pleasure."

"President Godard," I whispered and accepted the slight relaxation in his facial muscles as a warm greeting. He didn't offer to shake my hand.

Colin took half a step forward and offered his hand. "As always, an honour, sir."

"Mr Goddphin. Good to see you again." When the president had met Colin a year ago, it had been a few hours after we had saved the president's son. Colin had been in full disguise. Even though the names of Colin, Francine and Vinnie were never officially given to the president, I would've been surprised if he hadn't had knowledge of who was working under his direct command. The micro-expressions on the president's face told me he was being deceptive.

"We both know you know I'm Colin Frey, sir." Colin's tone held humour. "I'm the expert reappropriator."

"That's exactly what Colonel Millard calls you."

A short discussion at the door pulled my attention away from the president. In an interesting show of courtesy, Minister Lefebvre was insisting Daniel walked ahead of him into the room. I took note of Daniel's calculating expression as he gave a polite smile and led the Minister into the basement. Not once did Daniel's posture relax nor did he holster his weapon.

It was the first time I had seen Minister Lefebvre in person. Everything about him was average. His height, his hair colour, his weight, everything. Except his micro-expressions. Like most people in public positions, he'd learned to school his features, but no matter how controlled we were, no one could override the involuntary reactions triggered by our limbic brain.

A feeling of great discomfort overwhelmed me as quick introductions were made. Fortunately, Minister Lefebvre didn't insist on shaking everyone's hands. The young woman was introduced as Julie Bastin, Minister Lefebvre's personal assistant. The worried looks she was sending Henri exacerbated my disquiet. She was constantly shifting on her feet, unable to find a comfortable position. She clasped her hands tightly, her shoulders lifting to her ears. I thought she was about to lose consciousness from the severe mental strain exhibited in her body language.

"Sorry to ask you this, Mister President, but did you leave all your devices at home like we'd asked?" Not even for the president did Manny lose his slouch. He hunched his shoulders and looked much more tired than he'd done before the air raid alarm had sounded a second time.

President Godard patted his pockets. "I feel kind of naked without any gadget, Colonel. But yes, I left everything behind. As did the others."

Julie was nodding profusely, Henri swallowed, but it was Minister Lefebvre's reaction that had me inhale a sharp breath. His fleeting smirk didn't bode well. I tapped Colin on his arm and whispered, "He's lying."

"I beg your pardon?" Minister Lefebvre pulled his shoulders back.

"She says you're lying." Colin's tone was neutral, but his expression wary.

Daniel and Manny stepped closer to the minister. Manny held out his hand. "If you have any devices on you, now would be a good time to hand it over, sir."

I watched the short moment of indecision before Minister Lefebvre put his hand in his left jacket pocket and handed pieces of a phone to Manny. "I always carry three phones with me. You can ask Julie. We left in such a hurry that I only took out two. As you can see, I removed the battery from this phone."

"It made that phone completely useless," Pink said. He took the phone from Manny and turned it over in his hand. "Yup, without a battery, nothing and no one can access the phone or switch it on remotely. Where were you when you removed the battery?"

"A few blocks from where we had our meeting." Minister Lefebvre lifted one shoulder in a half shrug, indicating his uncertainty. "I'm not sure exactly where, but it was very far away from here."

I continued to stare at him, hoping to see the reason why I was not convinced by his explanation. His body language was congruent with his explanation, yet my subconscious and my training were giving me warning signs. The overload of information flooding my brain made it difficult to decide whether the minster's body language required priority.

Factual information seldom overwhelmed me. It was the sensory input that I was finding too much. There were too many people in the basement, too many nonverbal cues to decipher and too much data I needed to attach to the people, events and situations involved. I needed Mozart. I needed a few minutes alone with my music to make sense of everything floating around in my mind. But I knew I wasn't going to get it.

President Godard was busy explaining that he'd given Henri, Julie and Minister Lefebvre a short version of what Isabelle had told him. His trust in the minister and in their assistants was absolute. When he said this, Julie lost even more colour to her face and Henri stopped moving altogether. He was frozen, one of our three reactions to a threat.

"Is there anything new I need to know?" The president asked, looking at Francine.

Her mouth opened, closed and opened again. My well-spoken friend seemed to be at a complete loss for words when addressed by the president of France. Not even with Isabelle was she this awestruck.

"Um... Yes." Pink pushed his chair a bit forward to take the attention away from Francine. "We have a programme running to find out who are the account holders of those thirteen bank accounts in Samoa. We now have three very familiar names."

"Who are they?" Minister Lefebvre attempted casual interest. He pressed his arm tightly against his side, and I narrowed my eyes. It was as if he was trying to hold something closer to his body, possibly something in his right jacket pocket.

"Remi Dubois, René Motte and J.L. Legrange." Pink glanced at the computers behind him. "I won't be surprised if the next name is Claude Savreux."

Seeing the flash of dread on Minister Antoine Lefebvre's face as Pink gave the four names brought together the numerous separate streams of data to form a flash flood through my brain. The strength of it disoriented me and I might have lost my balance if it weren't for Colin's hand on my back, steadying me. I closed my eyes. It was as if I was mentally watching the different pieces of this case shift until everything was in its right place, forming a complete picture.

The high-level orders to stay away from Minister Savreux's murder, those orders filtering down all the way to Daniel's detective friend, Henri's conflicting body language as he also ordered us to focus solely on the Strasbourg heist. All of it made sense. The concern on Henri's face as he checked on Julie strengthened my suspicion about where Nikki's DMs came from.

The photo of the four friends and the photographer, the four friends' early jobs at FGMB, their connection to Elf, their connection to Gabon, the bank accounts both here in Strasbourg and in Samoa, the expensive lifestyles inconsistent with their traceable expenses, four of Mariam's files I'd read. That too fell into place. My breathing became erratic as the excitement of comprehension mixed with the fear of all the possible repercussions.

"Jenny?"

The concern in Colin's tone brought absolute silence to the basement. Only the computers' whirring could be heard. No sounds from the street penetrated Francine's safe workspace. I opened my eyes to see everyone staring at me, some with concern, others with fear.

As I inhaled to share what I'd concluded, a soft buzz broke into the silence. All eyes turned to Minister Lefebvre. He pushed his arm against his right jacket pocket, another fleeting smirk pulling at one corner of his mouth. I stared at his thumb pressing hard against his little finger. Safe blackness entered my peripheral vision, tempting me to hide in its warmth. I took a shuddering breath, fighting for control. I had to warn everyone.

The computers behind me made a ping sound, drawing the attention away from the minister.

"Oh, we have another name." Pink sounded excited and I heard his and Francine's chairs swivel.

"Oh, my God!" Francine's loud exclamation was immediately followed by the air raid alarm and the flashing red light. Sensory overload bore down on me and with immense effort I managed to take my focus away from the loud noise and look at the door. It was slightly ajar, open just wide enough for the three small cylinders to be thrown into the room. I immediately recognised what they were. Five nights ago, I had used exactly the same flash grenades when I had saved Vinnie from his attackers.

I screamed a warning, but no one heard my wheezy whisper above the air raid alarms. I dropped to the floor, and as I did in Vinnie's truck, closed my eyes tightly and covered my head with my arms, hoping to minimise the effect from the grenades. No sooner had I pressed my arms firmly against my ears than three consecutive explosions followed.

Irrationally, I wondered if Francine's soundproof basement had kept the loud noises from alerting the neighbours and hopefully bringing law enforcement to our aid. There was only a second of stunned silence before more noise erupted. It was overwhelming in its intensity. Julie let out a high-pitched scream, men shouted and I heard the distinct sounds of punches and grunts.

I lifted my head from the safety of my arms, shocked by the change in our situation. To my right and close to the sofa, Manny and Daniel were held at gunpoint by a man I recognised as one of the thugs who'd attacked Vinnie in the narrow street. He was joined by three other gunmen.

One of those was the second man from Vinnie's attack,

currently standing behind the president and Isabelle, the barrel of his gun pushed against the back of the president's head. The presidential couple was standing directly across from me, the seven-metre distance between us feeling like a kilometre. Next to Isabelle, Luc was on his knees, pressing his hand hard against his head, blood seeping through his fingers. The gunman had a second gun aimed at Luc.

Colin was crouched next to me, his hands over his ears. He was blinking profusely and shaking his head in annoyance. On the other side of the room, Henri was holding a trembling and crying Julie, also blinking fast in an attempt to regain his sight after the blinding light from the flash grenades. Minister Lefebvre was rubbing his one ear, but looked otherwise much less affected than everyone else.

Both Francine and Pink were in still their chairs, but were turned to the chaos in the room. Francine's expression was changing from shock to rage as she absorbed everything, her muscles tensing up. Pink put his arm out to stop her from getting up. He shook his head almost imperceptibly and slumped in his chair. The *orbicularis oculi* muscles contracted around Francine's eyes a millisecond before she copied Pink's posture. Both looked powerless and scared as the third gunman aimed his semi-automatic rifle at them.

"So nice of you to have a party for me, Doctor Lenard." Dukwicz walked past Minister Lefebvre, sneered at Manny and stopped in front of me. "So many people for me to play with."

I knew the type of playing he referred to was not about fun or games. Nor was it anything like the intellectual riddles Kubanov enjoyed. Dukwicz was a predator who enjoyed terrorising his prey. Weary of the constant fear weighing me down, I slowly stood up. I didn't want to give this man any more pleasure by cowering at his feet.

When Colin pushed himself up to stand next to me, Dukwicz raised his gun and aimed it at my head. "Anyone try anything and I pull this trigger. Before Doctor Lenard's lifeless body hits the floor, my friend behind me will also pull the trigger, dropping the president. Everyone clear on that? Or is someone going to make it more fun for me and try to be a hero?"

I knew he wasn't addressing me, but I felt the need to shake my head. A sideways glance confirmed that Daniel, Luc and Manny's holsters were empty. In the time Dukwicz and his associates had entered the room, they had not only overpowered all the trained law enforcement agents, but had also disarmed them. No matter how extensive the training, if caught by surprise, a second or two is all someone needed to gain advantage.

I didn't know whether Pink had come here armed, or if he still had a weapon. Dressed in civilian clothes and slouching in his chair, he didn't exhibit any cues that he had a weapon or that he was able to take action.

With every breath, it became harder to keep the panic at bay. I couldn't see a solution to this situation. We were completely at the mercy of a ruthless assassin and three heavily armed men. I didn't know if it were even possible to reason with him. But it might be possible to reason with the person behind this, the person giving Dukwicz orders. Ignoring the tremors of fear washing over my body, I slowly turned my head until I looked at Minister Lefebvre. His attempt at fear and looking like a hostage was hugely unsuccessful.

"You're responsible for this." It was painful to speak and I wasn't sure if anyone could hear me after the loud explosion. "You're the fifth man, the photographer. You're the one who put the camera in Minister Savreux's office. You're the one who ordered Savreux's murder and who ordered us away from investigating his case."

It was quiet in the basement. I had spoken slowly, hoping that Manny and Colin could read my lips even if they couldn't hear me. Minister Lefebvre took a step to the side, away from Henri and Julie. This time his smirk stayed. "Well, aren't you just clever. Think you have everything figured out?"

"Antoine?" The president spoke louder than normal. "What's happening?"

Minister Lefebvre's top lip curled as he faced the president. "You still don't see it, do you, Ray?"

"You?" The pain of betrayal was clear on President Godard's face. "You... We... Why?"

"Honestly? Because you're such a bleeding heart, Raymond. You're forever hoping that people will be good and kind and moral. I remember when you first started at FGMB, my colleagues told me you were always fighting for the underdog. Good thing I got out before you joined FGMB. I would've had you for breakfast."

"Wait." President Godard frowned. "I remember now. You worked at FGMB before I joined. You left after you lost that case to the American lawyer. That was in the late eighties, right? Wasn't that lawyer from Boston? Oh, God. Antoine, did you rob the Gardner museum?"

Minister Lefebvre shrugged. "I was proving a point to that obnoxious, loud Yank."

"I trusted you." While the president continued to express his dismay at Minister Lefebvre's treachery, I looked around the basement. A few metres from me, Manny's shoulders were hunched in absolute defeat. From his lowered eyelids, he sharply surveyed the room, careful not to give himself away.

Daniel was unable to appear defeated or uninterested, though he was successful in making his anger come across as fear. The slight trembling in his hands, his accelerated breathing and muscle tension could easily be misconstrued by an untrained eye. When he looked at Luc, I had to concentrate hard to control my reaction.

I glanced at Dukwicz to ensure he hadn't noticed any of my involuntary micro-expressions. He hadn't. Still aiming his weapon at my forehead, he was like everyone else watching the sad confrontation taking place between the president and the minister. His distraction gave me the freedom to observe the strange communication happening between Manny, Daniel, Luc and Pink.

I wasn't able to understand the countless nonverbal cues being communicated between them. I read people's body language and interpreted the emotions behind their micro-expressions. These four men seemed to be communicating messages, not emotions. It was Francine who communicated emotions when she was able to catch Manny's attention by frantically moving her little finger in what she told me was a 'pinkie-wave'.

"And that is why you shouldn't be president." Minister Lefebvre stepped closer to the centre of the room, bringing my attention back to their oddly polite argument. "You're so naïve. No secrets. Hah. Politics is built on secrets, my friend."

"No." Despite the barrel of the gun pressing against his

skull, the president shook his head, the corners of his mouth turned down. "You are no friend of mine."

"Friends don't do this to each other." Isabelle said through her teeth. Luc shifted slightly, but stayed on his knees. He looked towards Francine and Pink, and blinked slowly.

"Ah, Isabelle." Lefebvre's smile was cruel, his tone disparaging. "It will be such a pity that you died with your husband. Especially since you are the cause for all of this and justice won't be served by sending you to rot in jail. The good people of France will be devastated to find out that you dragged your husband to this basement to help hide your secrets. And such delicious secrets they are. Conspiring with the president of Gabon to bring down officials, stealing money and using a charity to launder it? Tsk, Tsk. The nation will be disappointed in their golden girl."

"You set this all up." Isabelle sounded breathless. "You created that false account to make it look as if I was taking money to help sway my husband's political decisions. You're vile."

"No need for name calling, my dear. Your loyal supporters will be so hurt to find out their Mother Theresa was nothing but a fraud. Someone who associated with lowlife criminals like art thieves and hackers." He stepped back, nodding at Dukwicz. "When some killers came looking for your hacker friend in her basement, you and the president were collateral damage. Hmm. Yes. This will suffice. The media will lap that story up. Of course, the Minister of Justice will be completely horrified at the death of his friend and role model, and of the betrayal of a woman he had held in high regard. Such a pity." He nodded slowly at the president. "Goodbye Raymond. Isabelle."

He took another step back, towards the door. From the

corner of my eye, I saw Manny gesture, but didn't have time to analyse it. The basement was suddenly dumped in complete darkness, disorienting in its unexpected lack of light. A gunshot broke the silence and I dropped to the ground, making myself as small a target as possible. All around me, I heard fighting, punches hitting flesh, grunts, four more gun shots and a lot of shouting.

I hugged my knees to my chest, feeling a shutdown coming on, but I fought it. Even though the darkness from my shutdowns was much kinder than this claustrophobic lack of light in Francine's basement, I didn't want to lose control. I started counting the seconds, giving my mind something tangible to focus on. Listening to the violence transpiring around me, I gave in to the need to count out loud, pushing the sounds past my tender vocal cords.

When I reached four hundred and twenty-three seconds, the lights came back on. I continued counting. I had to. What had been a cluttered basement before, now was in complete disarray. But that wasn't what caused me to cling onto the numbers. It was the blood spatter on the floor and walls. A few centimetres from my feet a small pool of blood drew me in until I had to blink to not feel like I was falling into it. I leaned back, still staring at it. Someone had slipped through the blood, the bloody shoeprint continuing to the door.

Whose blood was this? The realisation that one of my friends could be injured made me wildly look around the basement. Pink was helping the president off the floor, both of them unharmed. Luc already had Isabelle standing up, making sure she didn't have any injuries. His head wound was still bleeding, but looked less serious than it had appeared earlier. Henri and Julie were both sitting on the man who had pushed his weapon against the president's skull. Julie was hysterically hitting the man's back, shouting obscenities at him.

To my right, Daniel pushed his knees hard into the back of the man who'd had him and Manny at gunpoint. He took a computer cord from one of the boxes and tied the man's hands. Manny was taking similar action with Minister Lefebvre, handling him rather roughly and tightening the computer cord until the older man grunted. By the computers, Francine was smiling down maliciously at the man who had aimed his gun at her. He was on the floor at her feet, both his hands over his groin, pain evident on his face.

Next to me, Colin stood motionless, his face void of colour. I gasped when I saw his expression, my need to count lost in the face of the horror written on his face. I jumped up, searching his body for injuries. There was none. I stepped into his line of vision, forcing him to look away from the blood on the floor. He slowly lifted his eyes and swallowed. "I shot him, Jenny. I shot a man."

"Who did you shoot?" I forced out a loud whisper and winced at the pain.

He glanced down at the gun hanging loosely in his hand. "Dukwicz."

"Where is he?" I knew that despite Colin's criminal past, he had a deep dislike of force. The manner in which he was now staring at the gun was worrisome. "Colin?"

He shook his head as if he'd surfaced from a deep dive and looked at me. "I grabbed his gun when the lights went off. We struggled and the gun went off. If he's not here, I suppose he got out."

"Dukwicz's is gone." Manny was no longer slouching.

He pushed the minister to his knees and ordered him to stay. Manny looked around the room. "Everyone okay? Any injuries?"

"I think this man might consider gender reassignment surgery." Francine's smile widened as she rested her booted foot on the man's hands, causing him to whimper.

"Not them, supermodel. You."

"Oh." She looked down at herself. "I'm fine, handsome. Damn fine."

"Anyone got shot?"

Francine pointed behind her. "One of my computers is dead."

"Hmm. Doc? You all right?"

I blinked a few times before I nodded. I had suffered no injuries, but the mental strain of the past few days was building to a climax. My concern for Colin was adding to the pressure tightening around my chest.

"Jenny, look at me." Colin took my hand in his. "I'm fine. Just a little shook up, but I'm fine. Take deep breaths and hold on. I need you with me, okay?"

He was lying. One of the very few times Colin had lied to me and I suspected it was to keep me calm. Colin was more than just a little affected by shooting Dukwicz, but he was sincere when he'd said he needed me. This triggered defiance in me and I straightened my shoulders. I pulled my hands out of his, ignoring the small but genuine smile lifting the corners of his mouth.

Daniel secured his prisoner and took Francine's phone to call in his team. Francine immediately forgot about the man under her foot, rushed to her computer and pressed a red button next to it. She refused to answer Manny's questions, declaring her computers needed to be as useful as a housewife's. She also muttered about never coming back to this place.

The next few hours were more taxing than I could have anticipated. The president's security team got involved and numerous other high ranking officials made appearances. I became increasingly agitated despite my decision to remain in control. Having to painfully whisper answers to the same questions more than once was most vexing. Colin wouldn't allow anyone to separate us and did most of the talking, saving my voice and my temper.

Eventually, Isabelle intervened, supported by the president and six hours later we were free to go after promising to be available for any further questions. Colin and I stepped into the cold evening air and I took a deep breath. We walked quietly to Colin's SUV, the street crowded with black vehicles and men in suits.

Colin opened the passenger door for me, walked around the car, got in and didn't move. His nonverbal cues indicated great inner conflict. I didn't know what to do. Did he need me to talk to him or stay quiet? I didn't have any intuition handling sensitive moments like these. I thought it wisest to not interrupt Colin's thought process, so I leaned back against the seat and stared out into the night.

For three long minutes we sat in silence until Colin shifted to face me. "We are going on holiday. Far away from here. Preferably somewhere warm. I will do whatever you need so it will be okay for you, but we are going on a three week holiday, Jenny."

"Why?"

Colin burst out laughing. "Really? After all this stress, your life being in danger and you don't see the reason for a holiday?"

I thought about this for a moment. I could see how neurotypical people would need a break after the last two weeks we'd had. "Do you need a holiday?"

Colin leaned deeper into his seat. "Yes, love. I need a holiday. I need to be somewhere with you, knowing that you are safe and happy."

"I *am* safe and happy." I tilted my head back to consider my statement. "Yes. I truly feel safe and I am happy. Although I'm frustrated that Dukwicz escaped. But that doesn't affect my current happiness."

Colin's expression changed and I realised how much concern he'd exhibited when it was replaced by his affection for me. He leaned closer to me until our noses almost touched. "Thank you, love."

I didn't know why he would thank me for being happy, but I didn't ask. Instead I enjoyed the kiss from the one person whose physical touch I didn't mind, the one person whom I'd come to trust implicitly.

A loud knock against Colin's window interrupted us. A second later the backdoor opened and Manny got in. "Well then, let's go. I'm hungry. I hope the criminal is out of jail and cooking."

Chapter TWENTY-THREE

"I have like a million questions." Nikki fell into the dining room chair, her eyes bright. Vinnie and Nikki had been released hours earlier and had been anxiously waiting for our return. She had greeted us at the door and had given Manny a fierce hug that had made him blush. He'd returned the hug.

"First tell me that you were treated well at the police station." Manny sat down heavily in his usual chair at the table.

"The little punk was told to never return." Vinnie was stirring something in a pot on the stove. The aroma of the late dinner he was preparing was hugely appetising. "Those officers were seriously pissed off with her."

"What did you do?" Manny straightened, his eyes wide.

Nikki lifted one shoulder. "Played poker with them. They're just sore losers."

"If you were playing for money and not for Post-It notes, you would've cleaned out their bank accounts, punk."

I sat down next to Colin and allowed the normality of this to settle me. All the panic, looming shutdowns and need to hide in my head slowly moved into the background.

"I did win us some sandwiches and chocolates." Nikki turned to glare at Vinnie. "Most of which you ate."

"I'm bigger than you." Vinnie slapped his muscular abdomen. "Need more food."

"Where's Francine?" Nikki asked, rolling her eyes at Vinnie. "I think your cooking needs spices."

"She left before us," Manny said. "Took a taxi to get away from what she called 'Big Brother's minions'. That woman is paranoid."

Just then keys sounded in my front door and it opened. Francine walked in with Phillip. "Look who I found getting out of his car."

It took a few minutes to assure Phillip that we were all unharmed. Only when he asked me and I answered honestly, did he sit at the table and relax. Francine walked into the kitchen, pushed Vinnie out the way with her hip and peered into the pot. "I think this needs cumin."

"Stay away from my food, you spice witch."

Nikki put both elbows on the table and leaned towards us. "Spill. I want to know everything. I'm sick of watching the news on TV and not knowing if it's all like censored, the way Francine always says we receive the news."

"It's already on the news?" Colin asked.

"It's like all over the news and the internet, and I don't know what to believe. Did they really arrest the Minister of Justice?"

Francine came to the table and sat down. "Manny arrested him."

"No way!" Nikki looked at Manny, awestruck. "That is like the coolest thing ever."

I closed my eyes against Nikki's abundant use of the word 'like'. Her offensive use of the English language was mitigated by her relaxed posture and easy laughter.

"I'm equally curious," Phillip said.

"What do you want to know?" The dark rings under Manny's eyes and the lines around his mouth evidenced the toll this case had taken on him. The last six hours he had spent liaising with numerous law enforcement agencies, constantly speaking on a phone he'd taken from one of Daniel's team members.

"First, I just want to say how supercool it is to have everyone together. I was really worried." Nikki took her arms off the table and straightened. "Okay, now my questions. Is it true what they're saying on the news? That Minister Lefebvre was trying to kill the president? Have you found out yet who sent me those DM's? What about the president's wife? Do you think she will be coming here for tea?"

Nikki inhaled to continue her questions, but Manny interrupted her. "You sound like a journalist at a press conference."

"This scandal is any journalist's wet dream come true," Francine said. "Oh, what am I talking about? This scandal is *my* wet dream come true."

"Supermodel!" Manny glared at her.

"Doc G? Is it true about Minister Lefebvre?"

"It's complicated," I whispered. "He didn't plan to kill the president at first. He'd been working to discredit the president and his wife with a lot of fraudulent information. He was, however, responsible for the Boston heist."

"No way!" she said again. "That's like so bad."

I thought I would be able to ignore it, but my compulsion was too strong. I gave in and whispered, "Nikki, you cannot use 'like' in the manner you've been doing. It is grammatically an abomination, it sounds intellectually inferior and frankly, it is beneath your IQ."

She smiled. "I'm like so sorry, Doc G."

Everyone chuckled and I knew I had lost this battle. I delayed this argument for another day.

"Tell me more. Tell me more." Nikki looked at Manny.

Throughout the six hours, Daniel had given us frequent

updates as his colleagues located and arrested the other individuals implicated in this case. In turn, Manny had been in contact with the lead investigator, also receiving updates. I left it up to him to answer Nikki.

"René Motte and J.L. Legrange were arrested a few hours ago. They couldn't wait to give Lefebvre up. Apparently he'd been controlling them for the last ten years and there was nothing they could do to get out from under his domination. The investigator was shocked at how quickly the idiots started sharing information on whatever incriminating information they have on Lefebvre. But not before their lawyers made sure that a lesser charge for their information was on the table.

"Of the two, Legrange is in the better position. He and Savreux had kept insurance in case something like this happened. Savreux had all that financial detail in his rented cellar. Legrange kept their original communication and planning. As a lawyer he knew it would come in handy as a negotiation tool if he were ever to be caught. He and his lawyer are using that tool now. It will give the prosecution team a lot of material to work through."

"But why did they rob the Boston museum?" Nikki asked. "Was it for the money?"

Manny had relayed all the updates to us, including how surprisingly close Colin's unfounded hypothesis had been to the truth. The self-satisfied smile on Colin's face warned me he was going to point it out again. "Like I predicted, Motte, Savreux, Dubois, Legrange and Lefebvre were all wronged in some way in the late eighties."

"You didn't predict that about Lefebvre." This was the third time I reminded him of this.

"Only because we didn't know he was the fifth man." He

winked at Nikki. "Motte and Legrange told the investigator that they had originally planned this to thumb their noses at whoever they were angry with at that time. When they managed to pull it off and successfully leave America with five hundred million dollars' worth of art, they saw an opportunity. That was when they sat down and worked out a business plan for their art theft business."

"They had a business plan?" Phillip's eyebrows were raised, the tightness around his mouth revealing his indignation.

"They did." Manny scowled. "Bloody lawyers. With their legal studies and Dubois with his banking experience, they knew the loopholes to get around laws and stay undetected. They were well-prepared for their lives of crime.

"And?" Nikki asked. "Is Legrange walking free because he gave all that information?"

Manny snorted. "Not by a long shot. The charges might be lessened, or his sentence might be reduced, but this conspiracy is far too great to let them off scot-free."

"What about the president of Gabon and that minister guy?"

"Paul Ngondet was also arrested earlier in his hotel here in Strasbourg. The plan is to hand him over to the International Criminal Court so he can be tried for crimes against humanity," Manny said. President Mariam Boussombo's evidence was also going to be handed over to the ICC.

Six hours had been a long time and I'd had been able to look through Mariam's file. It was well-prepared and would have many repercussions. Not only did the file make an indisputable case against Minister Ngondet, but it also implicated numerous Gabonese and several French officials. J.L Legrange might have power now to negotiate on the current cases, but then he would have to face charges for his involvement in the crimes in Mariam's file.

"We were surprised when we got the names of the account holders of those thirteen accounts." Francine leaned back to allow Vinnie to place a plate in front of her. Nikki got up to help him set the table. "Motte, Savreux, Legrange, Dubois and Lefebvre had only twelve of the accounts. The thirteenth account belongs to Paul Ngondet."

"That child-killing bastard." Manny shook his head. "Ngondet told the officers who arrested him that the five men were to blame for everything. He claims to have been working under them for many years. Apparently, they forced him to sell stolen masterpieces and other artworks to his corrupt colleagues in Gabon. Of course that is utter bullshit."

Mariam's file indicated that Minister Ngondet had used the art sale money to fund his elaborate lifestyle, and also to fund some of the terrorist groups and other military factions to keep the war in central Africa alive. He had been receiving a lot of money from mediating arms deals, training child soldiers and other warmongering.

Manny took an angry breath. "In her research, President Boussombo had connected Paul Ngondet to Savreux and Legrange, but wasn't able to dig deep enough to find the cornerstone of their evil empire. She knew it was someone with strong connections in France and Gabon, but she didn't have the resources or enough trustworthy people to help her find out who it was."

"That is a shocking conspiracy," Phillip said after a few quiet moments. Vinnie and Nikki brought steaming dishes to the table and sat down.

"It seems like everything came to a head two years ago." Manny's eyes widened when he saw the content of the large oven dish. He waited for Nikki to dish up. "When Raymond Godard became president, these idiots knew that President Boussombo now had an ally who could help her clean up her country. They also knew that President Godard would push for transparency and their days of laundering bucket-loads of money was counted."

"How is the president of Gabon?" Nikki gave the serving spoon to Manny.

"Recovering quite well." One corner of Manny's mouth lifted when he dished a second spoon of Vinnie's lasagne onto his plate. "She should be returning to Gabon in a few days."

"Do you know who sent those DM's?" Nikki asked.

"Yes." My voice cracked and I took a sip of water. "It was Henri Fabron. He is quite unmoving in his loyalty towards the president. When he first met Julie, Minister Lefebvre's assistant, he didn't know whom she was working for. They started seeing each other romantically and that was when she decided to trust him with her concerns."

Julie had sobbed when she told her side of the story, happy to be relieved of that secret. I had watched her carefully while she talked and had seen no deception cues.

Colin put his arm around the back of my chair. "You shouldn't speak so much. Let me finish telling this story."

I nodded, grateful.

"Julie had been in the minister's house a few times and taken note of the masterpieces since her brother is an artist and she thought he would be interested. When she mentioned these to him, he told her all of the works she described were on some list of stolen art. When she told Fabron about her discoveries, he insisted on doing something. She was terrified that she was wrong and could lose her career and Henri didn't want to bring the investigation so close to the president and his wife.

He also didn't know if there was anyone he could really trust going through the normal channels of investigation."

"So the little shit decided to use us." Manny had especially taken offence that he had been manipulated by Henri. "He knew how much the president trusted us, but he didn't want to ask us directly. That's why he trapped us with reverse psychology to investigate."

Both Manny and Colin had been disappointed to find out that Henri Fabron had been assisting us all along. Their conflicting expressions of intense dislike and respect had been fascinating to observe. The president's assistant had reasoned, after his meetings with Manny, that the older man would investigate more vigorously if told not to. He had been right and Manny had been greatly displeased about this fact.

"Was he the reason Vin and I played poker with the policemen for twelve hours?"

"No," Manny said. "It was Lefebvre. When he was informed about your search for a connection between the president's wife and Elf, he knew that we were getting closer to his secret. He became desperate to stop us."

"I'm sorry, Doc G." Nikki put down her knife and fork, contrition clear on her face.

I took a sip of water. "I know, Nikki. We all learned a lesson from this."

"Oh, I did." She folded her arms. "I'm going to stick to drawing. For like forever. Why did nobody ever figure out that charity was on the take?"

"The Libreville Dignity Foundation wasn't on the take, lass."

"What does that mean?" I asked.

"That they were on the take?" Colin waited until I nodded.

"It means they were part of the fraud."

"We don't know yet..." My throat burned too much and I looked at Francine.

"We don't know yet if everyone there was involved," she said. "Or who exactly was involved. Lefebvre has organised their auditing since they were founded. There will also be a special investigation into their finances. The forensic auditors will trace all the money that has gone in and out of their accounts, including that sub-account. It might take a long time."

Nikki became pensive. "Why would they do this? I mean, I get the money part. Everyone wants to have shitloads of money. But why set up the president? Why hurt his wife? They're such nice people."

Manny and Colin became involved in a discussion about greed, politicians and that there were some questions that did not have answers. I leaned back against my chair and Colin put his hand on my shoulder. I felt drained. I wanted to get back to a routine of predictable cases, watching video footage, writing up reports of my analyses and living with regular hours. I didn't know if I liked Colin's idea of going on a holiday. It was going to be stressful for me.

Colin squeezed my shoulder as Francine and Nikki started clearing our plates. "I managed to phone and have an enlightening conversation with Sue."

"When?" I asked.

"While we were still in the basement. You were talking to Isabelle about Mariam's case."

"This Sue still doesn't want to come in?" Manny asked.

"Not in this lifetime, Millard." There was no hostility in Colin's answer, nor had there been any in Manny's question. The dynamics in our team had shifted. The biggest change had come from Manny. He was much less disparaging in his dealings with Colin and Vinnie.

The big surprise had been a few hours ago when Manny'd had an aggressive argument on the phone with an Interpol agent. He had moved to the far side of Francine's basement and had spoken in a hushed voice, but we'd been able to hear him. The task force was still looking into Colin and they refused to give Manny any access to their investigation. Neither Colin nor I had expected to hear Manny fight for him, especially not where he could be overheard doing so. Manny didn't know we'd heard the argument or that Colin had told Vinnie about it when he'd phoned to find out if Vinnie and Nikki were home.

"So? What did housewife by day, art thief by night Sue say?" Manny asked.

"I got in touch with her to let her know that these guys were arrested and she didn't have to worry about them being a threat any longer," Colin said. "She started crying from relief. She still doesn't know who had contacted her, but they had given her the details of her family's routine, her children's school activities and their favourite park. They threatened her family, and she said there was no choice. Her family comes first."

A ping sounded from the kitchen and Vinnie jumped up. "Dessert is ready."

Phillip asked Manny a few questions about the arrests made and the conversation continued around me. Colin raised an eyebrow when Manny deferred to him on questions about the art, but answered without commenting on this development.

"Pudding, old man." Vinnie put a bowl in front of Manny. "My Auntie Theresa's caramel apple pie pudding."

"My favourite." Manny picked up his spoon, his eyes fixed on the steaming baked dessert. He didn't realise Vinnie had made this meal especially for him and I knew Vinnie wasn't about to tell him. Manny's protection of Colin had brought forth a loyalty in Vinnie. It was clearly visible in his body language towards the older man. Pleasure relaxed Vinnie's face when Manny took a bite of the dessert and grunted his approval.

"I'm not your favourite dish?" Francine sat down next to Manny and ran a manicured nail down Manny's sleeve. "I'm much sweeter than that pie, handsome."

"Get away from me, you evil woman." Manny pulled his bowl away from Francine, turning his shoulder slightly to block her.

I absorbed the bantering around the table as I wondered how far-reaching the effects of this case would be. What other changes it would bring apart from Vinnie's attitude towards Manny, and the latter asking for Colin's input. How was this going to affect our work dynamics? Would we still be an effective team? One by one, other concerns came to the fore.

There were a lot of details in this case that needed to be clarified for the prosecutors. But that was not the main cause of my discomfort. Dukwicz was still out there. I didn't think I would be able to go on holiday until he was in prison, far away from me and the people around this table. I only hoped Colin would understand my aversion to leaving something unfinished. On the other hand, I wondered if this was maybe a good time for me to find a way to cope with my neurosis in order to give Colin something he clearly needed.

Nikki's loud laughter when Manny threatened Francine with arresting her for fashion violations brought me back to the present. I decided to address these distressing thoughts at a later time. Tomorrow I could start looking for Dukwicz again. Maybe I could look for a way to manage my compulsion for concluding something. Today I would enjoy this moment. This light-hearted meal with my friends.

~ ~ ~ ~ ~

Be first to find out when Genevieve's next adventure will be
published. Sign up for the newsletter at
http://estelleryan.com/contact.html

~ ~ ~ ~ ~

Listen to the Mozart pieces,
look at the paintings from this book
and read more about the Gardner Museum Heist and Flinck at:
http://estelleryan.com/the-flinck-connection.html

~ ~ ~ ~ ~

The Courbet Connection

Forged masterpieces. Kidnapped students. The dark net.

Nonverbal communications expert Doctor Genevieve Lenard's search for an international assassin is rudely interrupted by an autistic teenager who claims that forged masterpieces are being sold on the dark net—a secret internet few know exists. The resulting probe uncovers an underground marketplace offering much more sinister products and services. Including murder.

An official investigation into one of her team members and the discovery of dozens of missing students across Europe adds immense pressure on Genevieve to find out if one person is masterminding these seemingly unrelated cases. What starts out as a search for illegal art sales soon turns into a desperate hunt for clues to uncover the conspiracy to destroy her team member and murder more students. Timing becomes even more crucial when someone close to her disappears and the assassin she's been looking for is the key to preventing another senseless death.

The Courbet Connection

Excerpt from **Chapter ONE**

"Doctor Lenard! I want to speak to Doctor Genevieve Lenard! Where is she? The Red Sea is the warmest sea in the world! Doctor Lenard!"

I looked away from the computer monitors to glare at the glass doors to my left. The doors separating my viewing room from the team room had been sealed. Now they were slightly ajar, allowing the yelling to distract me.

"Doctor Lenard! You need me! Doctor Lenard!" The loud voice belonged to a young person. That much was clear to me. I rolled my shoulders to stretch the taut *trapezius* muscles in my neck.

My room was set up for maximum comfort and efficiency when viewing video footage. The glass doors had been specially fitted to seal so I could work in a soundproof—and uninterrupted—environment. I only went into the team room for meetings, which I often experienced to be chaotic, the constant digression a vexing waste of time.

More yelling ensued, but it was the lack of emotion, and the increase in volume of the young voice that completely drew my attention away from my work. I sighed and shook my head angrily. This disturbance was most unwelcome. The case I was working on was much more pressing than a stranger seeking me out and reciting strange geographical facts.

In front of me, ten monitors were arranged in a curve, filled with information we had gathered on Dukwicz. The notorious international assassin had evaded capture for more than a year. Not only had he killed people without remorse, he had terrorised me inside my own apartment and had stolen three clocks I had highly valued until he'd touched them.

It didn't matter that he had returned those clocks to my apartment. I had seen that action for what it was—an intimidation technique. It hadn't worked. If anything, it had made us more determined to find him.

His weakness for timepieces might very well be the key to catching him. Two days ago, Vinnie had heard from one of his contacts about a man offering to beat up non-paying clients for a fee or for a valuable timepiece. It was the latter form of payment that made me take notice.

Vinnie, the most intimidating member of our team, had convinced his contact to divulge information on how he had heard of this service, and how to get in touch with the service provider we suspected was Dukwicz. I had learned early on to never question Vinnie's methods in gaining information. It caused me much less mental distress not knowing.

"Doctor Lenard! I want to speak to you! Japan has six thousand eight hundred and fifty-two islands!" The yelling was much closer now, possibly in the hallway outside my viewing room. Movement in the team room drew my attention. Through the glass doors, I watched Vinnie get up from the round table used for our meetings and walk towards the hallway.

Other books in the Genevieve Lenard Series:

Book 1: The Gauguin Connection

Book 2: The Dante Connection

Book 3: The Braque Connection

Book 4: The Flinck Connection

Book 5: The Courbet Connection

Book 6: The Pucelle Connection

Book 7: The Léger Connection

Book 8: The Morisot Connection

and more…

~ ~ ~ ~

Find out more about Estelle at
www.estelleryan.com
Or visit her facebook page to chat with her:
www.facebook.com/EstelleRyanAuthor

BCPL
Baltimore County
Public Library

CPSIA information can be obtained
at www.ICGtesting.com
Printed in the USA
LVOW08s1929060617
537135LV00001B/48/P

9 781495 901737